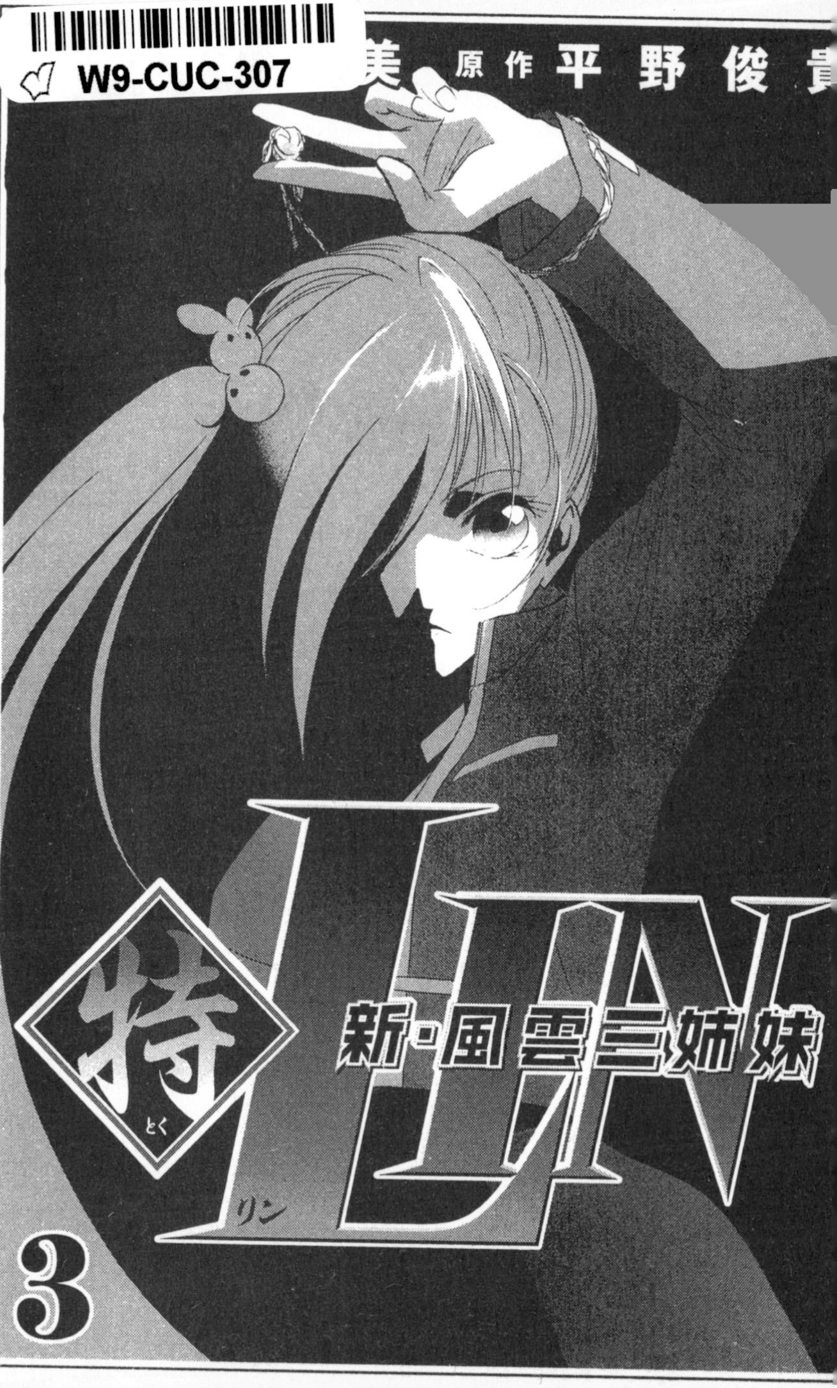
美 原作 平野俊貴
特
とく
LIN
リン
新·風雲三姉妹
3

Shaolin Sisters: Reborn Vol. 3
Written by Toshiki Hirano
Illustrated by Narumi Kakinouchi

Translation - Alethea Nibley
English Adaptation - Aaron Sparrow
Copy Editor - Eric Althoff
Retouch and Lettering - Irene Woori Choi
Production Artist - Jason Milligan
Cover Design - S. R. Cable

Editor - Tim Beedle
Digital Imaging Manager - Chris Buford
Production Managers - Jennifer Miller and Mutsumi Miyazaki
Managing Editor - Lindsey Johnston
VP of Production - Ron Klamert
Publisher and E.I.C. - Mike Kiley
President and C.O.O. - John Parker
C.E.O. - Stuart Levy

A  Manga

TOKYOPOP Inc.
5900 Wilshire Blvd. Suite 2000
Los Angeles, CA 90036

E-mail: info@TOKYOPOP.com
Come visit us online at www.TOKYOPOP.com

ISBN: 1-59532-509-3

First TOKYOPOP printing: November 2005
10 9 8 7 6 5 4 3 2 1
Printed in Canada

鈴 SHAOLIN SISTERS REBORN

Volume 3

by
Toshiki Hirano
&
Narumi Kakinouchi

TOKYOPOP®

HAMBURG // LONDON // LOS ANGELES // TOKYO

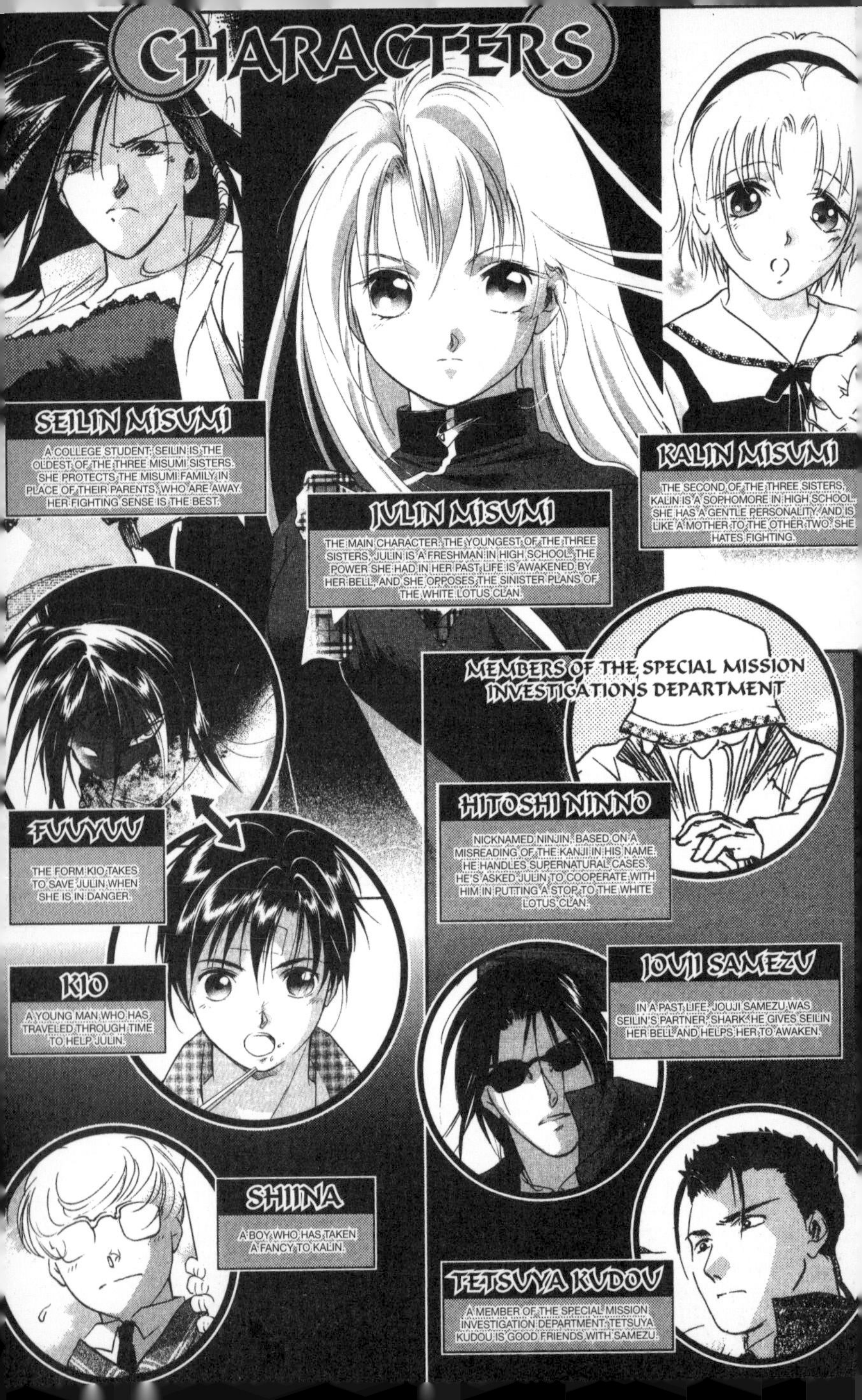
CHARACTERS
SEILIN MISUMI
A COLLEGE STUDENT, SEILIN IS THE OLDEST OF THE THREE MISUMI SISTERS. SHE PROTECTS THE MISUMI FAMILY IN PLACE OF THEIR PARENTS, WHO ARE AWAY. HER FIGHTING SENSE IS THE BEST.
JULIN MISUMI
THE MAIN CHARACTER. THE YOUNGEST OF THE THREE SISTERS, JULIN IS A FRESHMAN IN HIGH SCHOOL. THE POWER SHE HAD IN HER PAST LIFE IS AWAKENED BY HER BELL, AND SHE OPPOSES THE SINISTER PLANS OF THE WHITE LOTUS CLAN.
KALIN MISUMI
THE SECOND OF THE THREE SISTERS, KALIN IS A SOPHOMORE IN HIGH SCHOOL. SHE HAS A GENTLE PERSONALITY, AND IS LIKE A MOTHER TO THE OTHER TWO. SHE HATES FIGHTING.
MEMBERS OF THE SPECIAL MISSION INVESTIGATIONS DEPARTMENT
HITOSHI NINNO
NICKNAMED NINJIN, BASED ON A MISREADING OF THE KANJI IN HIS NAME. HE HANDLES SUPERNATURAL CASES. HE'S ASKED JULIN TO COOPERATE WITH HIM IN PUTTING A STOP TO THE WHITE LOTUS CLAN.
FUUYUU
THE FORM KIO TAKES TO SAVE JULIN WHEN SHE IS IN DANGER.
KIO
A YOUNG MAN WHO HAS TRAVELED THROUGH TIME TO HELP JULIN.
JOUJI SAMEZU
IN A PAST LIFE, JOUJI SAMEZU WAS SEILIN'S PARTNER, SHARK. HE GIVES SEILIN HER BELL AND HELPS HER TO AWAKEN.
SHIINA
A BOY WHO HAS TAKEN A FANCY TO KALIN.
TETSUYA KUDOU
A MEMBER OF THE SPECIAL MISSION INVESTIGATION DEPARTMENT, TETSUYA KUDOU IS GOOD FRIENDS WITH SAMEZU.

CHARACTERS

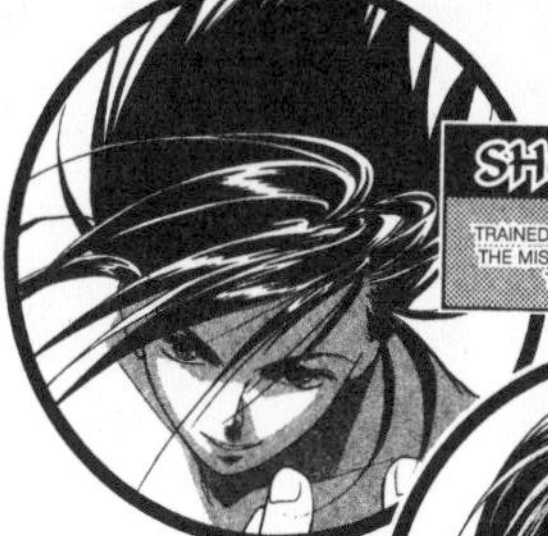

SHOURYUU LIN

TRAINED BY THE SAME MASTER WHO TRAINED THE MISUMIS, SHOURYUU HAS A BLACK BELL THE SAME SHAPE AS SEILIN'S.

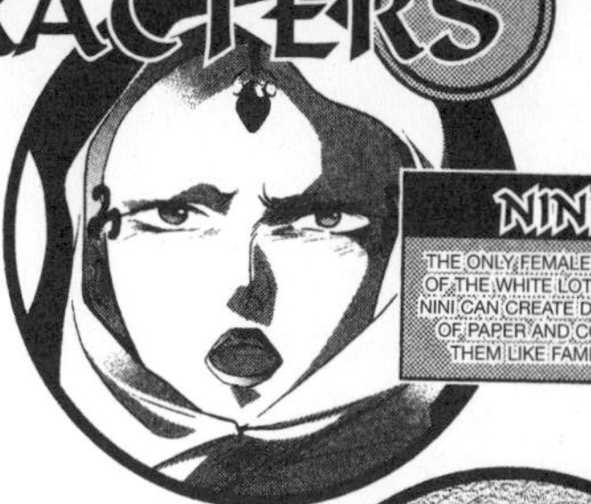

NINI

THE ONLY FEMALE MEME OF THE WHITE LOTUS CL NINI CAN CREATE DOLLS OF PAPER AND CONTR THEM LIKE FAMILIARS

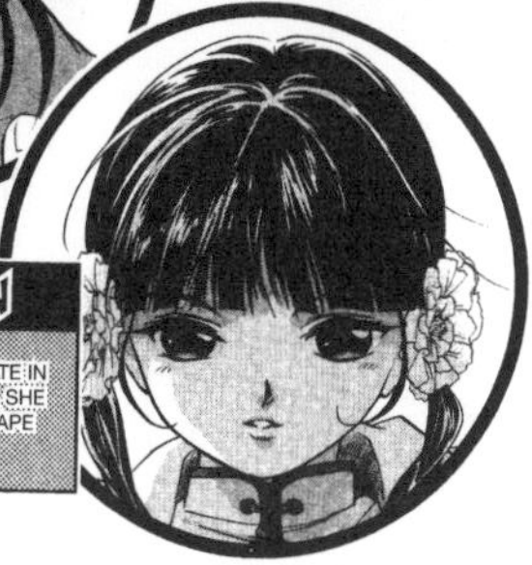

SHOUKO LIN

SHE CAME TO JAPAN TO PARTICIPATE IN THE KING OF KINGS TOURNAMENT. SHE HAS A BLACK BELL THE SAME SHAPE AS JULIN'S.

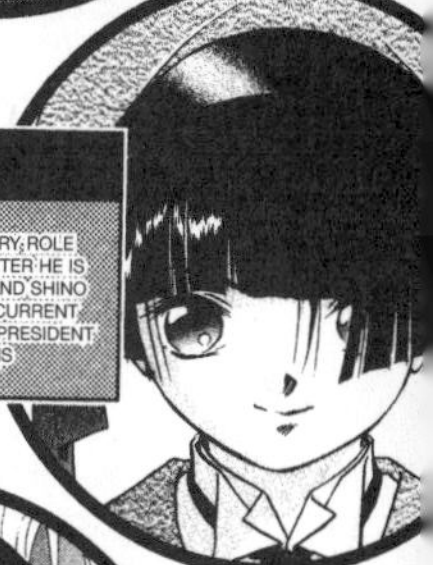

SANJI

SANJI HAS TAKEN AN ADVISORY ROLE IN THE WHITE LOTUS CLAN. AFTER HE IS AWAKENED, HE ASSISTS NINI AND SHINO IN THEIR AWAKENING. IN HIS CURRENT LIFE, HE IS THE TEN-YEAR-OLD PRESIDENT OF SANNOU CREATIONS

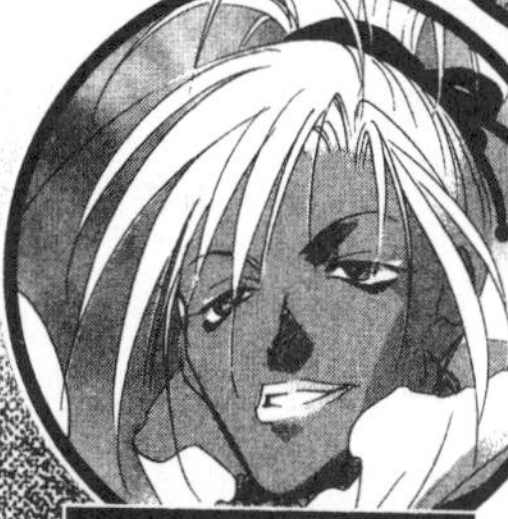

SHINO

A MEMBER OF THE WHITE LOTUS CLAN. BAI WANG HAS GIVEN SHINO THE POWER TO KILL ANY WARRIOR WIELDING A BELL, AND HAS ORDERED HIM TO BRING THE BELLS TO HER.

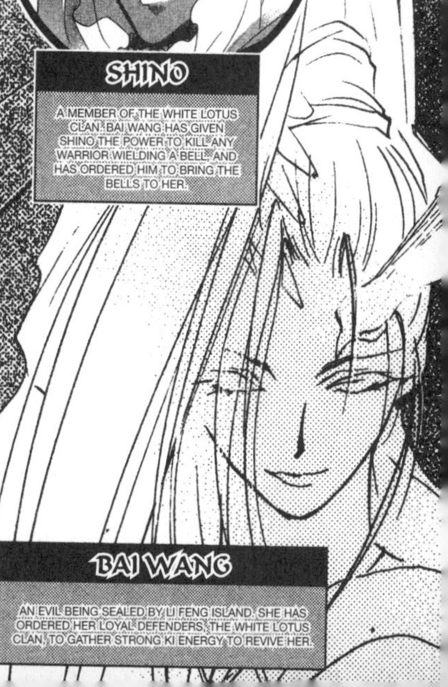

BAI WANG

AN EVIL BEING SEALED BY LI FENG ISLAND. SHE HAS ORDERED HER LOYAL DEFENDERS, THE WHITE LOTUS CLAN, TO GATHER STRONG KI ENERGY TO REVIVE HER.

THE STORY SO FAR:

THREE SISTERS, LOCKED IN BATTLE WITH THE EVIL BAI WANG, ARE PULLED THROUGH A RIFT IN TIME, ONLY TO AWAKEN, REINCARNATED, IN THE PRESENT DAY WITH NO MEMORIES OF THEIR PAST LIVES. TWO OF THE SISTERS, JULIN AND SEILIN, ARE APPROACHED BY THE SPECIAL MISSION INVESTIGATIONS DEPARTMENT — A SELECT DIVISION OF THE POLICE DEPARTMENT DEVOTED TO INVESTIGATING SUPERNATURAL OCCURRENCES. THROUGH THE ASSISTANCE OF THE DEPARTMENT, BOTH SISTERS "AWAKEN" TO THE REALIZATION OF WHO THEY ARE.

MEANWHILE, SANJI, NINI AND SHINO JOURNEY TO THE FORBIDDEN ISLAND OF LI FENG IN SEARCH OF THEIR DARK MASTER, BAI WANG. SEALED IN A STONE STATUE, SHE INSTRUCTS THEM TO HOLD A TOURNAMENT TO GATHER KI ENERGY FROM STRONG FIGHTERS TO AWAKEN HER.

TWO OF THESE STRONG FIGHTERS ARE SHOURYUU AND SHOUKO LIN, SIBLINGS WHO HAVE TRAINED UNDER THE SAME MASTER AS THE MISUMIS. INTRIGUINGLY, BOTH SHOURYUU AND SHOUKO HAVE BELLS AS WELL, BUT THEIRS ARE BELLS OF DARKNESS, NOT OF LIGHT. WHEN THE LINS FIND THEMSELVES IN TROUBLE, JULIN AND SEILIN COME TO THEIR AID, ONLY TO FIND THEMSELVES TRANSPORTED TEMPORARILY TO ANOTHER WORLD BY THE COMBINED POWER OF THEIR BELLS. WHAT IS THE SECRET OF THESE MYSTERIOUS WEAPONS?

CONTENTS

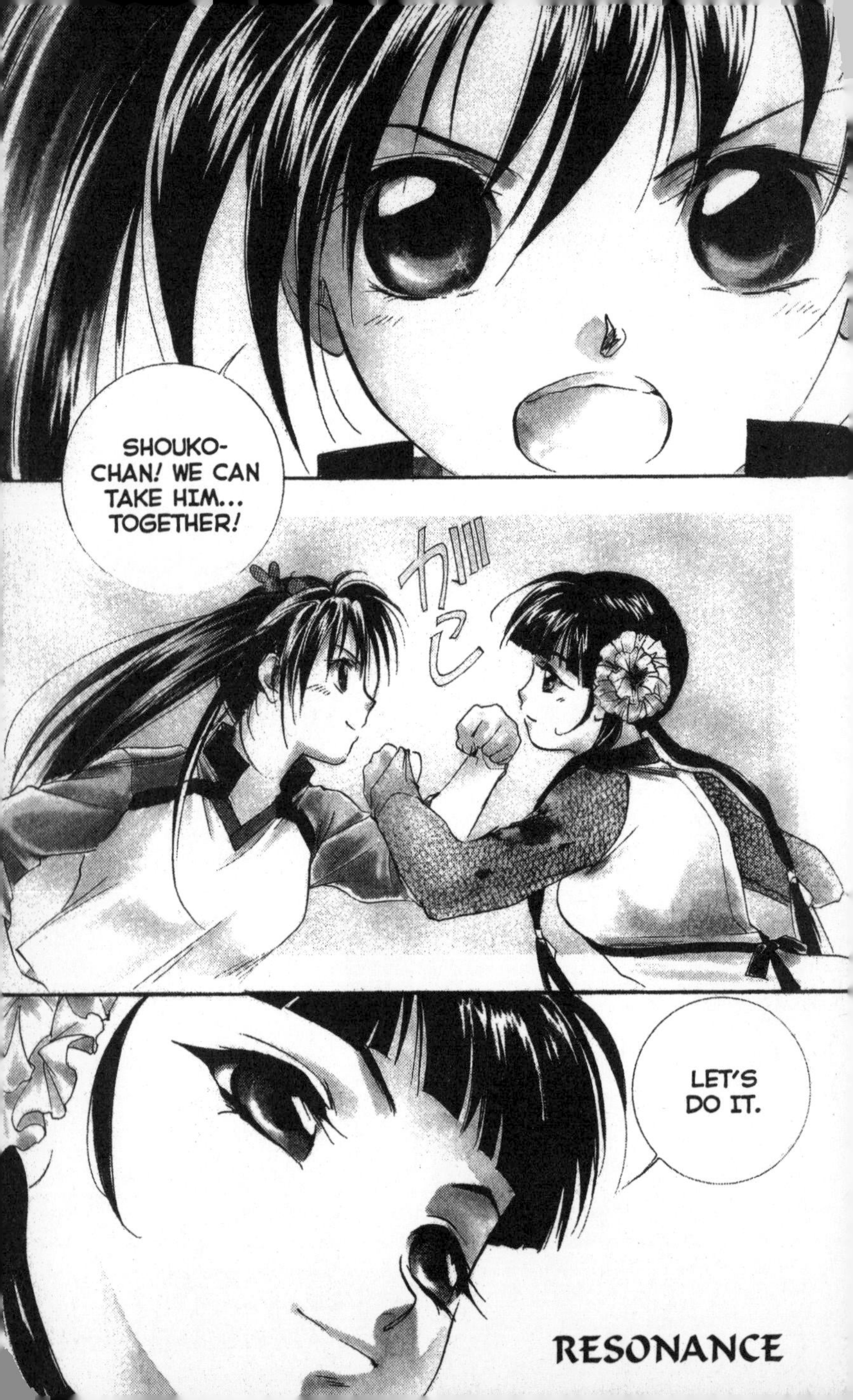
SHOUKO-CHAN! WE CAN TAKE HIM... TOGETHER!
がし
LET'S DO IT.
RESONANCE

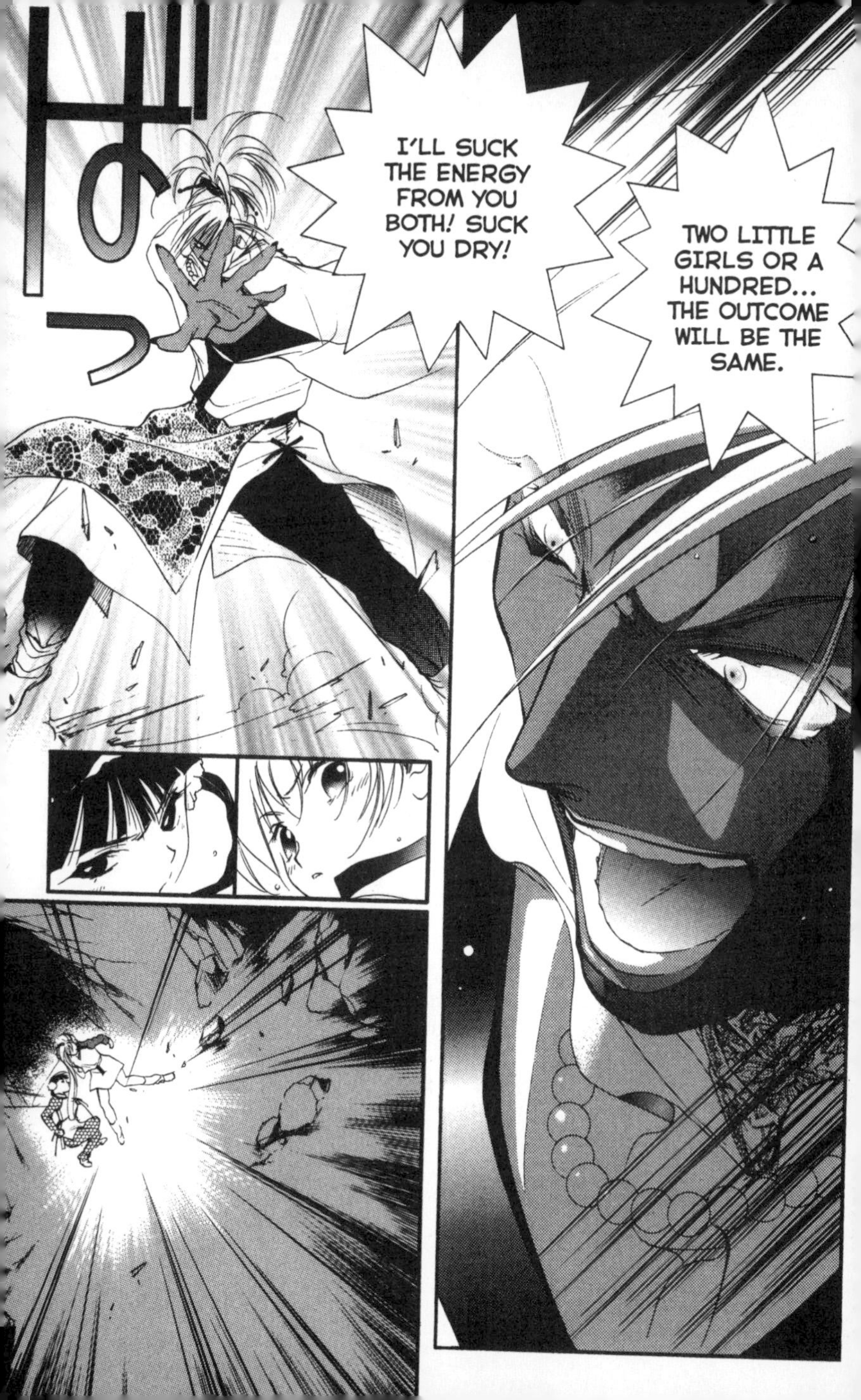
TWO LITTLE GIRLS OR A HUNDRED... THE OUTCOME WILL BE THE SAME.
I'LL SUCK THE ENERGY FROM YOU BOTH! SUCK YOU DRY!

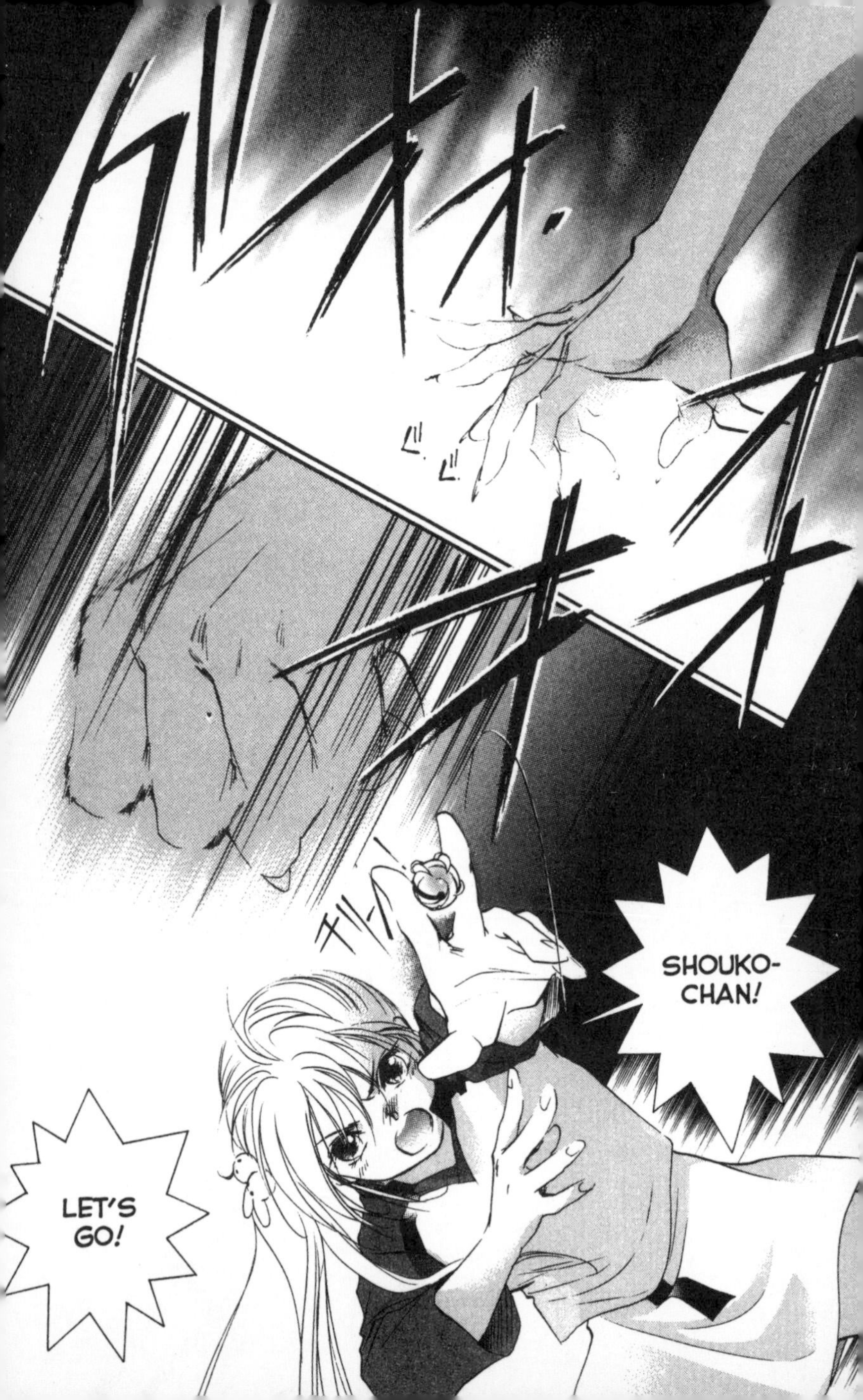
SHOUKO-CHAN!
LET'S GO!

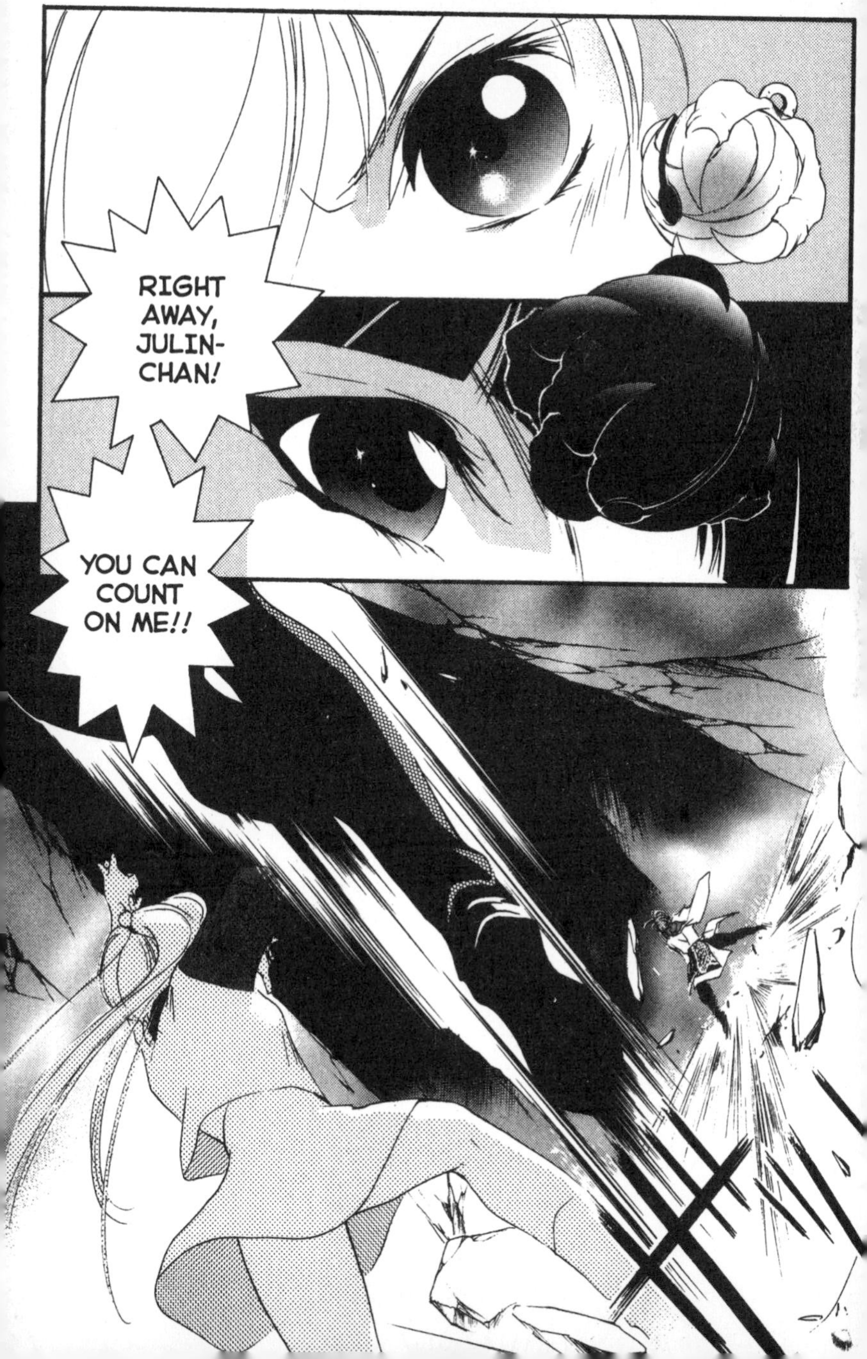
RIGHT AWAY, JULIN-CHAN!
YOU CAN COUNT ON ME!!

HEH.

FOOLISH LITTLE GIRLS, PLAYING A MAN'S GAME.

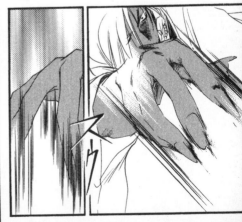

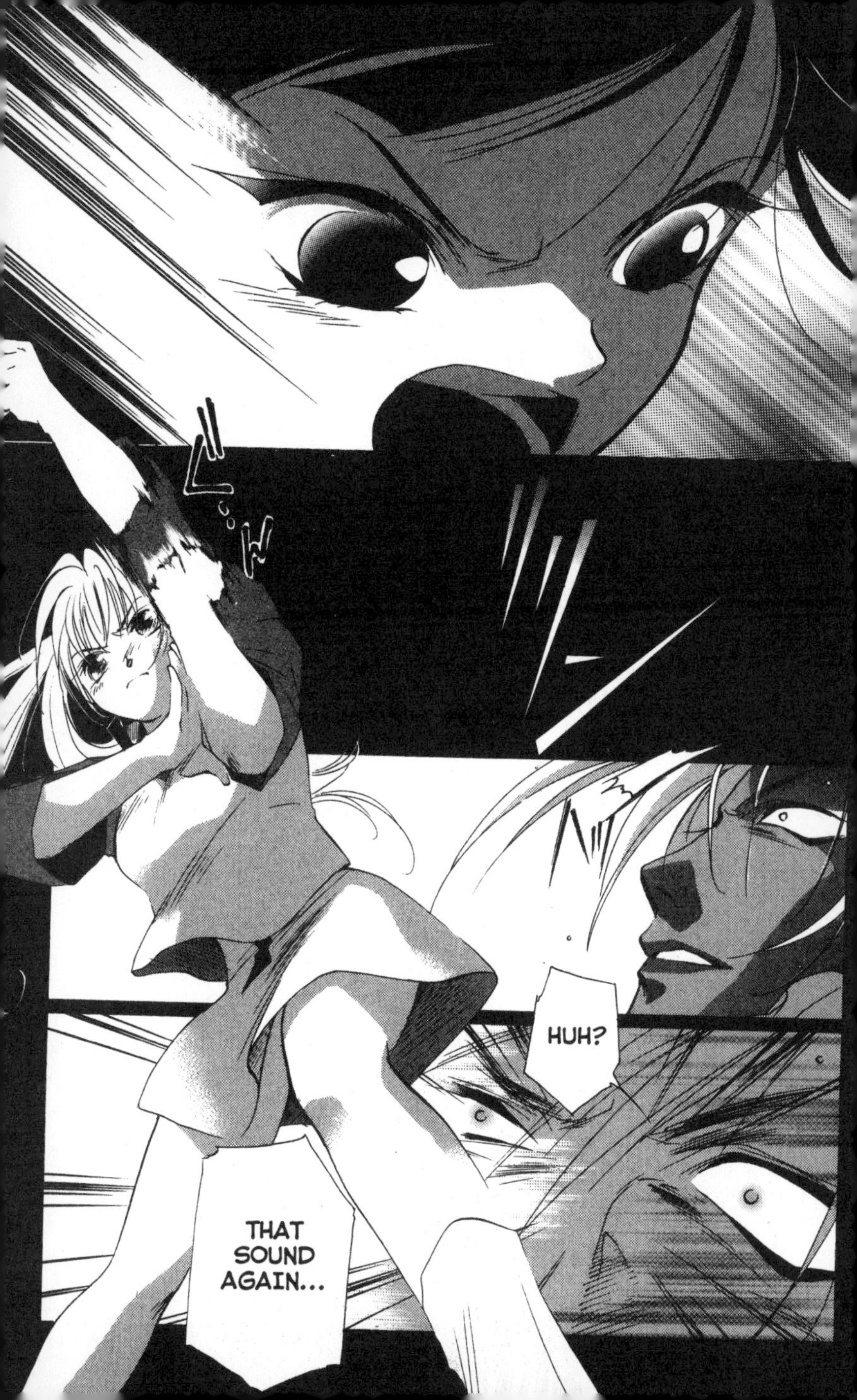
HUH?
THAT SOUND AGAIN...

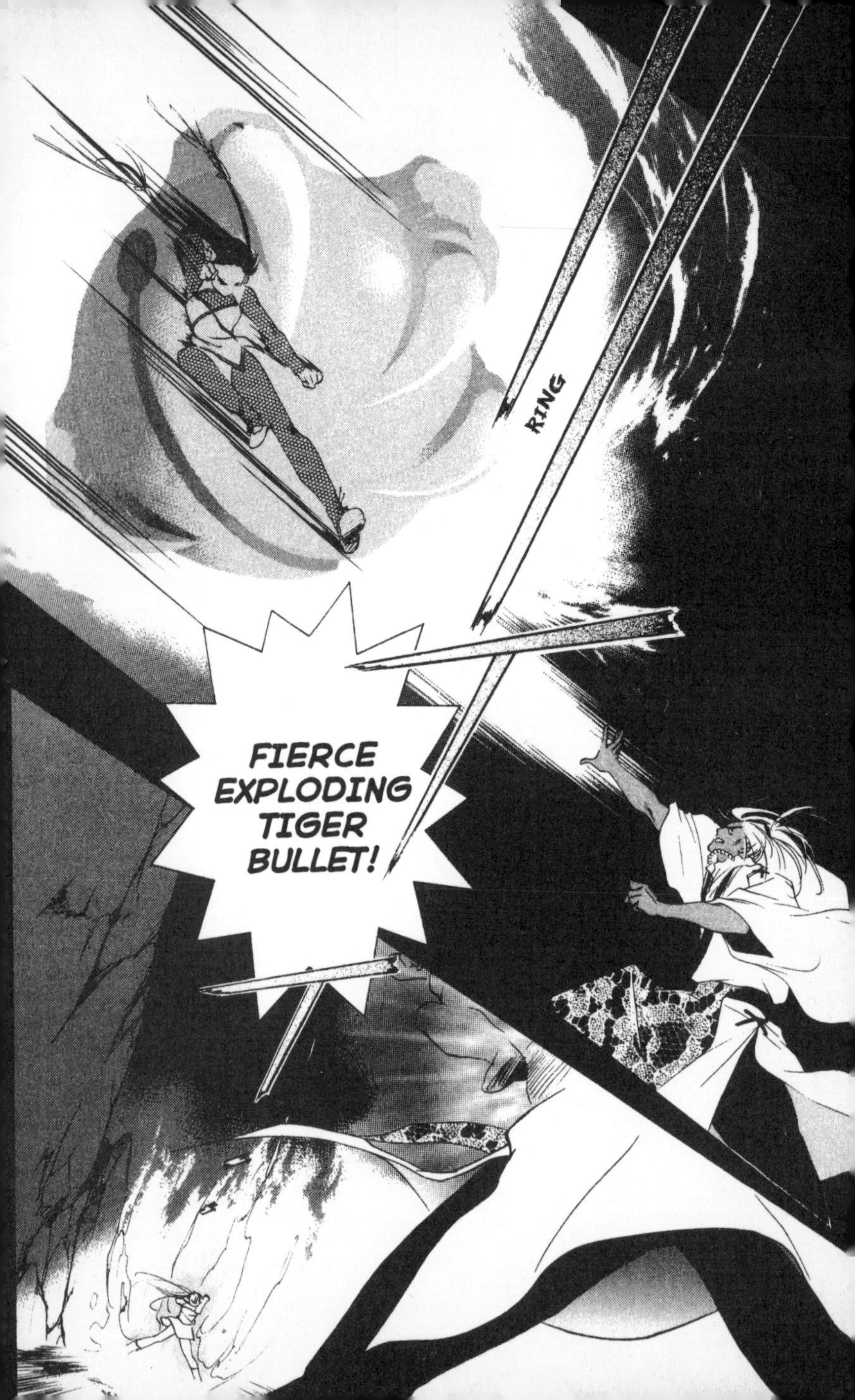
RING
FIERCE EXPLODING TIGER BULLET!

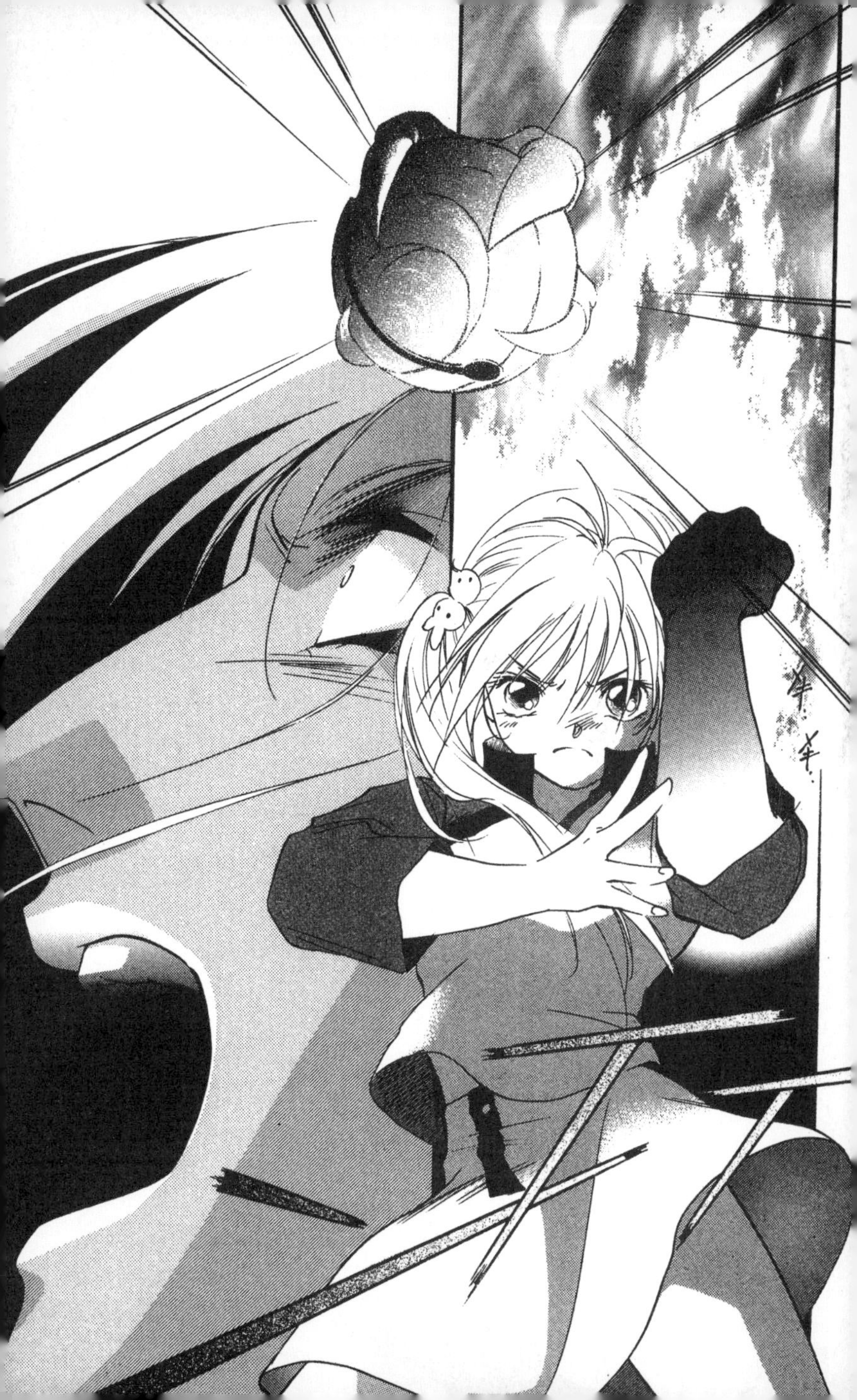

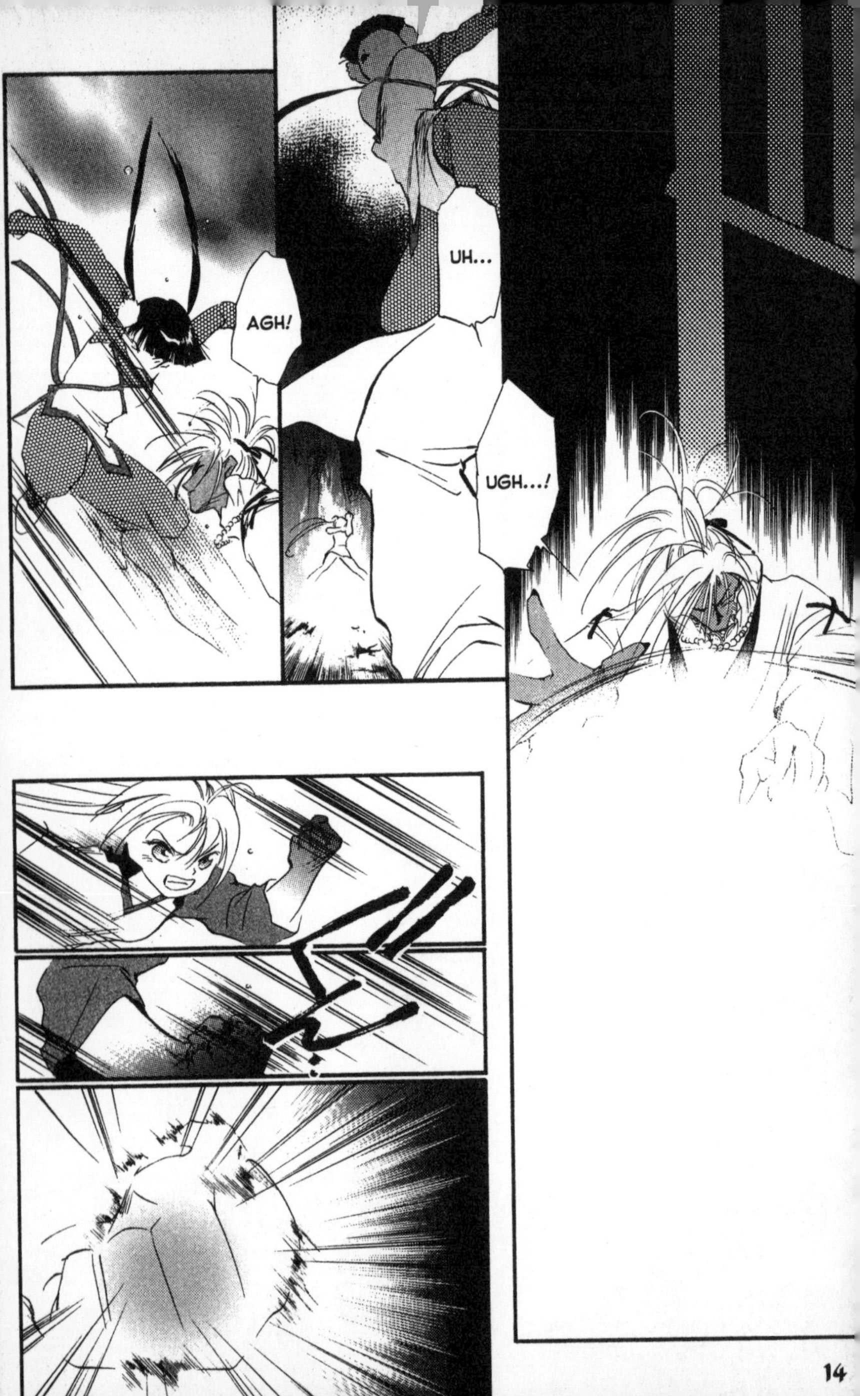
UH...
UGH...!
AGH!

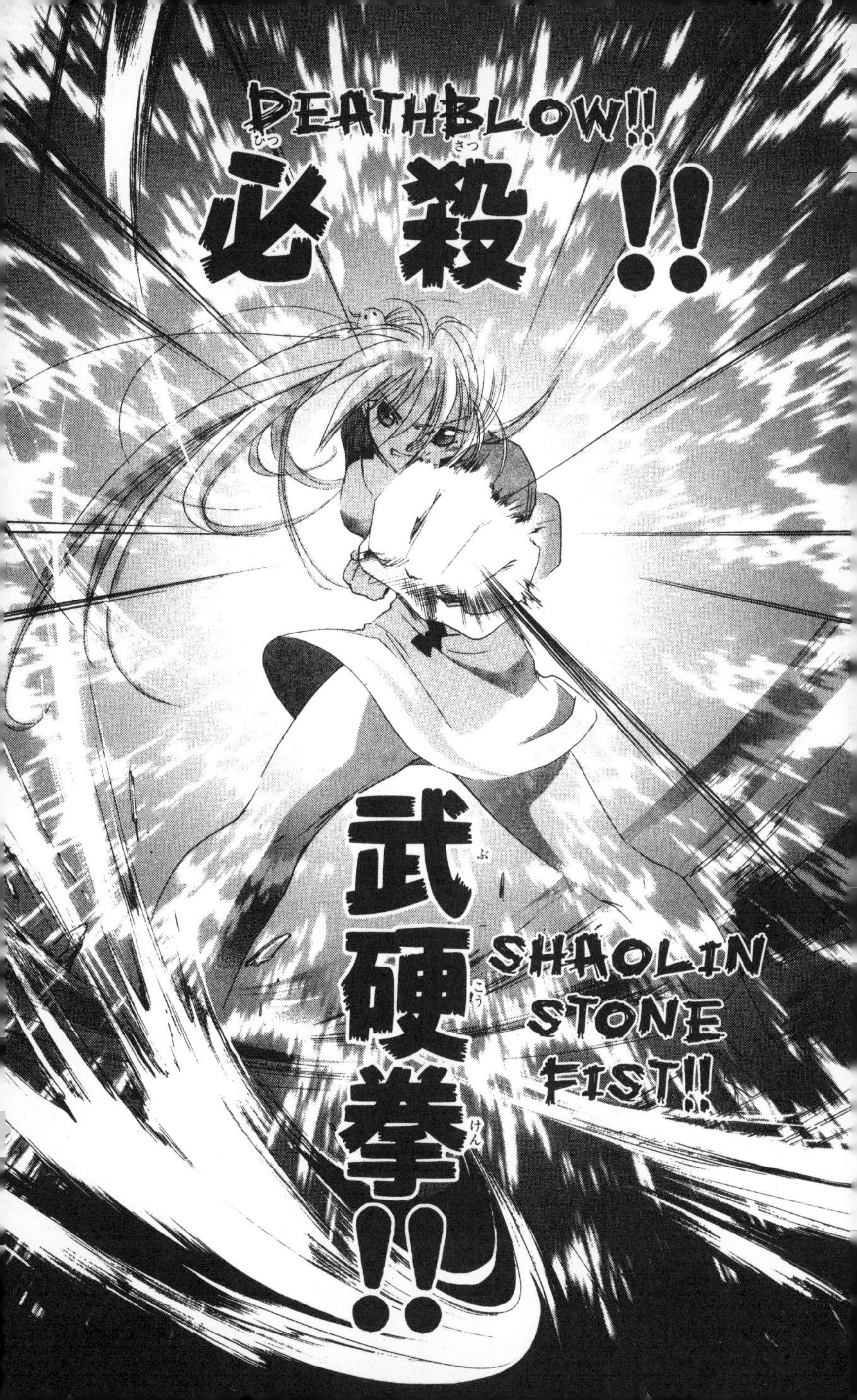
DEATHBLOW!!
必殺!!
武硬拳!!
SHAOLIN STONE FIST!!

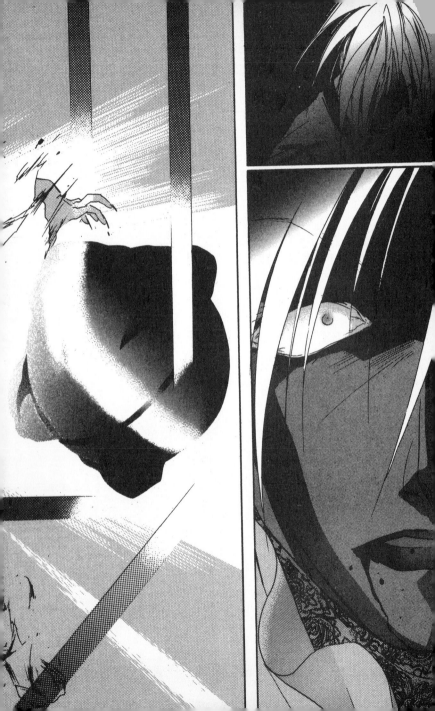

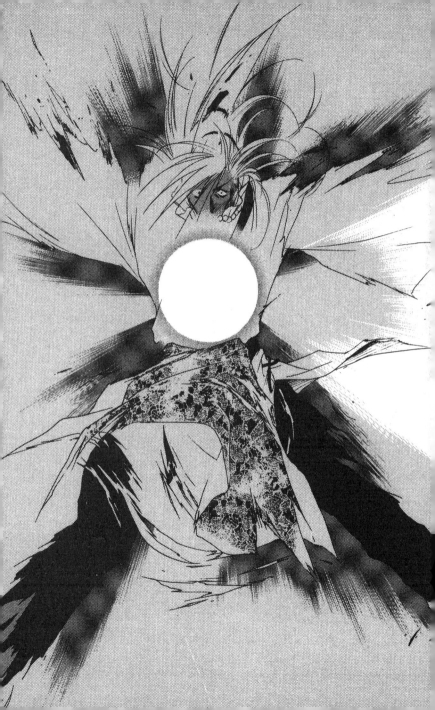

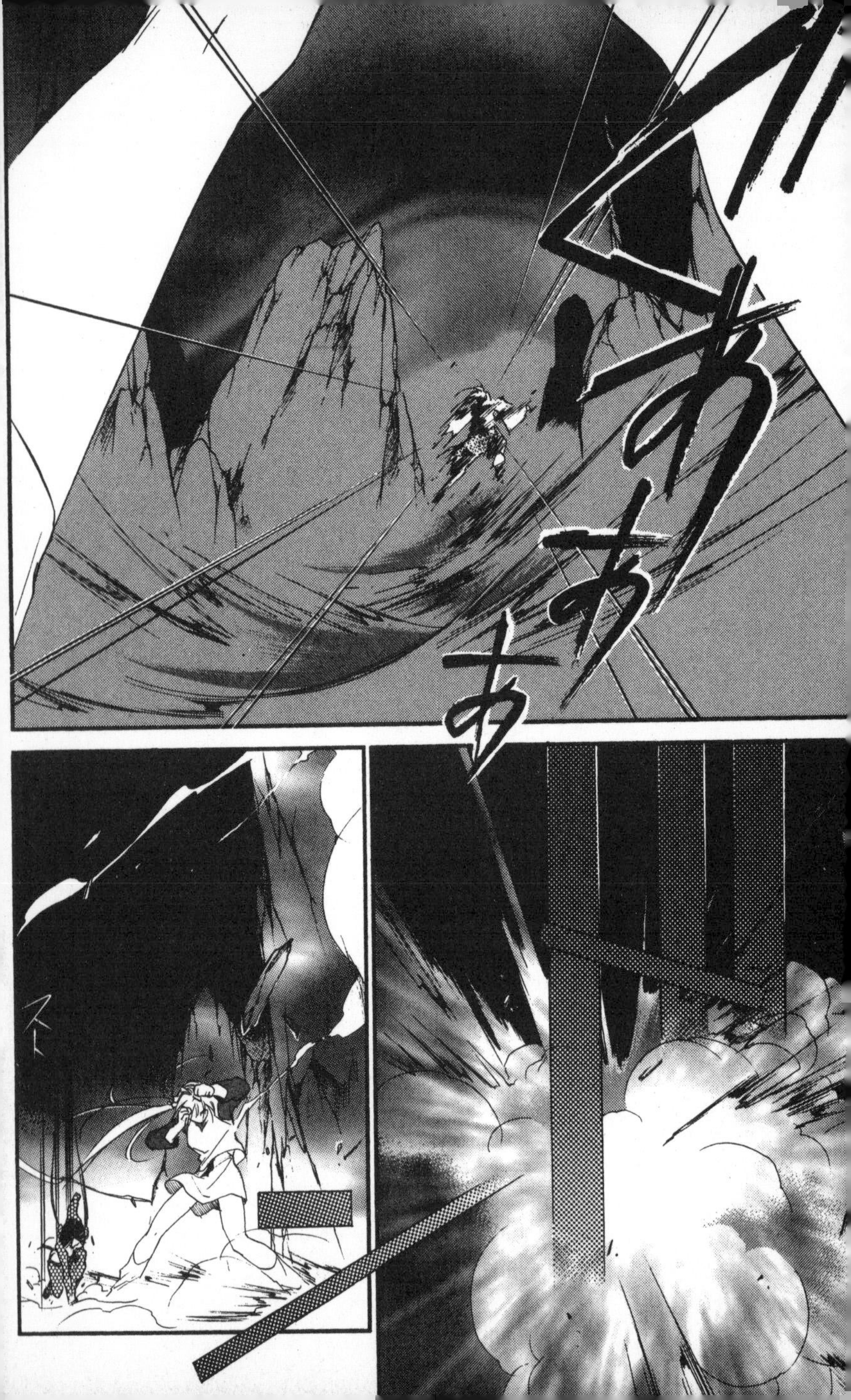
ぐあああ
スト

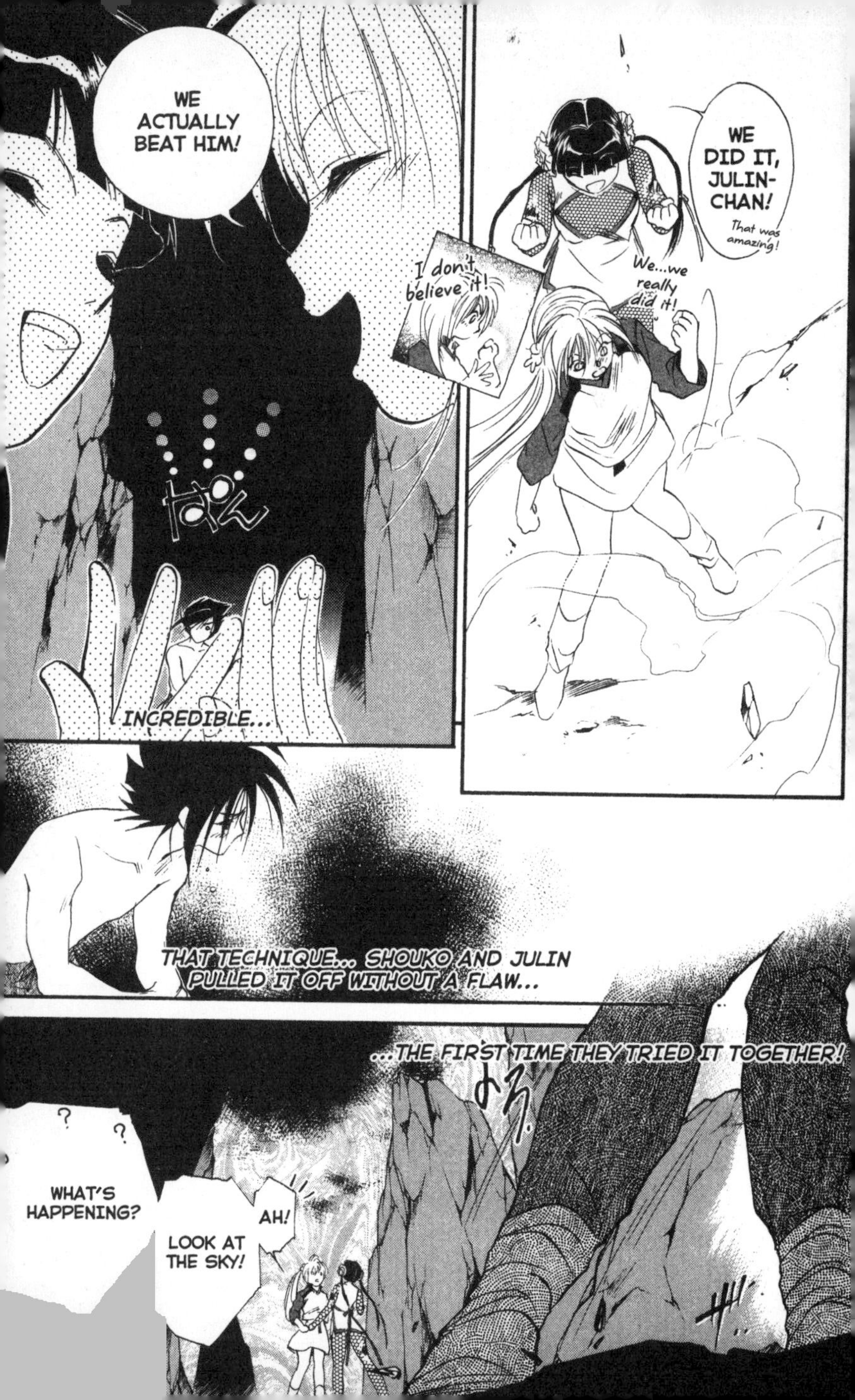
WE DID IT, JULIN-CHAN!
That was amazing!
We...we really did it!
I don't believe it!
WE ACTUALLY BEAT HIM!
ぱん
INCREDIBLE...
THAT TECHNIQUE... SHOUKO AND JULIN PULLED IT OFF WITHOUT A FLAW...
...THE FIRST TIME THEY TRIED IT TOGETHER!
よろ
AH!
LOOK AT THE SKY!
?
?
WHAT'S HAPPENING?

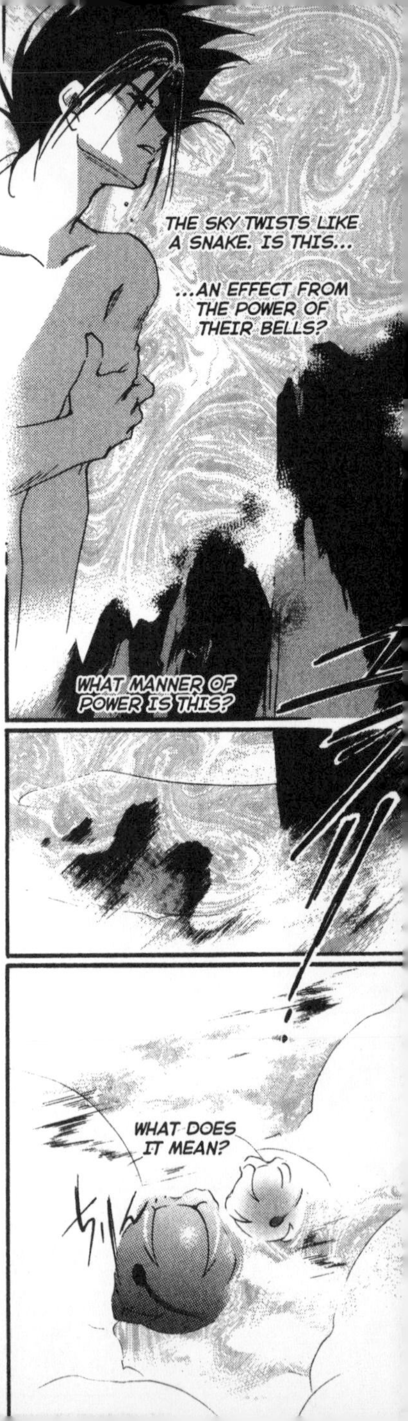
THE SKY TWISTS LIKE A SNAKE. IS THIS...
...AN EFFECT FROM THE POWER OF THEIR BELLS?
WHAT MANNER OF POWER IS THIS?
WHAT DOES IT MEAN?

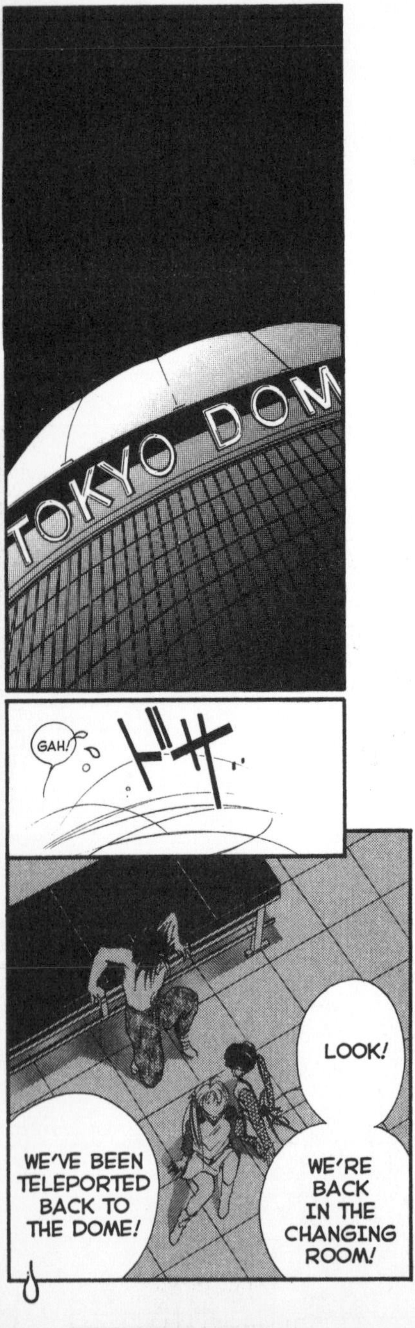
TOKYO DOM
GAH!
LOOK!
WE'RE BACK IN THE CHANGING ROOM!
WE'VE BEEN TELEPORTED BACK TO THE DOME!

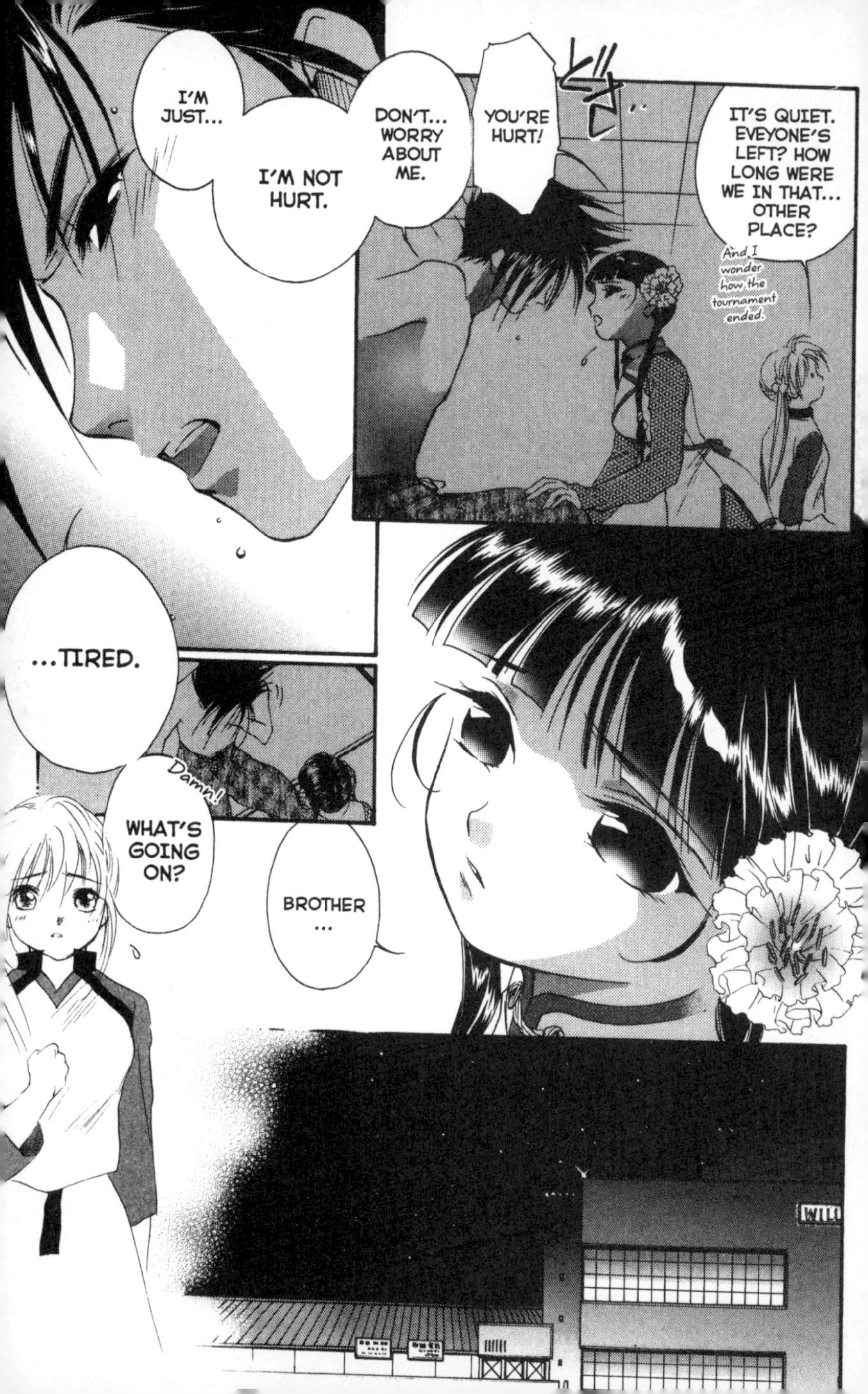
IT'S QUIET. EVEYONE'S LEFT? HOW LONG WERE WE IN THAT... OTHER PLACE?
And I wonder how the tournament ended.
YOU'RE HURT!
DON'T... WORRY ABOUT ME.
I'M NOT HURT.
I'M JUST...
...TIRED.
BROTHER ...
Damn!
WHAT'S GOING ON?

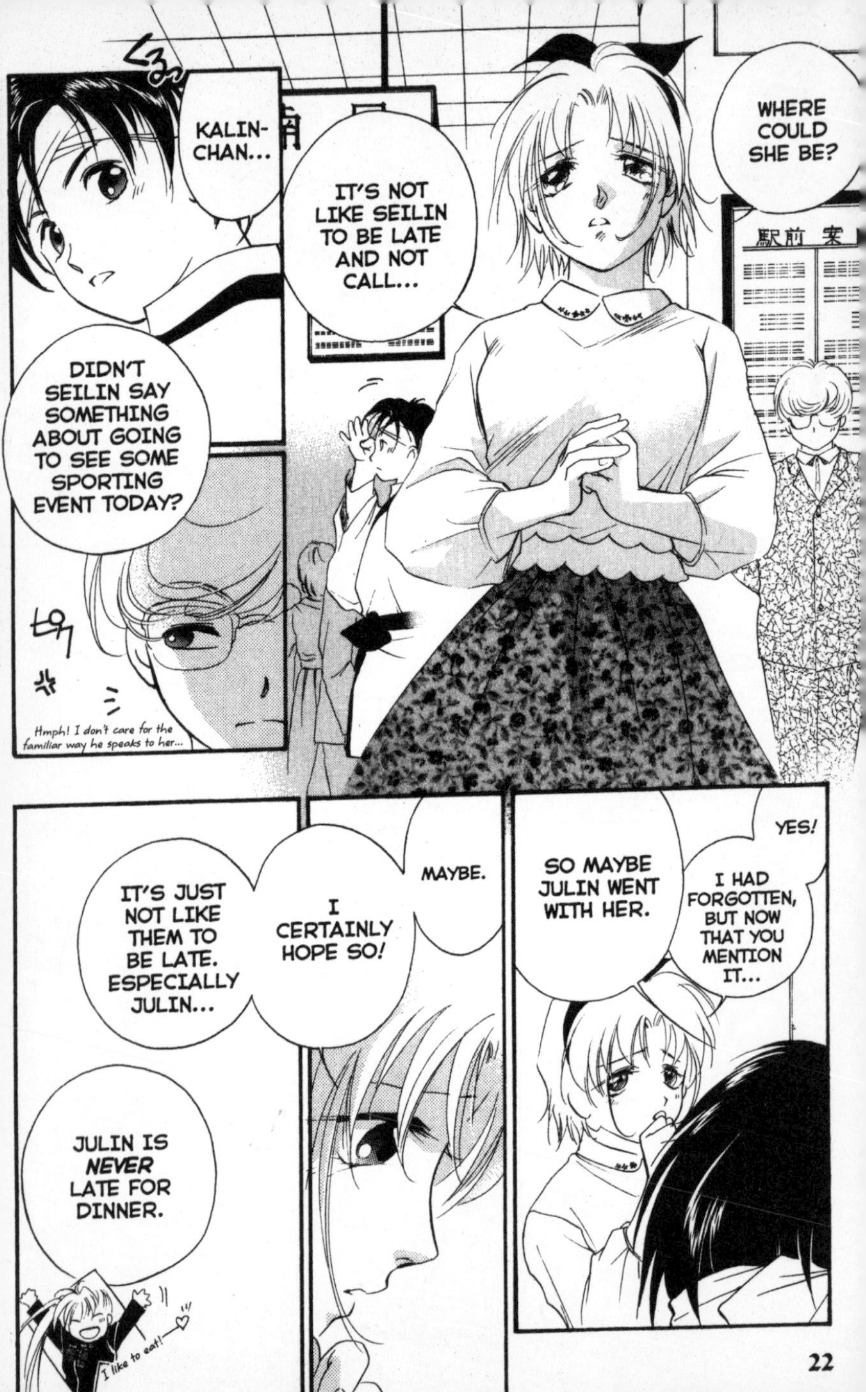
WHERE COULD SHE BE?
IT'S NOT LIKE SEILIN TO BE LATE AND NOT CALL...
KALIN-CHAN...
DIDN'T SEILIN SAY SOMETHING ABOUT GOING TO SEE SOME SPORTING EVENT TODAY?
Hmph! I don't care for the familiar way he speaks to her...
YES!
I HAD FORGOTTEN, BUT NOW THAT YOU MENTION IT...
SO MAYBE JULIN WENT WITH HER.
MAYBE.
I CERTAINLY HOPE SO!
IT'S JUST NOT LIKE THEM TO BE LATE. ESPECIALLY JULIN...
JULIN IS NEVER LATE FOR DINNER.
I like to eat!

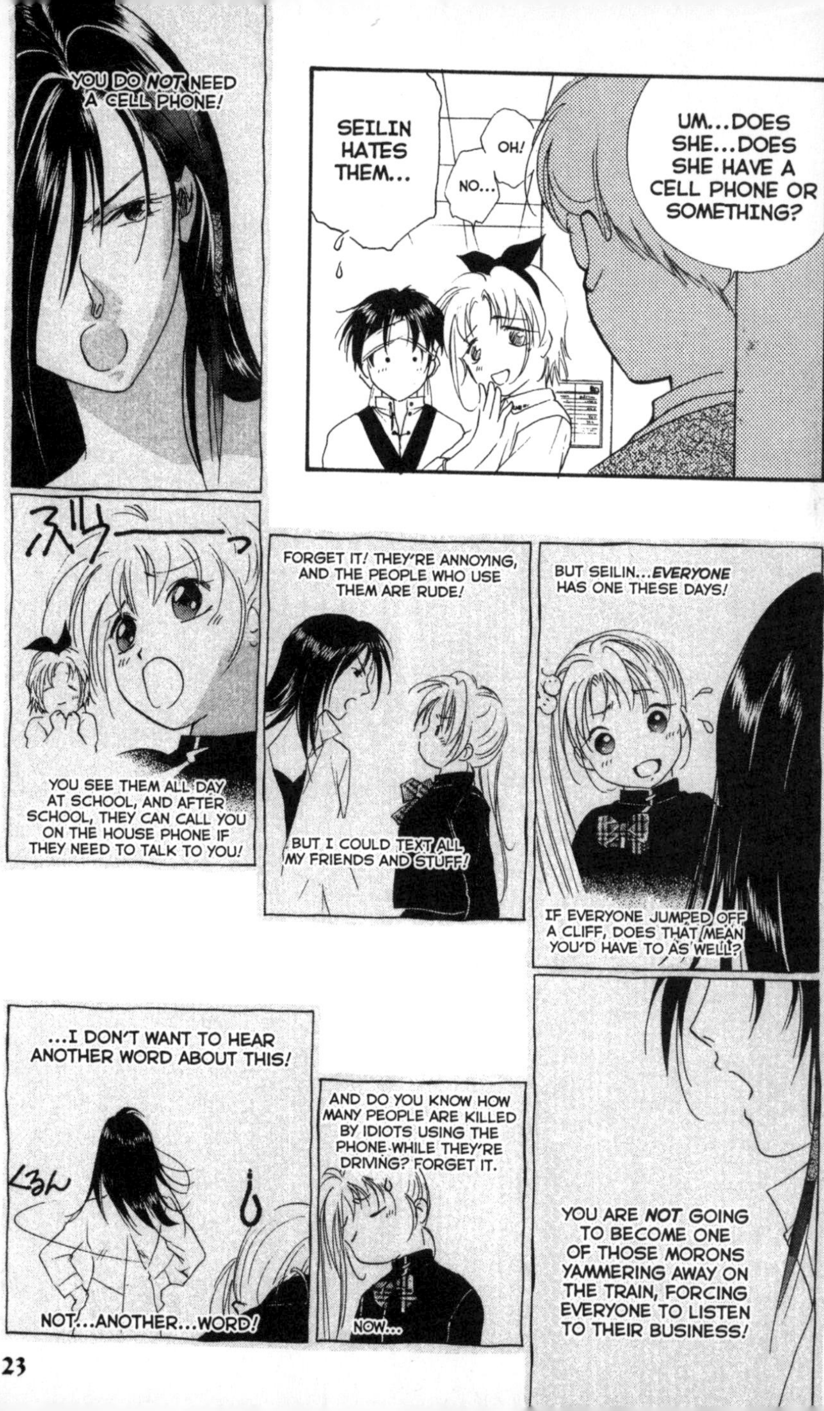
UM...DOES SHE...DOES SHE HAVE A CELL PHONE OR SOMETHING?
OH!
NO...
SEILIN HATES THEM...
YOU DO *NOT* NEED A CELL PHONE!
BUT SEILIN...*EVERYONE* HAS ONE THESE DAYS!
IF EVERYONE JUMPED OFF A CLIFF, DOES THAT MEAN YOU'D HAVE TO AS WELL!?
FORGET IT! THEY'RE ANNOYING, AND THE PEOPLE WHO USE THEM ARE RUDE!
BUT I COULD TEXT ALL MY FRIENDS AND STUFF!
YOU SEE THEM ALL DAY AT SCHOOL, AND AFTER SCHOOL, THEY CAN CALL YOU ON THE HOUSE PHONE IF THEY NEED TO TALK TO YOU!
YOU ARE *NOT* GOING TO BECOME ONE OF THOSE MORONS YAMMERING AWAY ON THE TRAIN, FORCING EVERYONE TO LISTEN TO THEIR BUSINESS!
AND DO YOU KNOW HOW MANY PEOPLE ARE KILLED BY IDIOTS USING THE PHONE WHILE THEY'RE DRIVING? FORGET IT.
NOW...
...I DON'T WANT TO HEAR ANOTHER WORD ABOUT THIS!
くるん
NOT...ANOTHER...WORD!

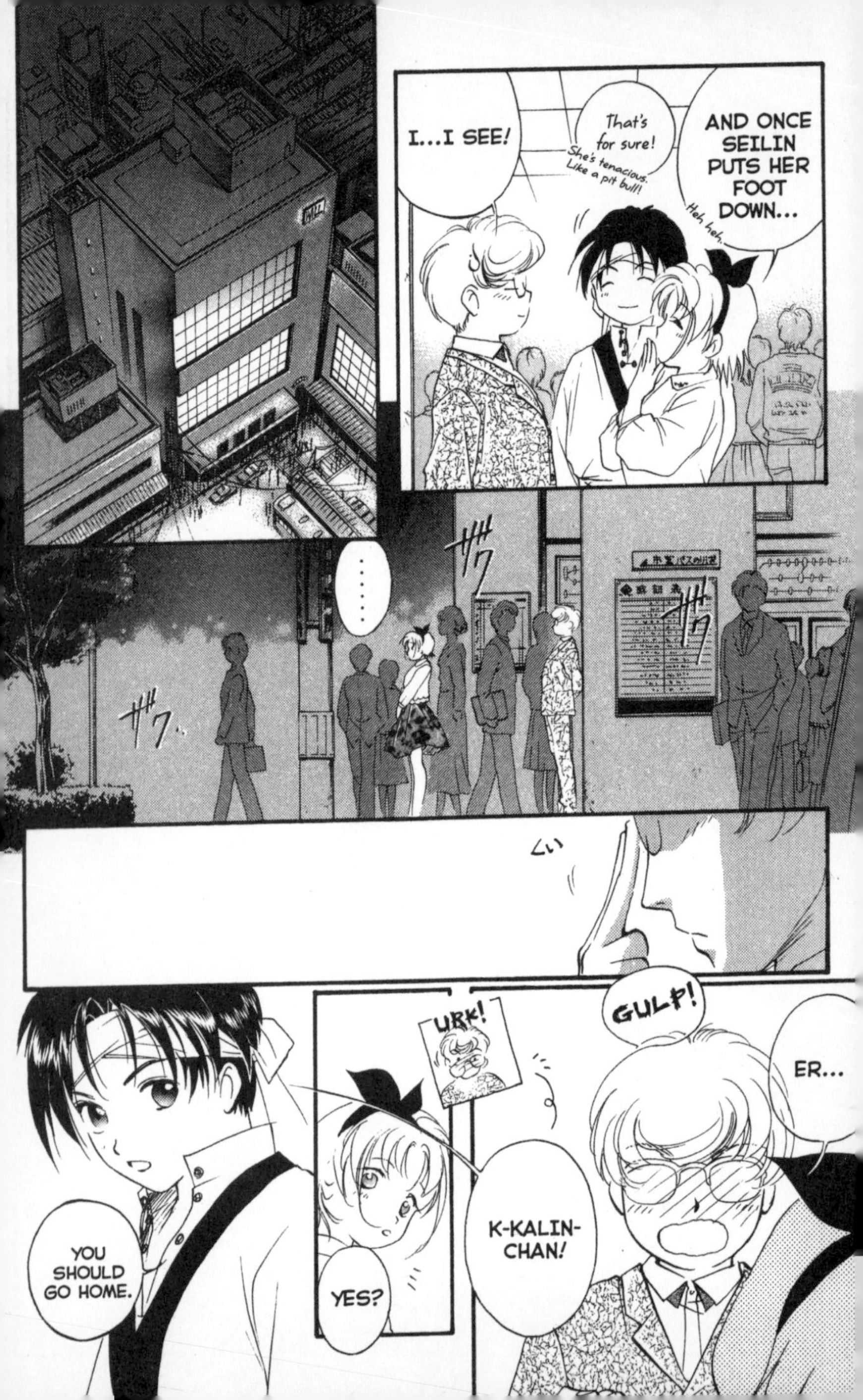
AND ONCE SEILIN PUTS HER FOOT DOWN...
Heh heh.
That's for sure!
She's tenacious. Like a pit bull!!
I...I SEE!
ザワ
ザワ
......
ザワ..
くい
ER...
GULP!
K-KALIN-CHAN!
URK!
YES?
YOU SHOULD GO HOME.

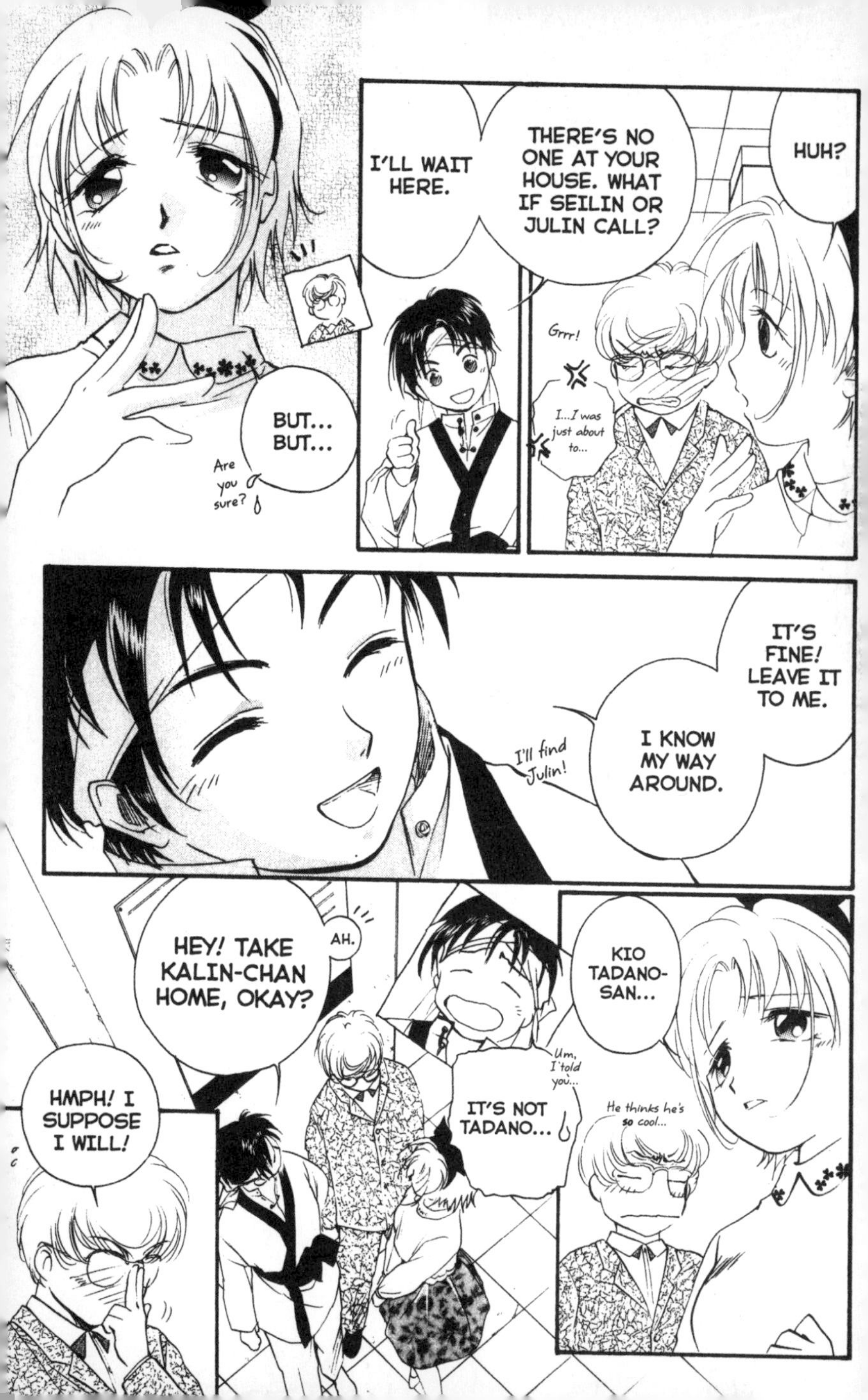
HUH?
THERE'S NO ONE AT YOUR HOUSE. WHAT IF SEILIN OR JULIN CALL?
Grrr!
I...I was just about to...
I'LL WAIT HERE.
BUT... BUT...
Are you sure?
IT'S FINE! LEAVE IT TO ME.
I KNOW MY WAY AROUND.
I'll find Julin!
KIO TADANO-SAN...
He thinks he's so cool...
AH.
HEY! TAKE KALIN-CHAN HOME, OKAY?
Um, I told you...
IT'S NOT TADANO...
HMPH! I SUPPOSE I WILL!

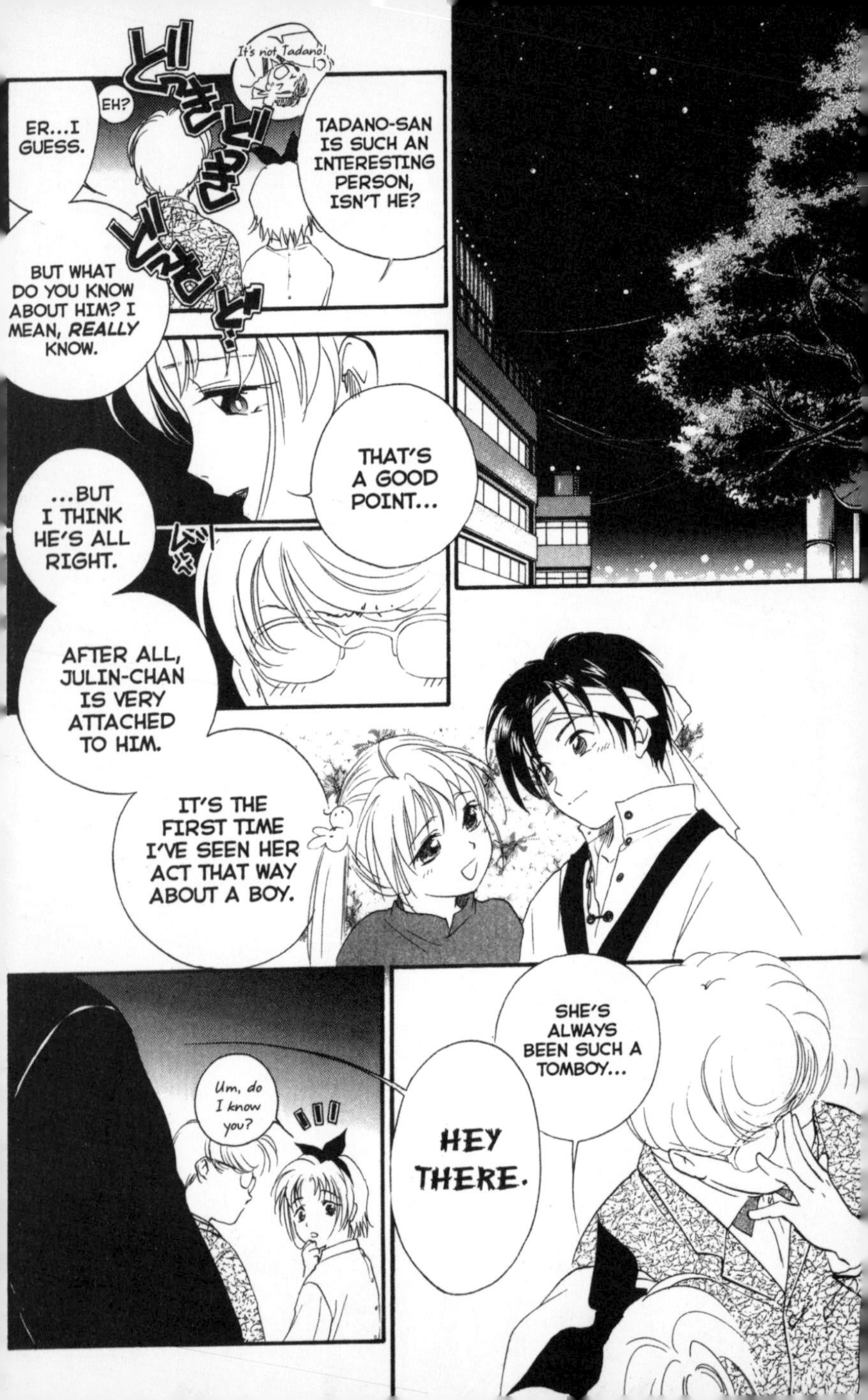
TADANO-SAN IS SUCH AN INTERESTING PERSON, ISN'T HE?
It's not Tadano!
EH?
ER...I GUESS.
BUT WHAT DO YOU KNOW ABOUT HIM? I MEAN, *REALLY* KNOW.
THAT'S A GOOD POINT...
...BUT I THINK HE'S ALL RIGHT.
AFTER ALL, JULIN-CHAN IS VERY ATTACHED TO HIM.
IT'S THE FIRST TIME I'VE SEEN HER ACT THAT WAY ABOUT A BOY.
SHE'S ALWAYS BEEN SUCH A TOMBOY...
HEY THERE.
Um, do I know you?

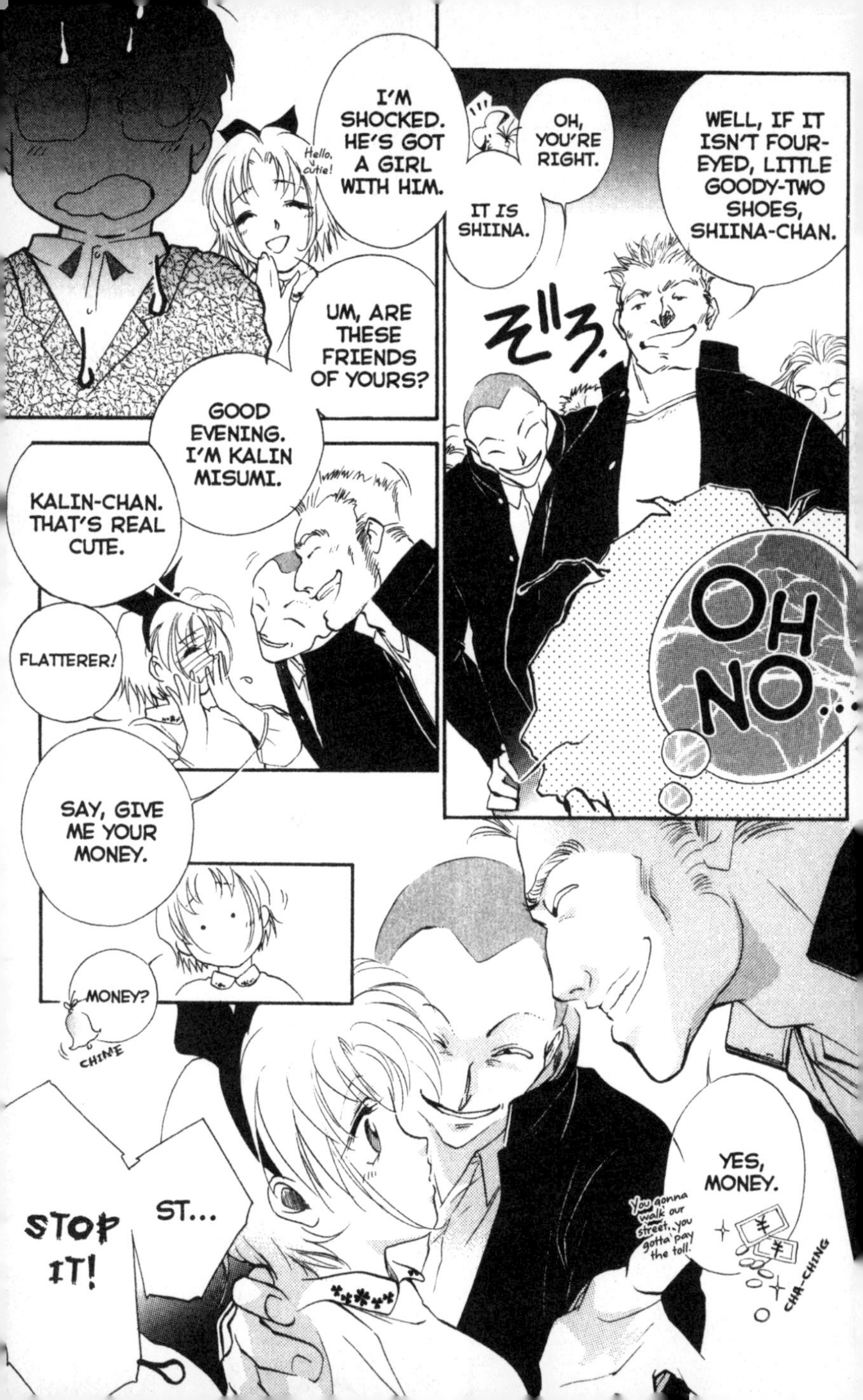
WELL, IF IT ISN'T FOUR-EYED, LITTLE GOODY-TWO SHOES, SHIINA-CHAN.
OH, YOU'RE RIGHT.
IT *IS* SHIINA.
ぞろ
OH NO...
I'M SHOCKED. HE'S GOT A GIRL WITH HIM.
Hello, cutie!
UM, ARE THESE FRIENDS OF YOURS?
GOOD EVENING. I'M KALIN MISUMI.
KALIN-CHAN. THAT'S REAL CUTE.
FLATTERER!
SAY, GIVE ME YOUR MONEY.
MONEY?
CHIME
YES, MONEY.
You gonna walk our street, you gotta pay the toll.
CHA-CHING
ST...
STOP IT!

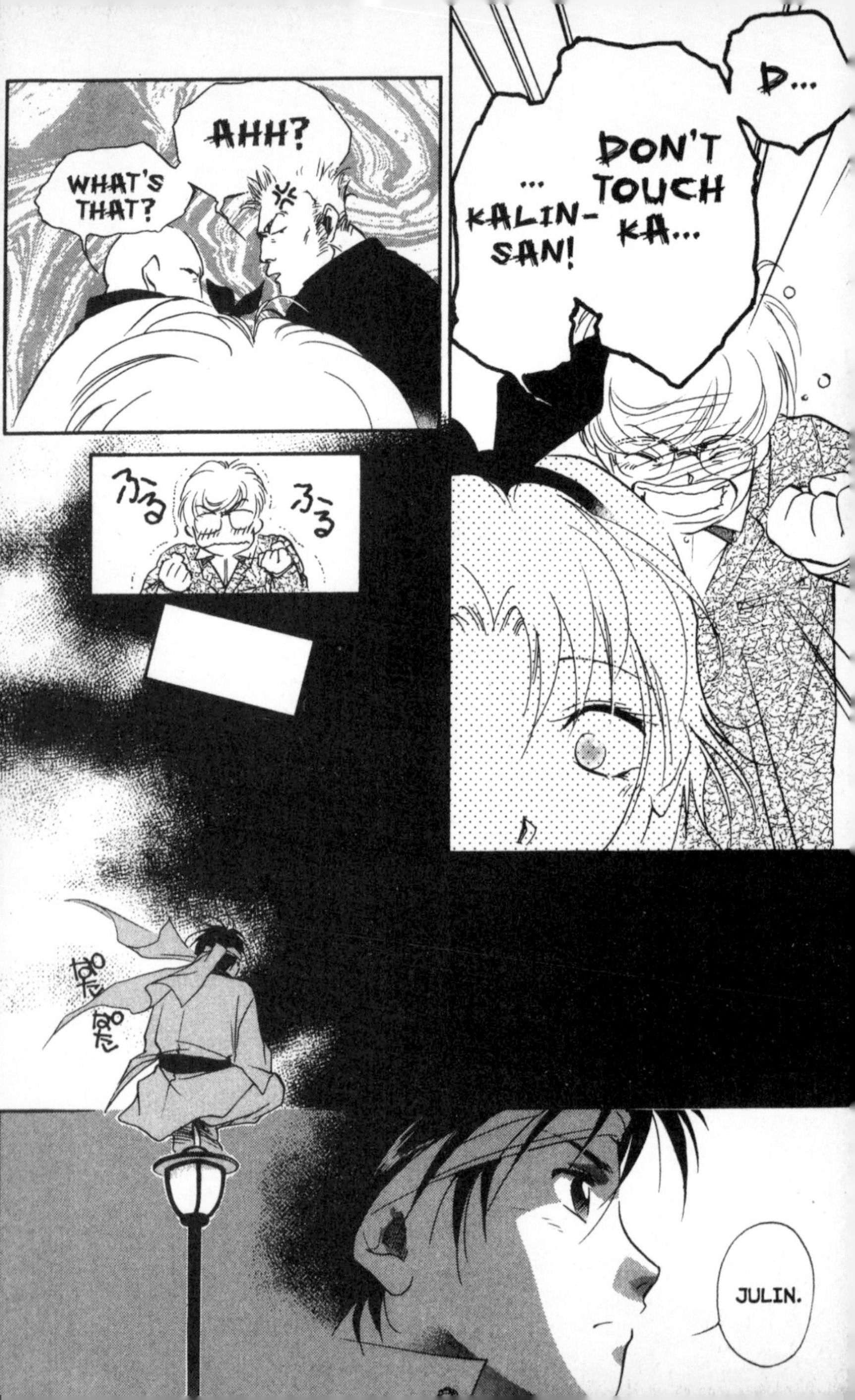
D...
DON'T TOUCH KA...
... KALIN-SAN!
AHH?
WHAT'S THAT?
ふる ふる
ぱた ぱた
JULIN.

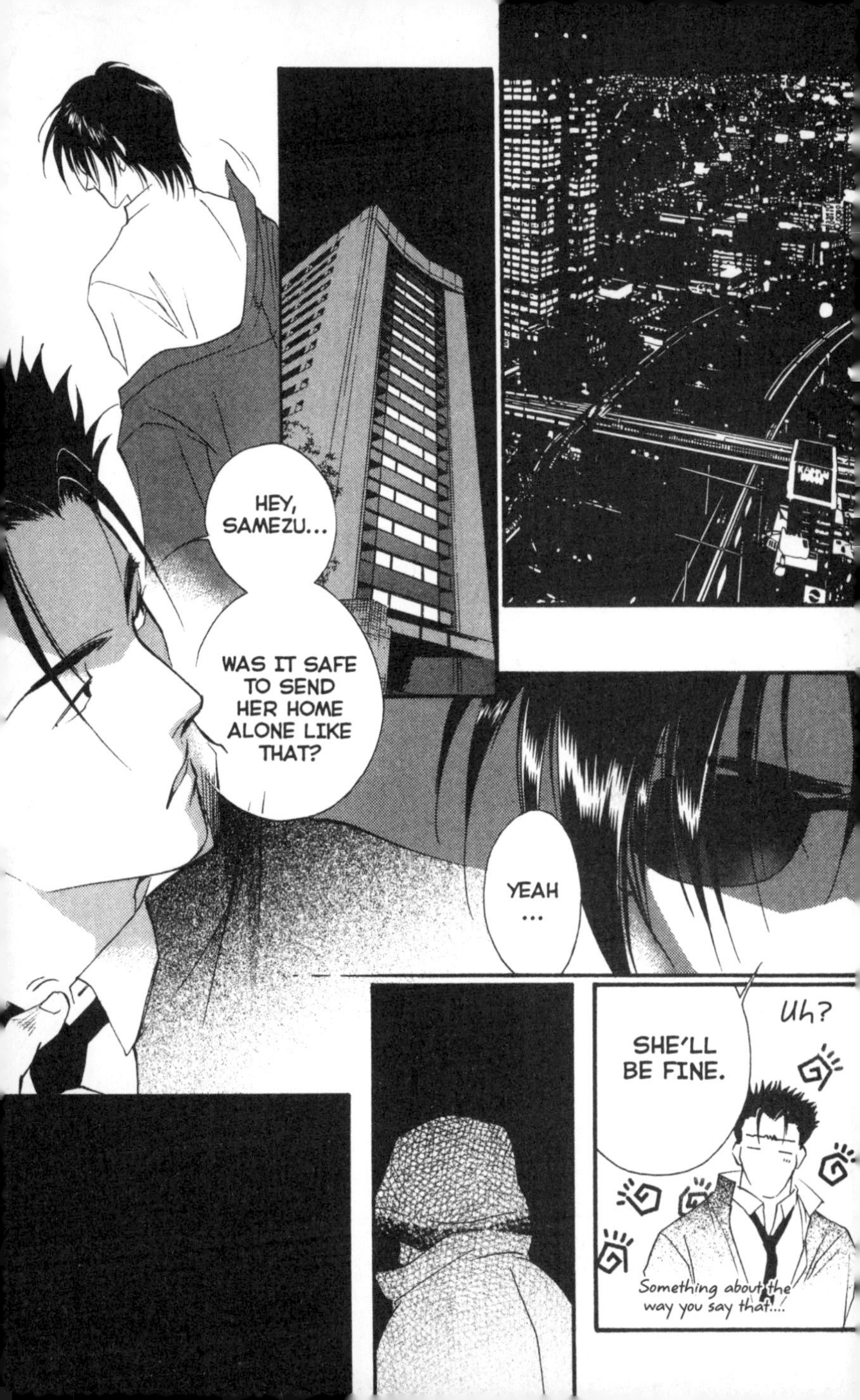
HEY, SAMEZU...
WAS IT SAFE TO SEND HER HOME ALONE LIKE THAT?
YEAH ...
SHE'LL BE FINE.
Uh?
Something about the way you say that...!

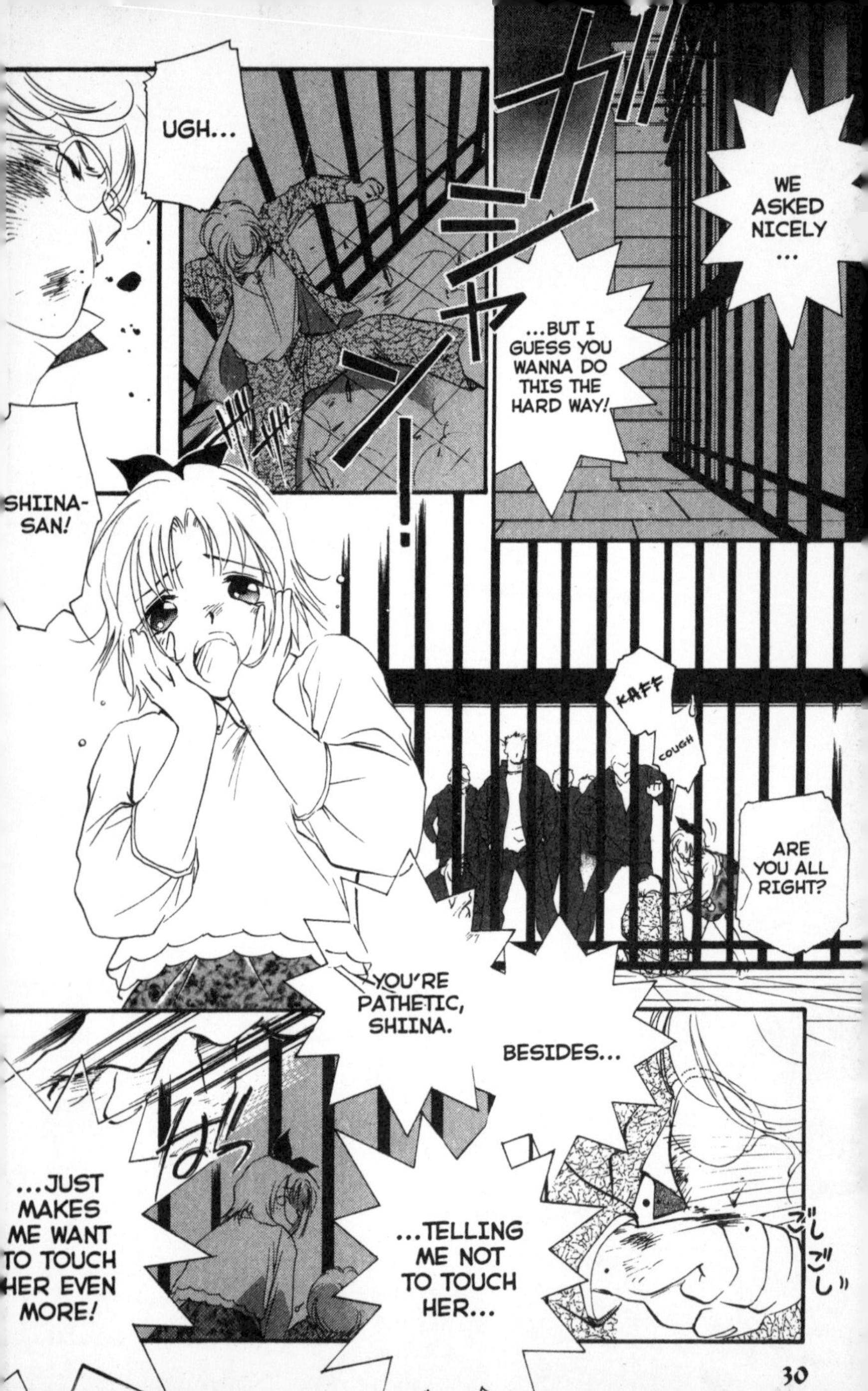
WE ASKED NICELY ...
...BUT I GUESS YOU WANNA DO THIS THE HARD WAY!
ガシャーン!
UGH...
KAFF
COUGH
ARE YOU ALL RIGHT?
SHIINA-SAN!
YOU'RE PATHETIC, SHIINA.
BESIDES...
ごしごし
...TELLING ME NOT TO TOUCH HER...
...JUST MAKES ME WANT TO TOUCH HER EVEN MORE!

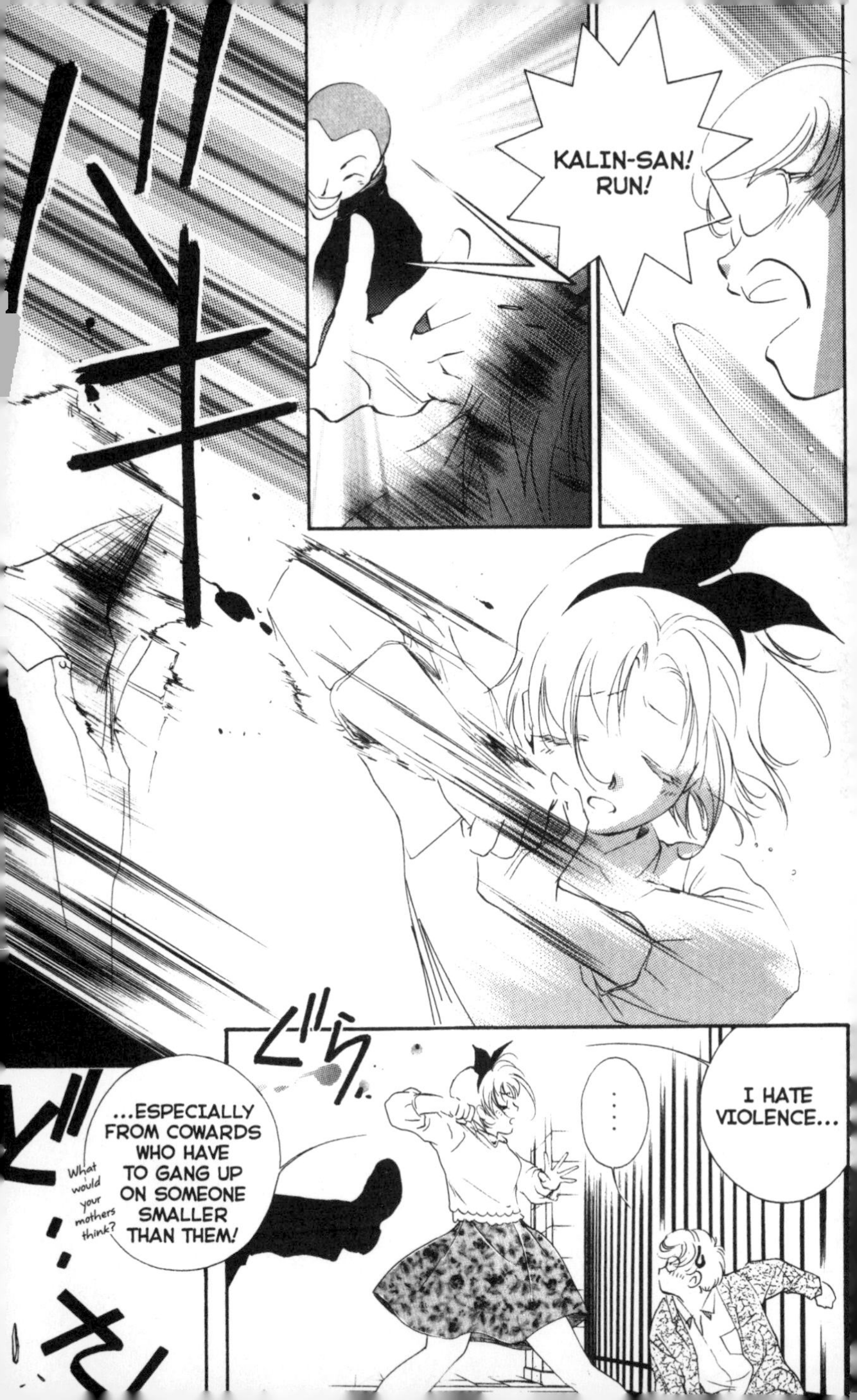
KALIN-SAN! RUN!
I HATE VIOLENCE...
....
...ESPECIALLY FROM COWARDS WHO HAVE TO GANG UP ON SOMEONE SMALLER THAN THEM!
What would your mothers think?

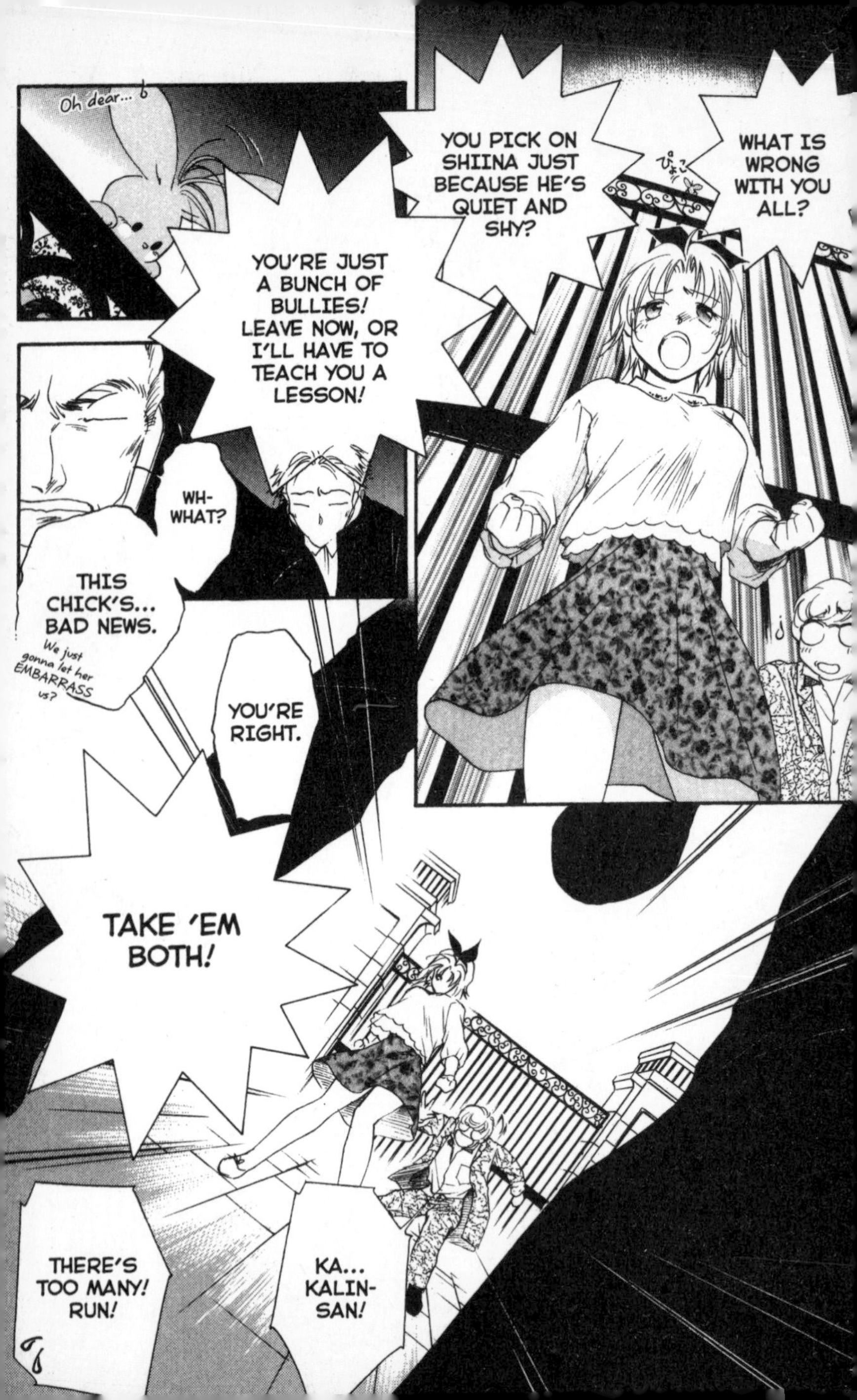
WHAT IS WRONG WITH YOU ALL?
YOU PICK ON SHIINA JUST BECAUSE HE'S QUIET AND SHY?
YOU'RE JUST A BUNCH OF BULLIES! LEAVE NOW, OR I'LL HAVE TO TEACH YOU A LESSON!
Oh dear...
WH- WHAT?
THIS CHICK'S... BAD NEWS.
We just gonna let her EMBARRASS us?
YOU'RE RIGHT.
TAKE 'EM BOTH!
KA... KALIN-SAN!
THERE'S TOO MANY! RUN!

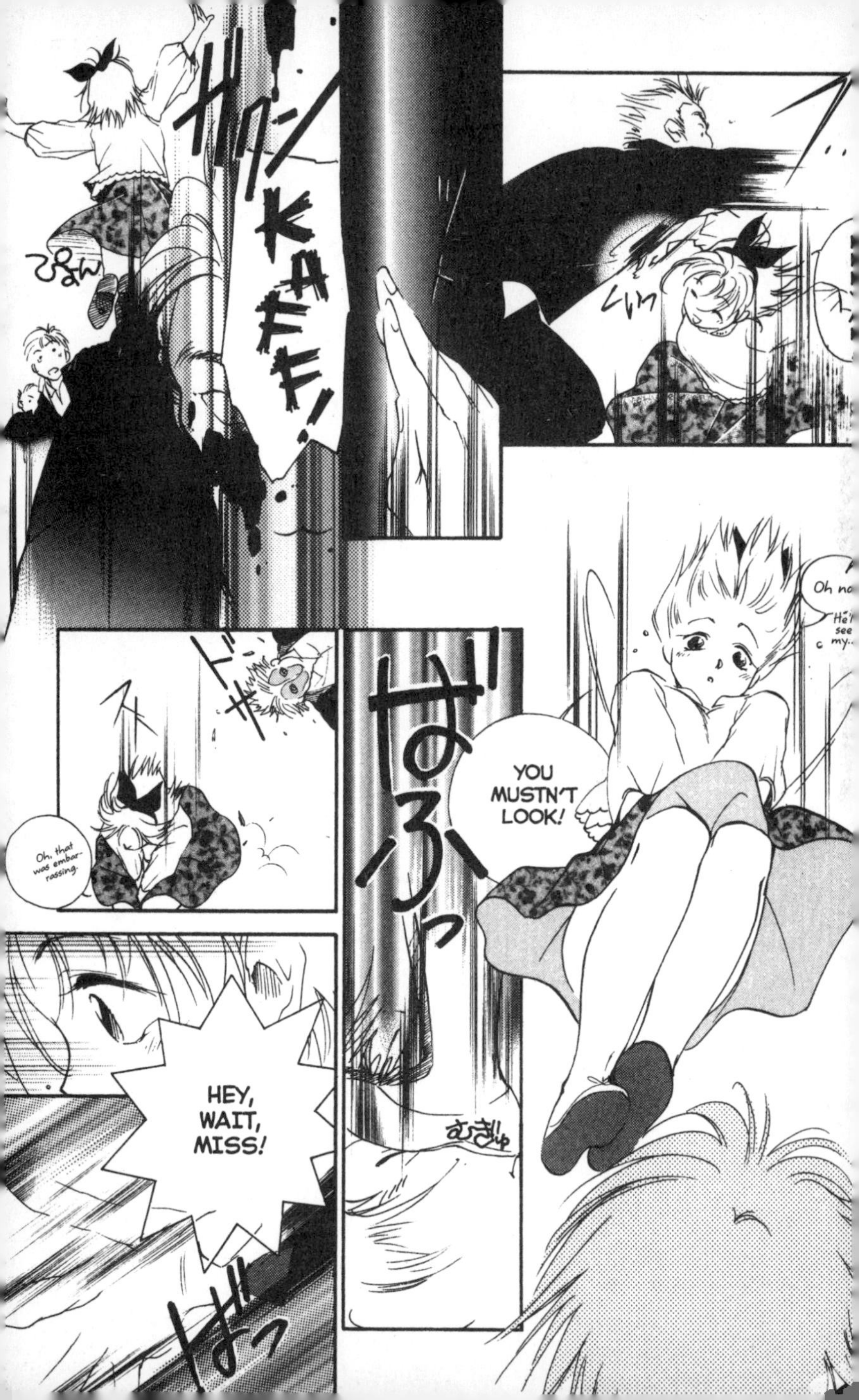
...
KAFFE!
ぴょん
Oh no
He' see my...
YOU MUSTN'T LOOK!
はふっ
むぎゅ
Oh, that was embarrassing.
HEY, WAIT, MISS!
ばっ

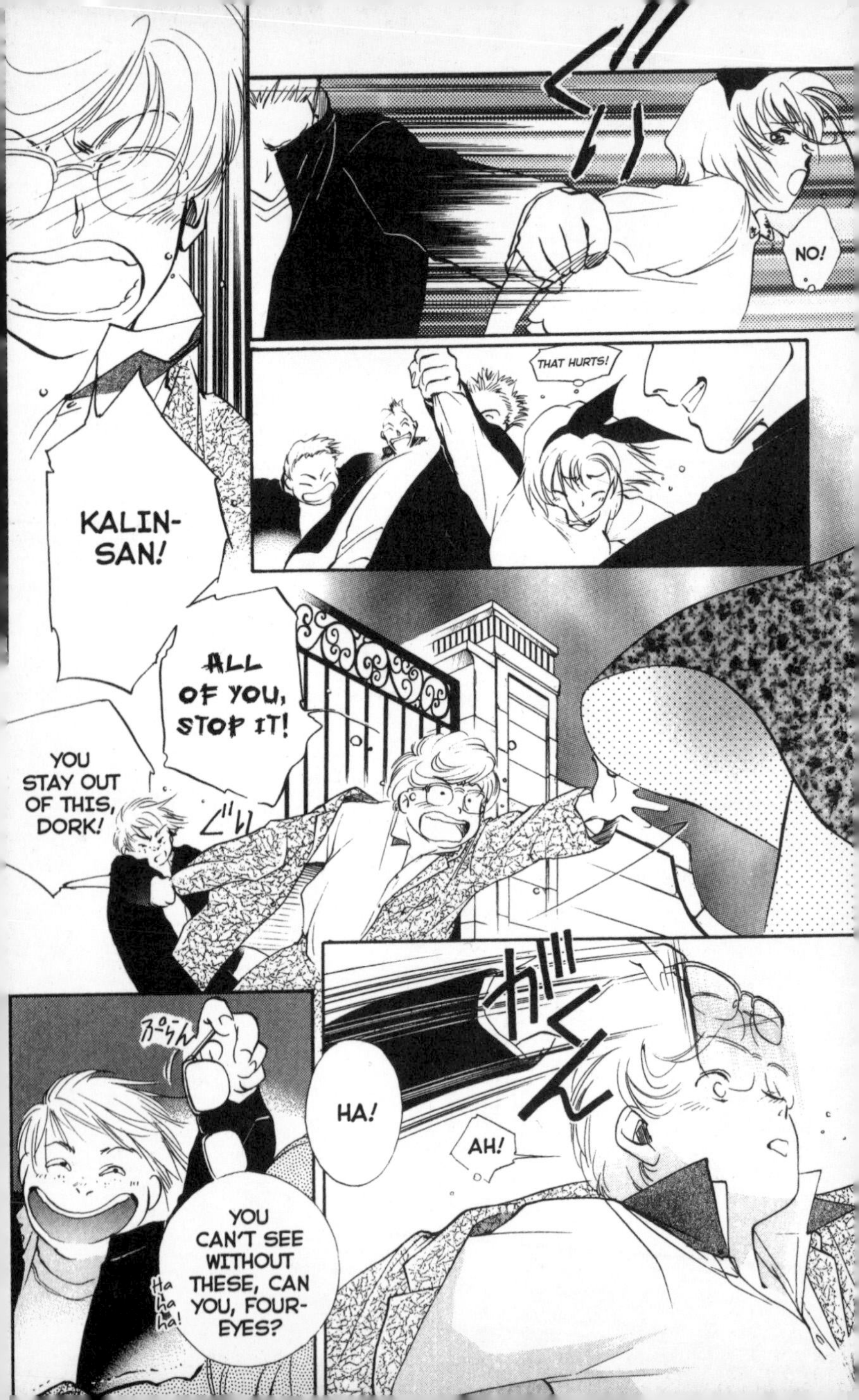
NO!
THAT HURTS!
KALIN-SAN!
ALL OF YOU, STOP IT!
YOU STAY OUT OF THIS, DORK!
ぐい
AH!
HA!
ぷらん
YOU CAN'T SEE WITHOUT THESE, CAN YOU, FOUR-EYES?
Ha ha ha!

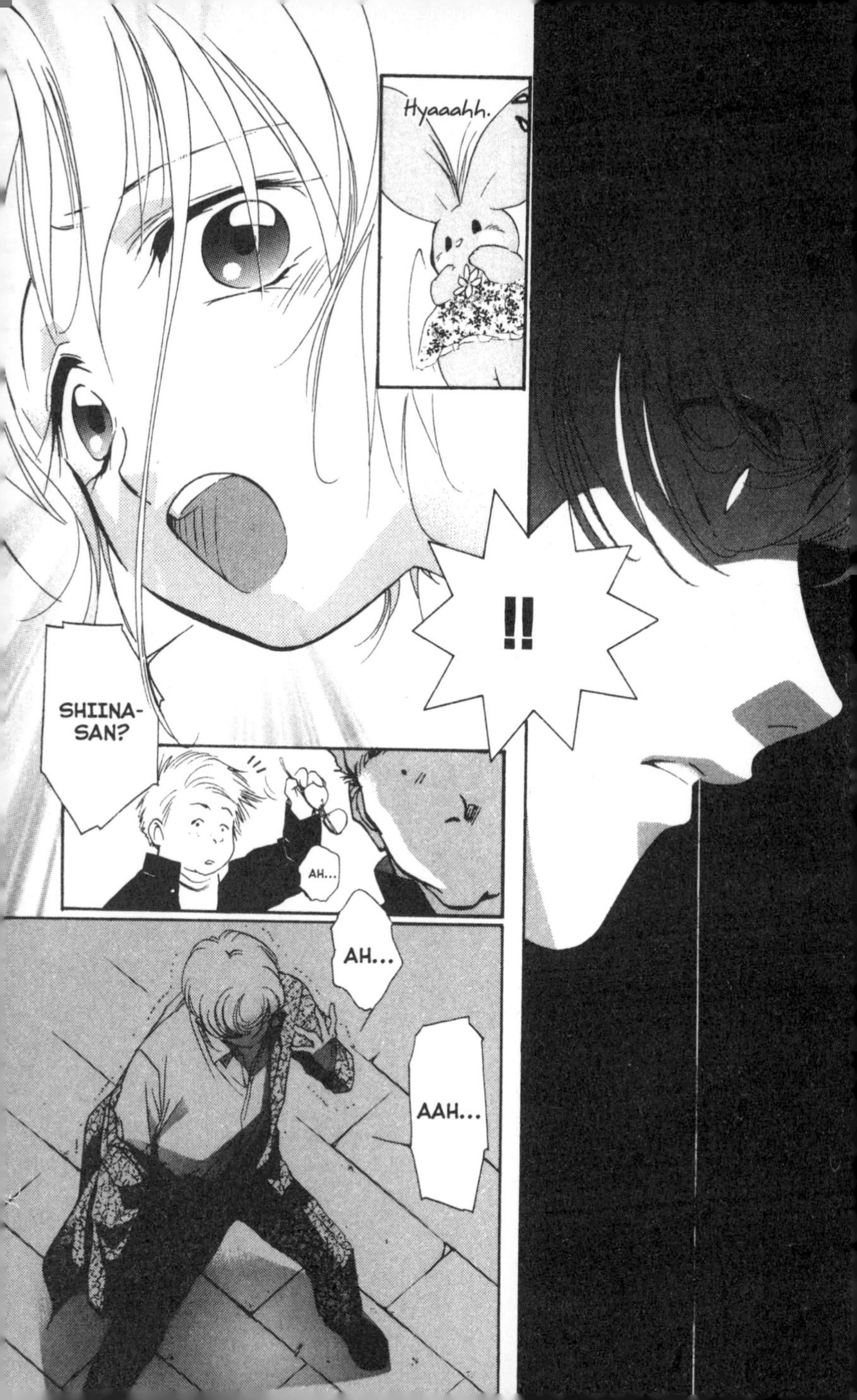

!!
Hyaaahh.
SHIINA-SAN?
AH...
AH...
AAH...

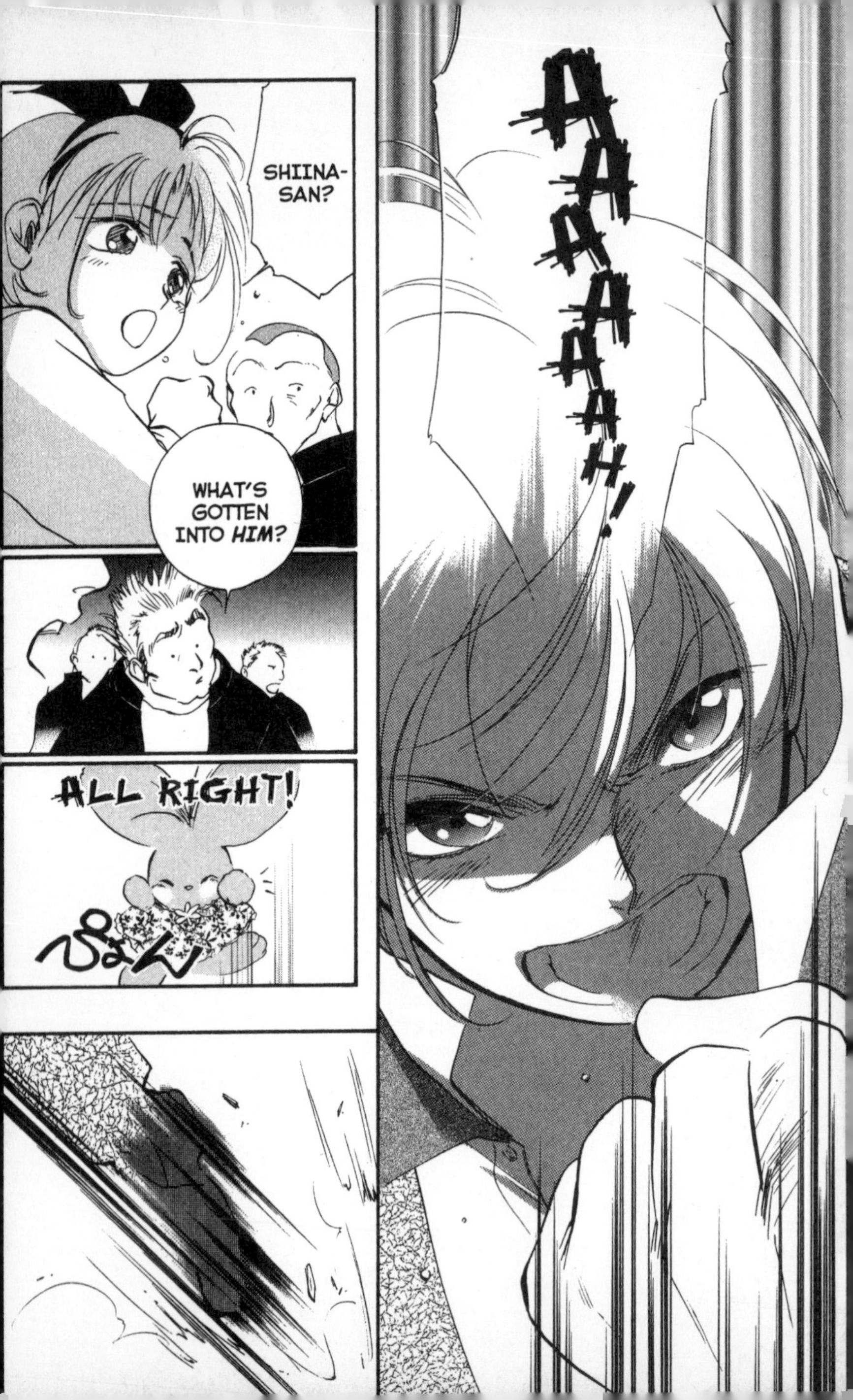
AAAAAAH!
SHIINA-SAN?
WHAT'S GOTTEN INTO *HIM*?
ALL RIGHT!
ぴょん

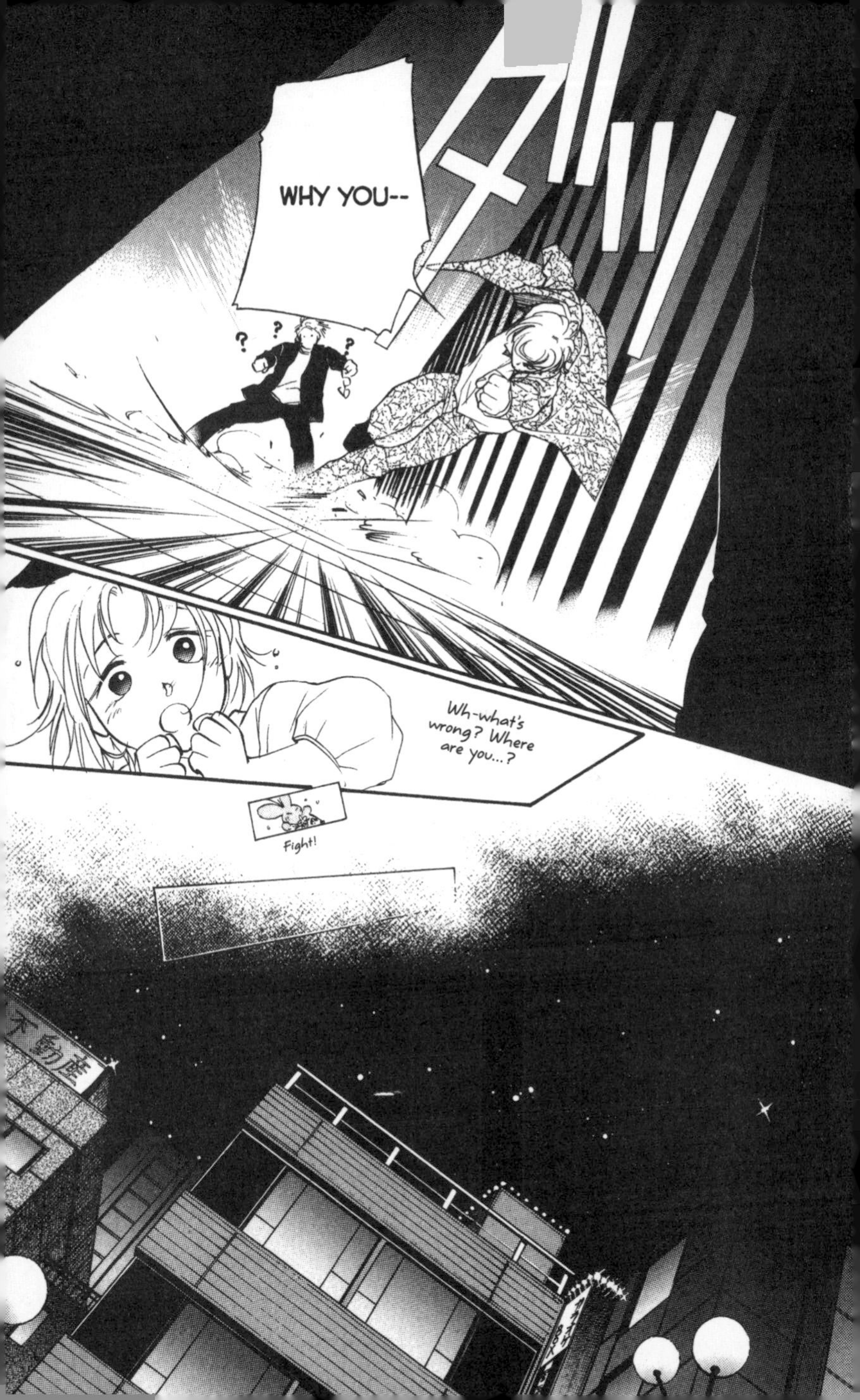
WHY YOU--
Wh-what's wrong? Where are you...?
Fight!
不動産

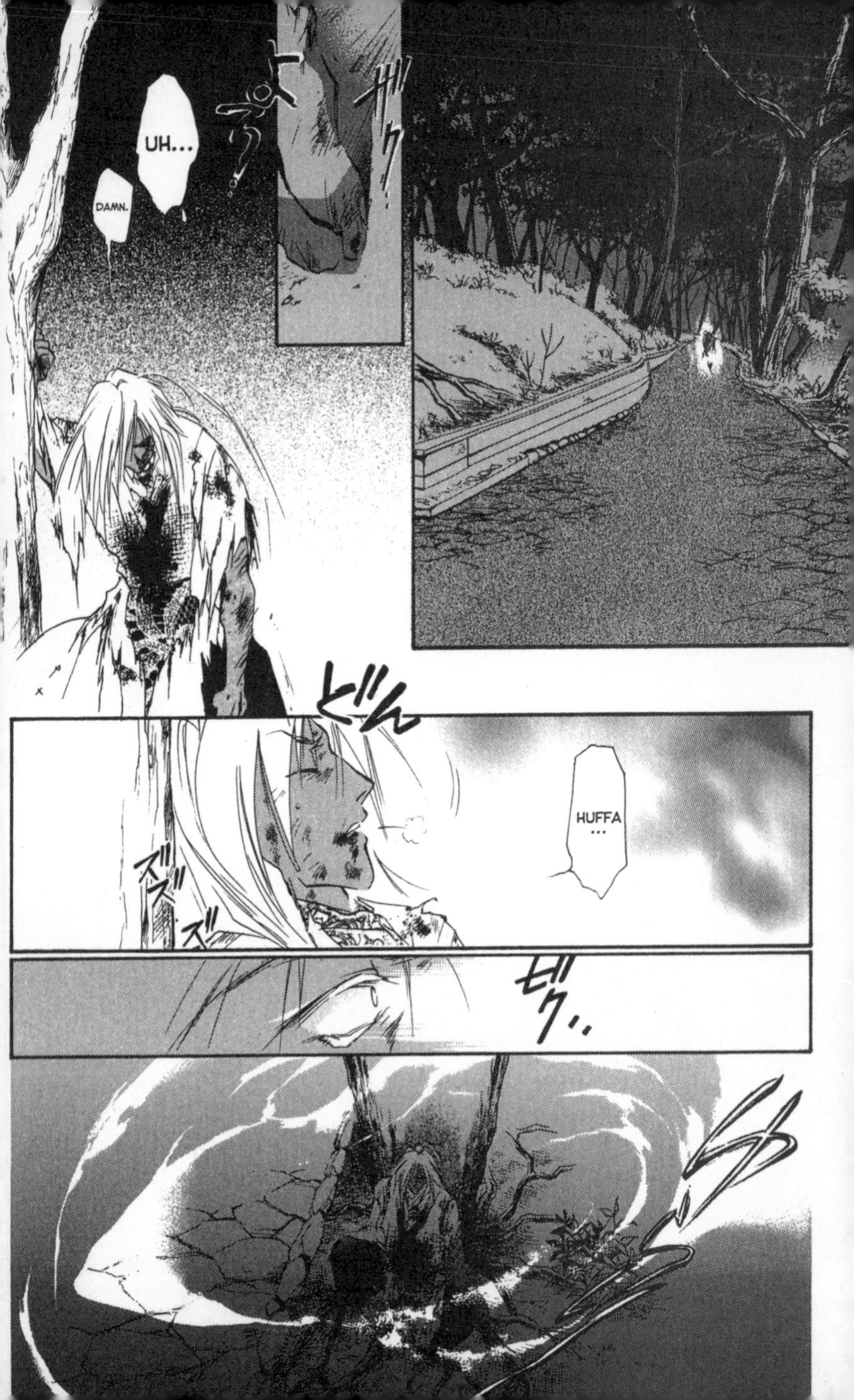
UH...
DAMN.
HUFFA ...

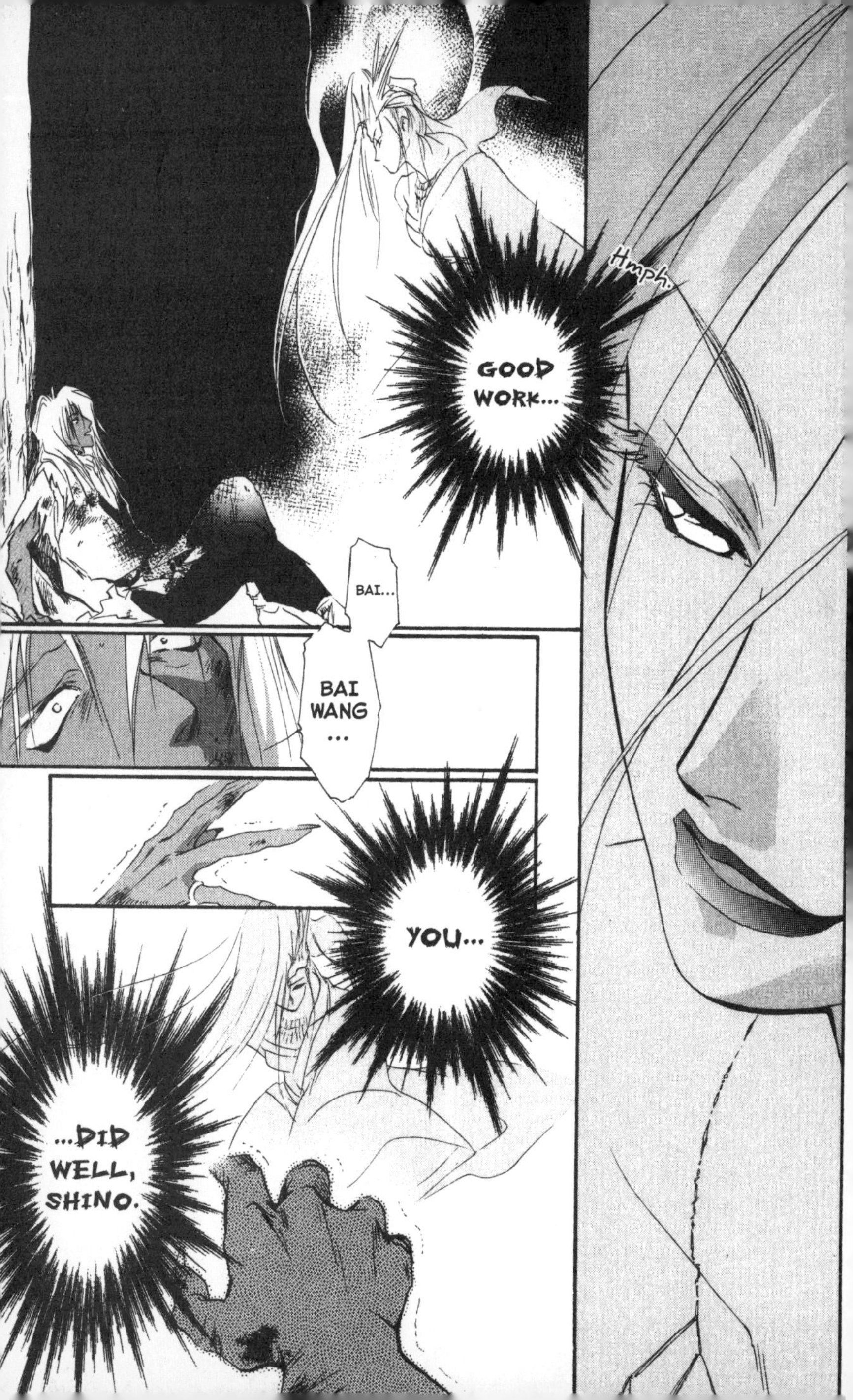
Hmph.
GOOD WORK...
BAI...
BAI WANG...
YOU...
...DID WELL, SHINO.

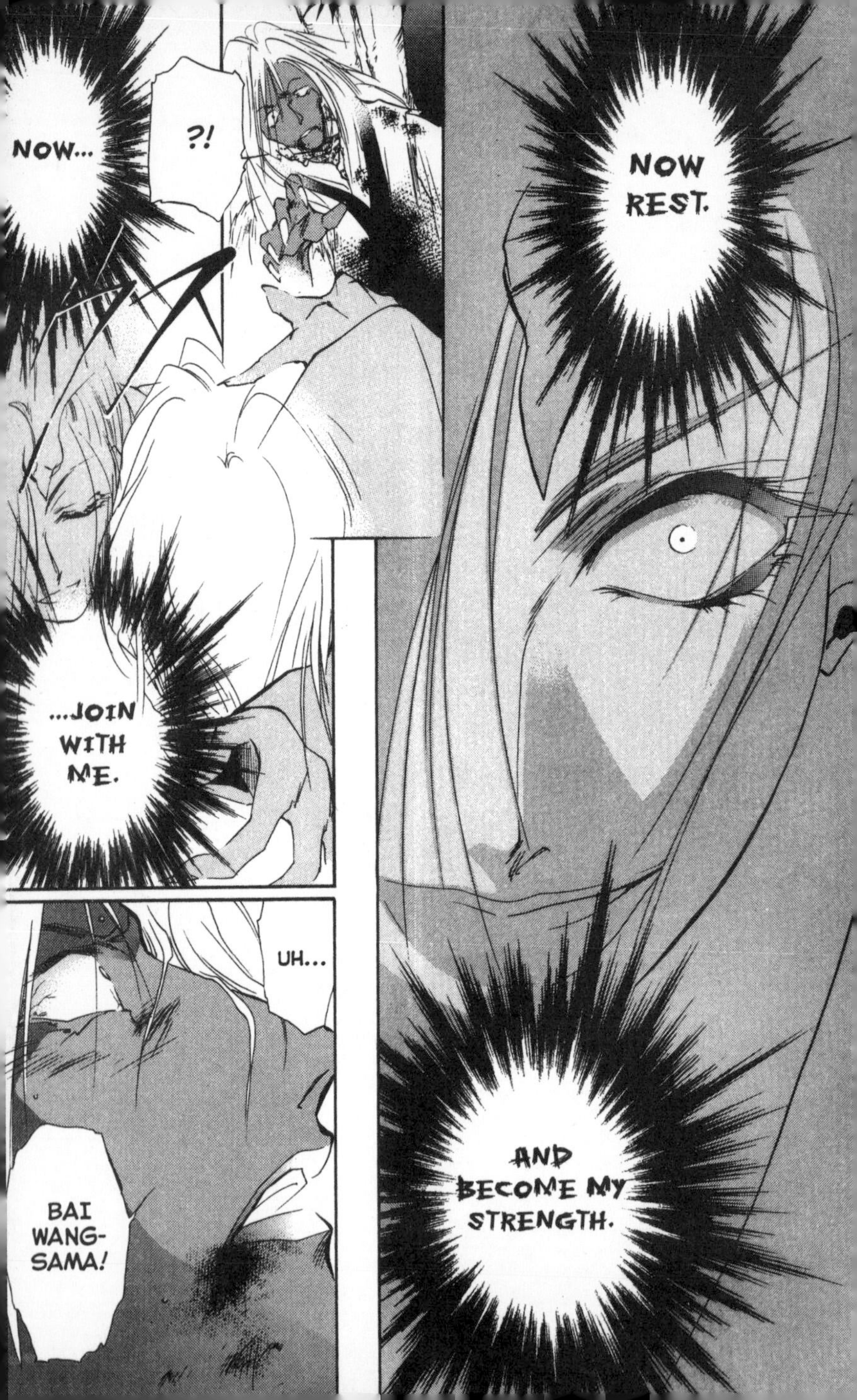
NOW REST.
AND BECOME MY STRENGTH.
?!
NOW...
...JOIN WITH ME.
UH...
BAI WANG-SAMA!

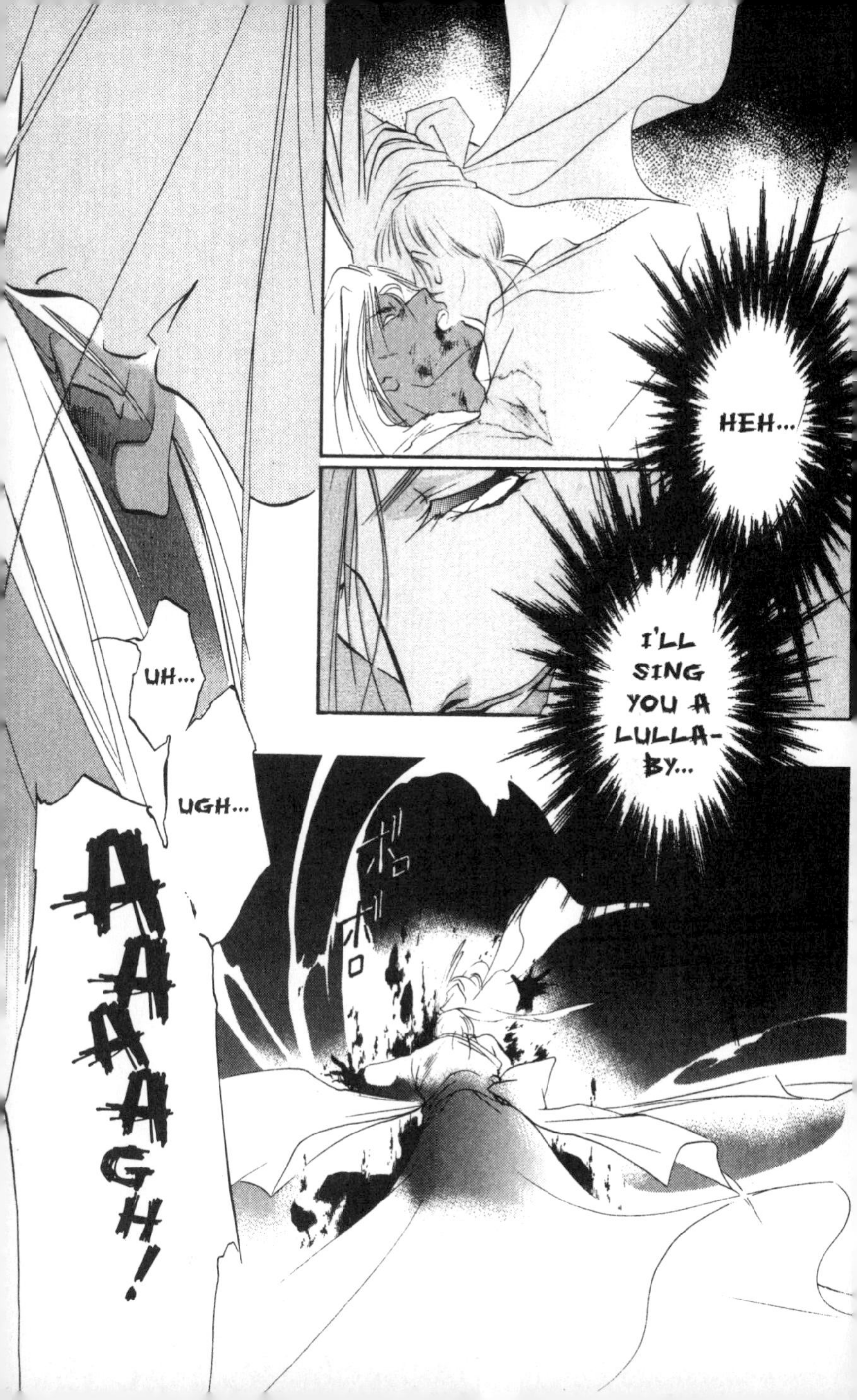
HEH...
I'LL SING YOU A LULLA-BY...
UH...
UGH...
AAAAGH!

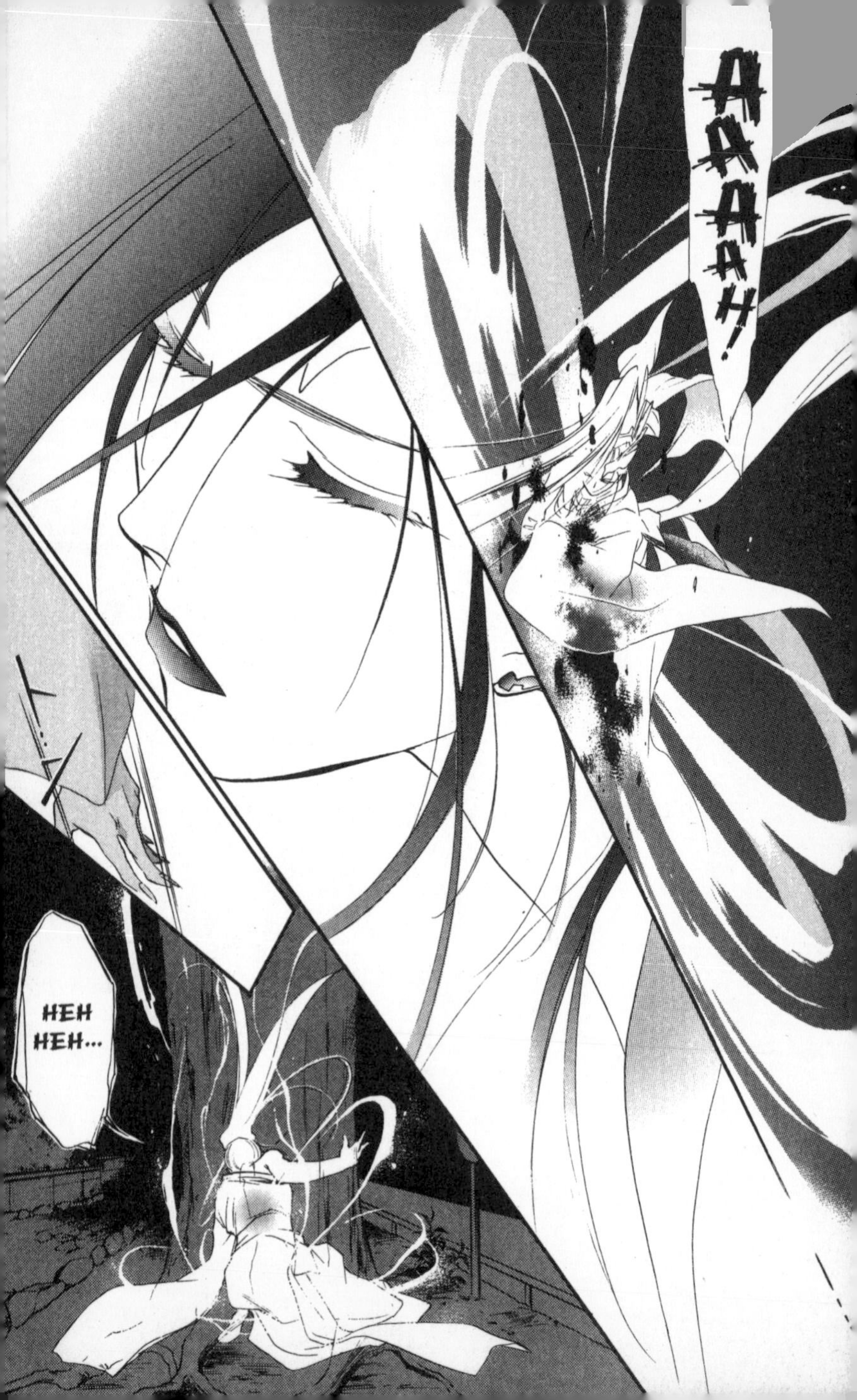
AAAAAH!
HEH HEH...

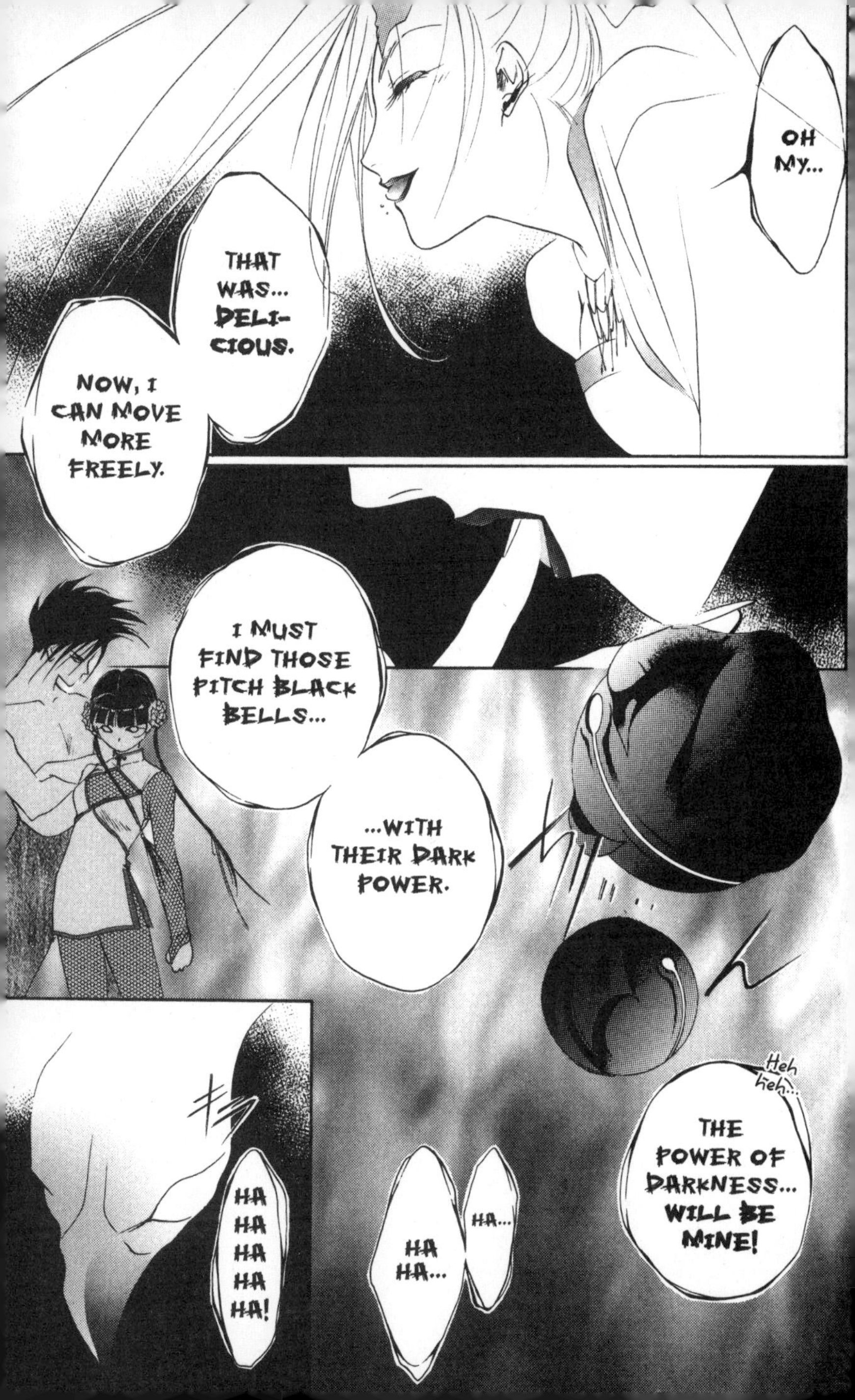
OH MY...
THAT WAS... DELICIOUS.
NOW, I CAN MOVE MORE FREELY.
I MUST FIND THOSE PITCH BLACK BELLS...
...WITH THEIR DARK POWER.
Heh heh...
THE POWER OF DARKNESS... WILL BE MINE!
HA...
HA HA...
HA HA HA HA HA!

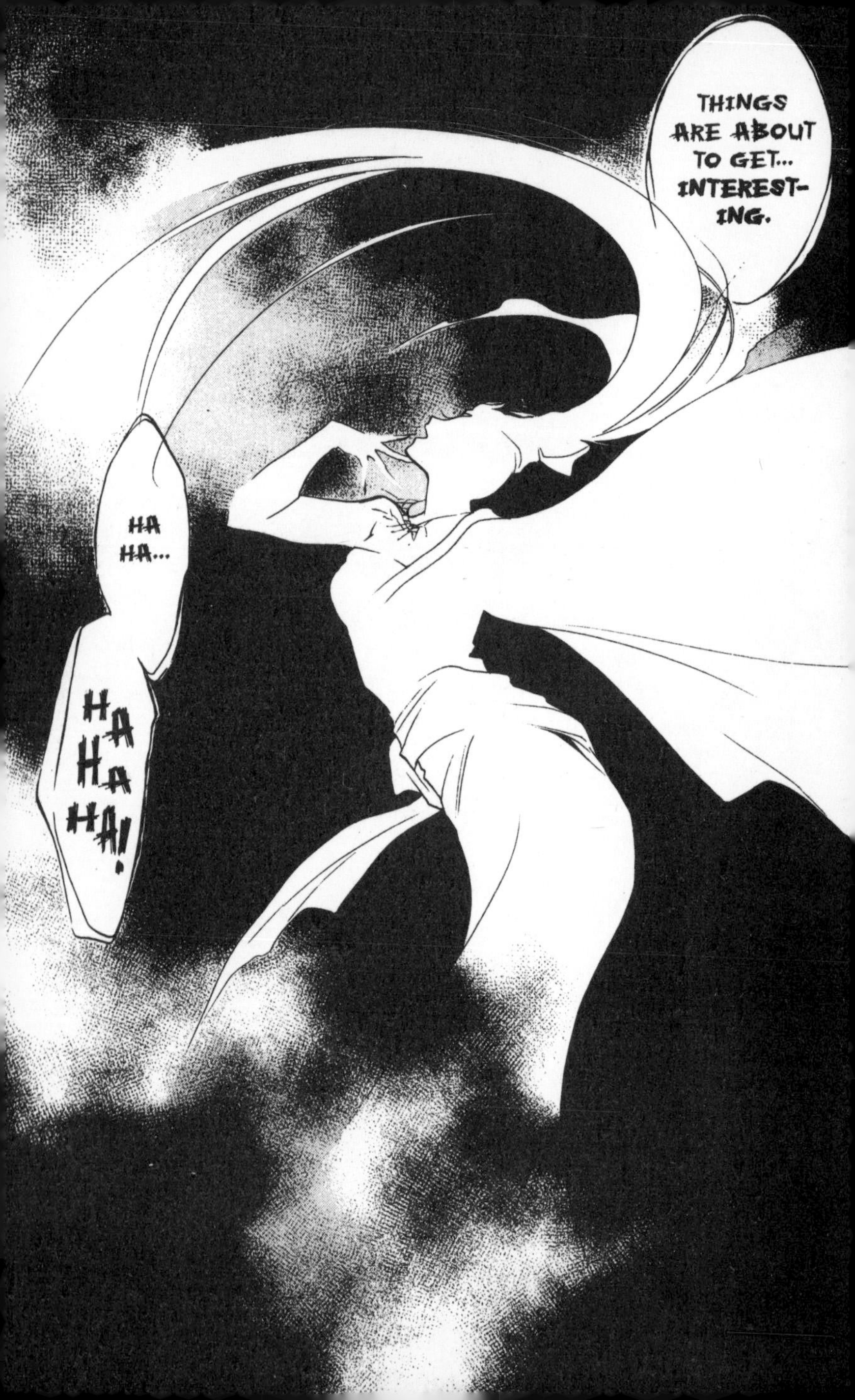
THINGS ARE ABOUT TO GET... INTEREST-ING.
HA HA...
HA HA HA!

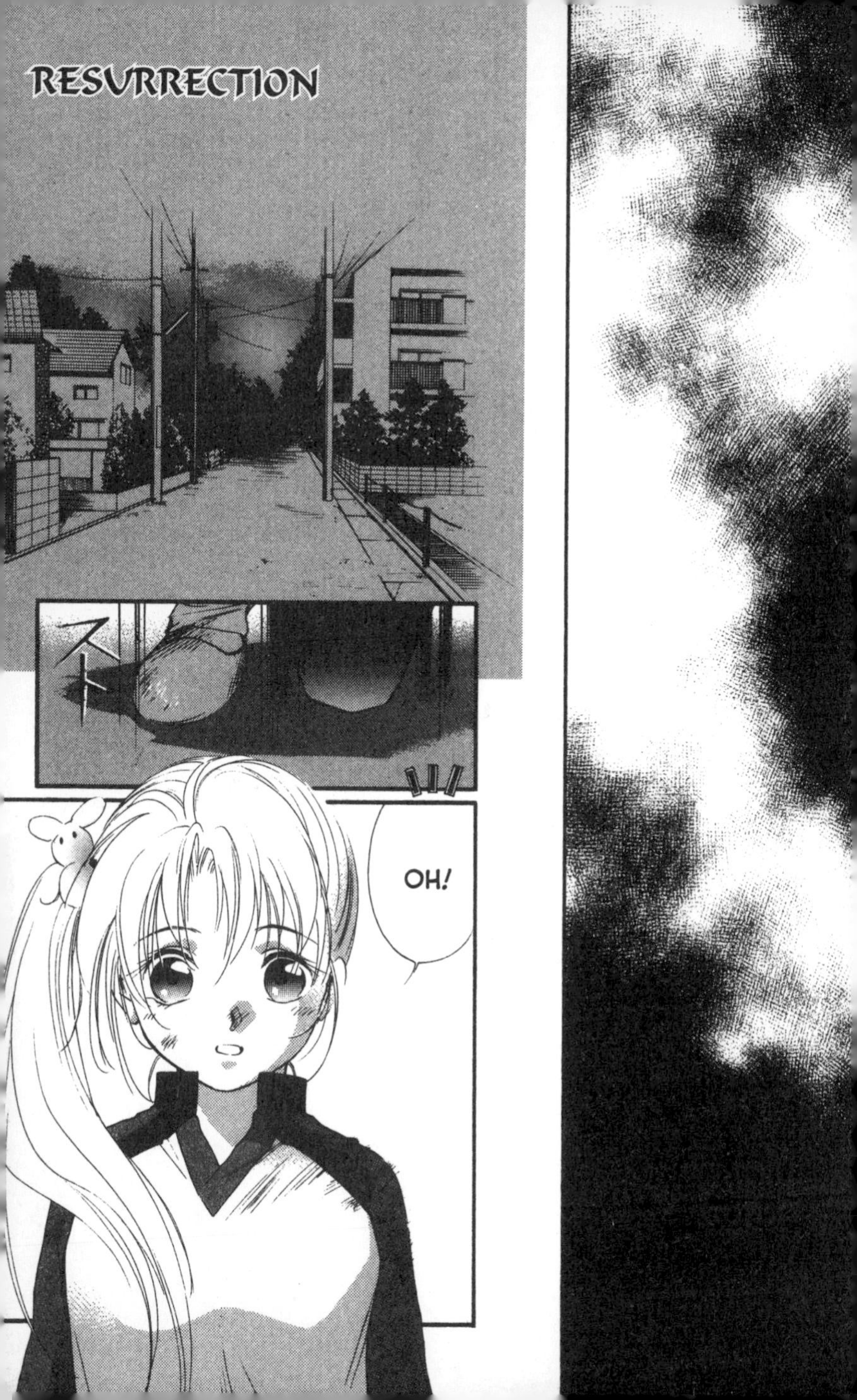
RESURRECTION
スト
OH!

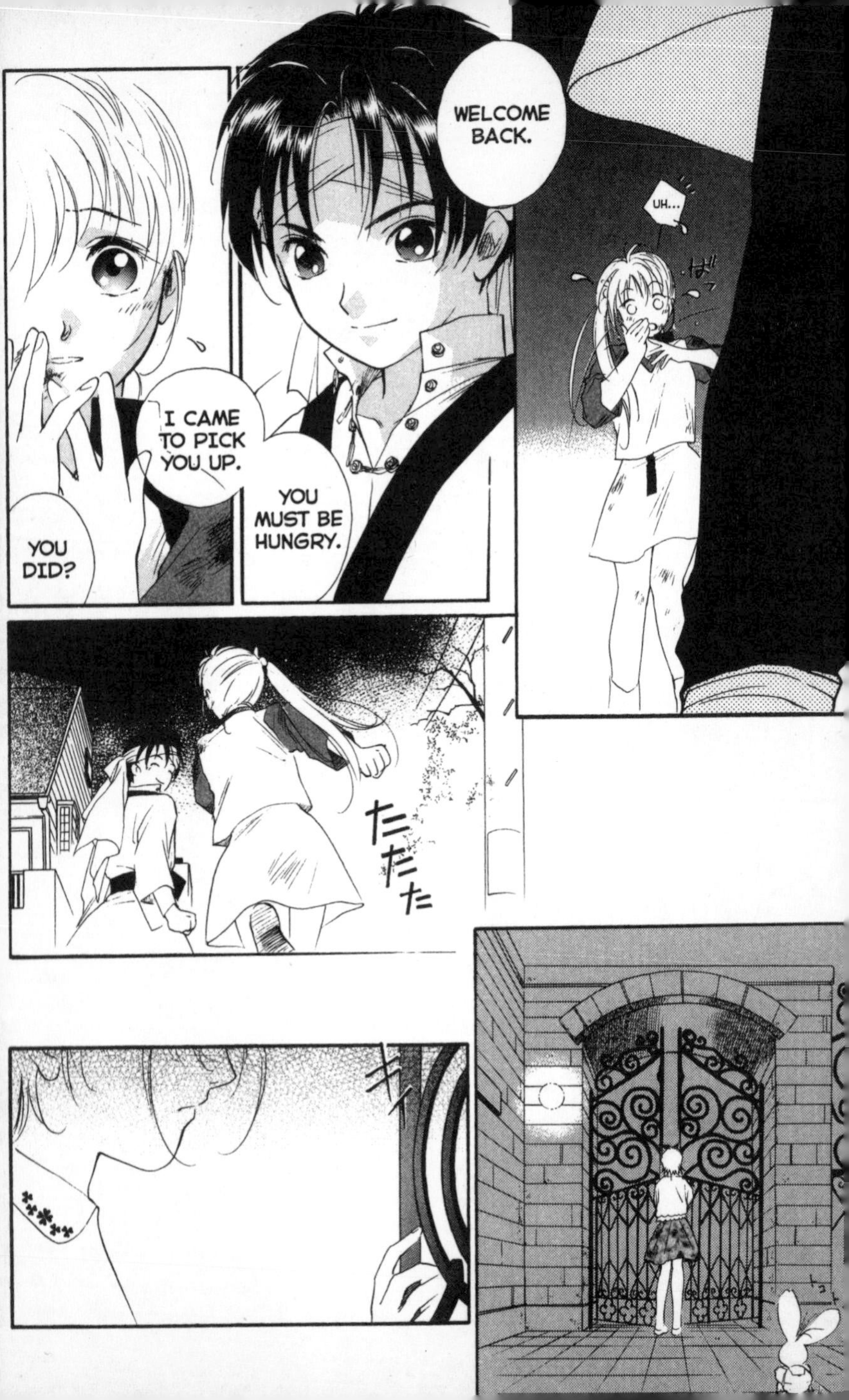
WELCOME BACK.
UH...
I CAME TO PICK YOU UP.
YOU MUST BE HUNGRY.
YOU DID?
たたた
キィ

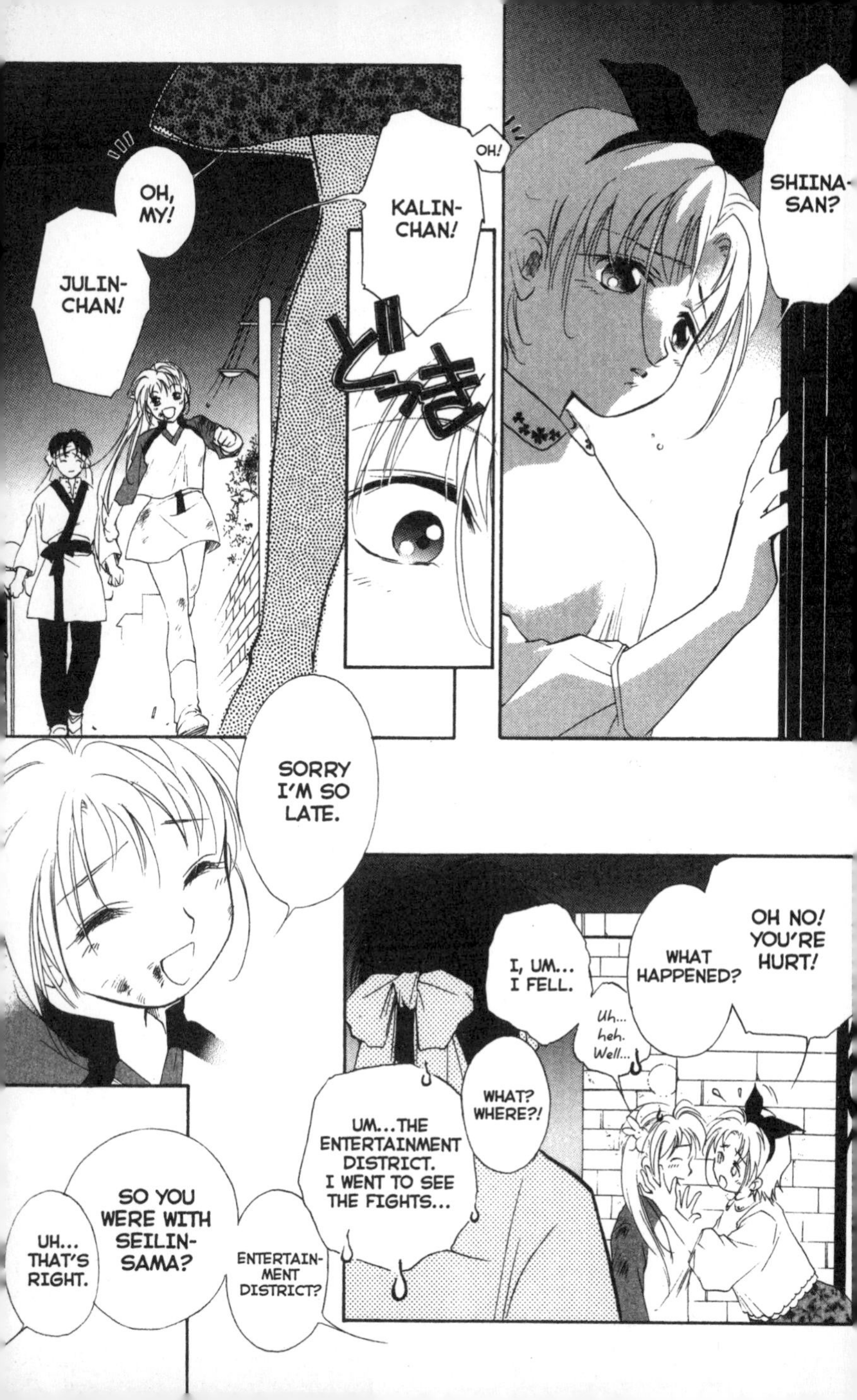
SHIINA-SAN?
OH!
KALIN-CHAN!
どっき
OH, MY!
JULIN-CHAN!
SORRY I'M SO LATE.
OH NO! YOU'RE HURT!
WHAT HAPPENED?
I, UM... I FELL.
Uh... heh. Well...
WHAT? WHERE?!
UM...THE ENTERTAINMENT DISTRICT. I WENT TO SEE THE FIGHTS...
ENTERTAIN-MENT DISTRICT?
SO YOU WERE WITH SEILIN-SAMA?
UH... THAT'S RIGHT.

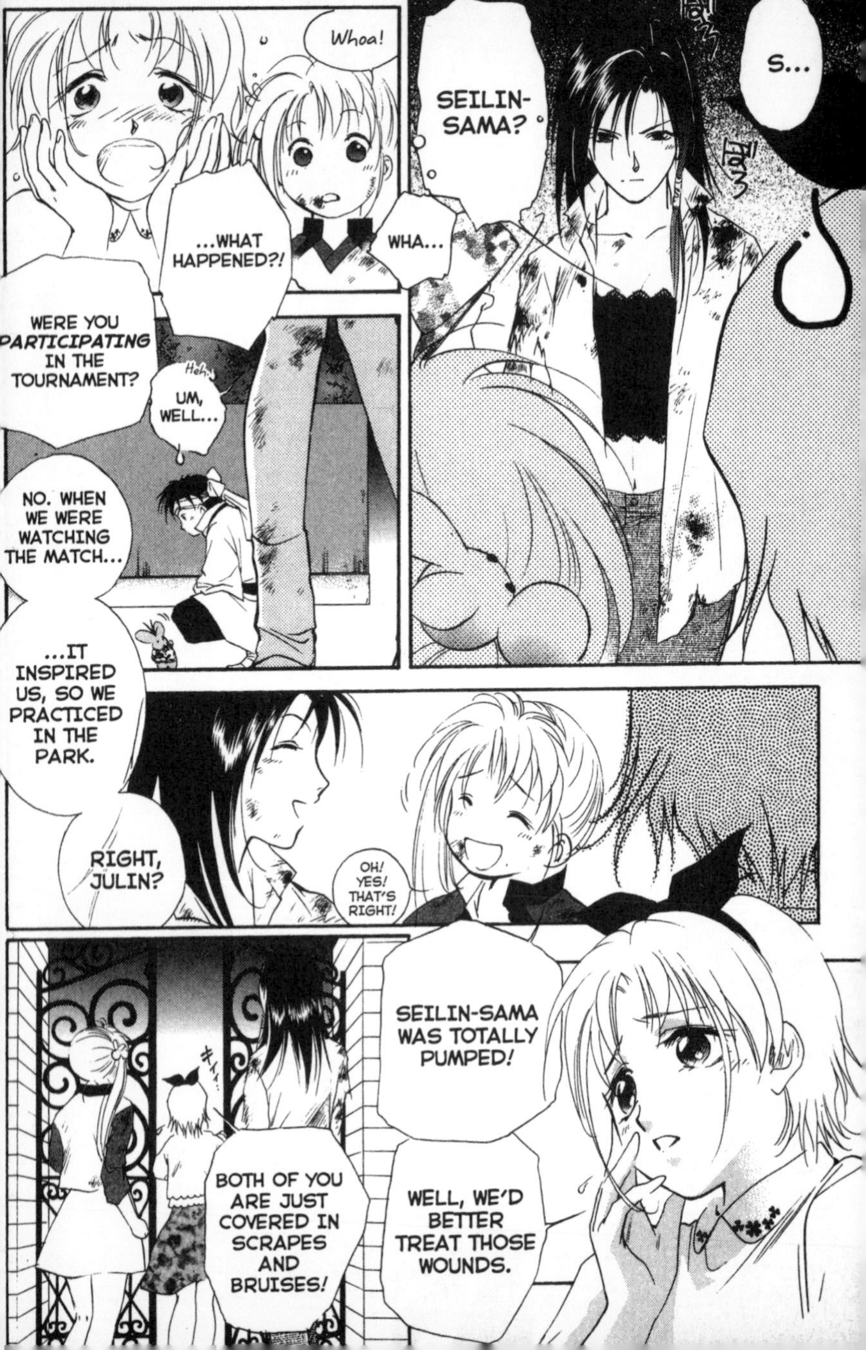
S...
SEILIN-SAMA?
Whoa!
WHA...
...WHAT HAPPENED?!
WERE YOU PARTICIPATING IN THE TOURNAMENT?
Heh.
UM, WELL...
NO. WHEN WE WERE WATCHING THE MATCH...
...IT INSPIRED US, SO WE PRACTICED IN THE PARK.
RIGHT, JULIN?
OH! YES! THAT'S RIGHT!
SEILIN-SAMA WAS TOTALLY PUMPED!
BOTH OF YOU ARE JUST COVERED IN SCRAPES AND BRUISES!
WELL, WE'D BETTER TREAT THOSE WOUNDS.

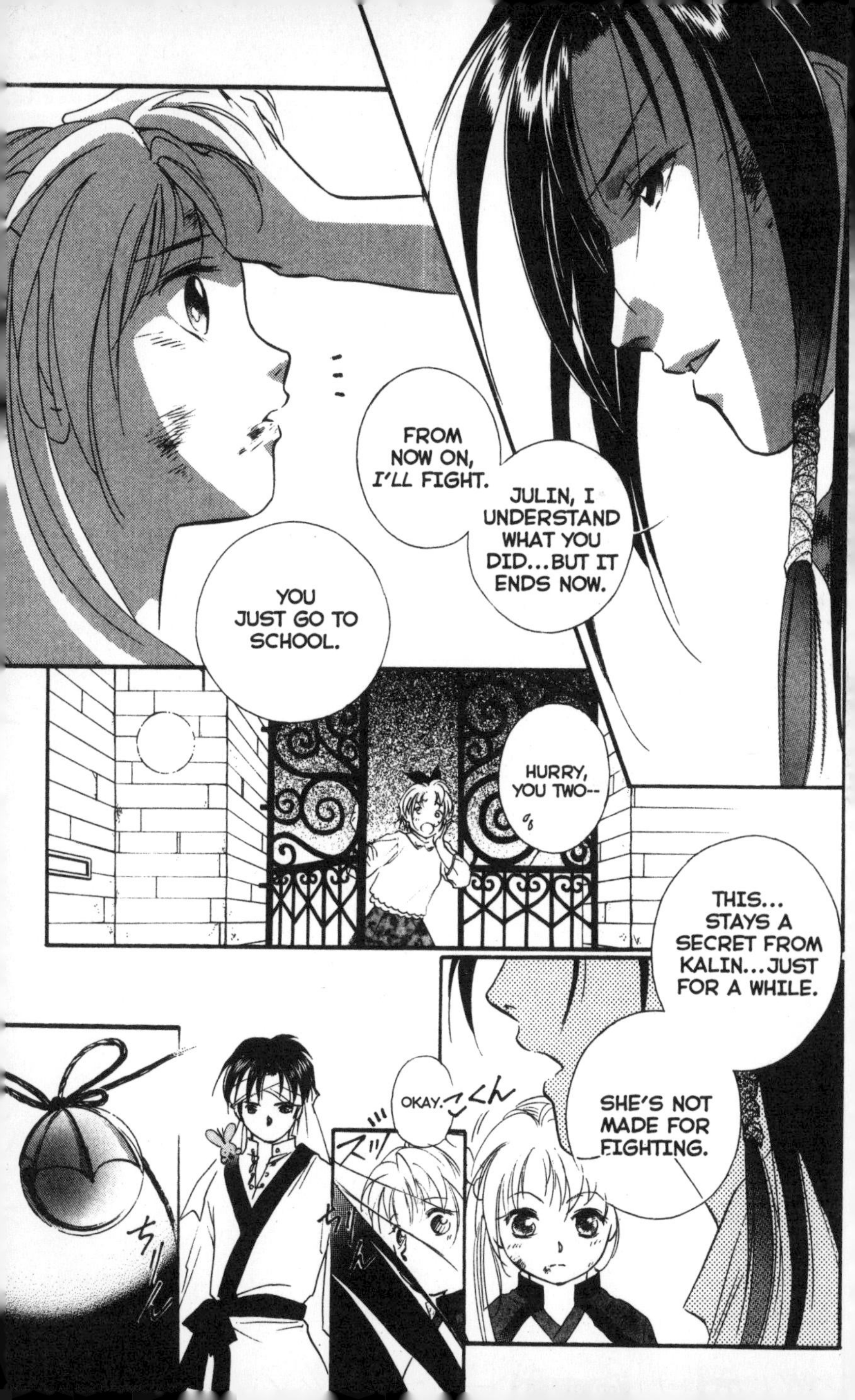

JULIN, I UNDERSTAND WHAT YOU DID...BUT IT ENDS NOW.
FROM NOW ON, *I'LL* FIGHT.
YOU JUST GO TO SCHOOL.
...
HURRY, YOU TWO--
THIS... STAYS A SECRET FROM KALIN...JUST FOR A WHILE.
SHE'S NOT MADE FOR FIGHTING.
OKAY.

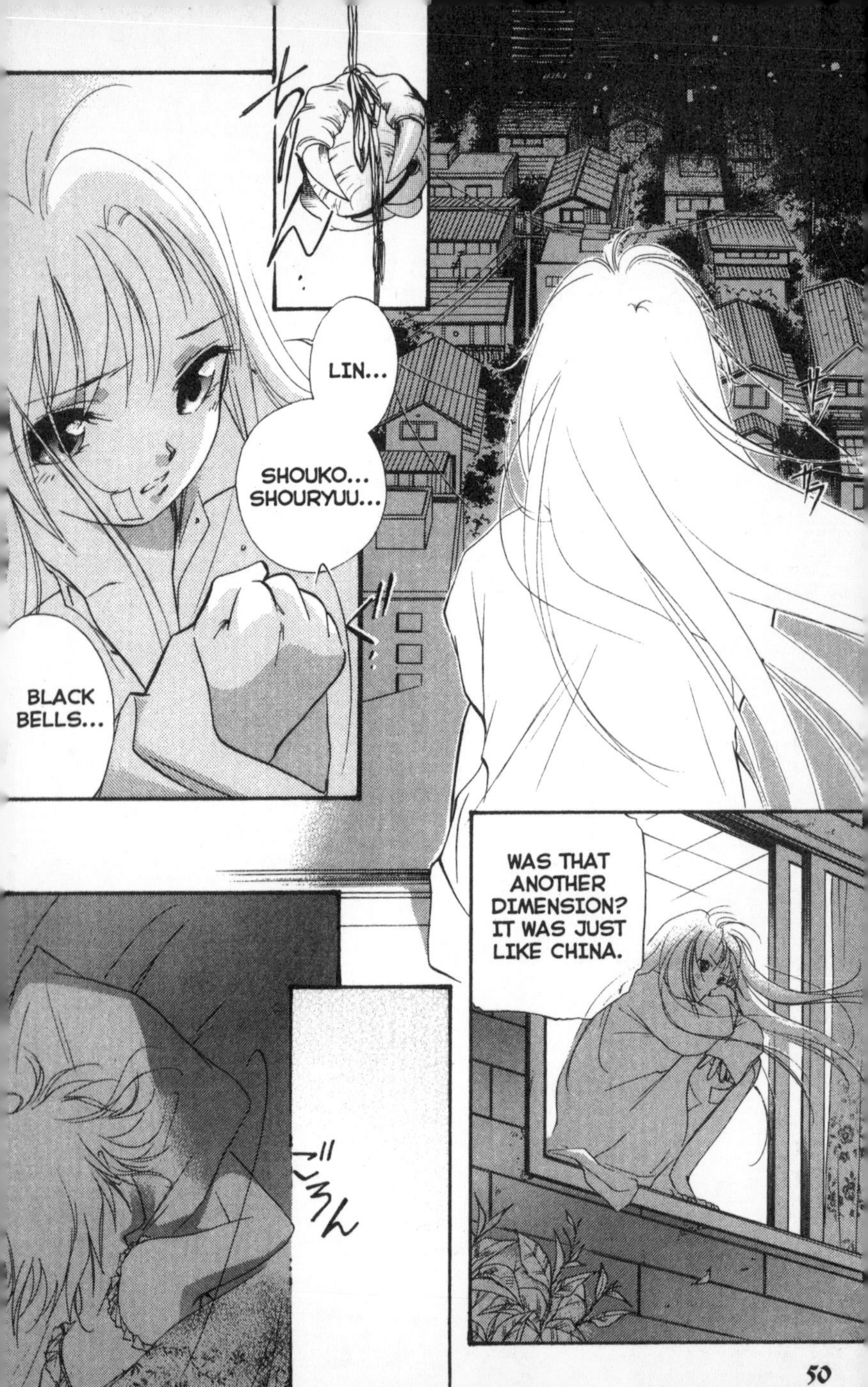
LIN...
SHOUKO... SHOURYUU...
BLACK BELLS...
WAS THAT ANOTHER DIMENSION? IT WAS JUST LIKE CHINA.

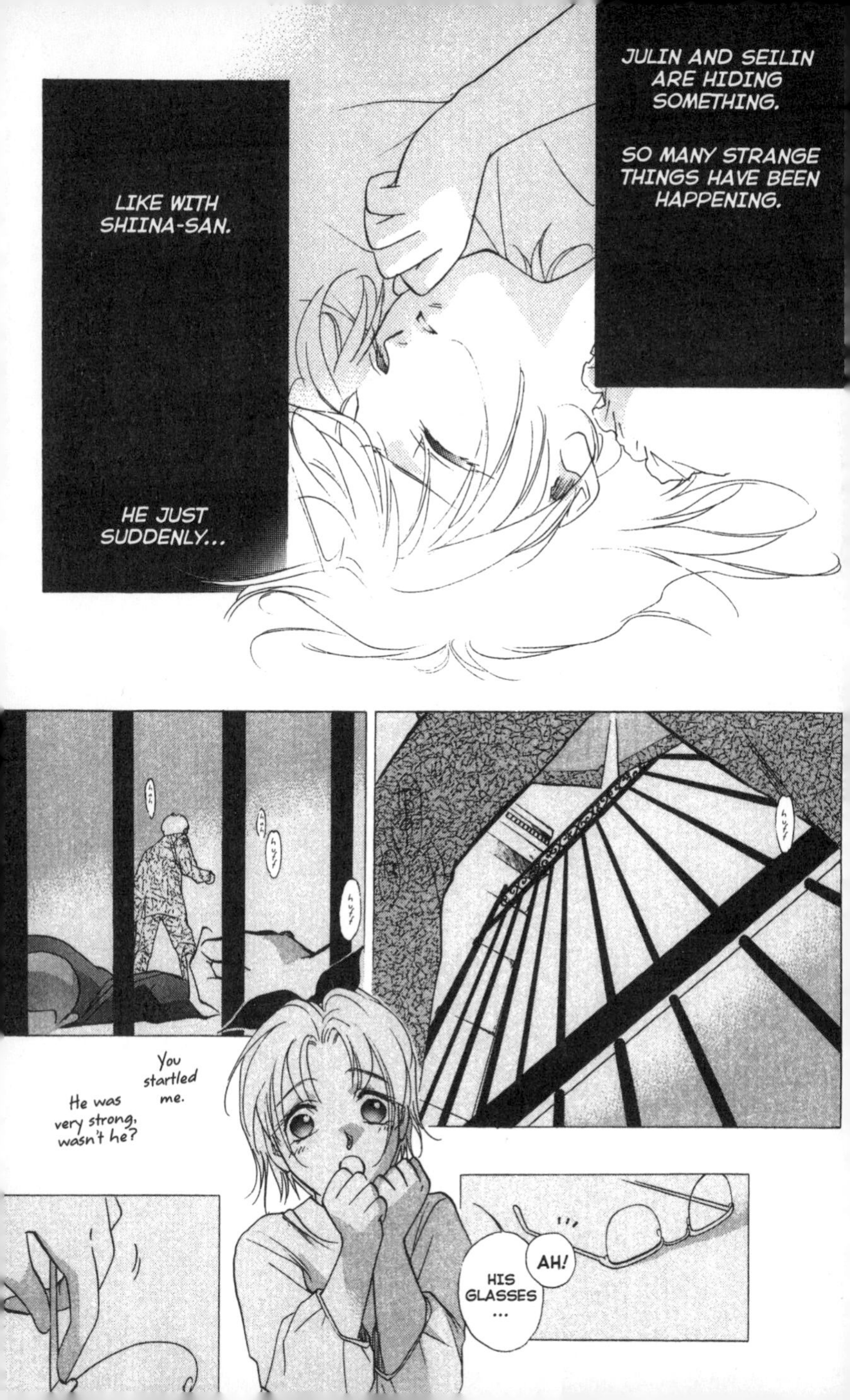
JULIN AND SEILIN ARE HIDING SOMETHING.
SO MANY STRANGE THINGS HAVE BEEN HAPPENING.
LIKE WITH SHIINA-SAN.
HE JUST SUDDENLY...
You startled me.
He was very strong, wasn't he?
AH!
HIS GLASSES ...

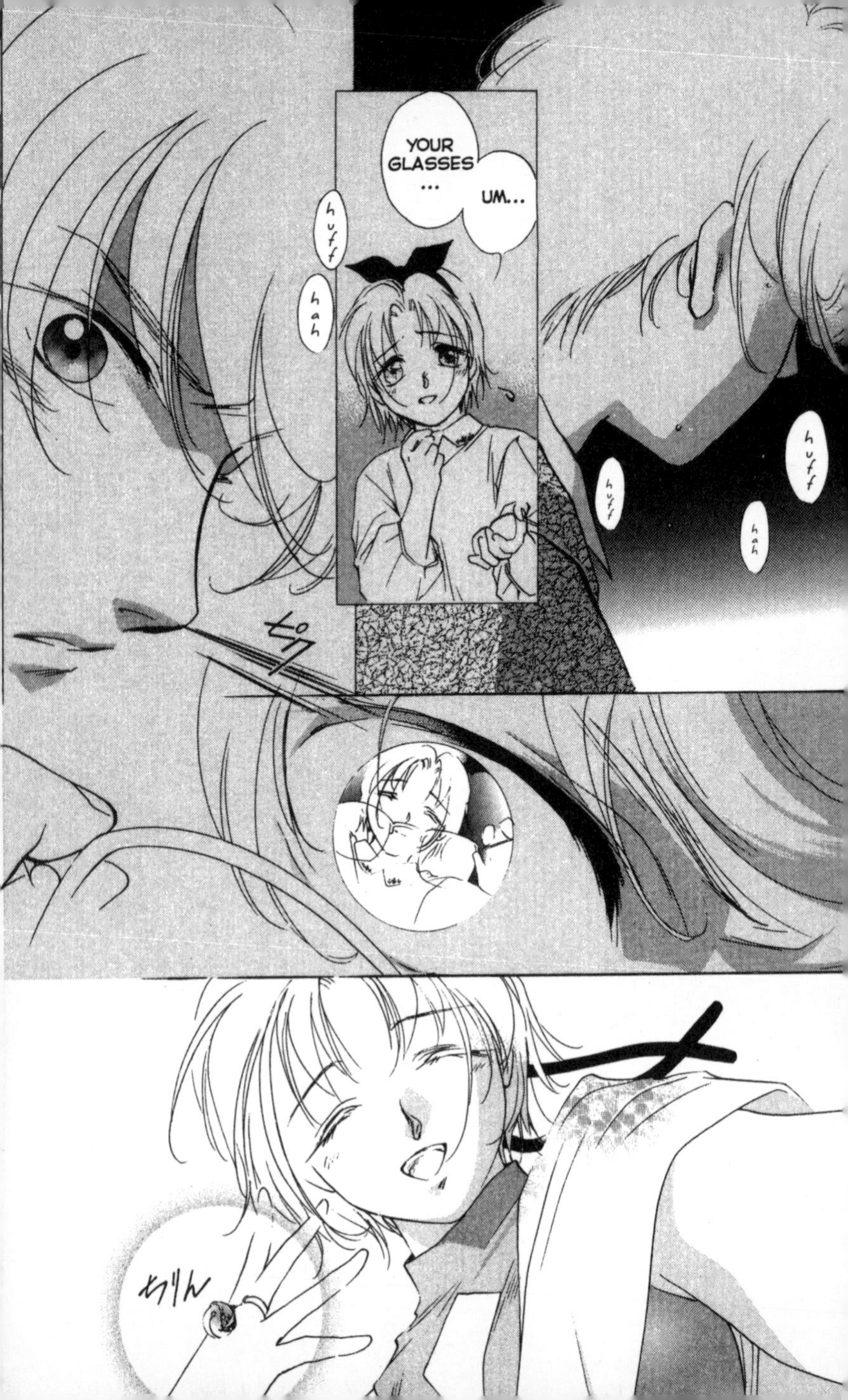
huff
huff
hah
YOUR GLASSES ...
UM...
huff
hah
ピク
ちりん

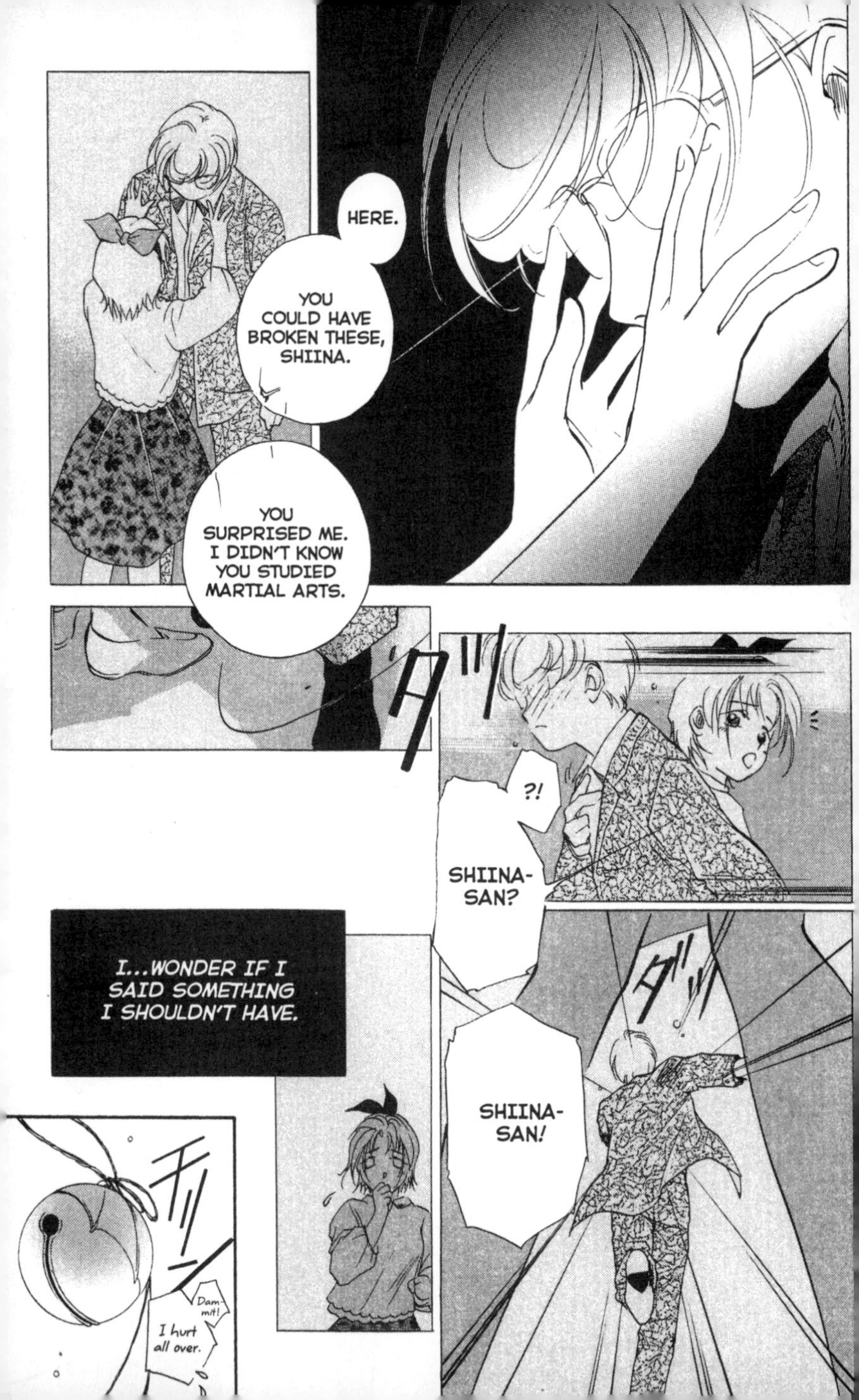
HERE.
YOU COULD HAVE BROKEN THESE, SHIINA.
YOU SURPRISED ME. I DIDN'T KNOW YOU STUDIED MARTIAL ARTS.
?!
SHIINA-SAN?
SHIINA-SAN!
I...WONDER IF I SAID SOMETHING I SHOULDN'T HAVE.
Dam-mit!
I hurt all over.

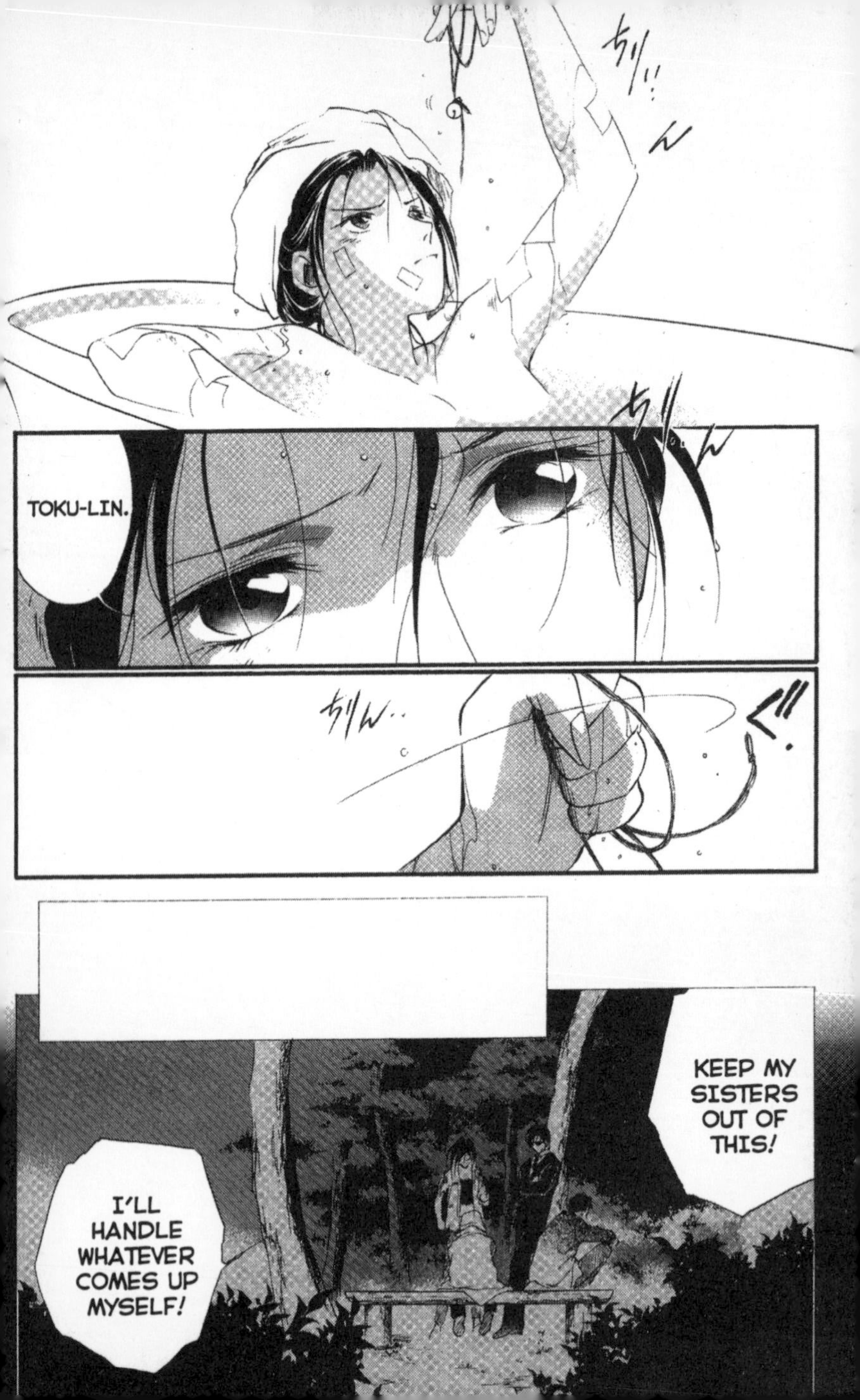
TOKU-LIN.
ちりん..
KEEP MY SISTERS OUT OF THIS!
I'LL HANDLE WHATEVER COMES UP MYSELF!

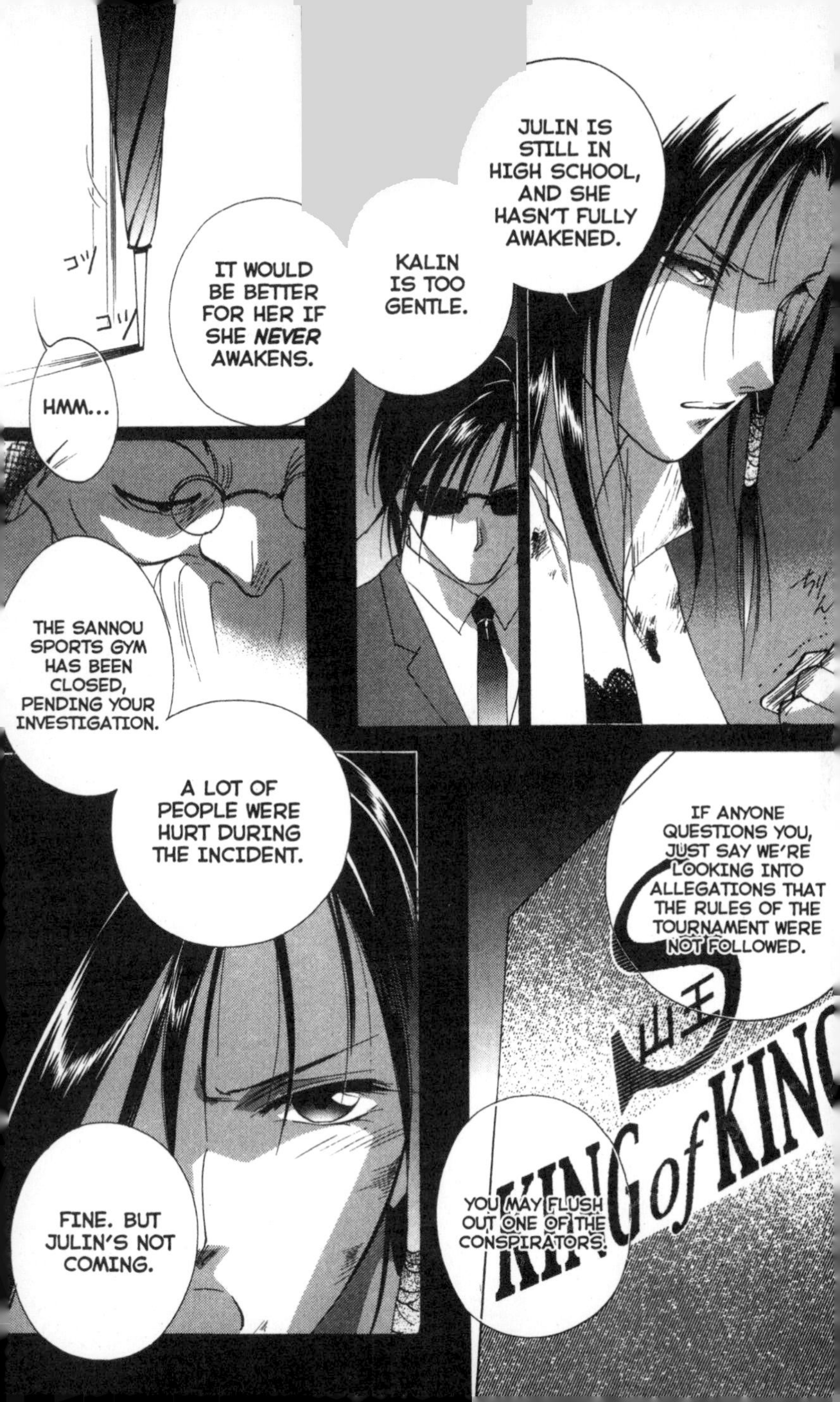
JULIN IS STILL IN HIGH SCHOOL, AND SHE HASN'T FULLY AWAKENED.
ちりん
KALIN IS TOO GENTLE.
IT WOULD BE BETTER FOR HER IF SHE *NEVER* AWAKENS.
コツ
コツ
HMM...
THE SANNOU SPORTS GYM HAS BEEN CLOSED, PENDING YOUR INVESTIGATION.
A LOT OF PEOPLE WERE HURT DURING THE INCIDENT.
IF ANYONE QUESTIONS YOU, JUST SAY WE'RE LOOKING INTO ALLEGATIONS THAT THE RULES OF THE TOURNAMENT WERE NOT FOLLOWED.
山王
YOU MAY FLUSH OUT ONE OF THE CONSPIRATORS.
FINE. BUT JULIN'S NOT COMING.

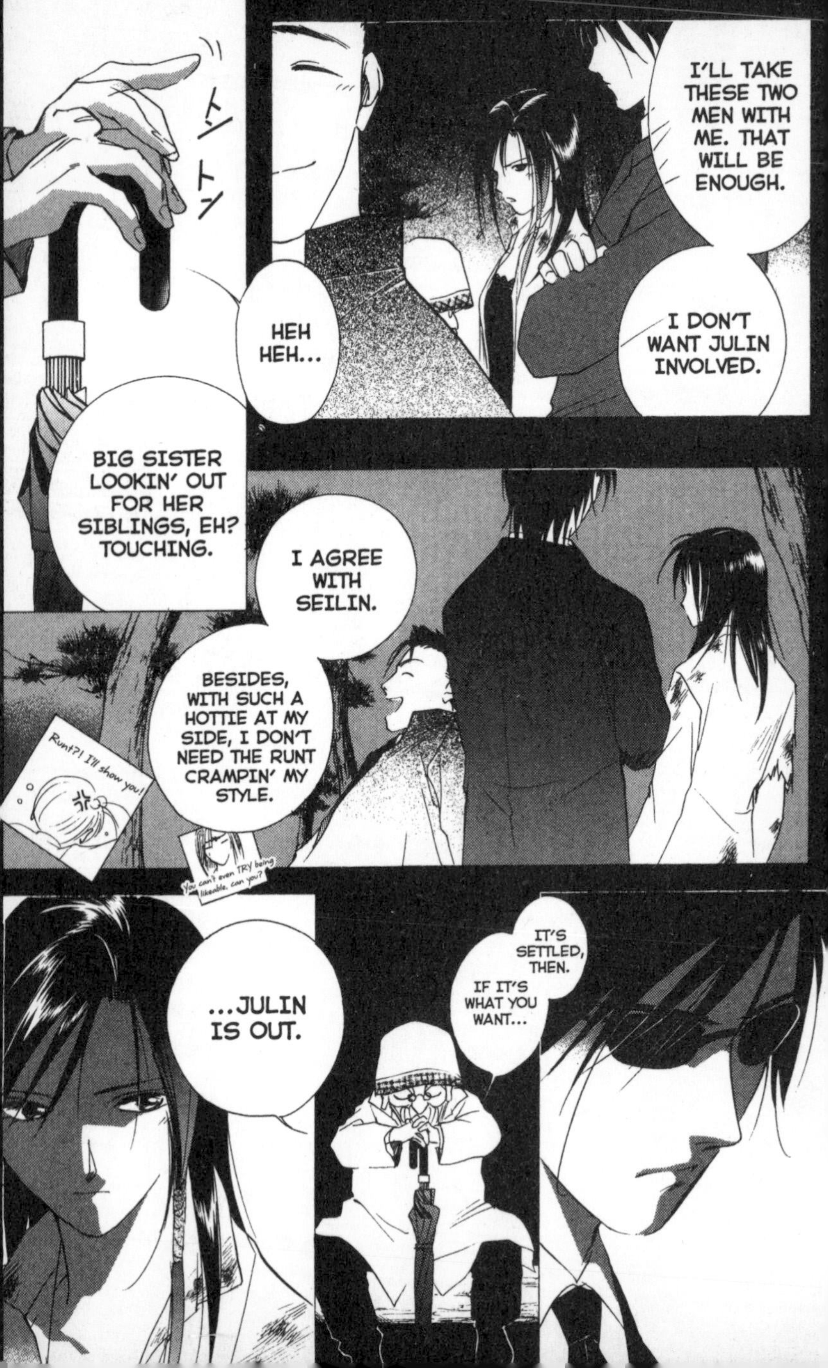

I'LL TAKE THESE TWO MEN WITH ME. THAT WILL BE ENOUGH.
I DON'T WANT JULIN INVOLVED.
HEH HEH...
トン トン
BIG SISTER LOOKIN' OUT FOR HER SIBLINGS, EH? TOUCHING.
I AGREE WITH SEILIN.
BESIDES, WITH SUCH A HOTTIE AT MY SIDE, I DON'T NEED THE RUNT CRAMPIN' MY STYLE.
Runt?! I'll show you!
You can't even TRY being likeable, can you?
IT'S SETTLED, THEN.
IF IT'S WHAT YOU WANT...
...JULIN IS OUT.

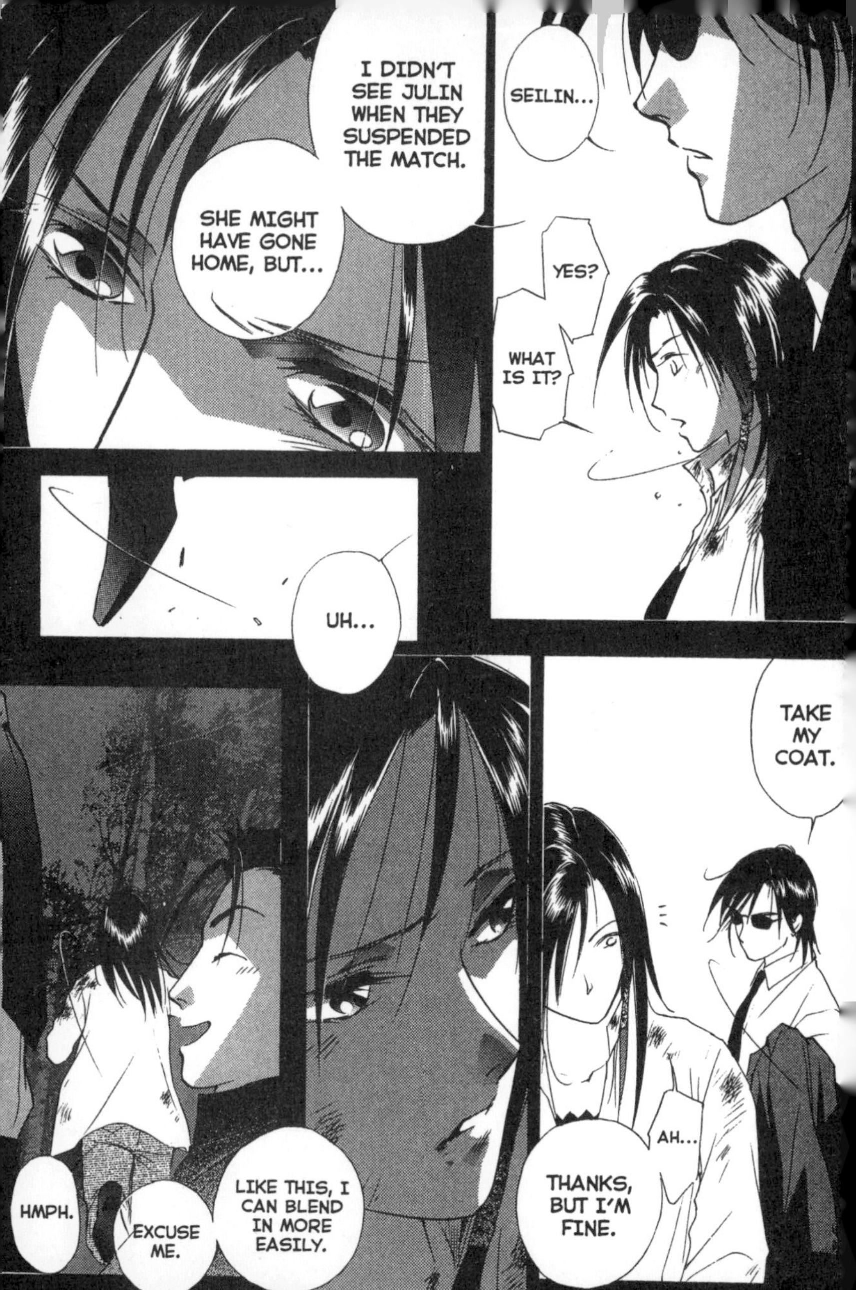
SEILIN...
YES?
WHAT IS IT?
I DIDN'T SEE JULIN WHEN THEY SUSPENDED THE MATCH.
SHE MIGHT HAVE GONE HOME, BUT...
UH...
TAKE MY COAT.
AH...
THANKS, BUT I'M FINE.
LIKE THIS, I CAN BLEND IN MORE EASILY.
EXCUSE ME.
HMPH.

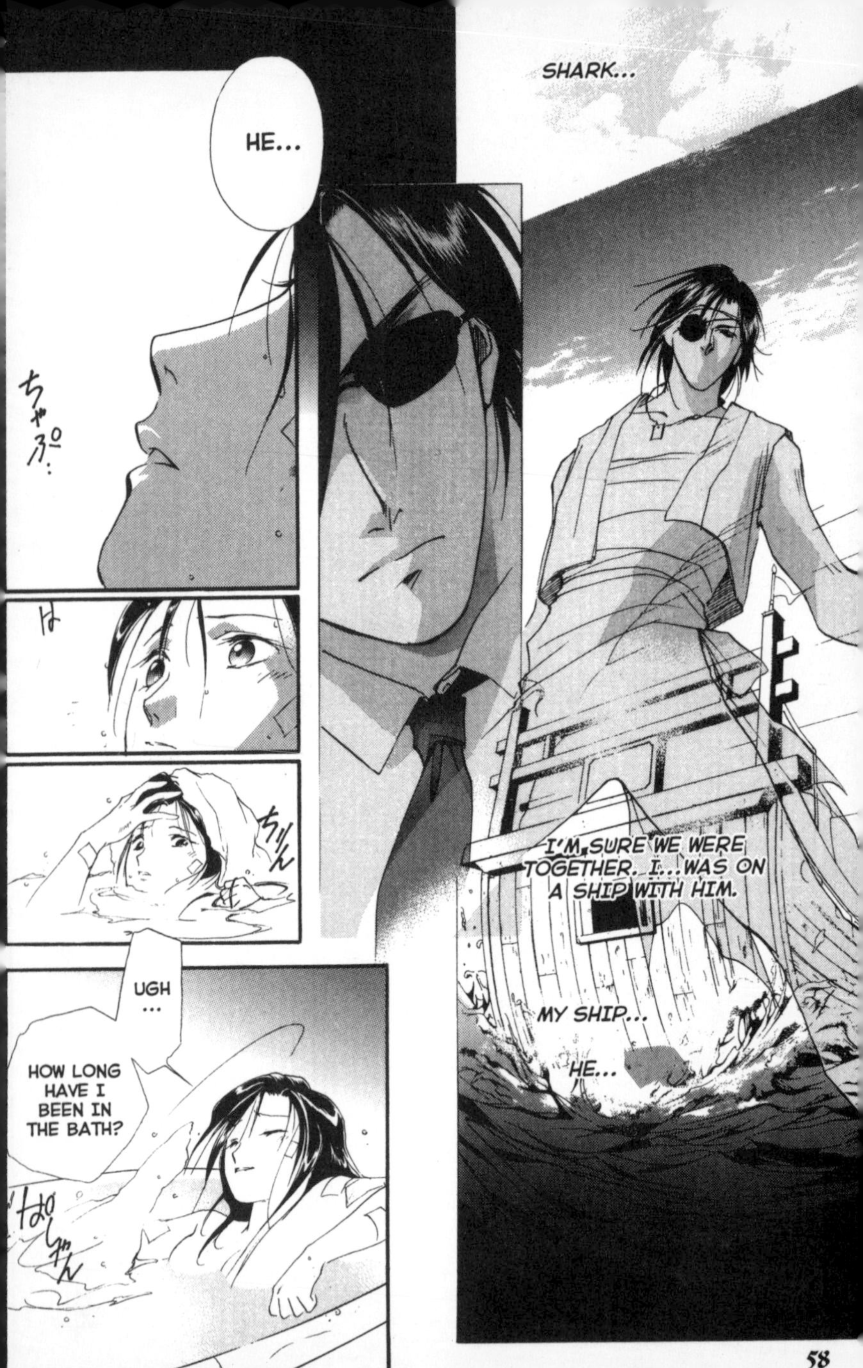
SHARK...
I'M SURE WE WERE TOGETHER. I...WAS ON A SHIP WITH HIM.
MY SHIP...
HE...
HE...
ちゃぷ
は
ちりん
UGH ...
HOW LONG HAVE I BEEN IN THE BATH?
ぱしゃん

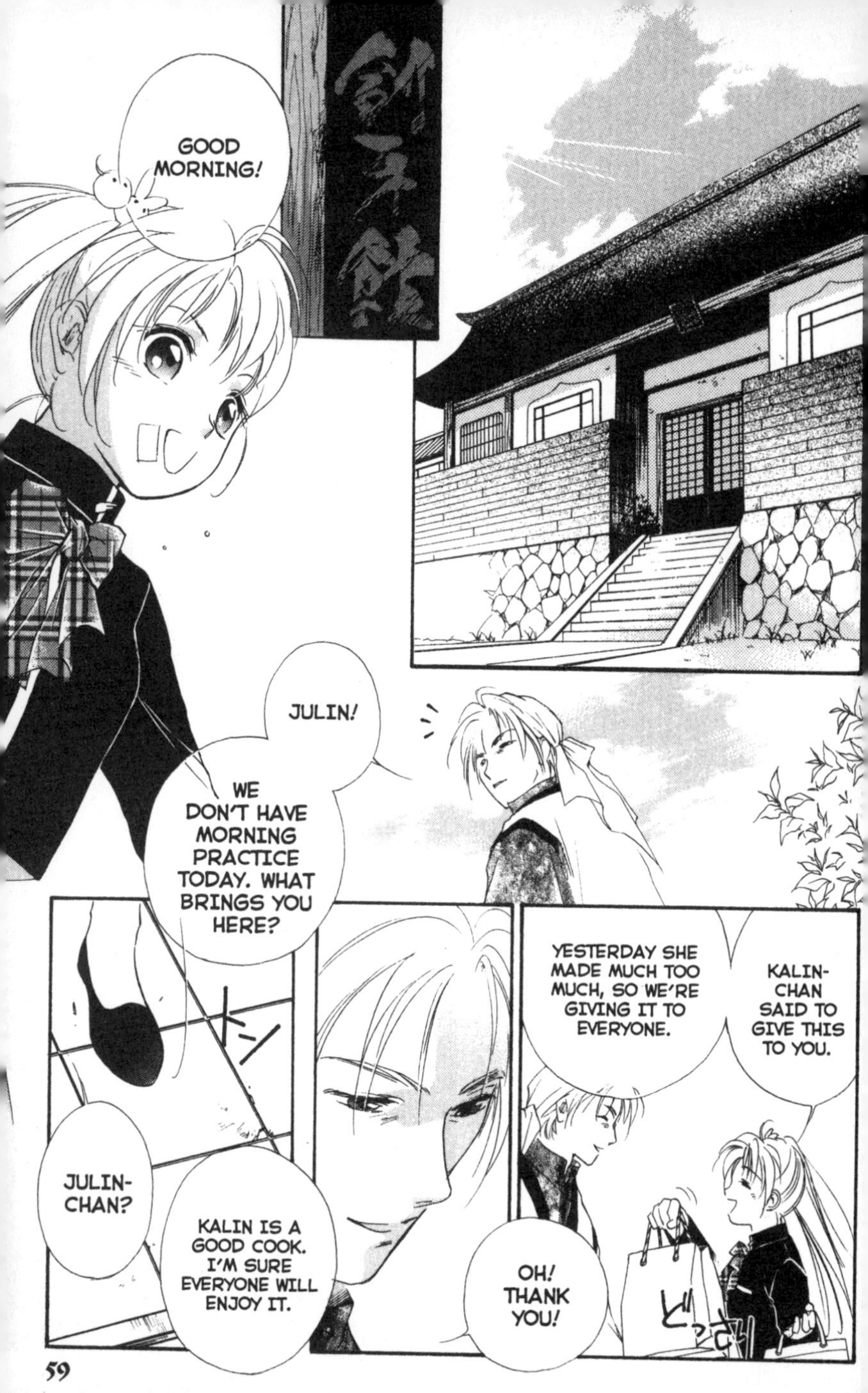
GOOD MORNING!
JULIN!
WE DON'T HAVE MORNING PRACTICE TODAY. WHAT BRINGS YOU HERE?
KALIN-CHAN SAID TO GIVE THIS TO YOU.
YESTERDAY SHE MADE MUCH TOO MUCH, SO WE'RE GIVING IT TO EVERYONE.
OH! THANK YOU!
KALIN IS A GOOD COOK. I'M SURE EVERYONE WILL ENJOY IT.
JULIN-CHAN?

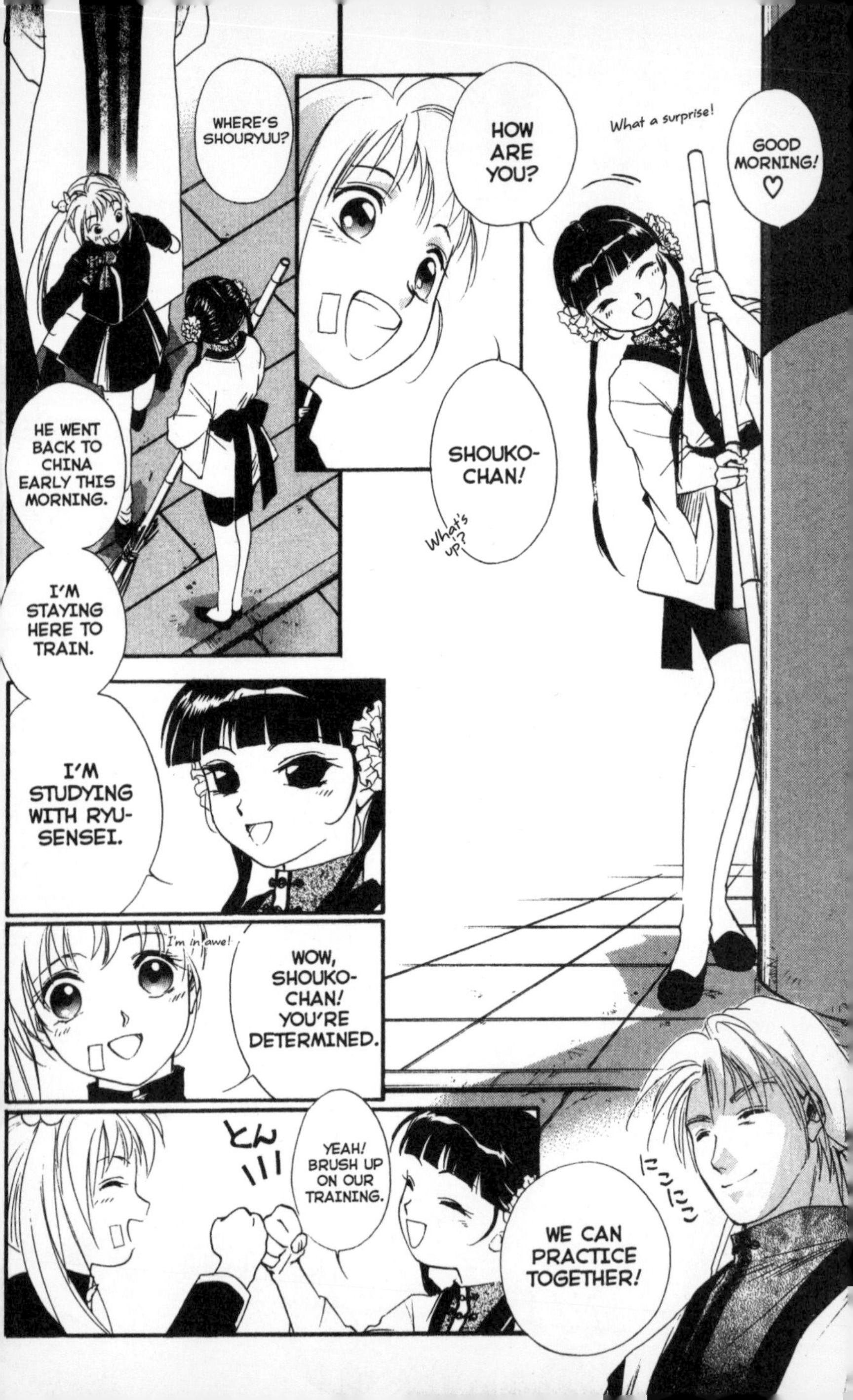
GOOD MORNING! ♡
What a surprise!
HOW ARE YOU?
SHOUKO-CHAN!
What's up?
WHERE'S SHOURYUU?
HE WENT BACK TO CHINA EARLY THIS MORNING.
I'M STAYING HERE TO TRAIN.
I'M STUDYING WITH RYU-SENSEI.
I'm in awe!
WOW, SHOUKO-CHAN! YOU'RE DETERMINED.
にこにこ
WE CAN PRACTICE TOGETHER!
とん
YEAH! BRUSH UP ON OUR TRAINING.

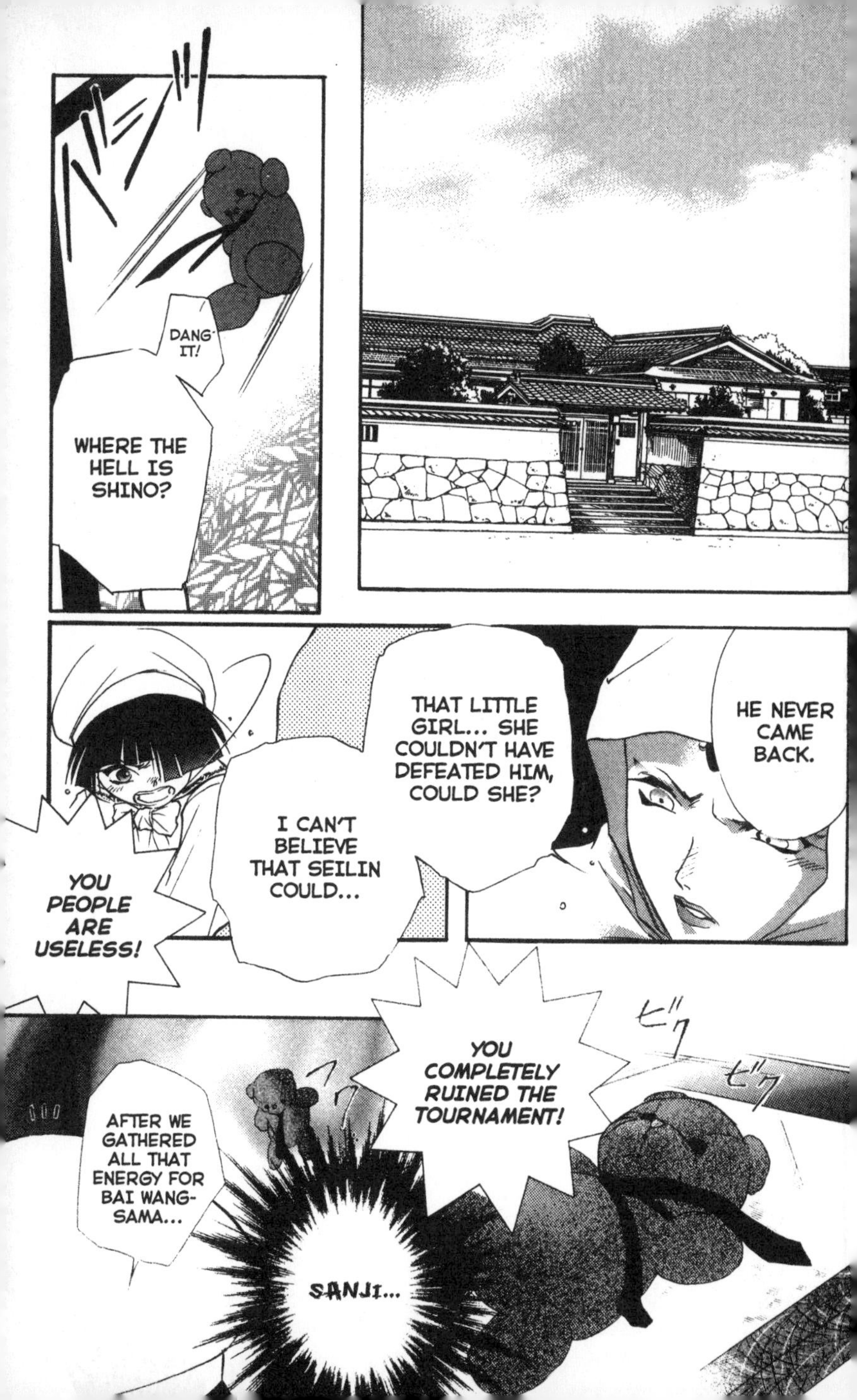
DANG IT!
WHERE THE HELL IS SHINO?
HE NEVER CAME BACK.
THAT LITTLE GIRL... SHE COULDN'T HAVE DEFEATED HIM, COULD SHE?
I CAN'T BELIEVE THAT SEILIN COULD...
YOU PEOPLE ARE USELESS!
ビク
ビク
YOU COMPLETELY RUINED THE TOURNAMENT!
AFTER WE GATHERED ALL THAT ENERGY FOR BAI WANG-SAMA...
SANJI...

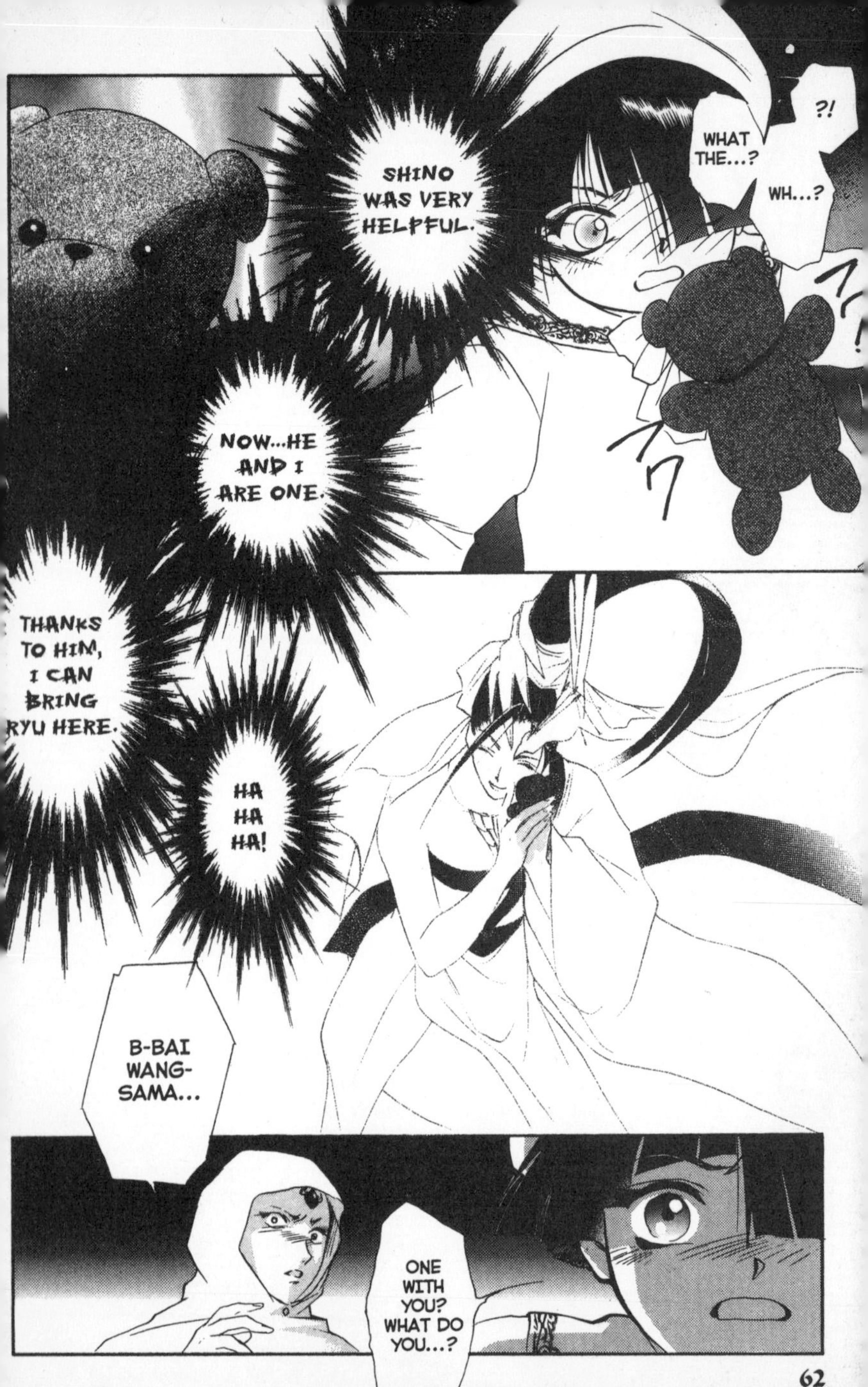
?!
WHAT THE...?
WH...?
SHINO WAS VERY HELPFUL.
NOW...HE AND I ARE ONE.
THANKS TO HIM, I CAN BRING RYU HERE.
HA HA HA!
B-BAI WANG-SAMA...
ONE WITH YOU? WHAT DO YOU...?

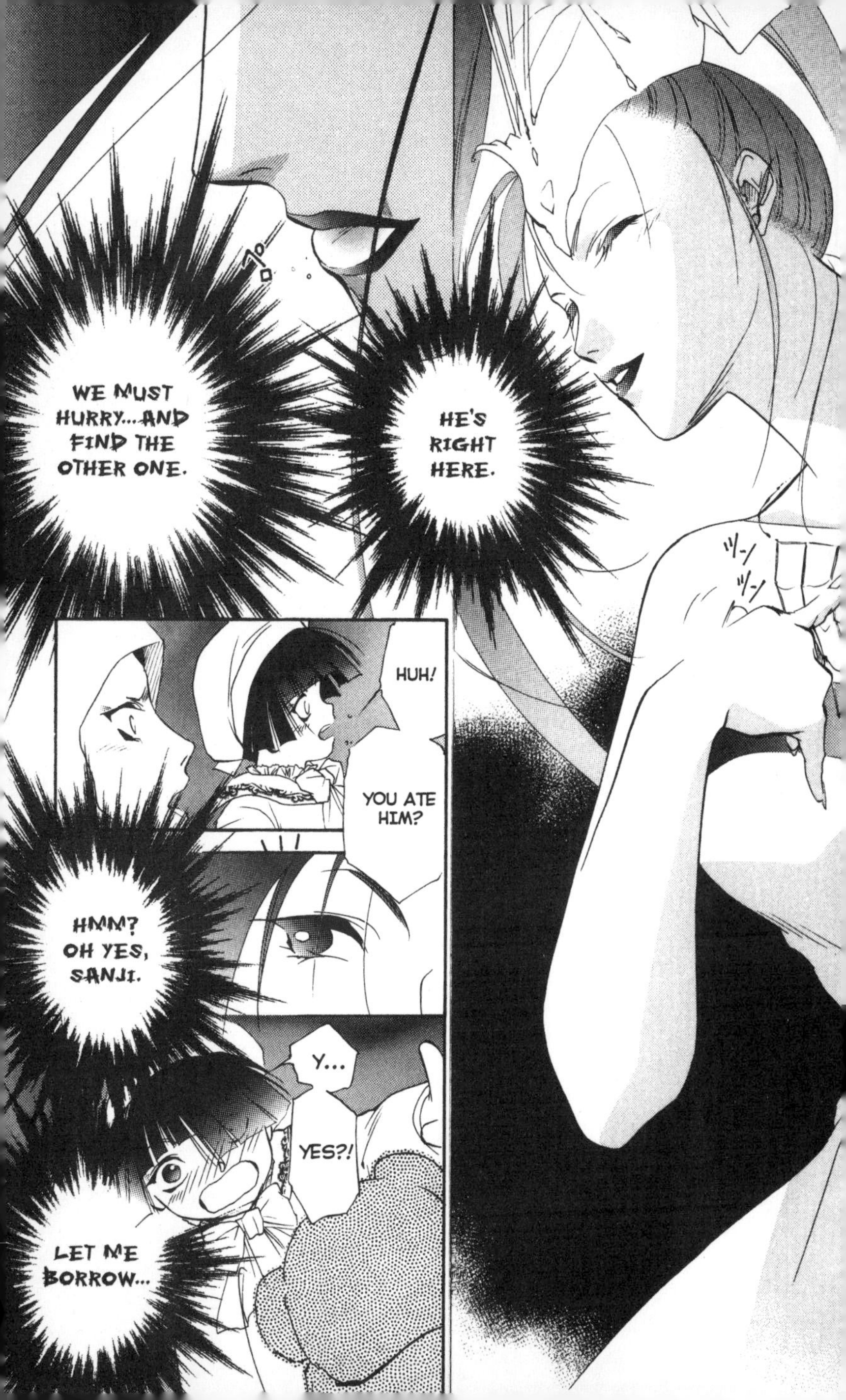
WE MUST HURRY...AND FIND THE OTHER ONE.
HE'S RIGHT HERE.
HUH!
YOU ATE HIM?
HMM? OH YES, SANJI.
Y...
YES?!
LET ME BORROW...

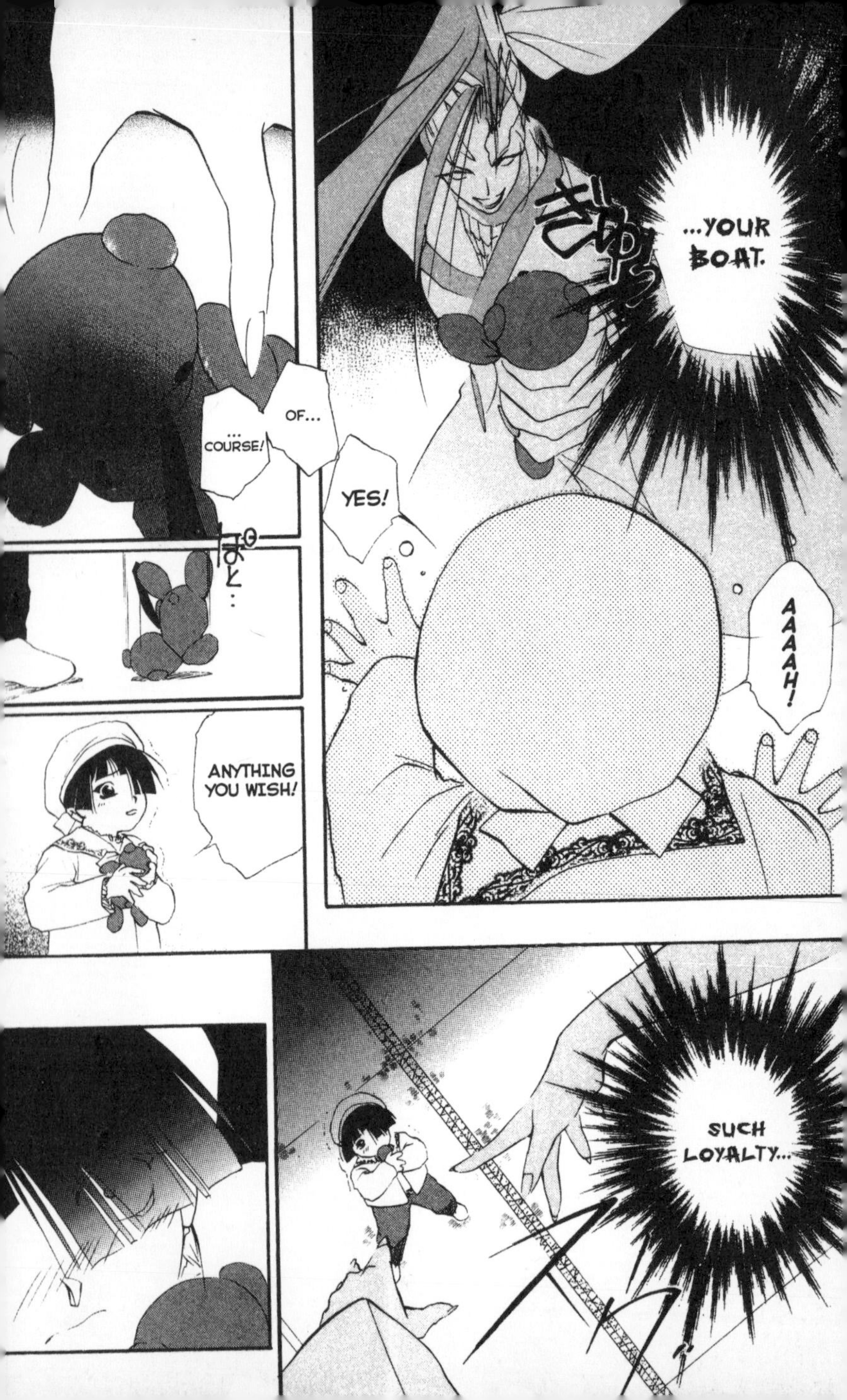
...YOUR BOAT.
きゅ
YES!
AAAAH!
OF...
...COURSE!
ぽと…
ANYTHING YOU WISH!
SUCH LOYALTY...

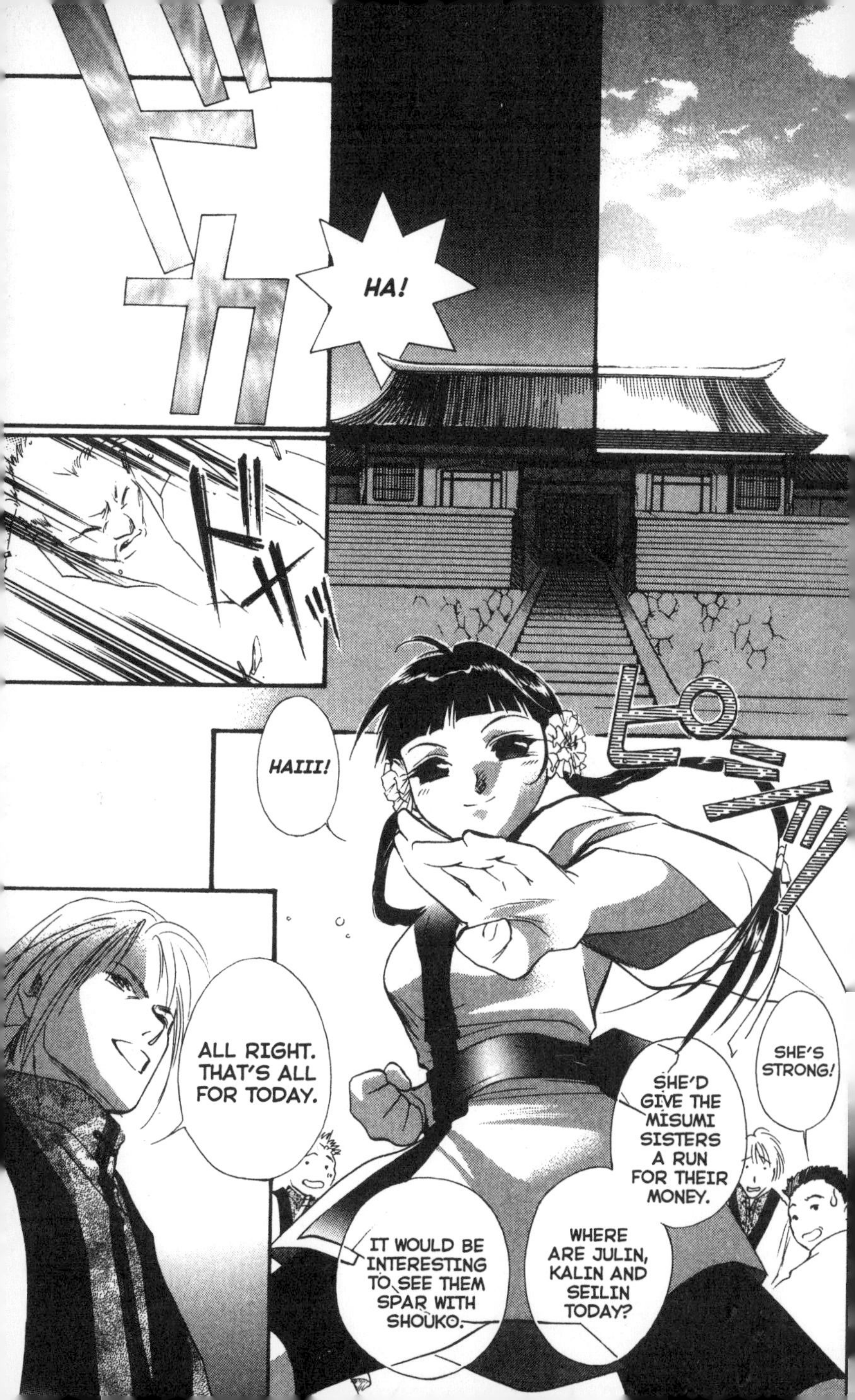
HA!
HAIII!
SHE'S STRONG!
SHE'D GIVE THE MISUMI SISTERS A RUN FOR THEIR MONEY.
WHERE ARE JULIN, KALIN AND SEILIN TODAY?
IT WOULD BE INTERESTING TO SEE THEM SPAR WITH SHOUKO.
ALL RIGHT. THAT'S ALL FOR TODAY.

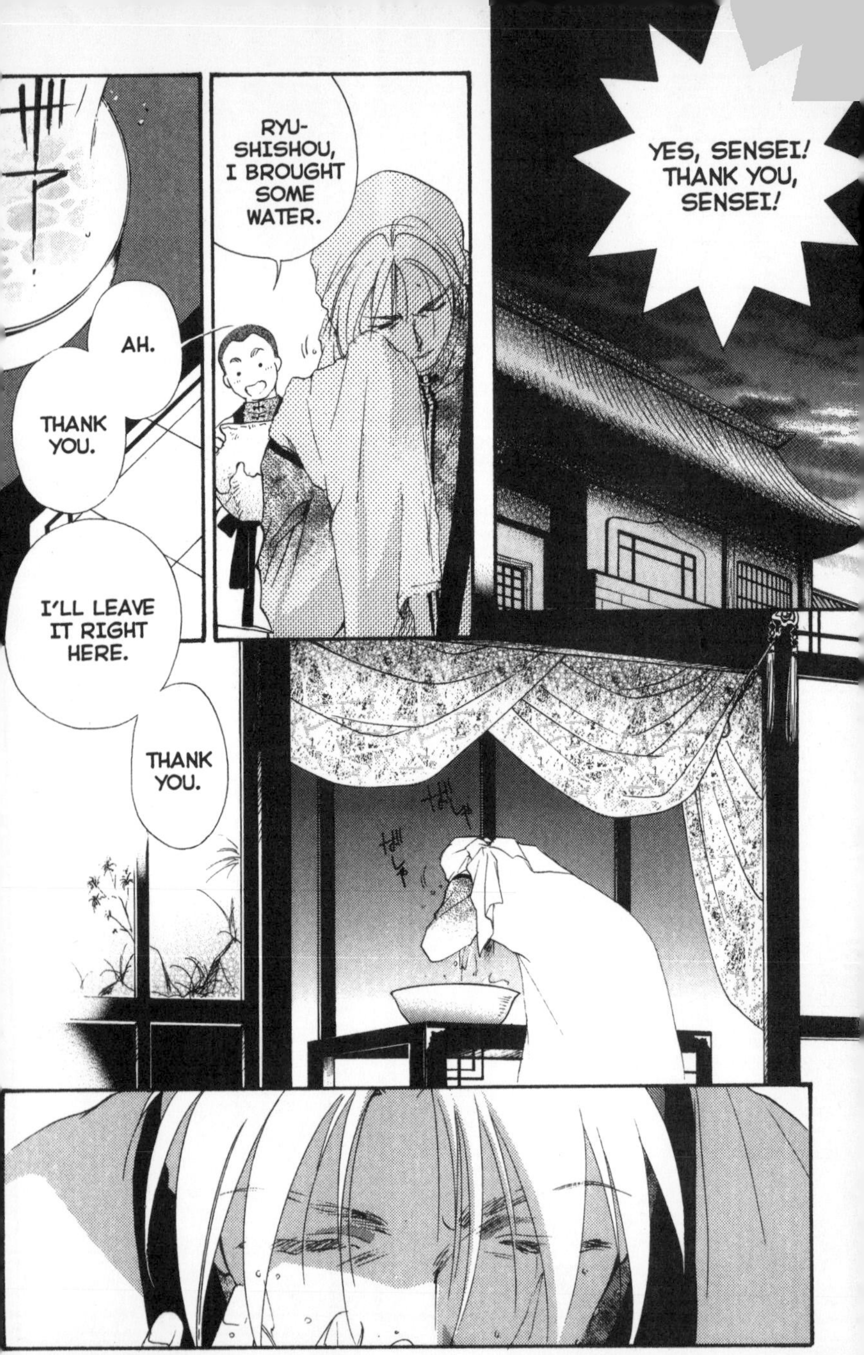
YES, SENSEI! THANK YOU, SENSEI!
RYU-SHISHOU, I BROUGHT SOME WATER.
AH.
THANK YOU.
I'LL LEAVE IT RIGHT HERE.
THANK YOU.

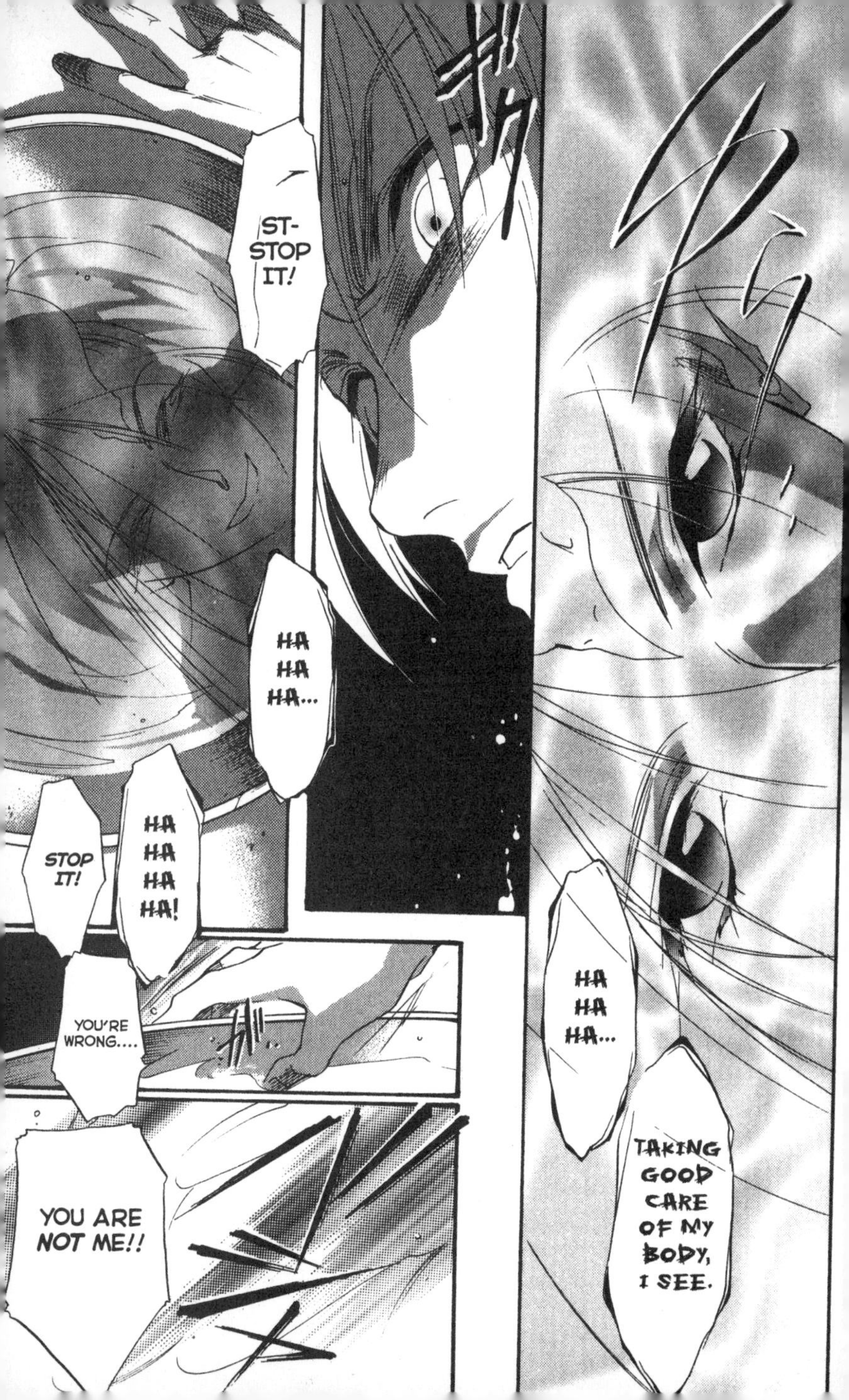
HA HA HA...
TAKING GOOD CARE OF MY BODY, I SEE.
ST- STOP IT!
HA HA HA...
HA HA HA HA!
STOP IT!
YOU'RE WRONG....
YOU ARE NOT ME!!

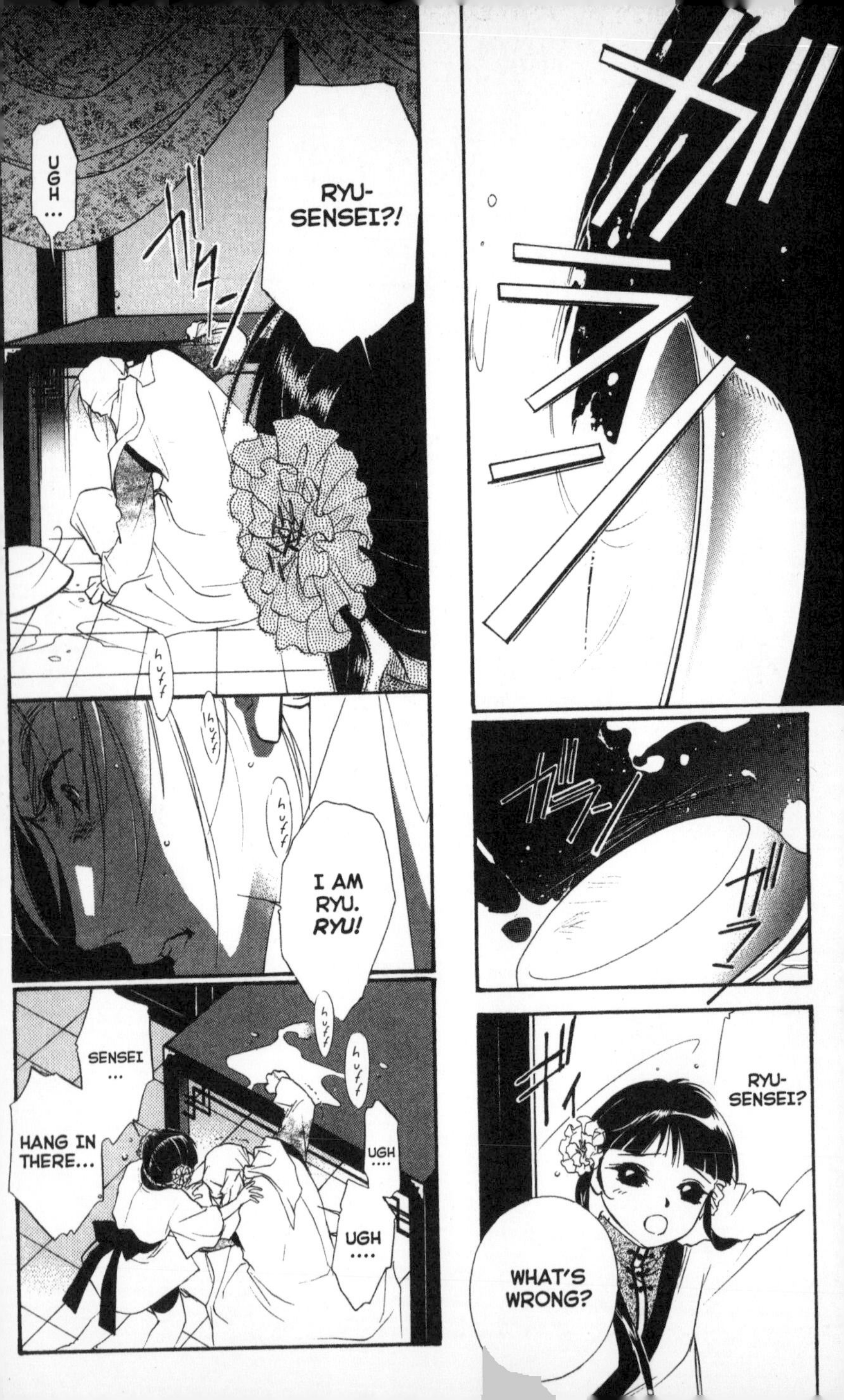
RYU-SENSEI?!
UGH ...
huff
huff
huff
I AM RYU. RYU!
RYU-SENSEI?
WHAT'S WRONG?
huff
huff
UGH ....
UGH ....
SENSEI ...
HANG IN THERE...

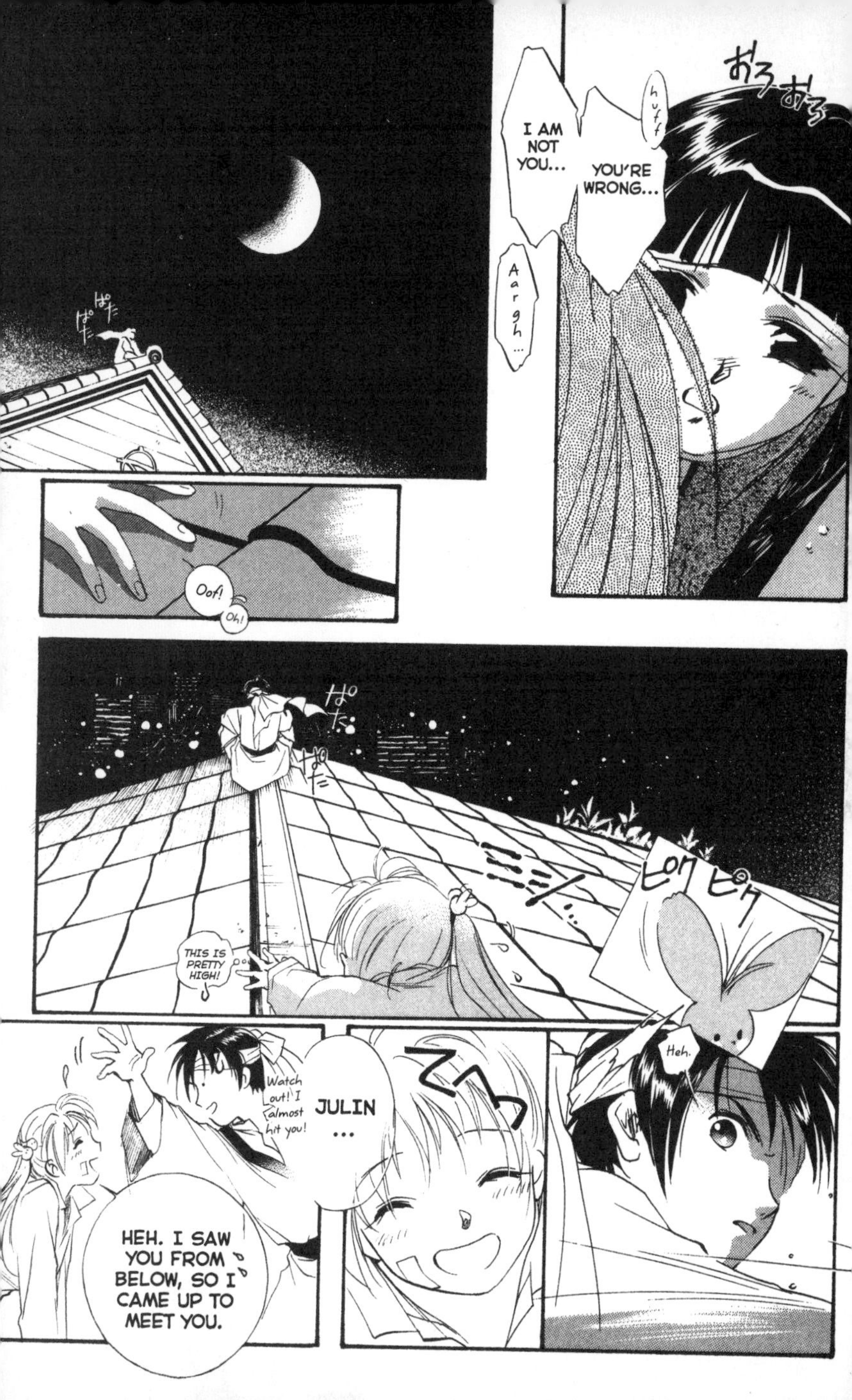

おろおろ
huff
YOU'RE WRONG...
I AM NOT YOU...
Aargh...
ぱた ぱた
Oof!
Oh!
ぱた ぱた
ピク ピク
ミミ...
THIS IS PRETTY HIGH!
Heh.
てへっ
JULIN ...
Watch out! I almost hit you!
HEH. I SAW YOU FROM BELOW, SO I CAME UP TO MEET YOU.

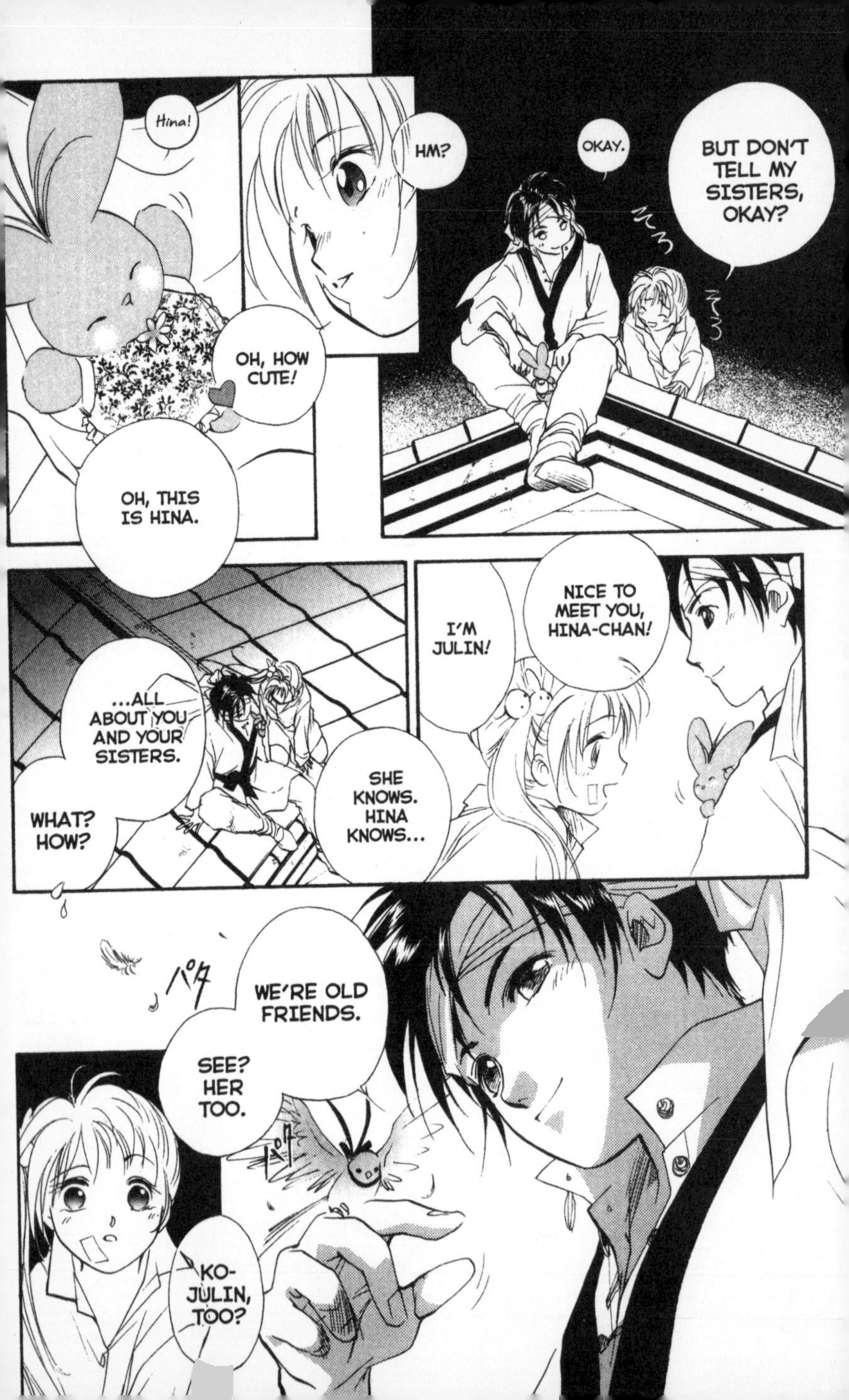
BUT DON'T TELL MY SISTERS, OKAY?
OKAY.
HM?
Hina!
OH, HOW CUTE!
OH, THIS IS HINA.
NICE TO MEET YOU, HINA-CHAN!
I'M JULIN!
SHE KNOWS. HINA KNOWS...
...ALL ABOUT YOU AND YOUR SISTERS.
WHAT? HOW?
パタ
WE'RE OLD FRIENDS.
SEE? HER TOO.
KO-JULIN, TOO?

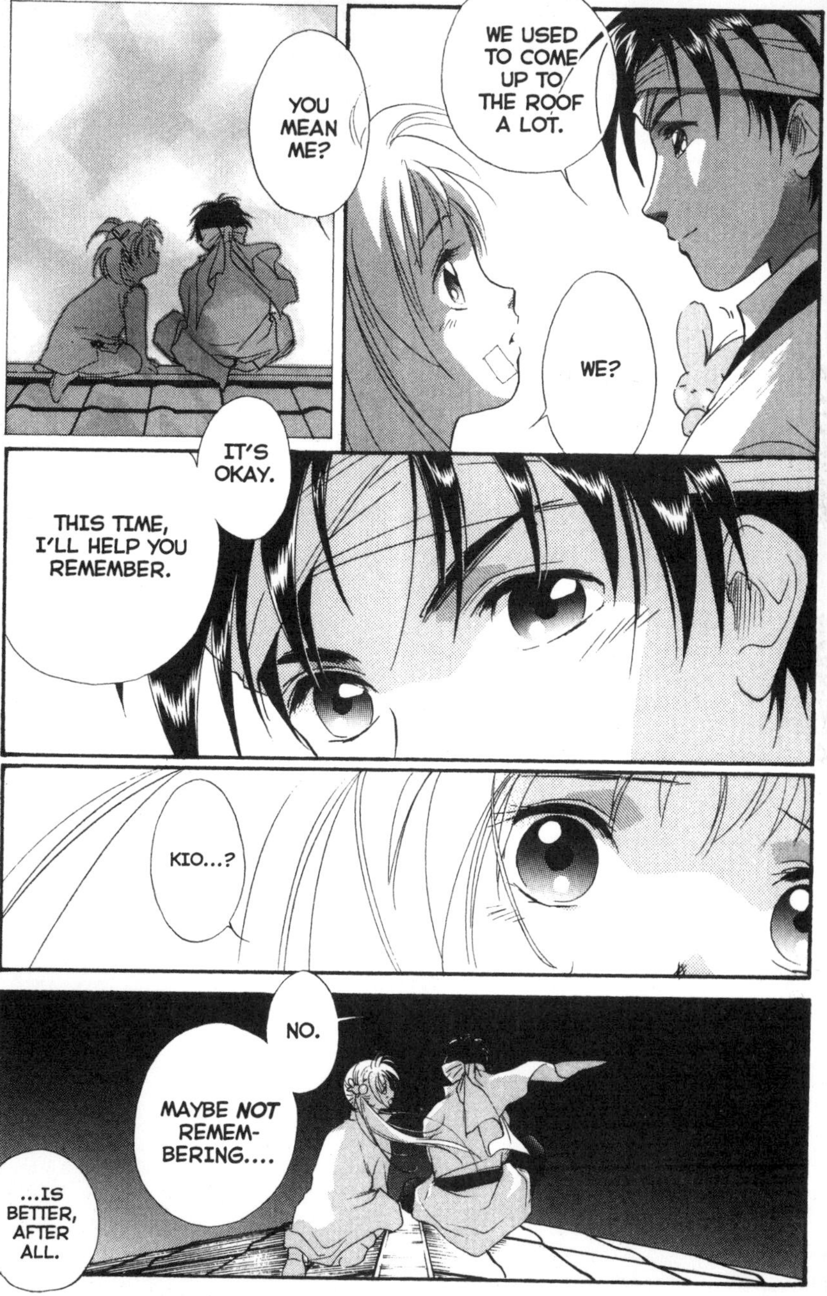
WE USED TO COME UP TO THE ROOF A LOT.
YOU MEAN ME?
WE?
IT'S OKAY.
THIS TIME, I'LL HELP YOU REMEMBER.
KIO...?
NO.
MAYBE *NOT* REMEMBERING....
...IS BETTER, AFTER ALL.

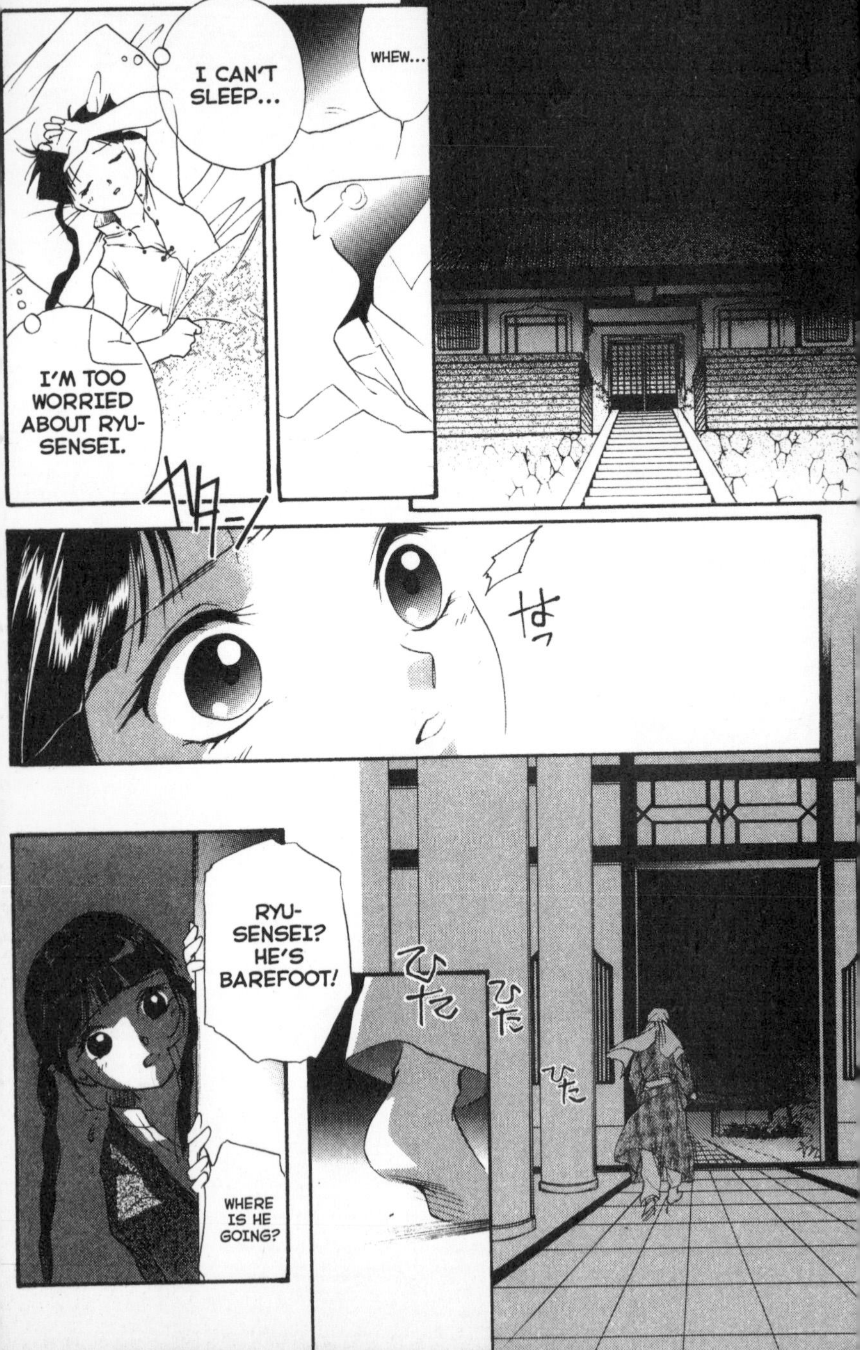
WHEW...
I CAN'T SLEEP...
I'M TOO WORRIED ABOUT RYU-SENSEI.
カターン
はっ
ひた
ひた
ひた
RYU-SENSEI? HE'S BAREFOOT!
WHERE IS HE GOING?

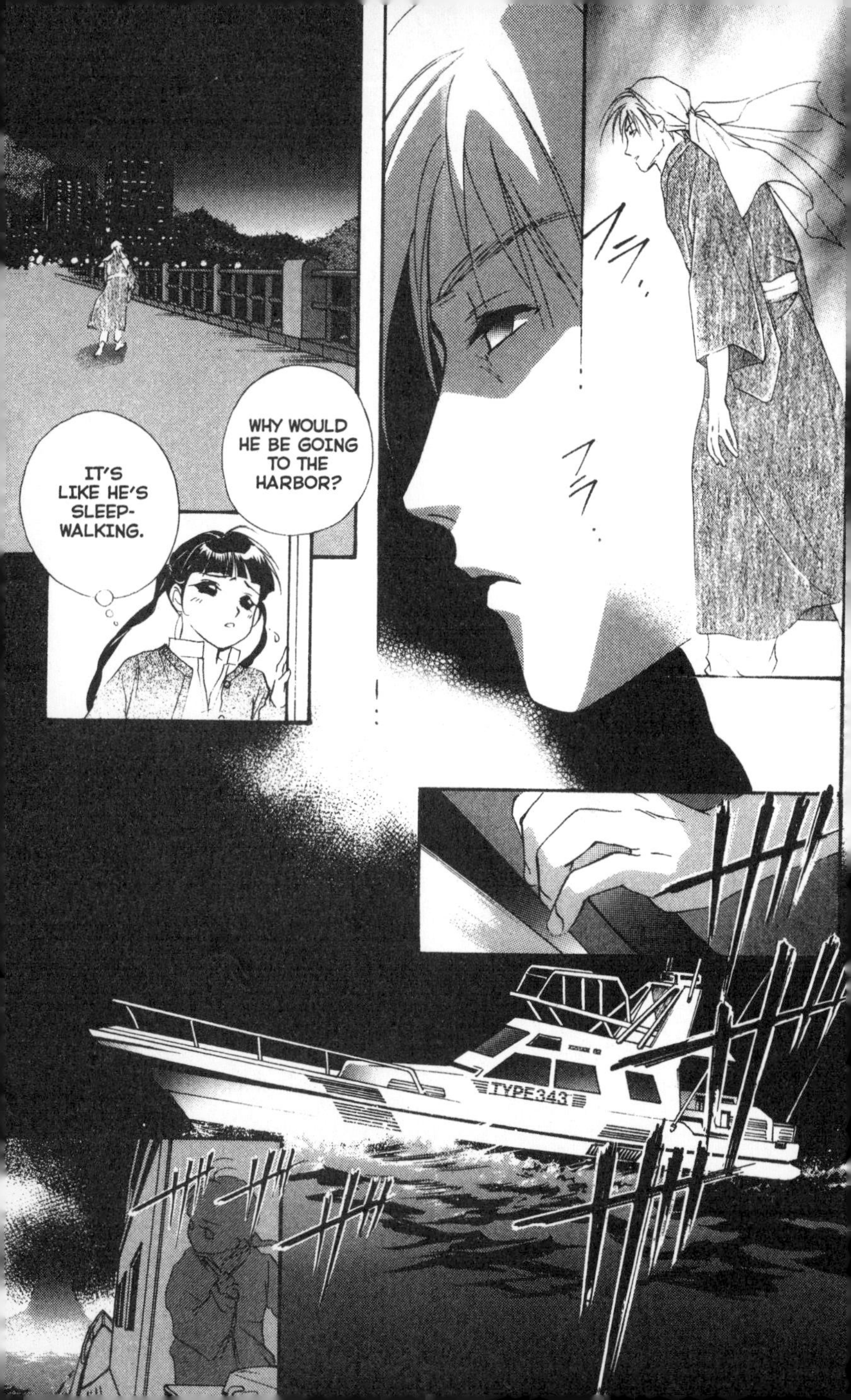
WHY WOULD HE BE GOING TO THE HARBOR?
IT'S LIKE HE'S SLEEP-WALKING.
TYPE 343

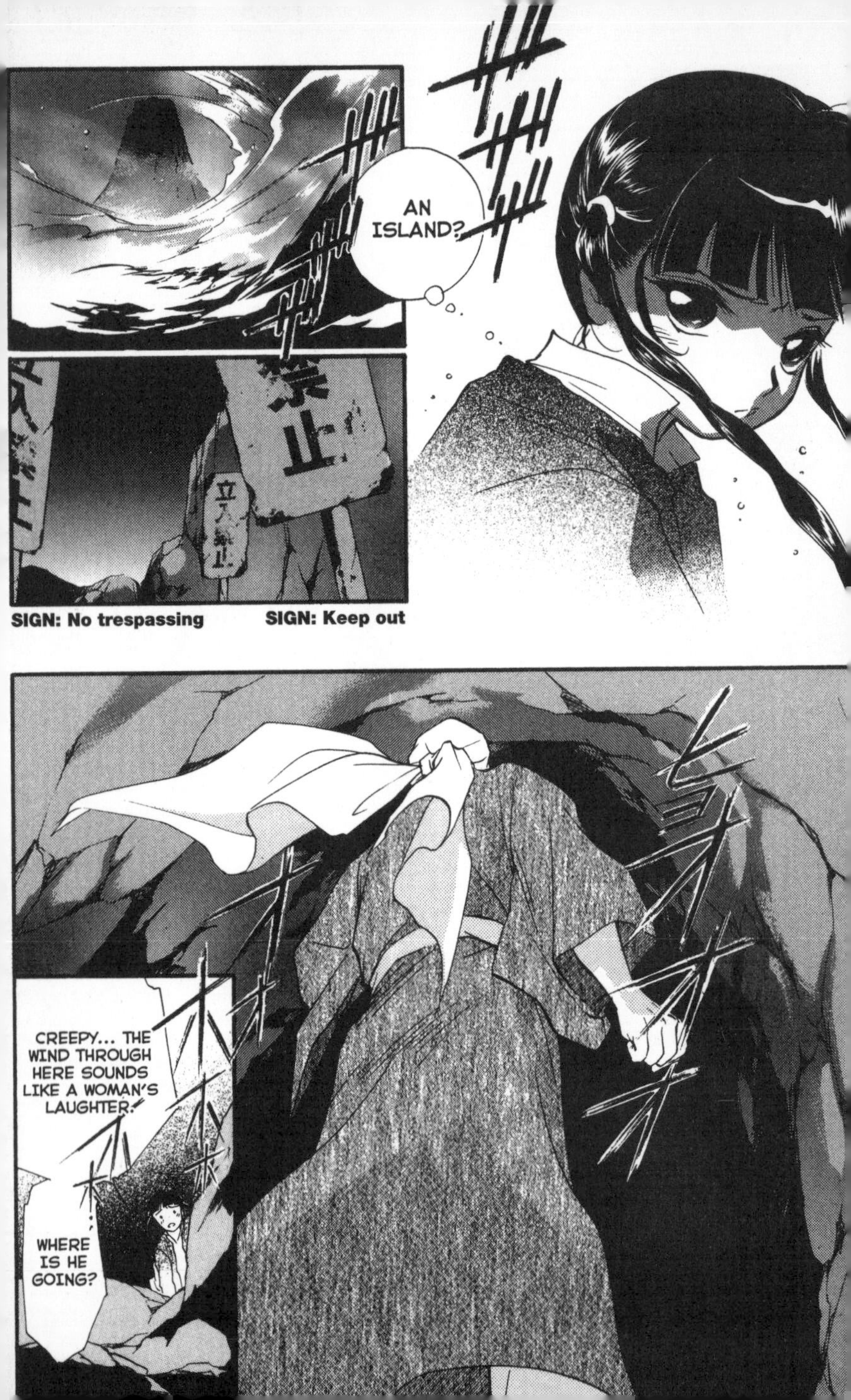
AN ISLAND?
SIGN: Keep out
SIGN: No trespassing
CREEPY... THE WIND THROUGH HERE SOUNDS LIKE A WOMAN'S LAUGHTER.
WHERE IS HE GOING?

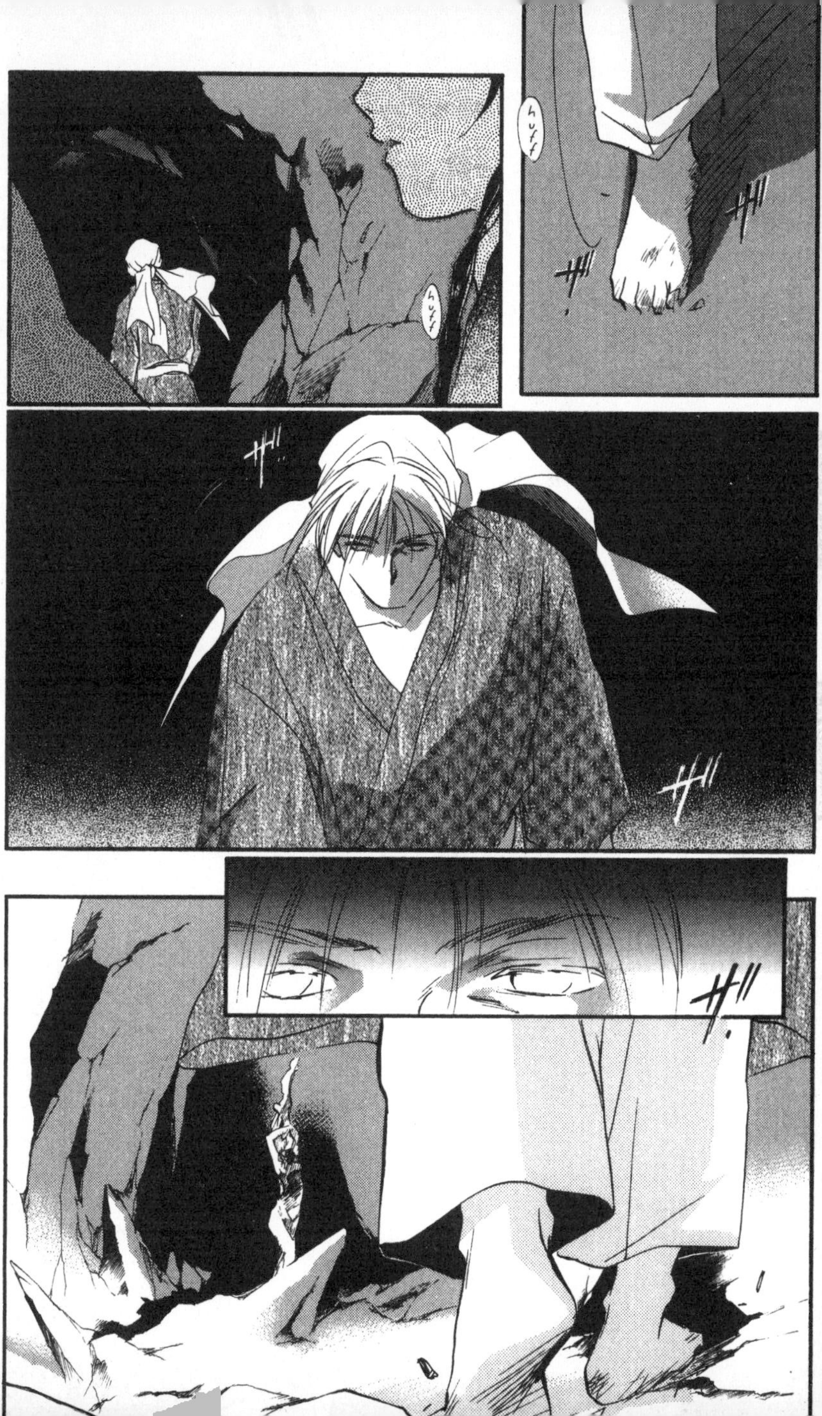
huff
huff

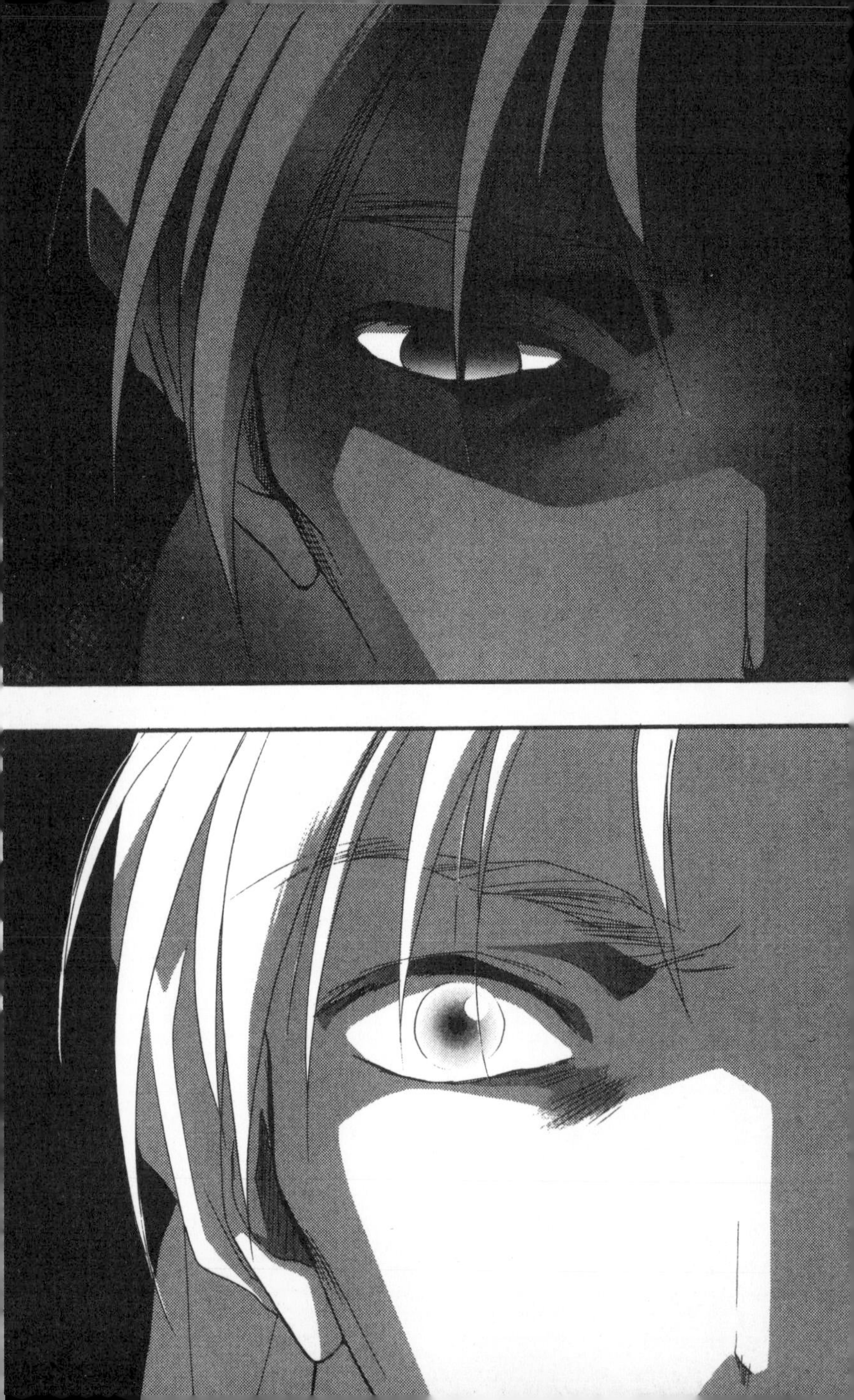

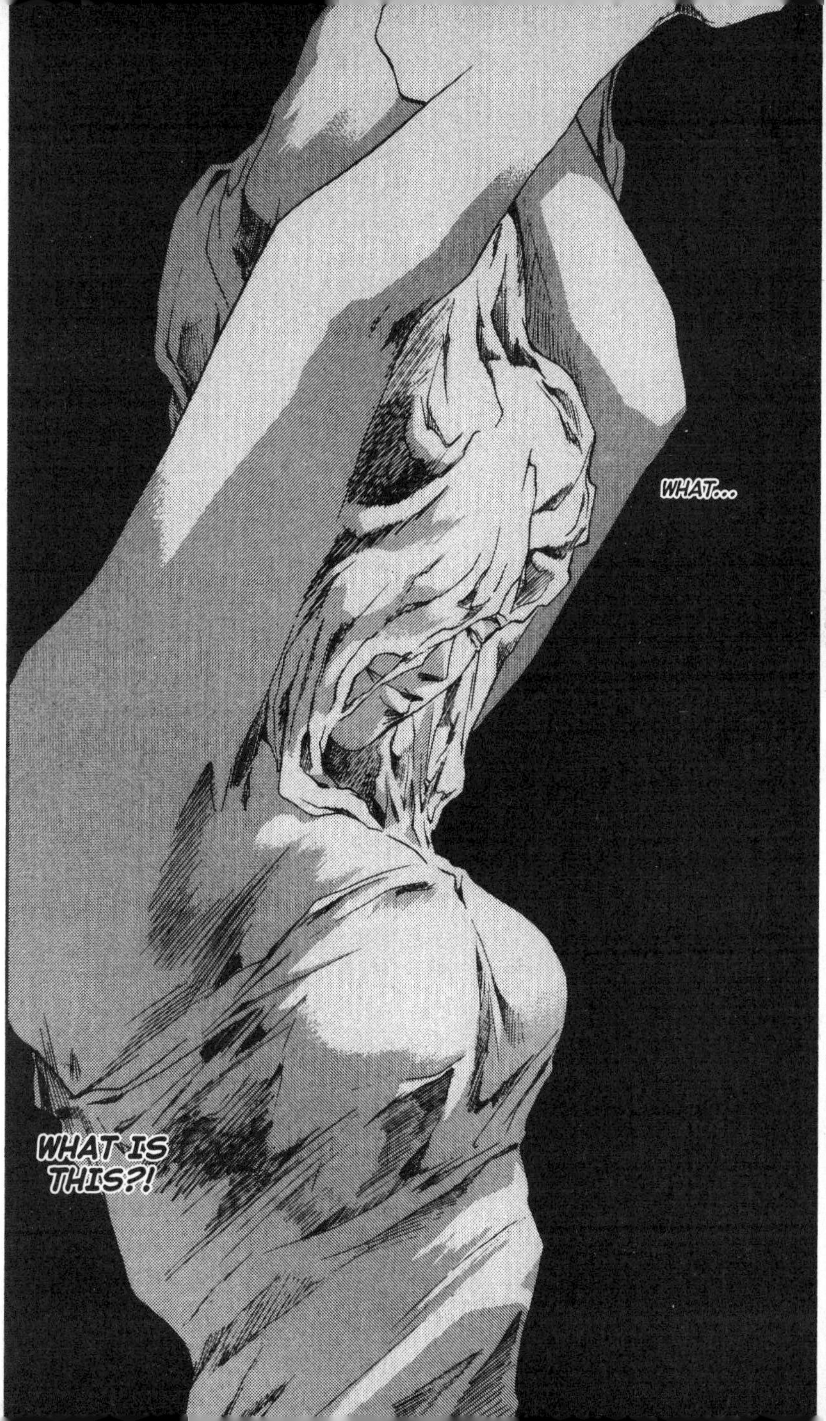
WHAT...
WHAT IS THIS?!

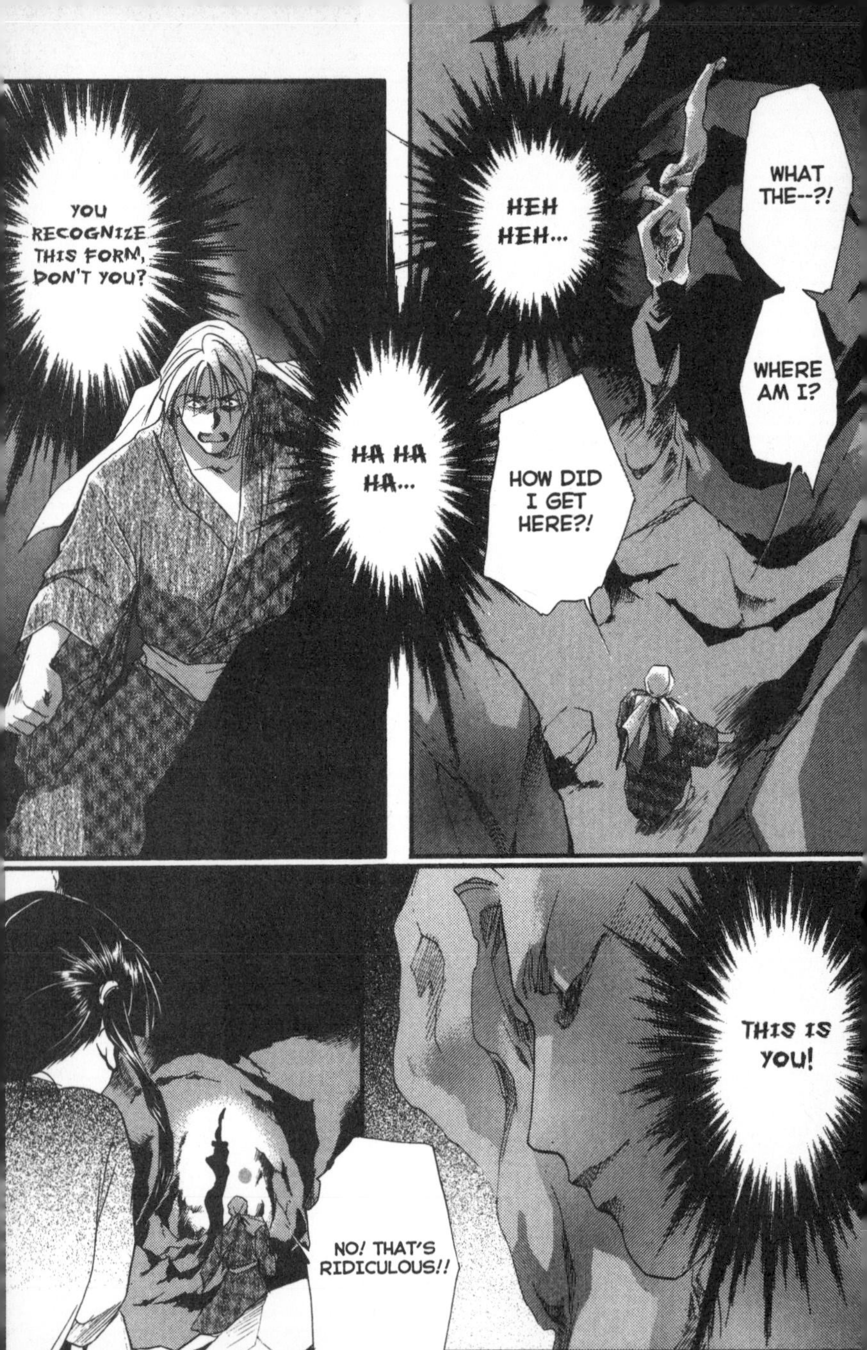
WHAT THE--?!
WHERE AM I?
HEH HEH...
HOW DID I GET HERE?!
HA HA HA...
YOU RECOGNIZE THIS FORM, DON'T YOU?
THIS IS YOU!
NO! THAT'S RIDICULOUS!!

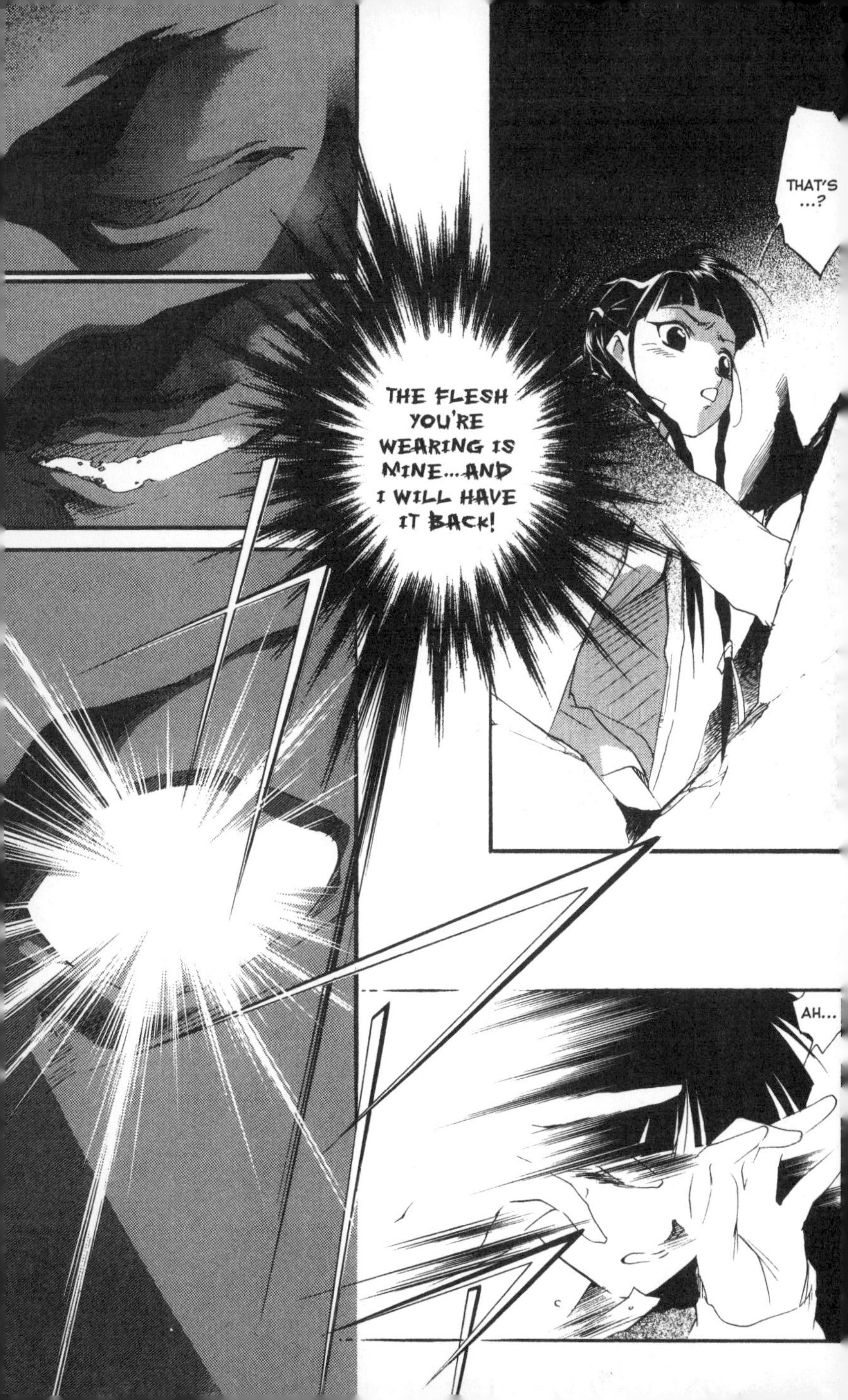
THAT'S ...?
THE FLESH YOU'RE WEARING IS MINE... AND I WILL HAVE IT BACK!
AH...

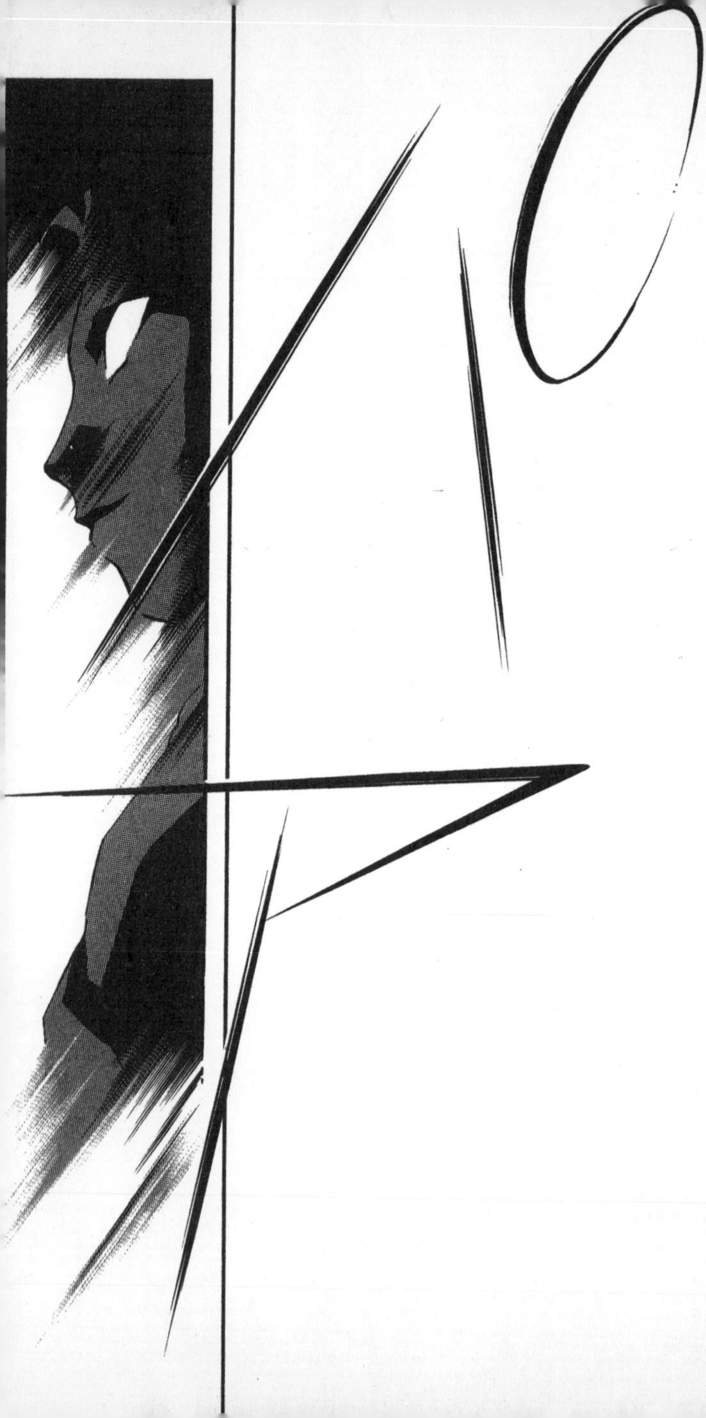

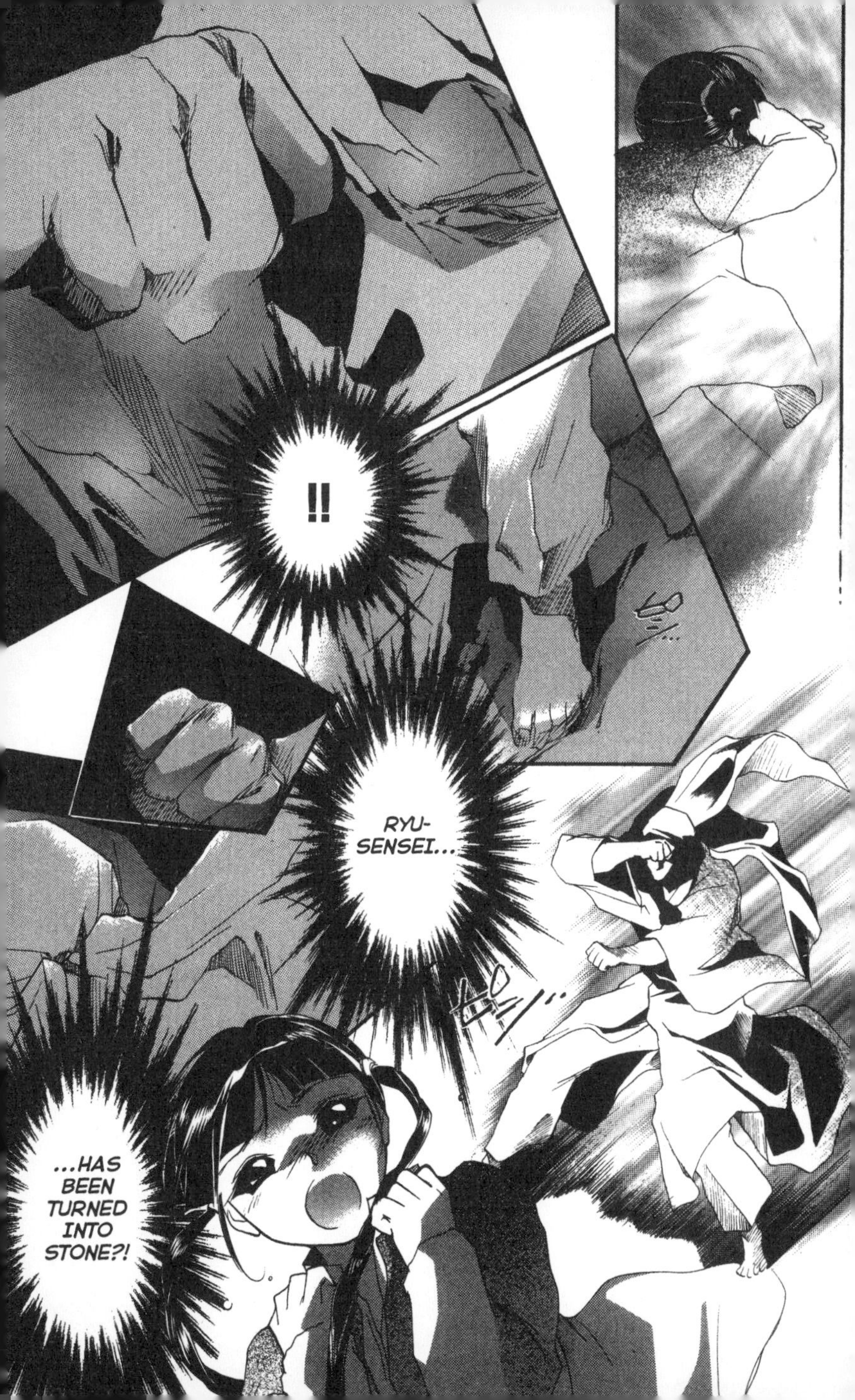
!!
RYU-SENSEI...
...HAS BEEN TURNED INTO STONE?!

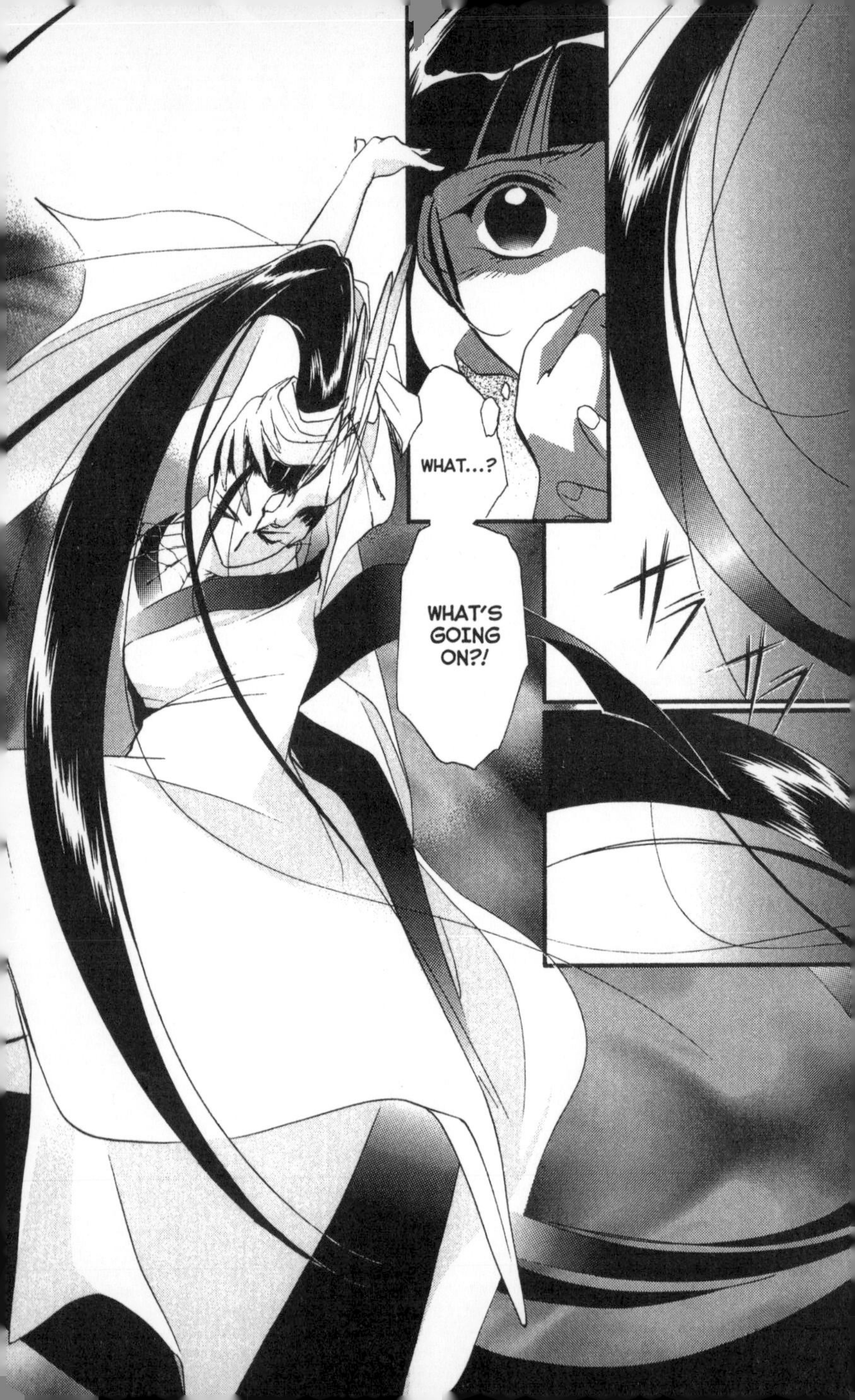
WHAT...?
WHAT'S GOING ON?!

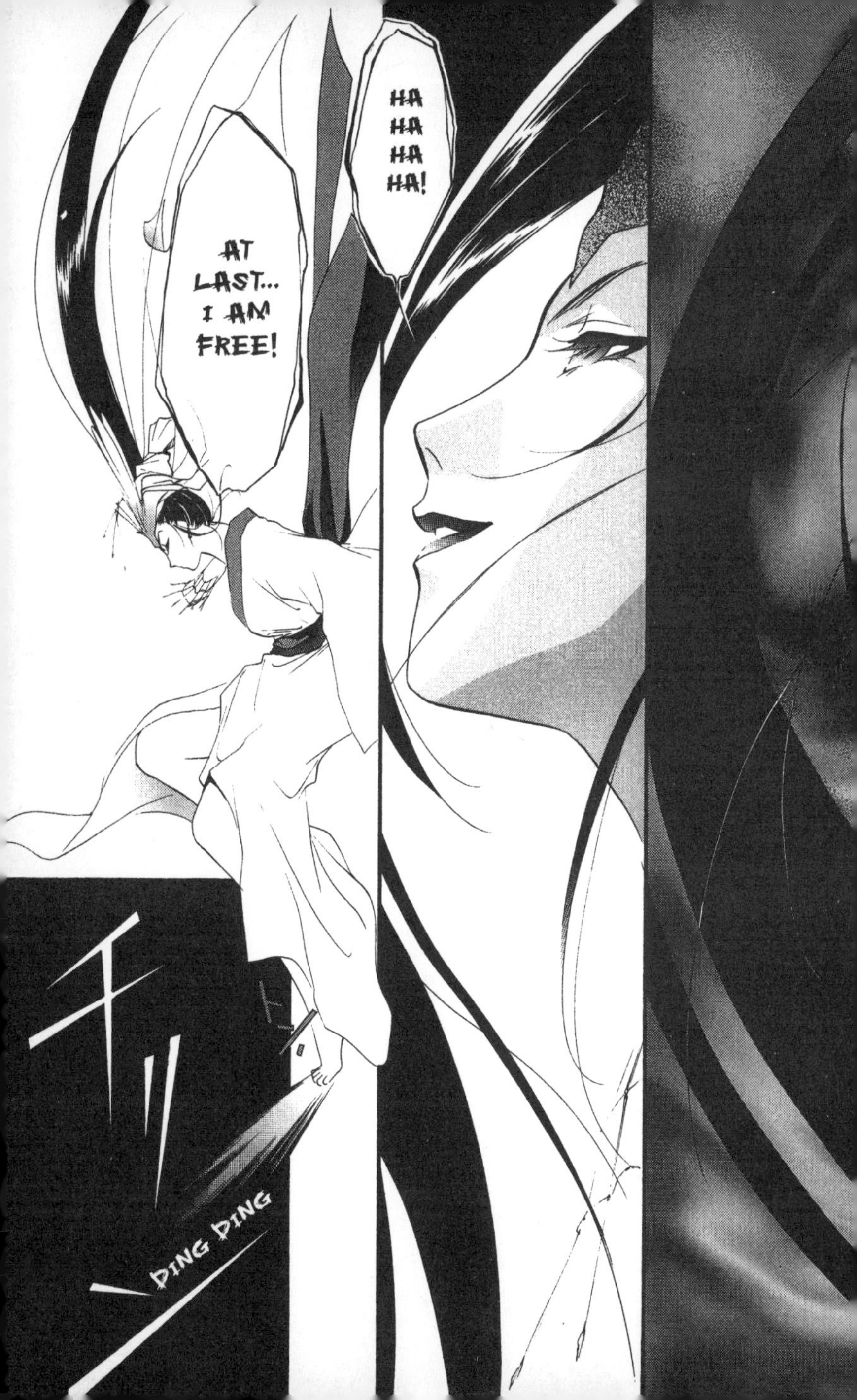
HA HA HA HA!
AT LAST... I AM FREE!
チッ
DING DING

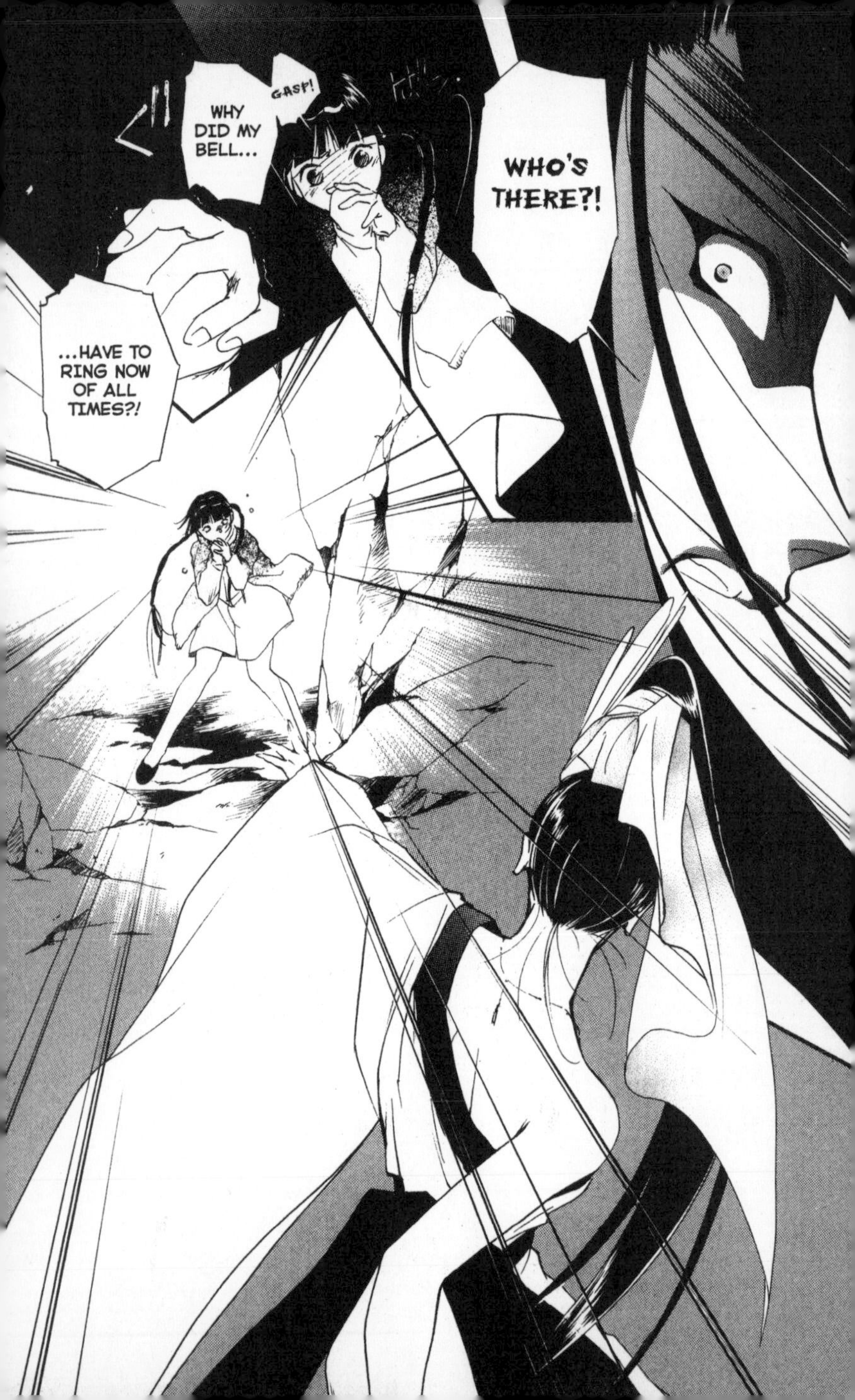
WHO'S THERE?!
GASP!
WHY DID MY BELL...
...HAVE TO RING NOW OF ALL TIMES?!

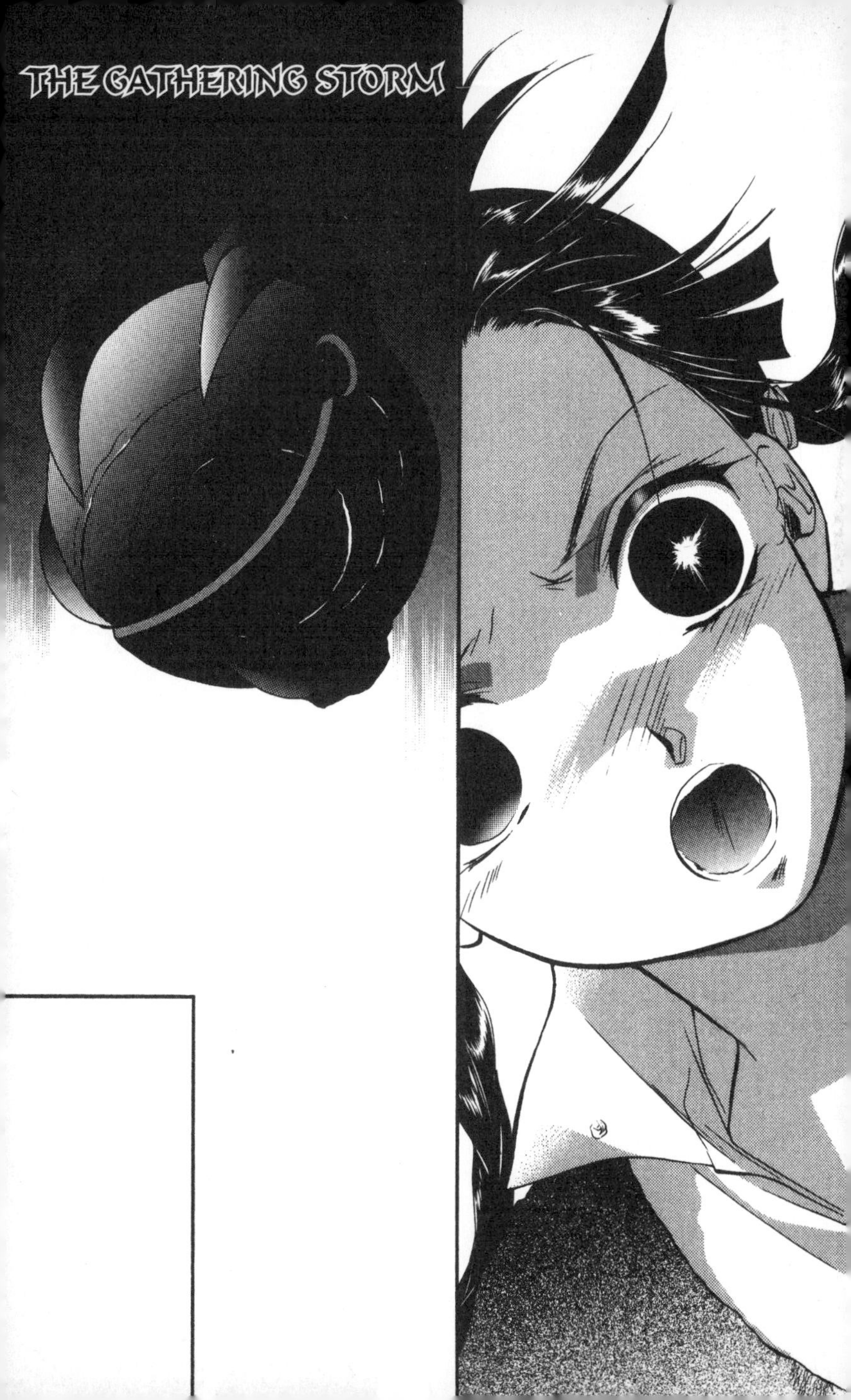
THE GATHERING STORM

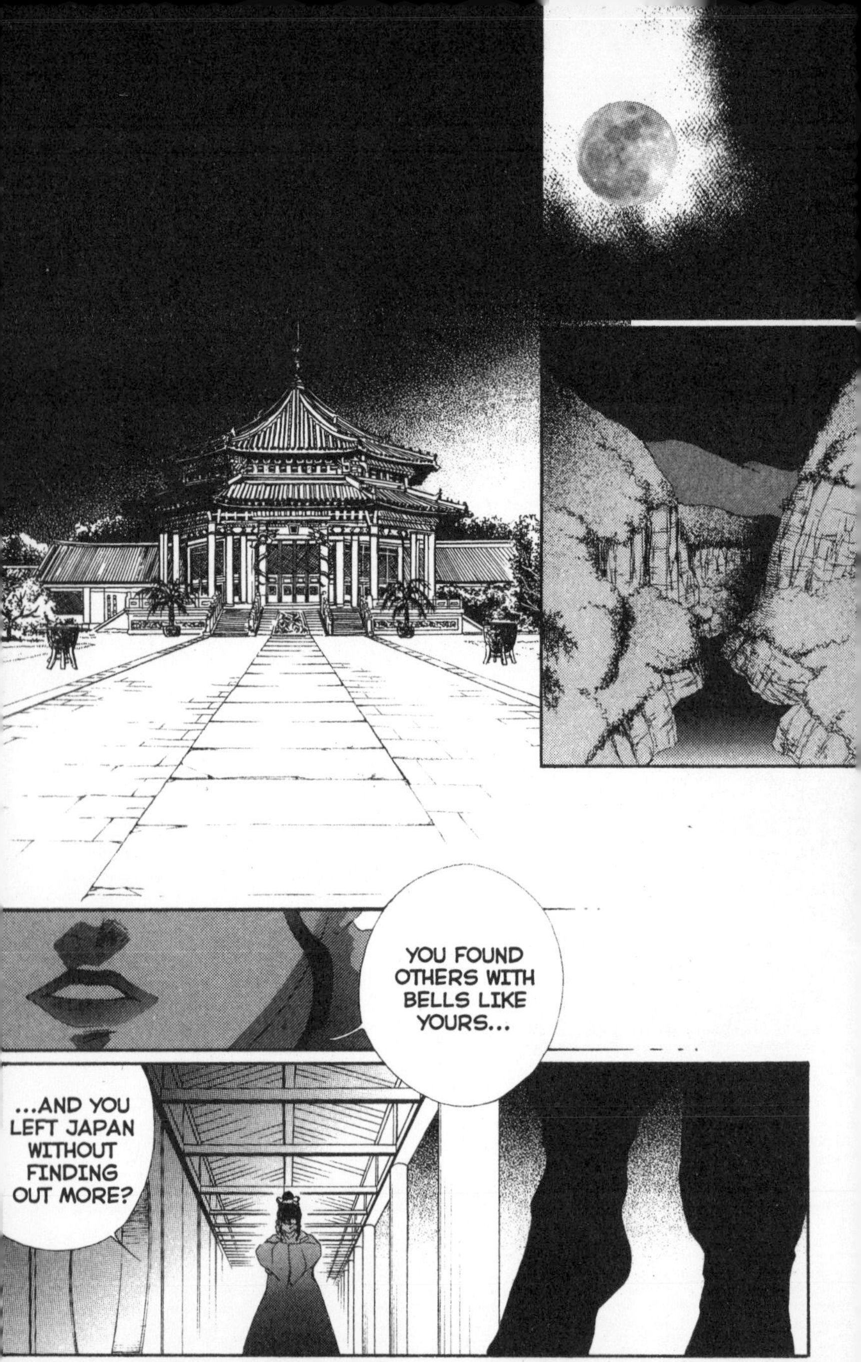
YOU FOUND OTHERS WITH BELLS LIKE YOURS...
...AND YOU LEFT JAPAN WITHOUT FINDING OUT MORE?

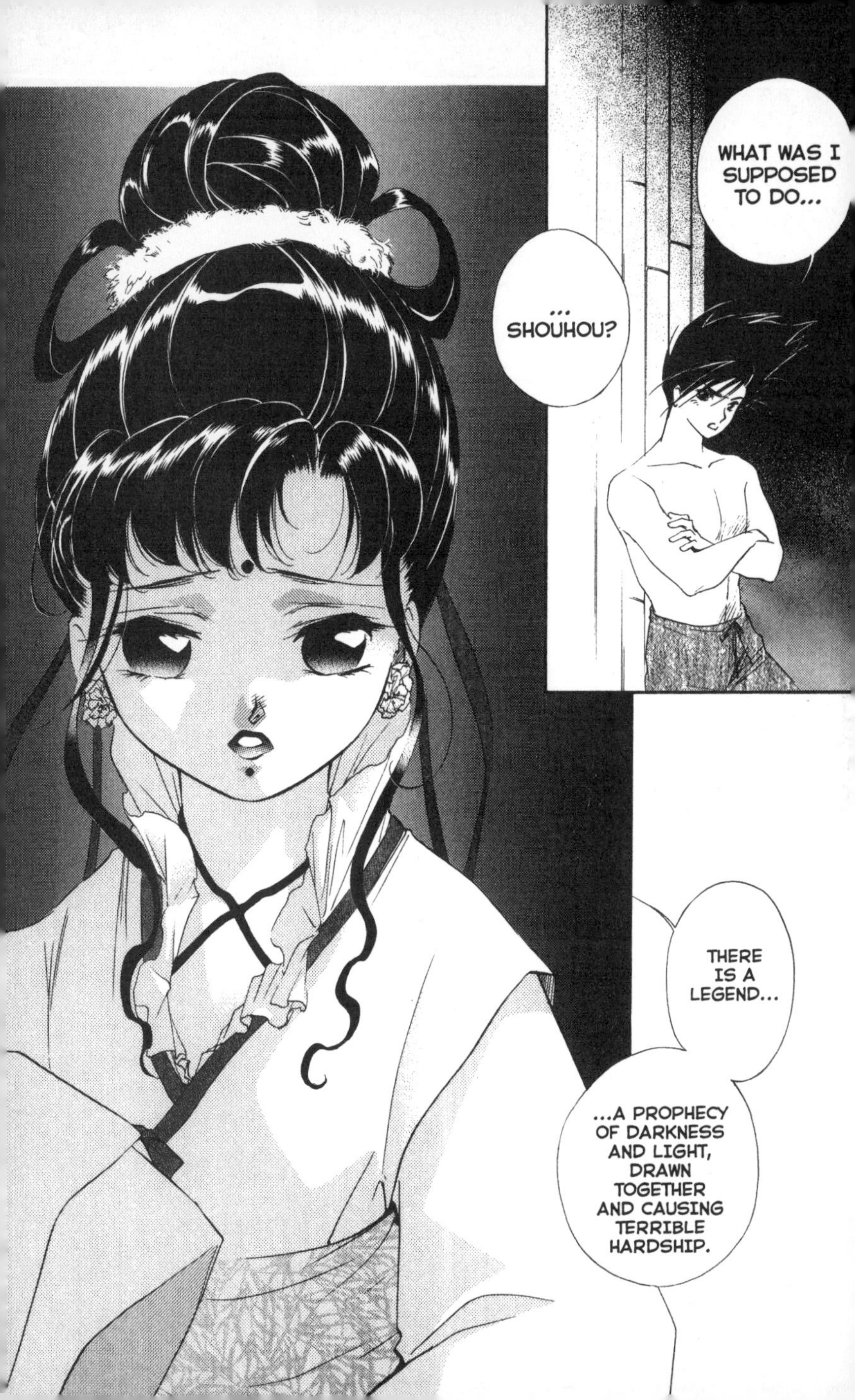
WHAT WAS I SUPPOSED TO DO...
... SHOUHOU?
THERE IS A LEGEND...
...A PROPHECY OF DARKNESS AND LIGHT, DRAWN TOGETHER AND CAUSING TERRIBLE HARDSHIP.

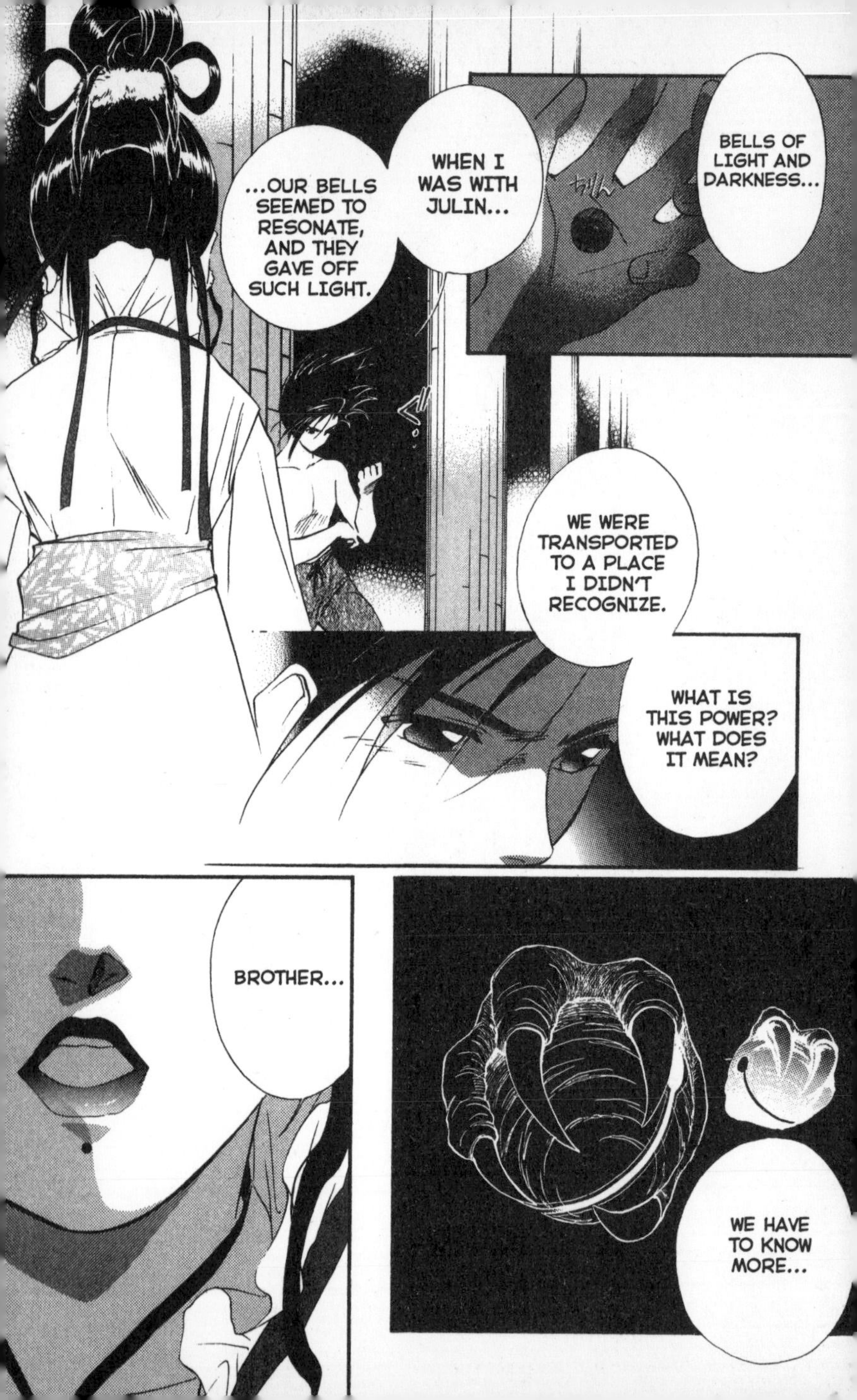
BELLS OF LIGHT AND DARKNESS...
ちりん
WHEN I WAS WITH JULIN...
...OUR BELLS SEEMED TO RESONATE, AND THEY GAVE OFF SUCH LIGHT.
WE WERE TRANSPORTED TO A PLACE I DIDN'T RECOGNIZE.
WHAT IS THIS POWER? WHAT DOES IT MEAN?
WE HAVE TO KNOW MORE...
BROTHER...

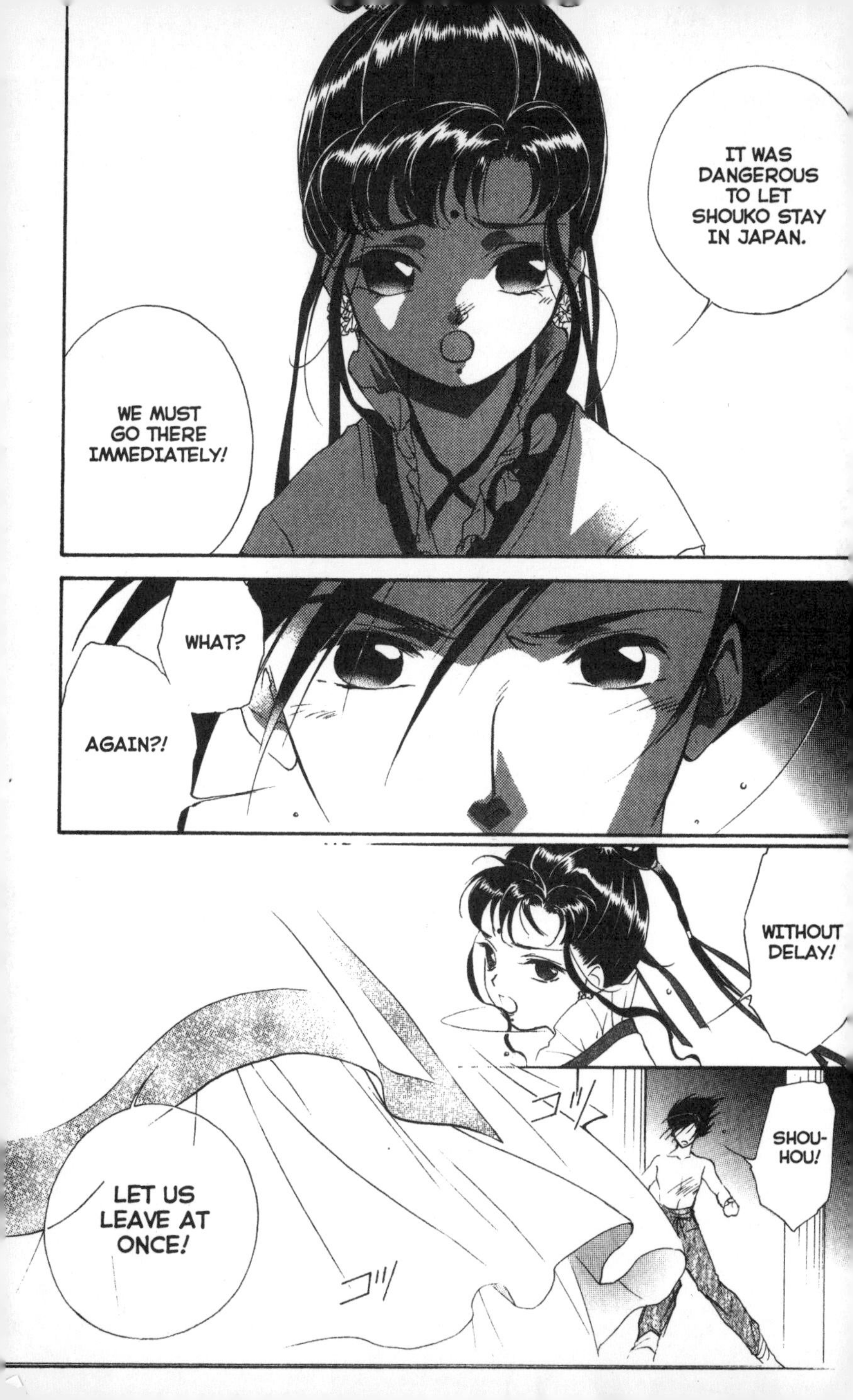
IT WAS DANGEROUS TO LET SHOUKO STAY IN JAPAN.
WE MUST GO THERE IMMEDIATELY!
WHAT?
AGAIN?!
WITHOUT DELAY!
SHOU-HOU!
LET US LEAVE AT ONCE!

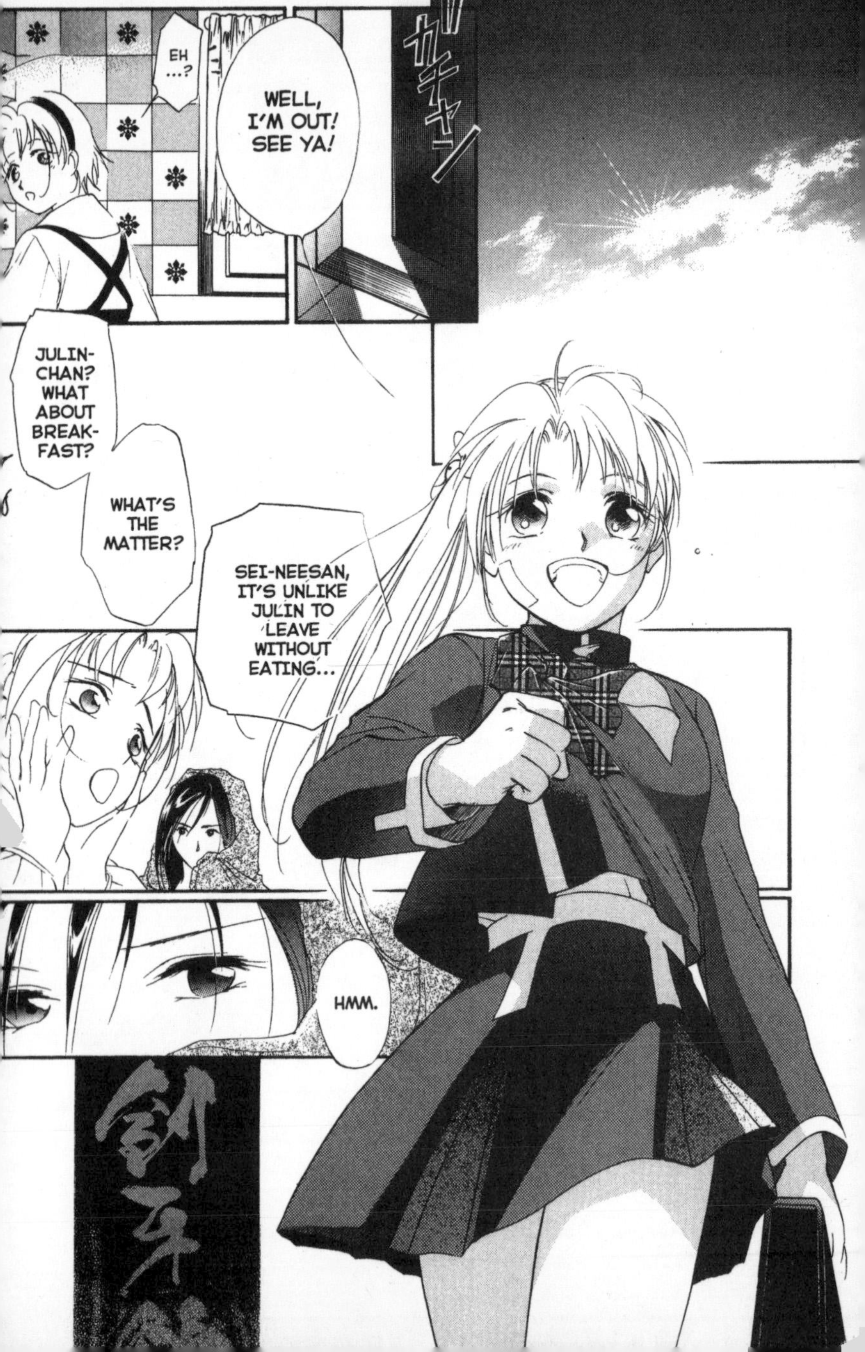
ガチャン
WELL, I'M OUT! SEE YA!
EH ...?
JULIN-CHAN? WHAT ABOUT BREAK-FAST?
WHAT'S THE MATTER?
SEI-NEESAN, IT'S UNLIKE JULIN TO LEAVE WITHOUT EATING...
HMM.

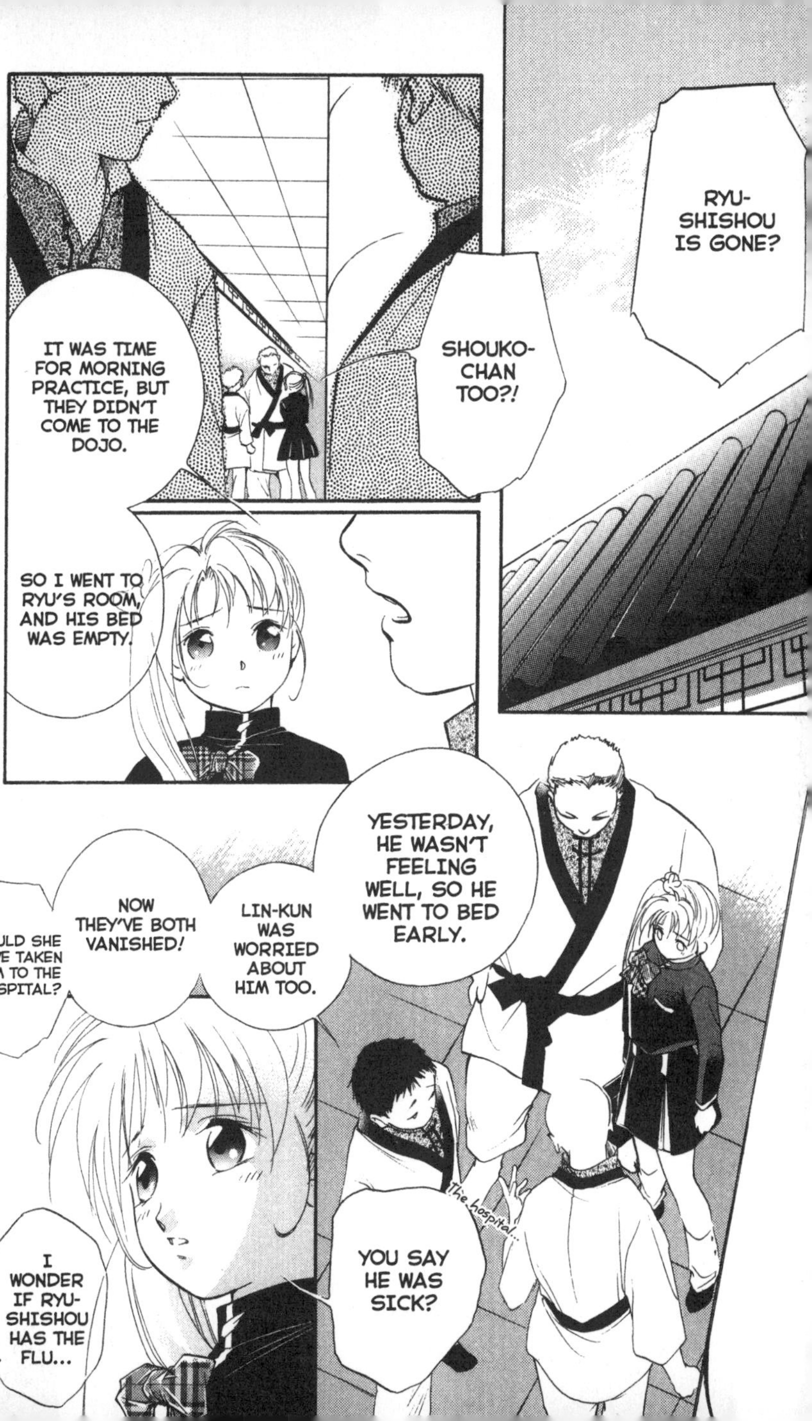
RYU-SHISHOU IS GONE?
SHOUKO-CHAN TOO?!
IT WAS TIME FOR MORNING PRACTICE, BUT THEY DIDN'T COME TO THE DOJO.
SO I WENT TO RYU'S ROOM, AND HIS BED WAS EMPTY.
YESTERDAY, HE WASN'T FEELING WELL, SO HE WENT TO BED EARLY.
LIN-KUN WAS WORRIED ABOUT HIM TOO.
NOW THEY'VE BOTH VANISHED!
COULD SHE HAVE TAKEN HIM TO THE HOSPITAL?
YOU SAY HE WAS SICK?
The hospital...
I WONDER IF RYU-SHISHOU HAS THE FLU...

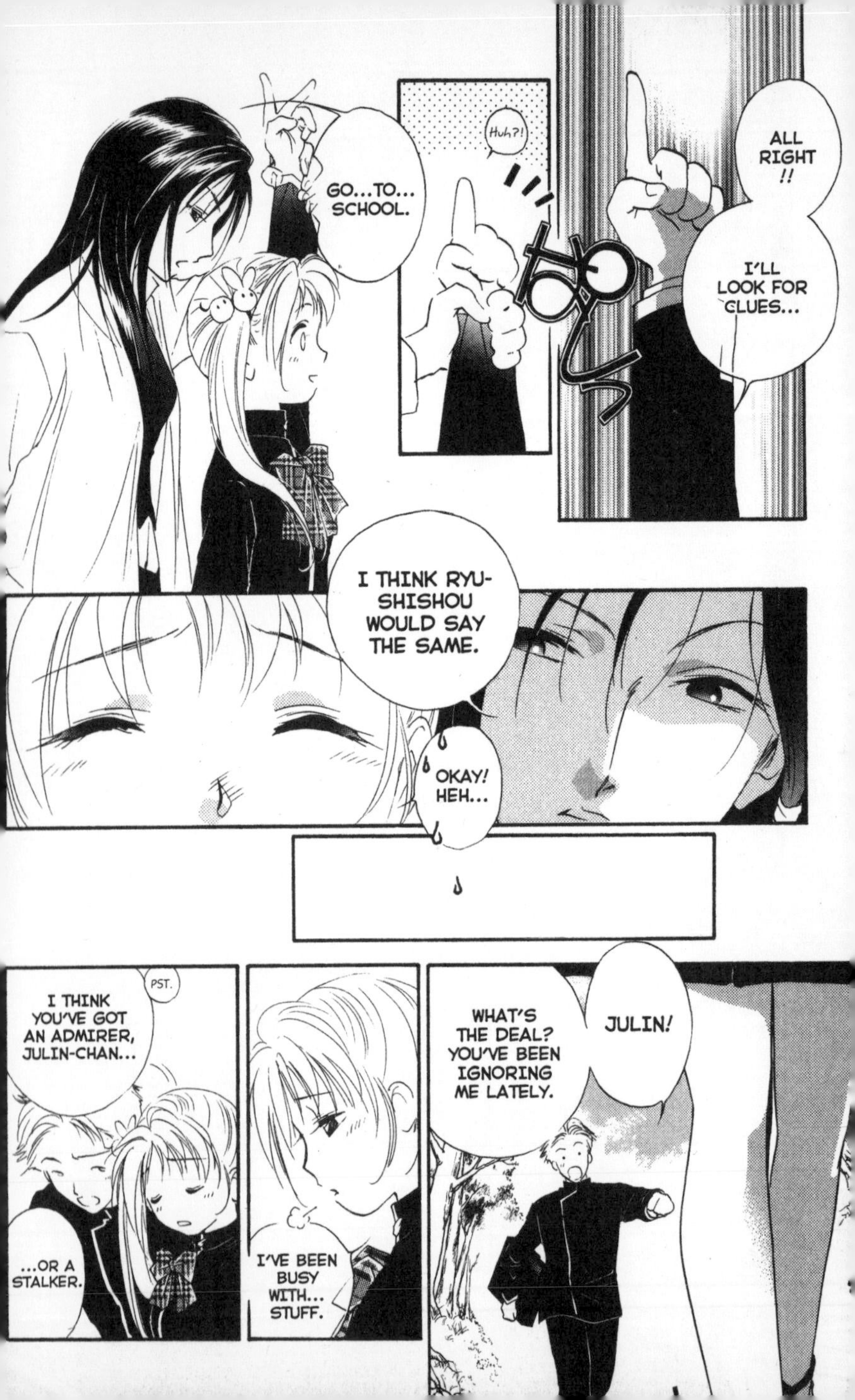
ALL RIGHT !!
I'LL LOOK FOR CLUES...
Huh?!
GO...TO... SCHOOL.
I THINK RYU-SHISHOU WOULD SAY THE SAME.
OKAY! HEH...
JULIN!
WHAT'S THE DEAL? YOU'VE BEEN IGNORING ME LATELY.
I'VE BEEN BUSY WITH... STUFF.
PST.
I THINK YOU'VE GOT AN ADMIRER, JULIN-CHAN...
...OR A STALKER.

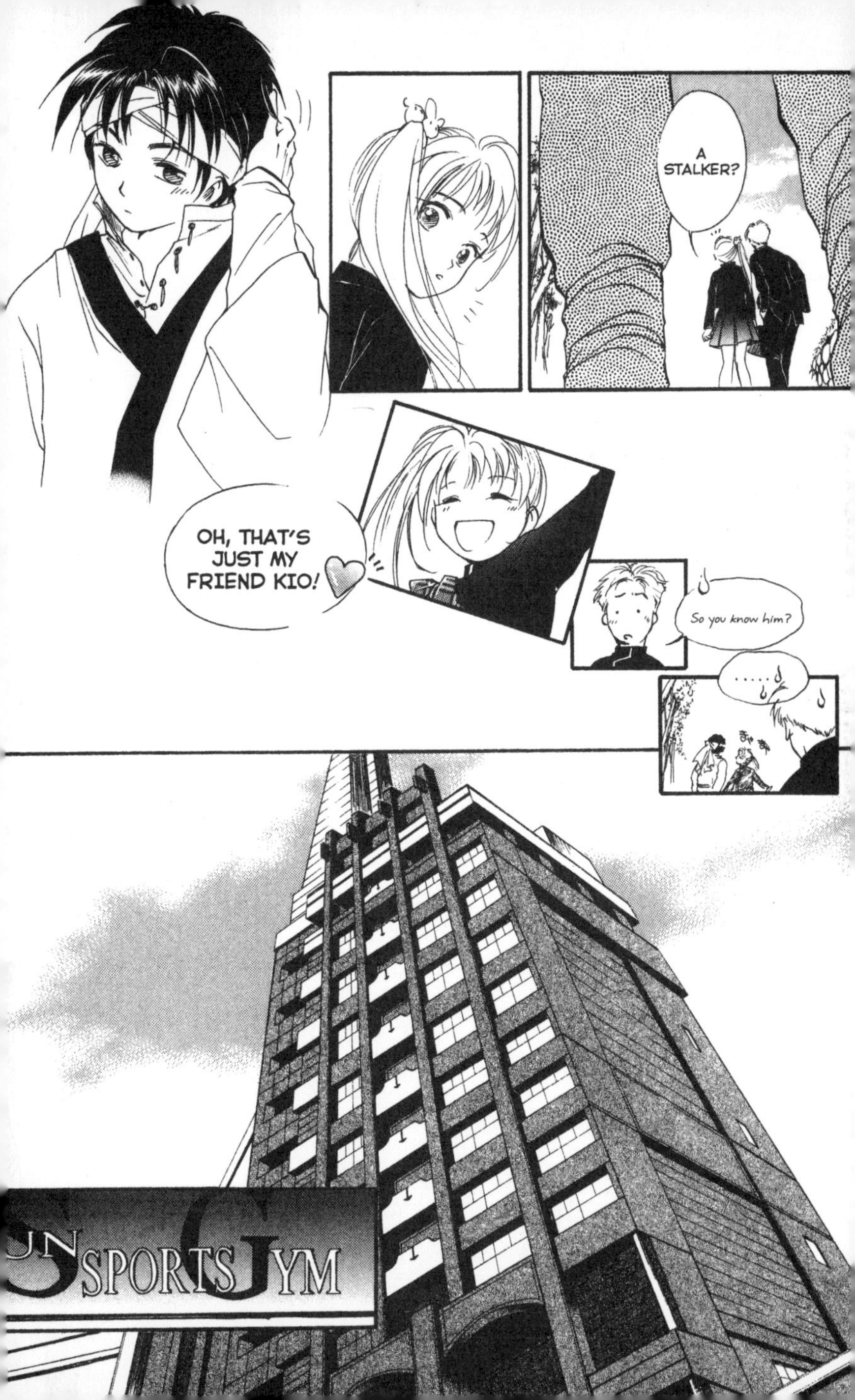
A STALKER?
OH, THAT'S JUST MY FRIEND KIO!
So you know him?
.....
SUN SPORTS GYM

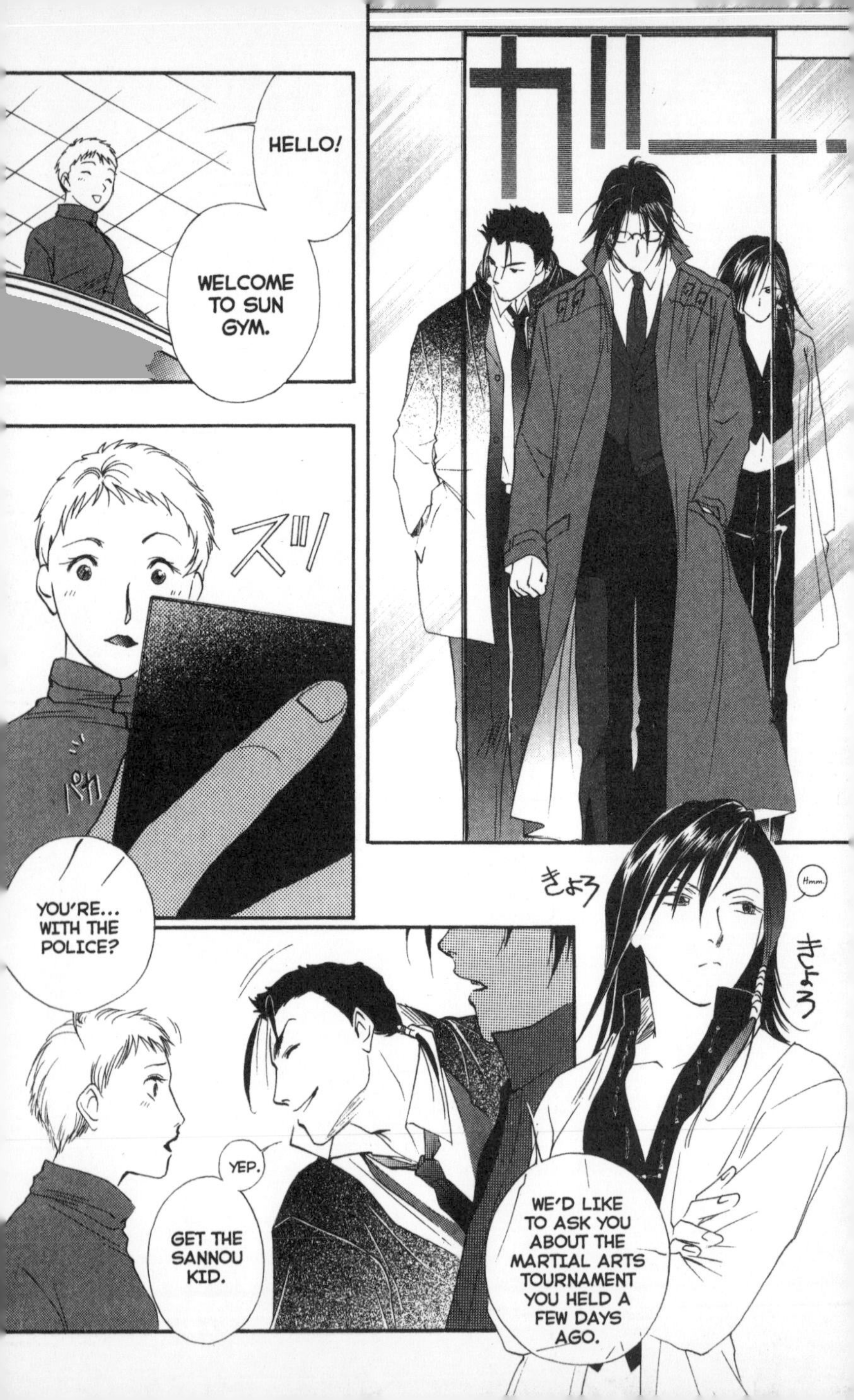
HELLO!
WELCOME TO SUN GYM.
ズッ
きょろ
Hmm.
きょろ
YOU'RE... WITH THE POLICE?
WE'D LIKE TO ASK YOU ABOUT THE MARTIAL ARTS TOURNAMENT YOU HELD A FEW DAYS AGO.
YEP.
GET THE SANNOU KID.

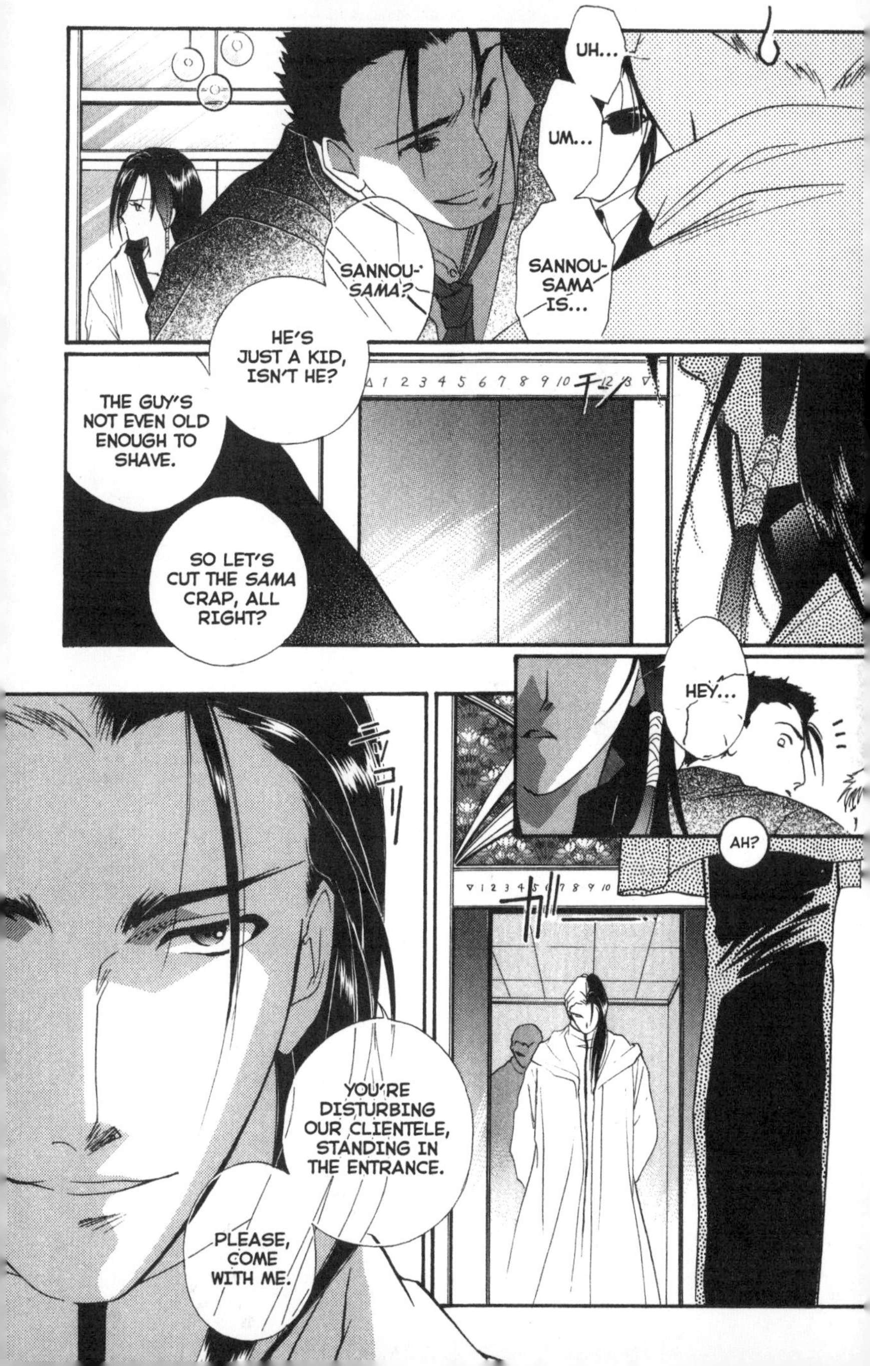
UH...
UM...
SANNOU-SAMA IS...
SANNOU-SAMA?
HE'S JUST A KID, ISN'T HE?
THE GUY'S NOT EVEN OLD ENOUGH TO SHAVE.
SO LET'S CUT THE SAMA CRAP, ALL RIGHT?
HEY...
AH?
YOU'RE DISTURBING OUR CLIENTELE, STANDING IN THE ENTRANCE.
PLEASE, COME WITH ME.

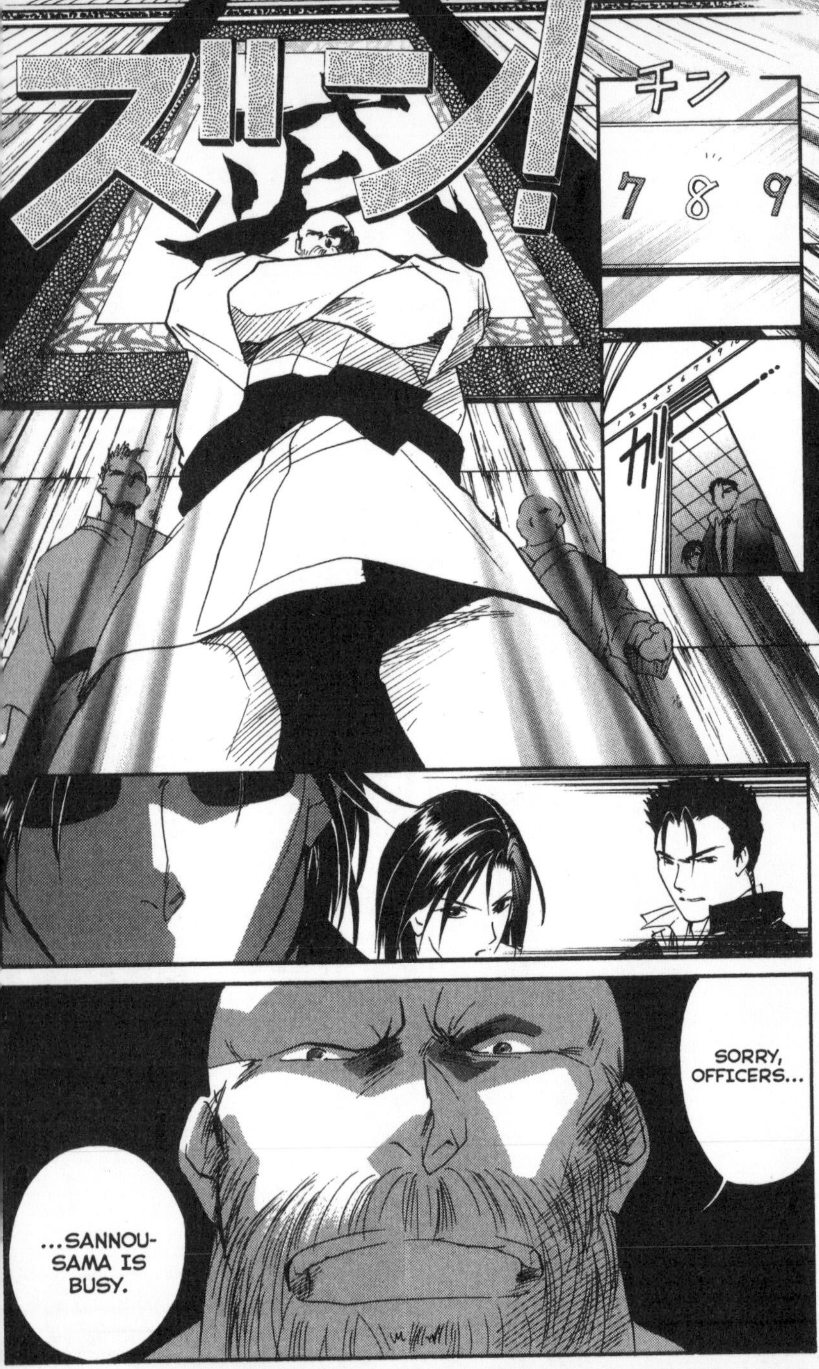
ズゥーン!
チン
7
8
9
カ
SORRY, OFFICERS...
...SANNOU-SAMA IS BUSY.

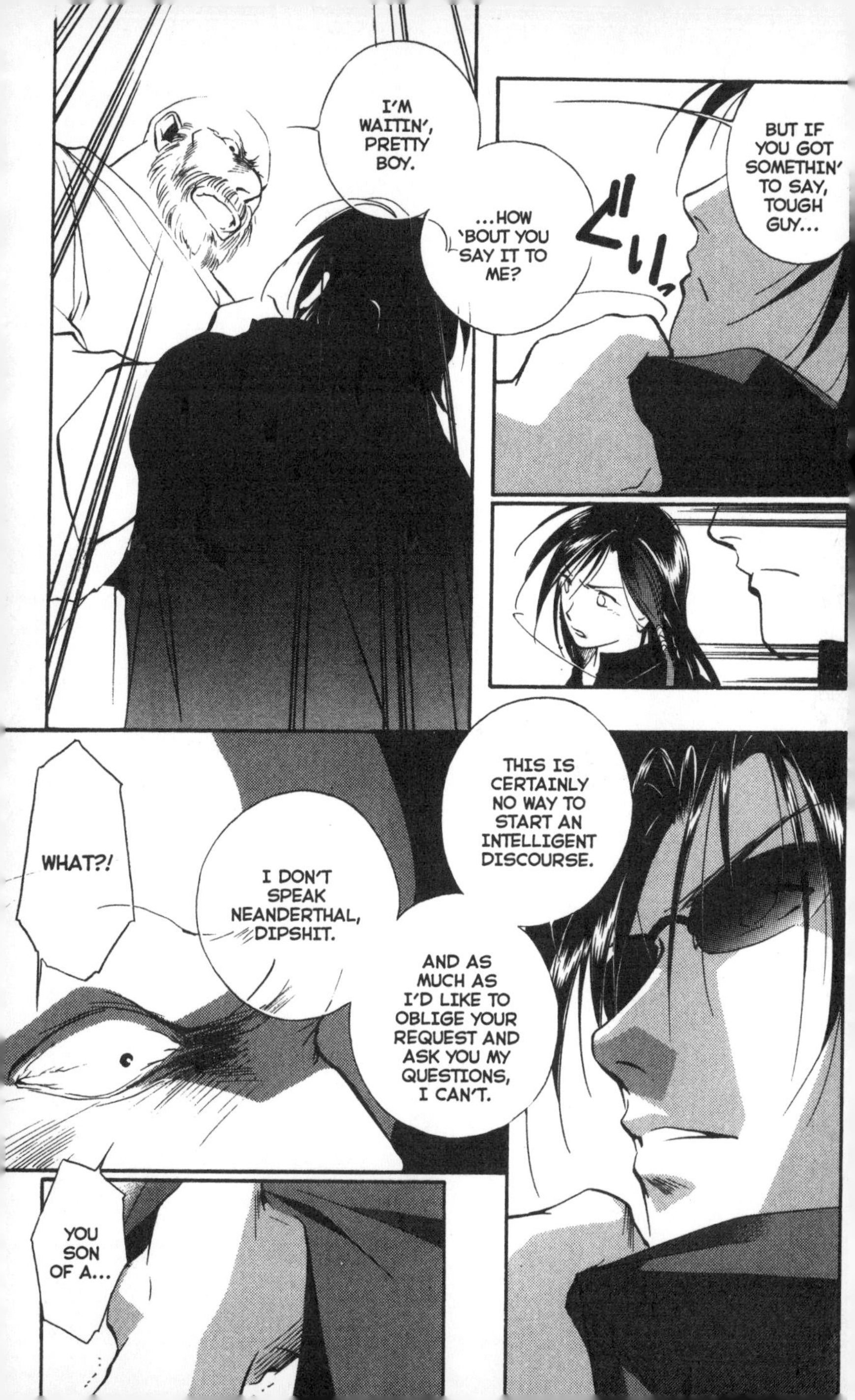
BUT IF YOU GOT SOMETHIN' TO SAY, TOUGH GUY...
...HOW 'BOUT YOU SAY IT TO ME?
ぐい
I'M WAITIN', PRETTY BOY.
THIS IS CERTAINLY NO WAY TO START AN INTELLIGENT DISCOURSE.
I DON'T SPEAK NEANDERTHAL, DIPSHIT.
WHAT?!
AND AS MUCH AS I'D LIKE TO OBLIGE YOUR REQUEST AND ASK YOU MY QUESTIONS, I CAN'T.
YOU SON OF A...

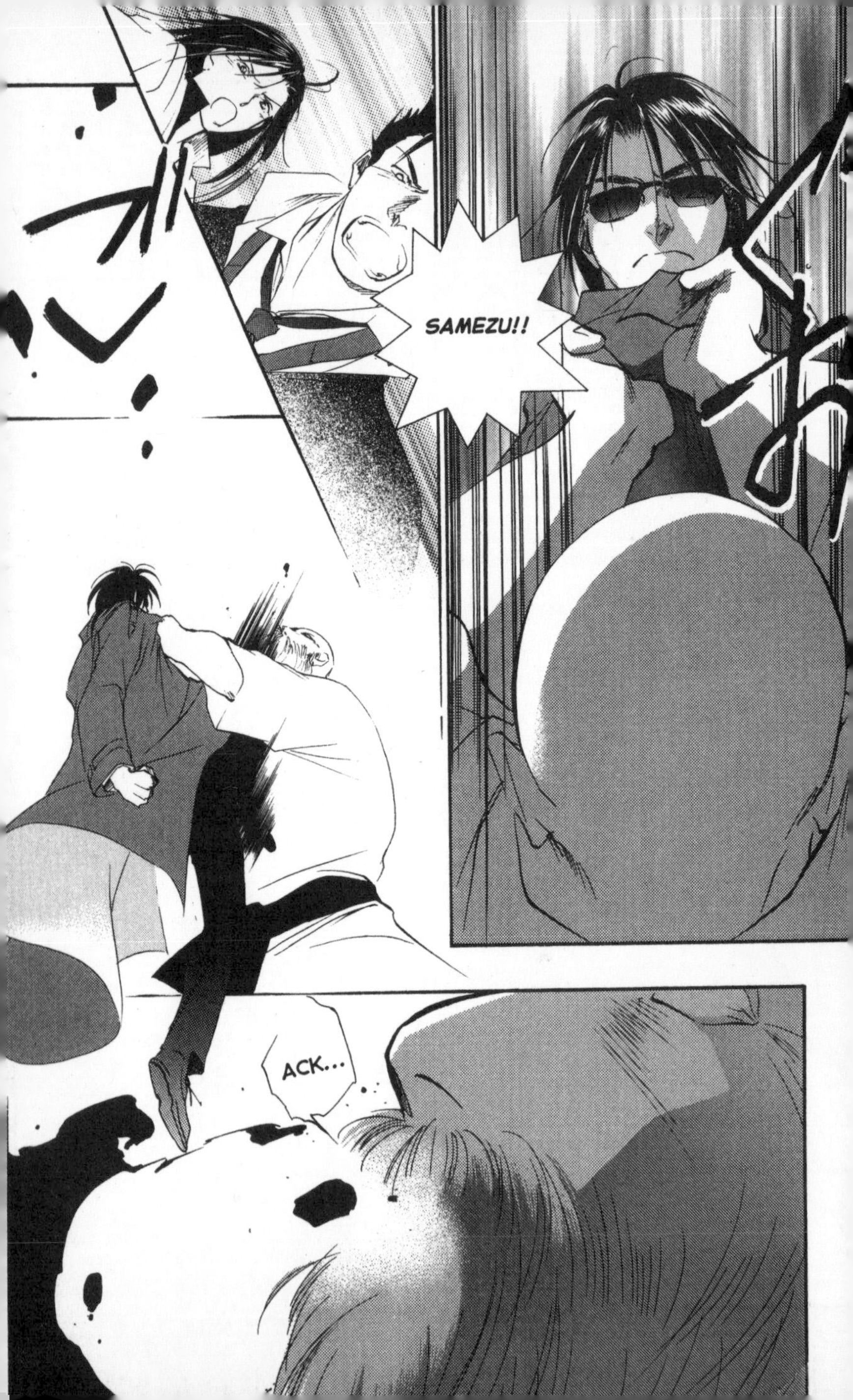
SAMEZU!!
ACK...

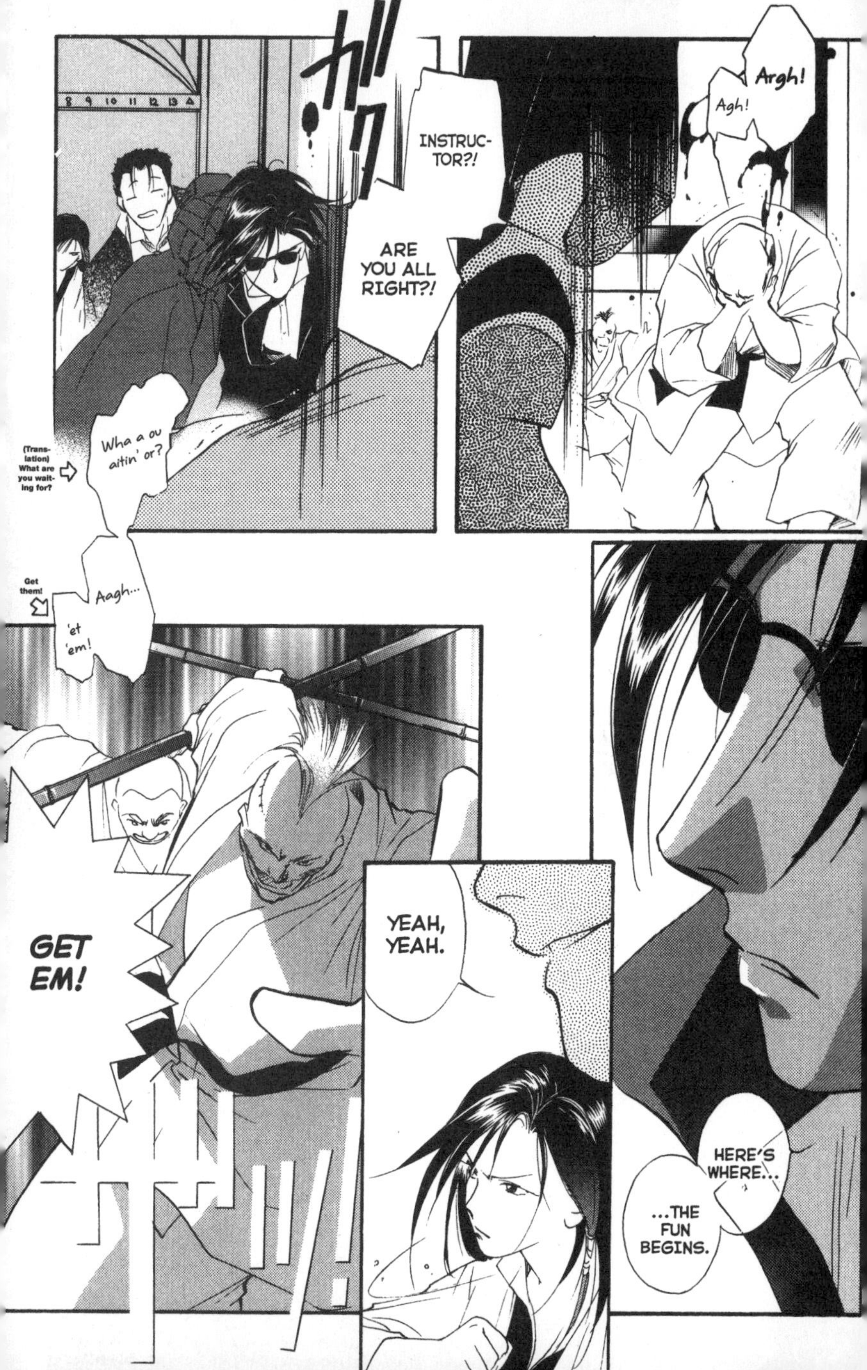
Argh!
Agh!
INSTRUCTOR?!
ARE YOU ALL RIGHT?!
Wha a ou aitin' or?
(Translation) What are you waiting for?
HERE'S WHERE...
...THE FUN BEGINS.
Aagh...
'et 'em!
Get them!
GET EM!
YEAH, YEAH.

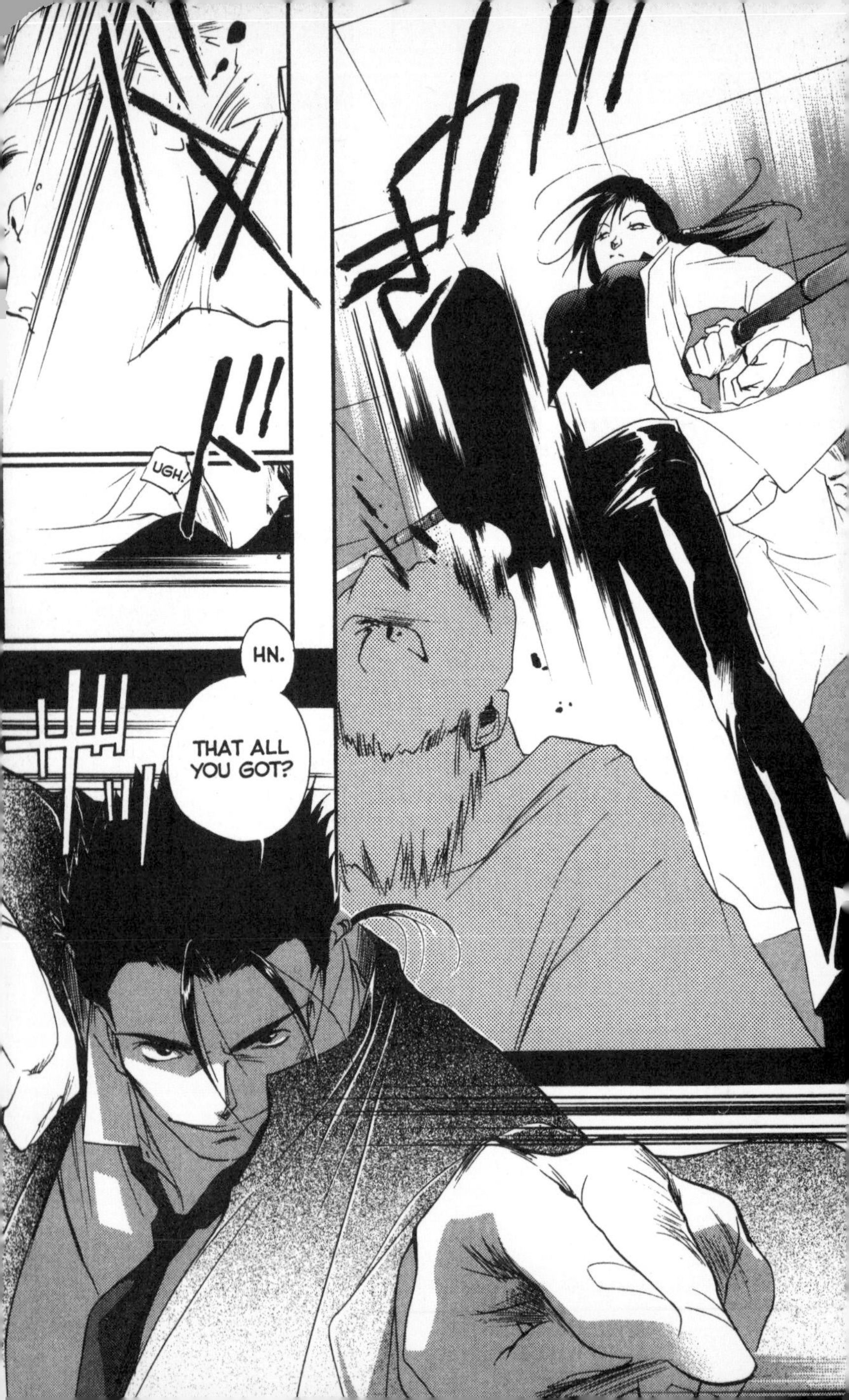
UGH!
HN.
THAT ALL YOU GOT?

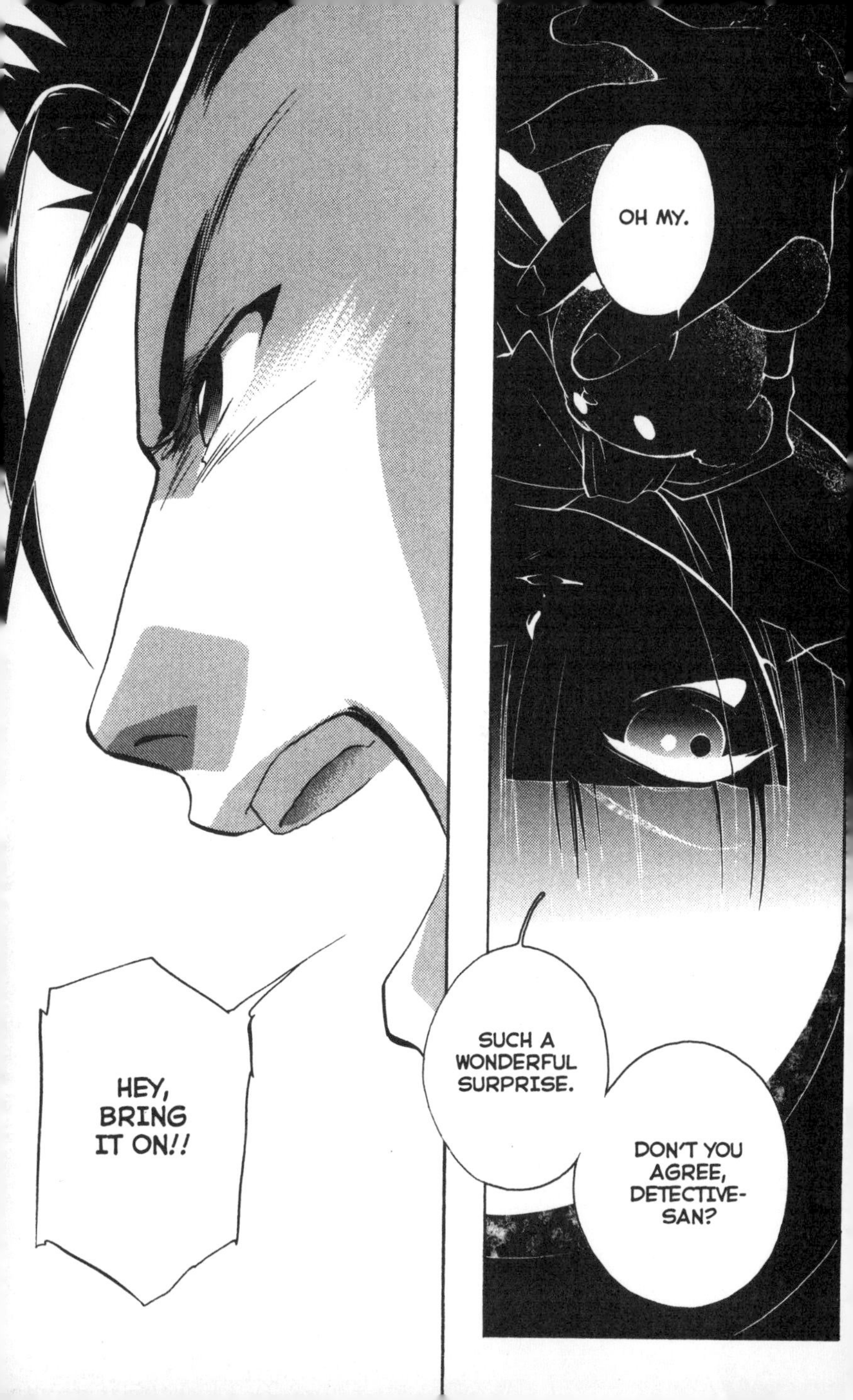
OH MY.
SUCH A WONDERFUL SURPRISE.
DON'T YOU AGREE, DETECTIVE-SAN?
HEY, BRING IT ON!!

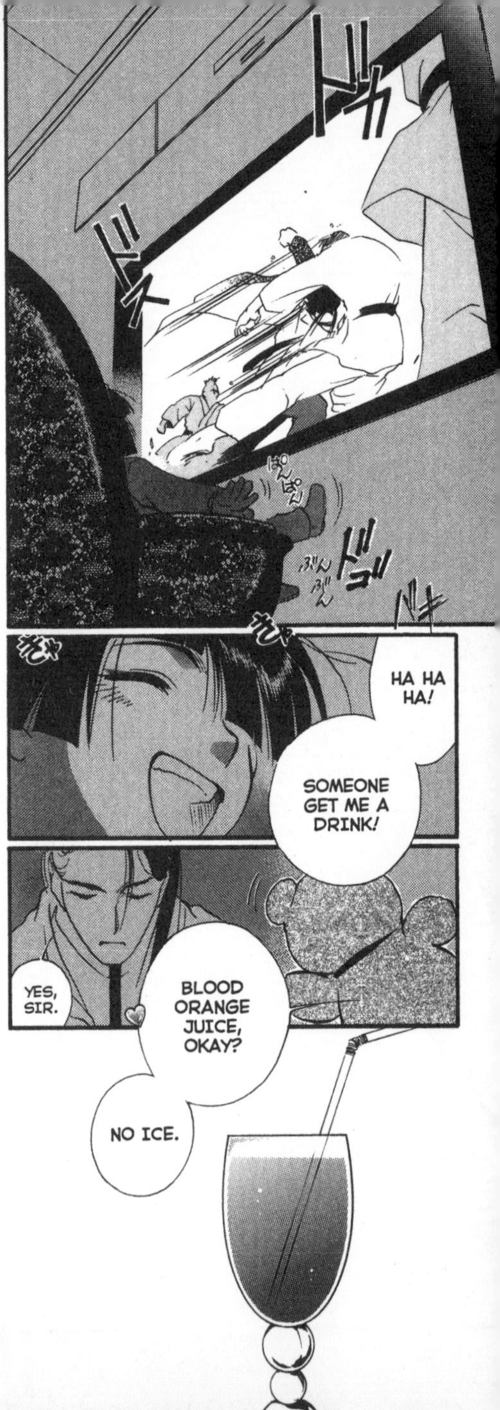
ドカ
ドス
ぱんぱん
ぶんぶん
ドゴ
バキ
HA HA HA!
SOMEONE GET ME A DRINK!
YES, SIR.
BLOOD ORANGE JUICE, OKAY?
NO ICE.

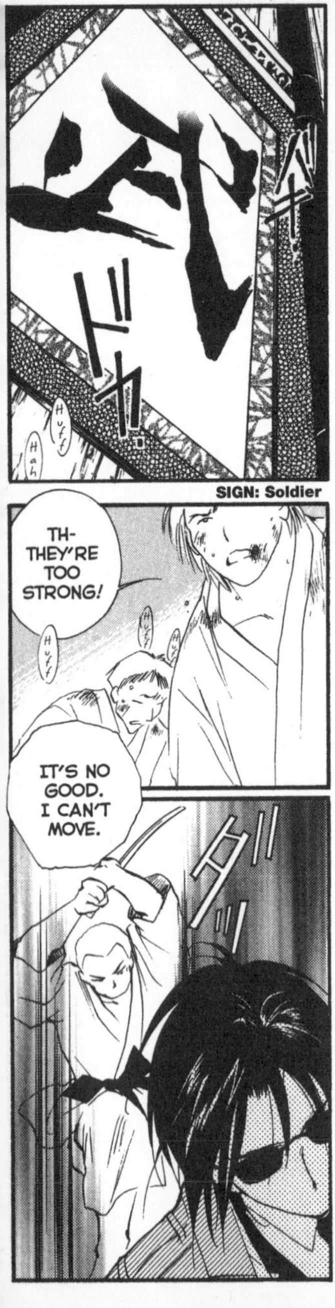
バキ
ドカ
Huff
Hah
SIGN: Soldier
TH-THEY'RE TOO STRONG!
Huff
Huff
IT'S NO GOOD. I CAN'T MOVE.
ダッ

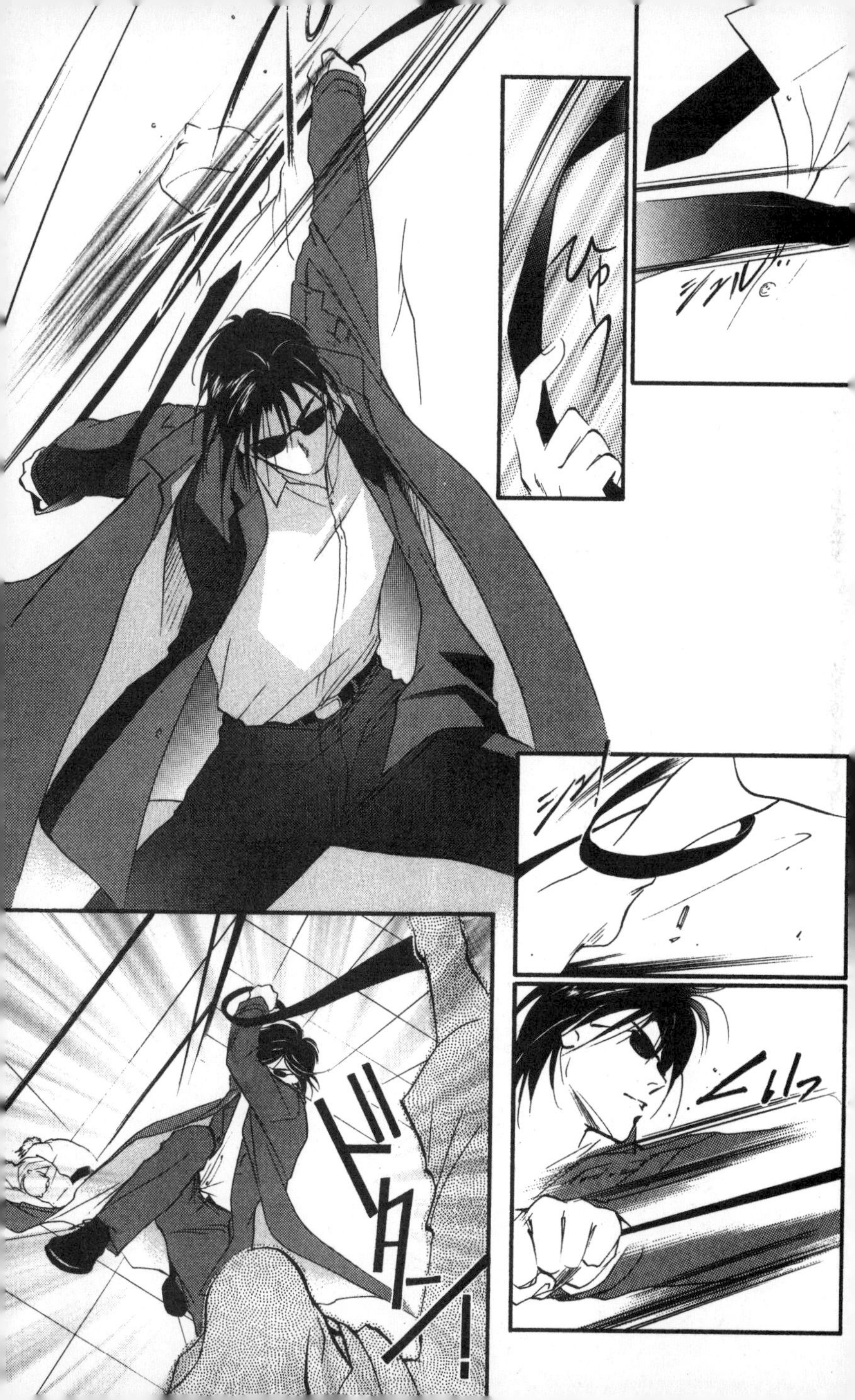
シュルッ
ひゅっ
シュッ
ぐいっ
ドカー!

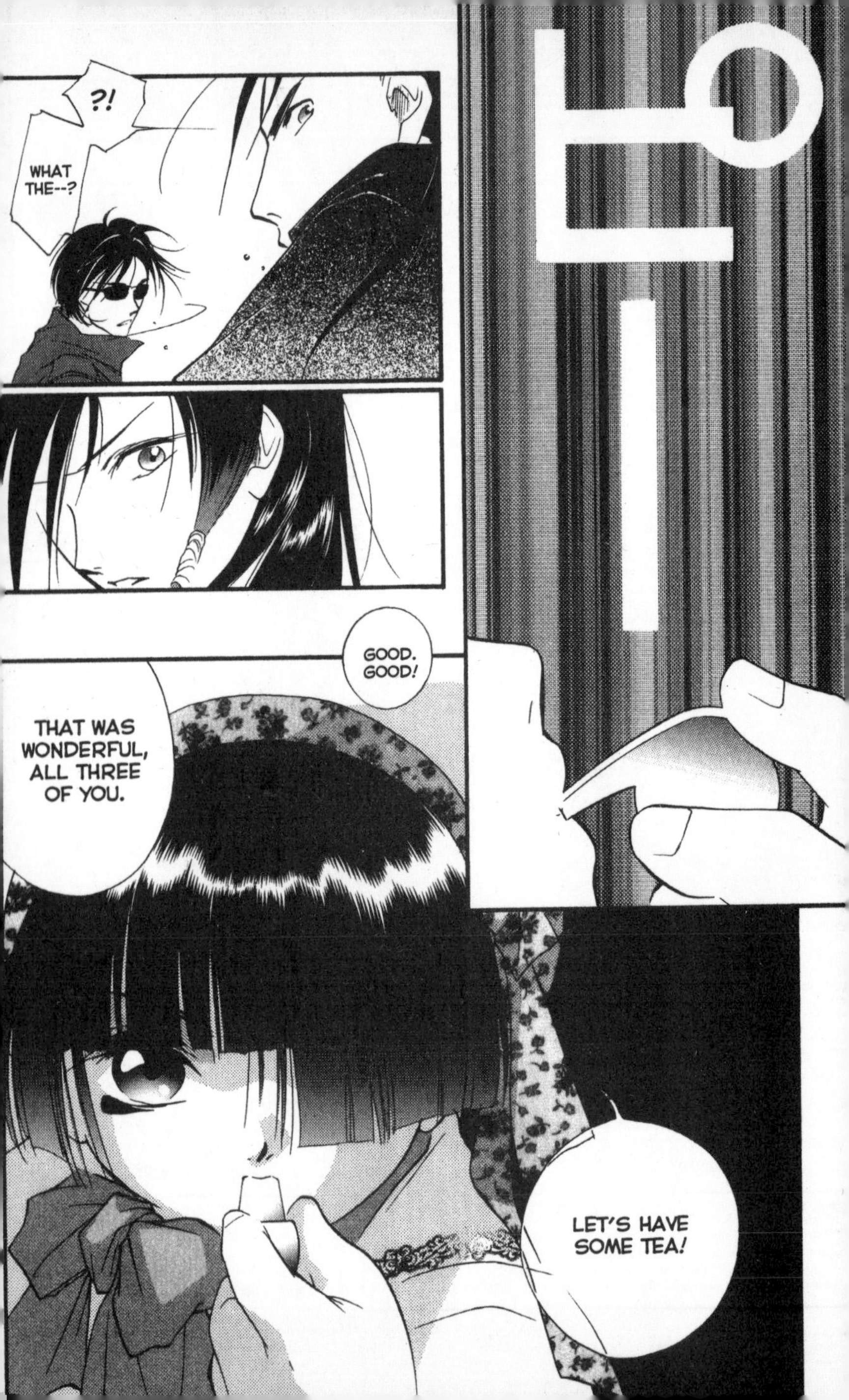
?!
WHAT THE--?
GOOD. GOOD!
THAT WAS WONDERFUL, ALL THREE OF YOU.
LET'S HAVE SOME TEA!

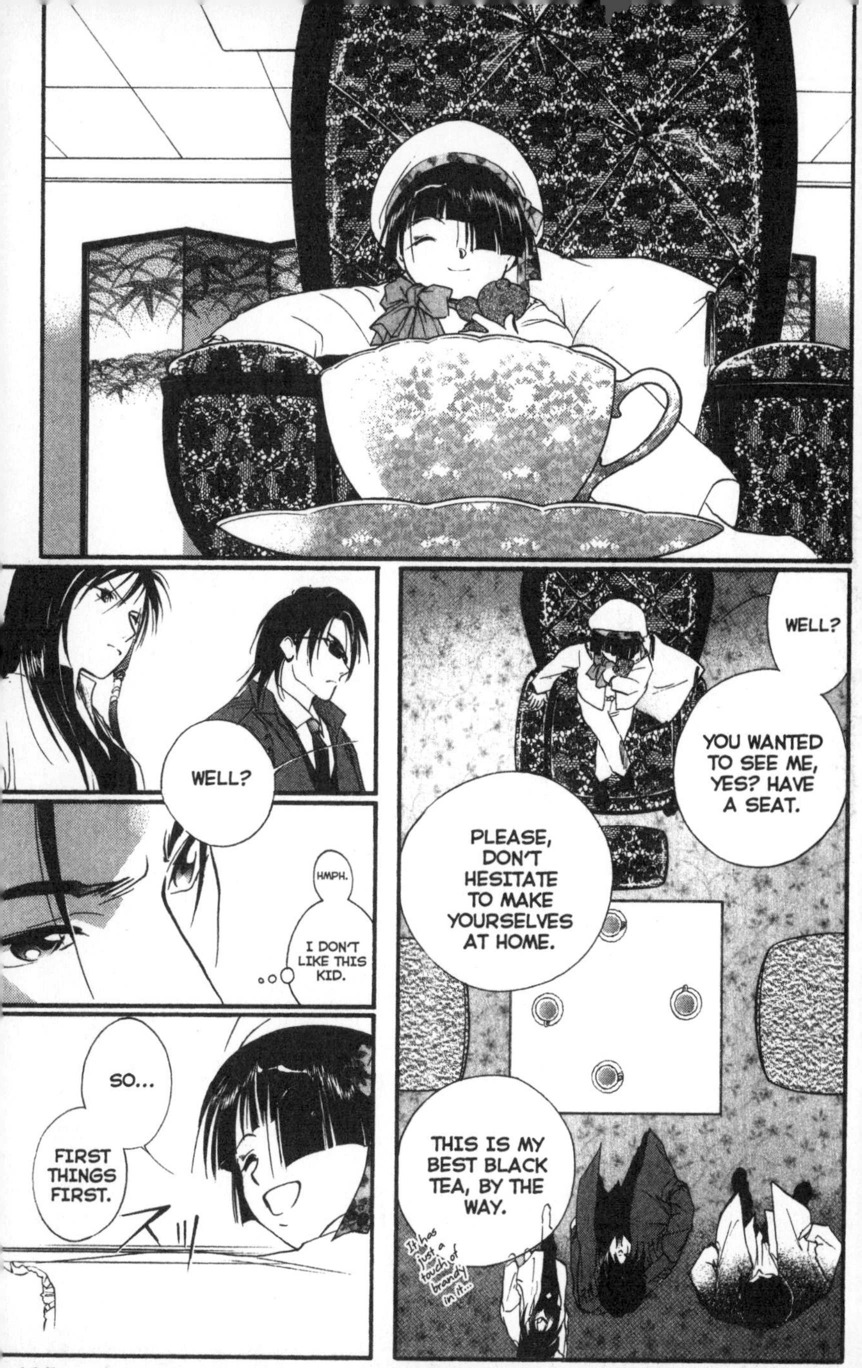
WELL?
YOU WANTED TO SEE ME, YES? HAVE A SEAT.
PLEASE, DON'T HESITATE TO MAKE YOURSELVES AT HOME.
THIS IS MY BEST BLACK TEA, BY THE WAY.
It has just a touch of brandy in it...
WELL?
HMPH.
I DON'T LIKE THIS KID.
SO...
FIRST THINGS FIRST.

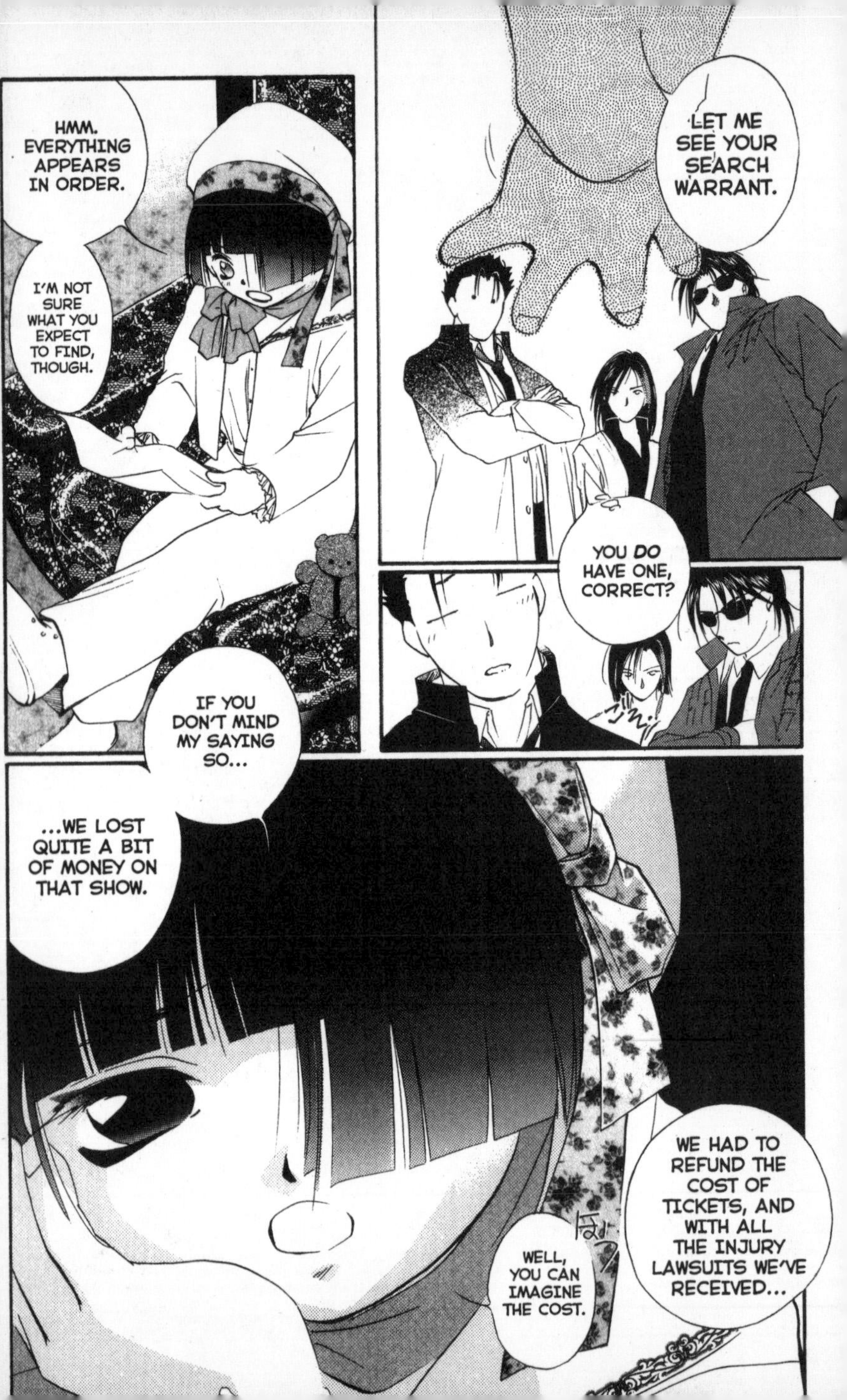
LET ME SEE YOUR SEARCH WARRANT.
YOU *DO* HAVE ONE, CORRECT?
HMM. EVERYTHING APPEARS IN ORDER.
I'M NOT SURE WHAT YOU EXPECT TO FIND, THOUGH.
IF YOU DON'T MIND MY SAYING SO...
...WE LOST QUITE A BIT OF MONEY ON THAT SHOW.
WE HAD TO REFUND THE COST OF TICKETS, AND WITH ALL THE INJURY LAWSUITS WE'VE RECEIVED...
WELL, YOU CAN IMAGINE THE COST.

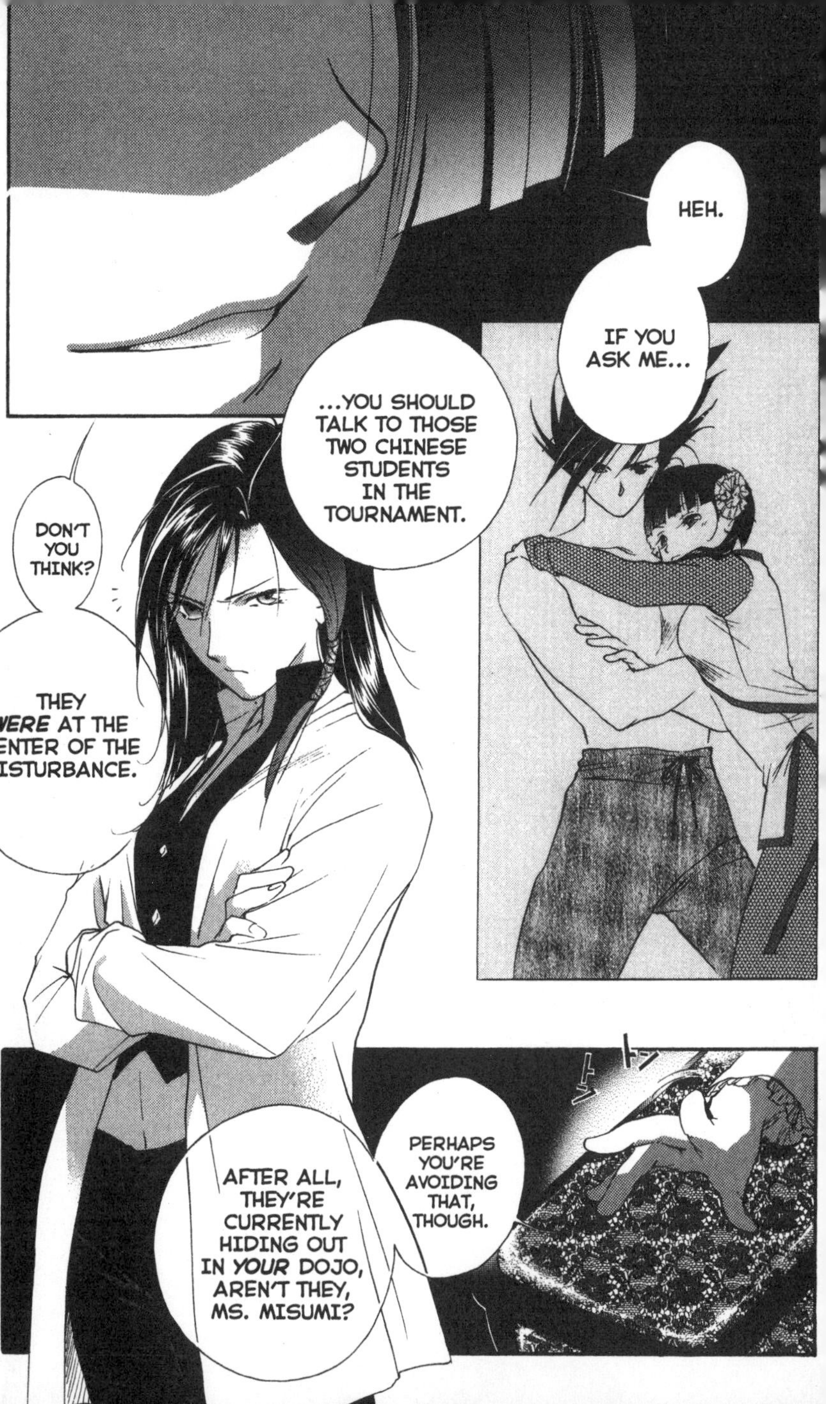
HEH.
IF YOU ASK ME...
...YOU SHOULD TALK TO THOSE TWO CHINESE STUDENTS IN THE TOURNAMENT.
DON'T YOU THINK?
THEY *WERE* AT THE CENTER OF THE DISTURBANCE.
PERHAPS YOU'RE AVOIDING THAT, THOUGH.
AFTER ALL, THEY'RE CURRENTLY HIDING OUT IN *YOUR* DOJO, AREN'T THEY, MS. MISUMI?

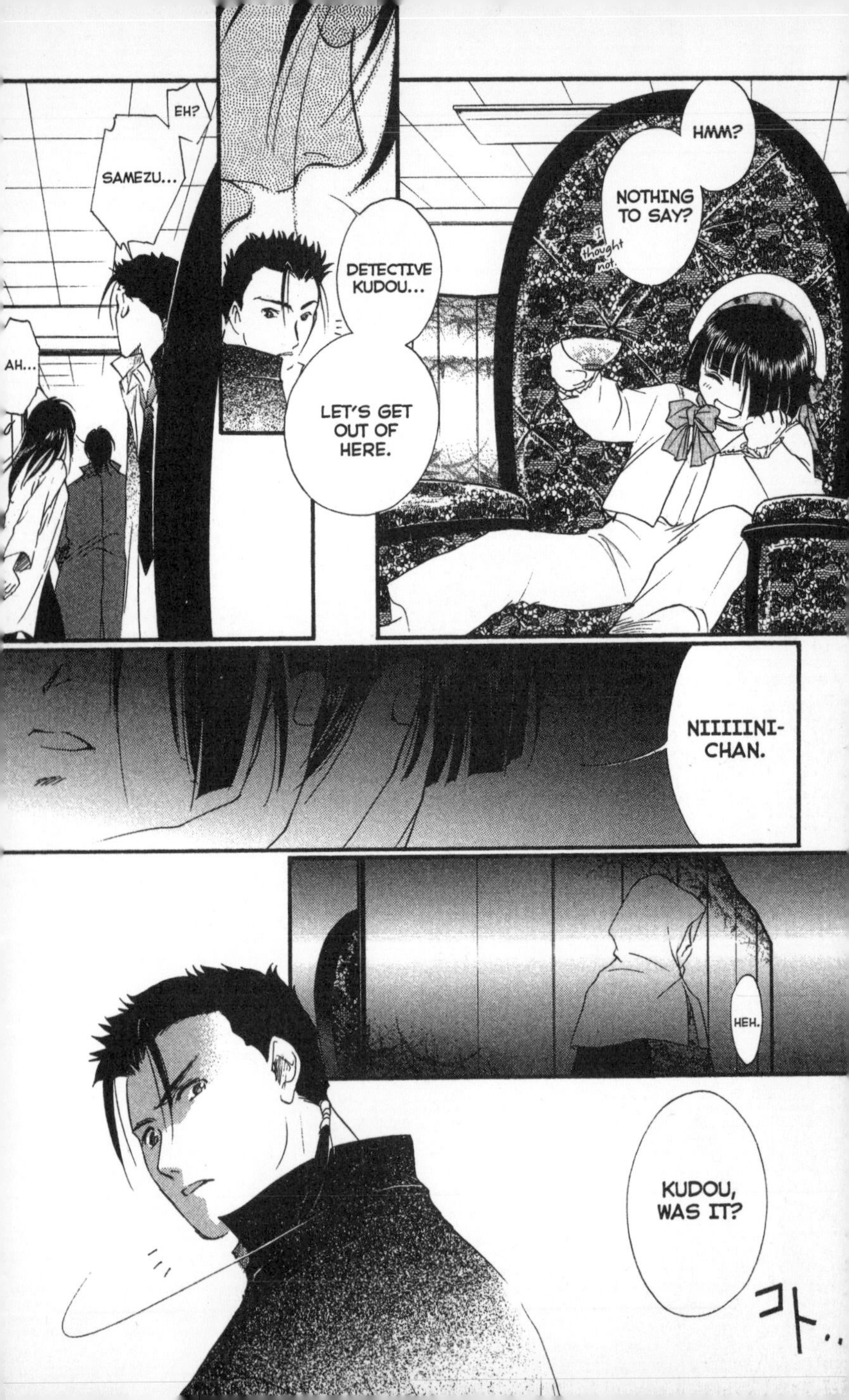
HMM?
NOTHING TO SAY?
I thought not.
DETECTIVE KUDOU...
LET'S GET OUT OF HERE.
EH?
SAMEZU...
AH...
NIIIIINI-CHAN.
HEH.
KUDOU, WAS IT?
コト..

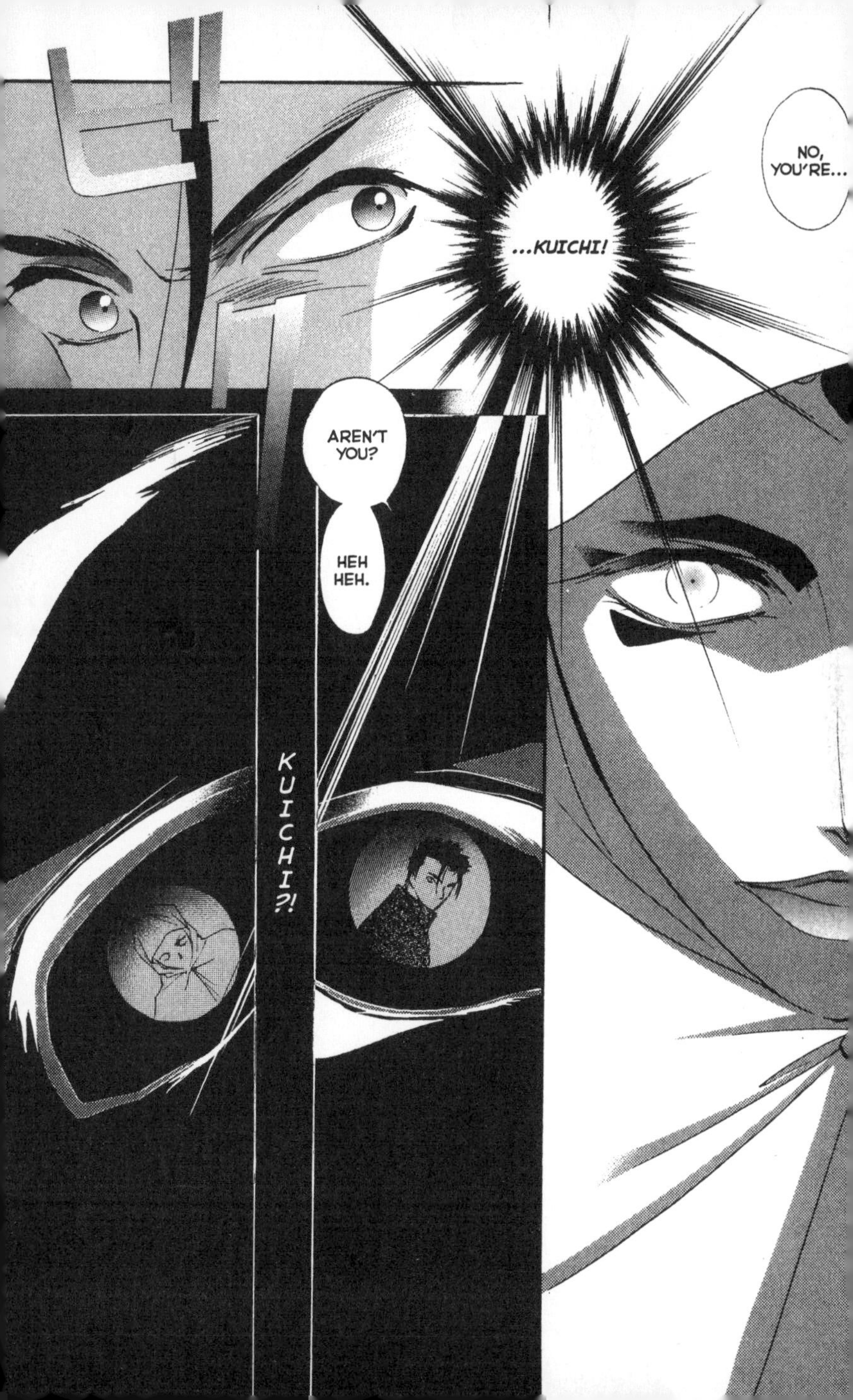
NO, YOU'RE...
...KUICHI!
AREN'T YOU?
HEH HEH.
KUICHI?!

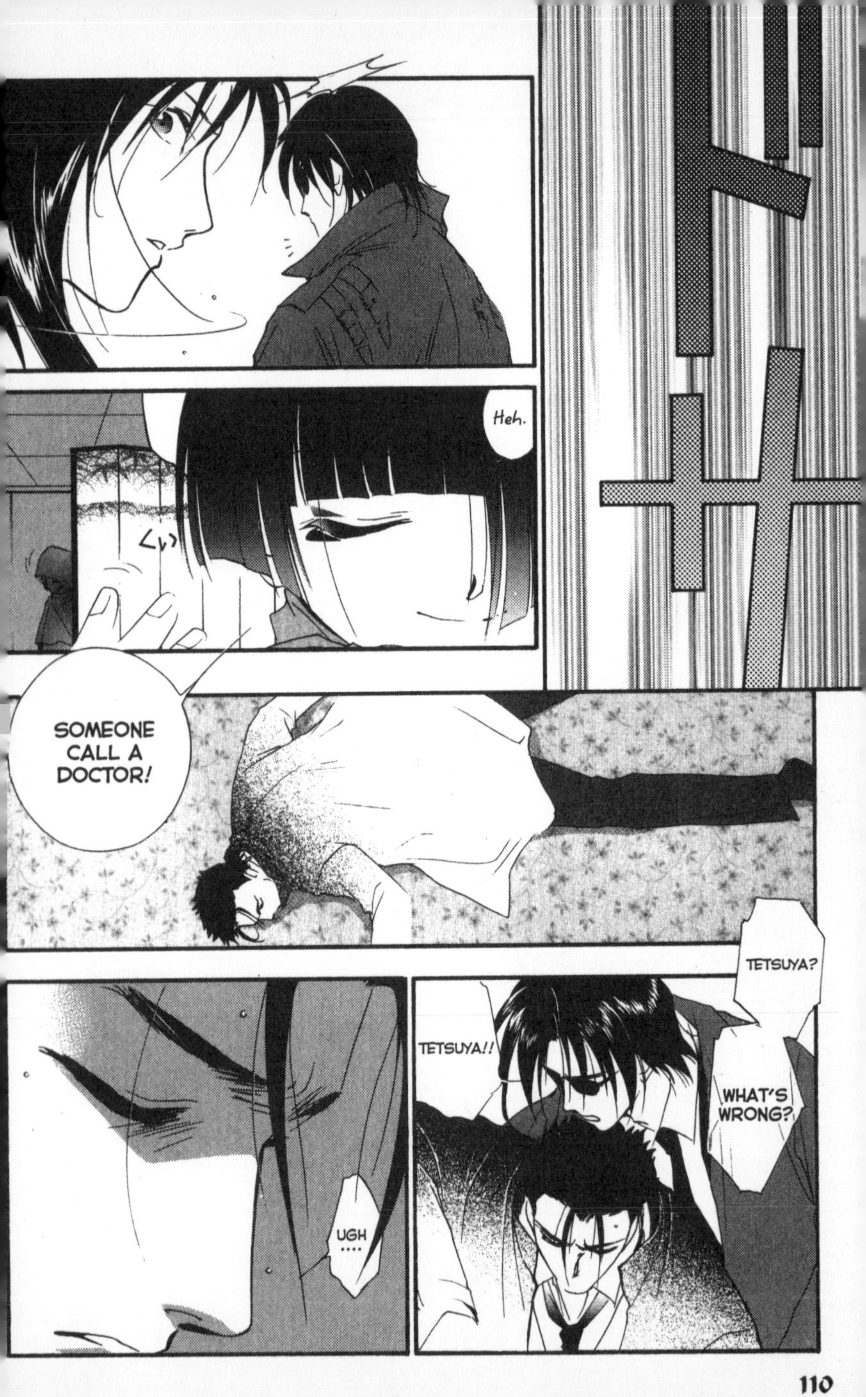
Heh.
SOMEONE CALL A DOCTOR!
TETSUYA?
WHAT'S WRONG?
TETSUYA!!
UGH....

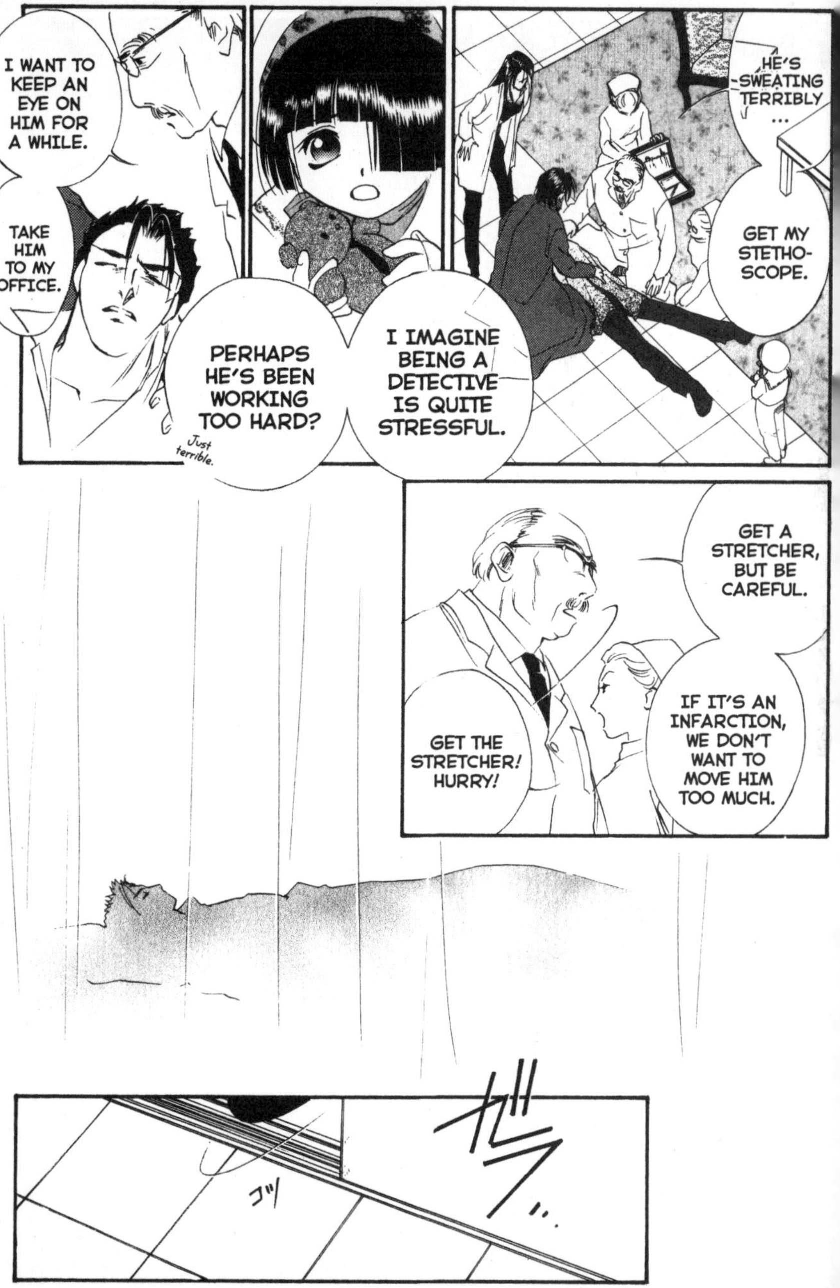
HE'S SWEATING TERRIBLY...
GET MY STETHO-SCOPE.
I IMAGINE BEING A DETECTIVE IS QUITE STRESSFUL.
PERHAPS HE'S BEEN WORKING TOO HARD?
Just terrible.
I WANT TO KEEP AN EYE ON HIM FOR A WHILE.
TAKE HIM TO MY OFFICE.
GET A STRETCHER, BUT BE CAREFUL.
IF IT'S AN INFARCTION, WE DON'T WANT TO MOVE HIM TOO MUCH.
GET THE STRETCHER! HURRY!
ゴツ

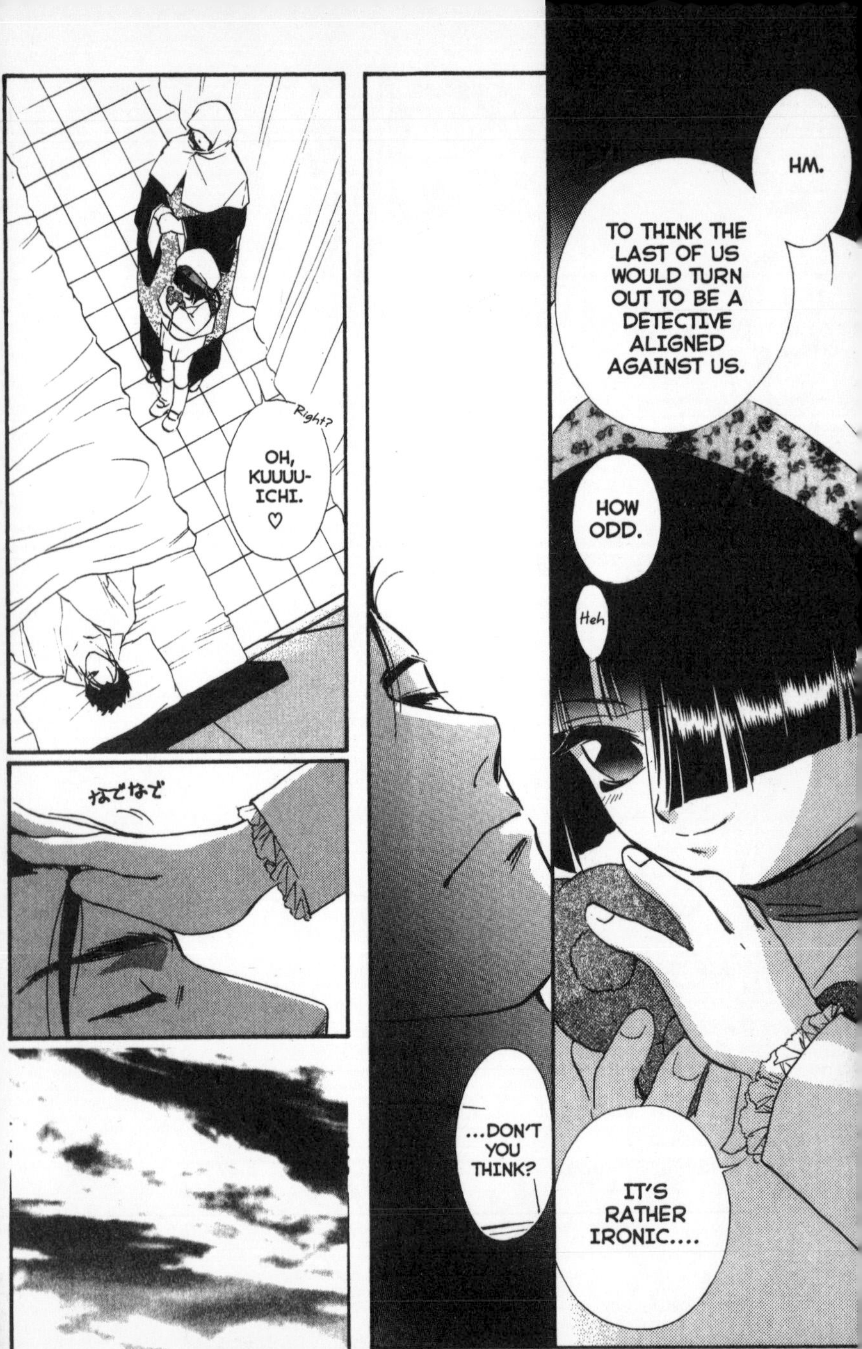
HM.
TO THINK THE LAST OF US WOULD TURN OUT TO BE A DETECTIVE ALIGNED AGAINST US.
HOW ODD.
Heh
IT'S RATHER IRONIC....
...DON'T YOU THINK?
OH, KUUUU-ICHI. ♡
Right?
なでなで

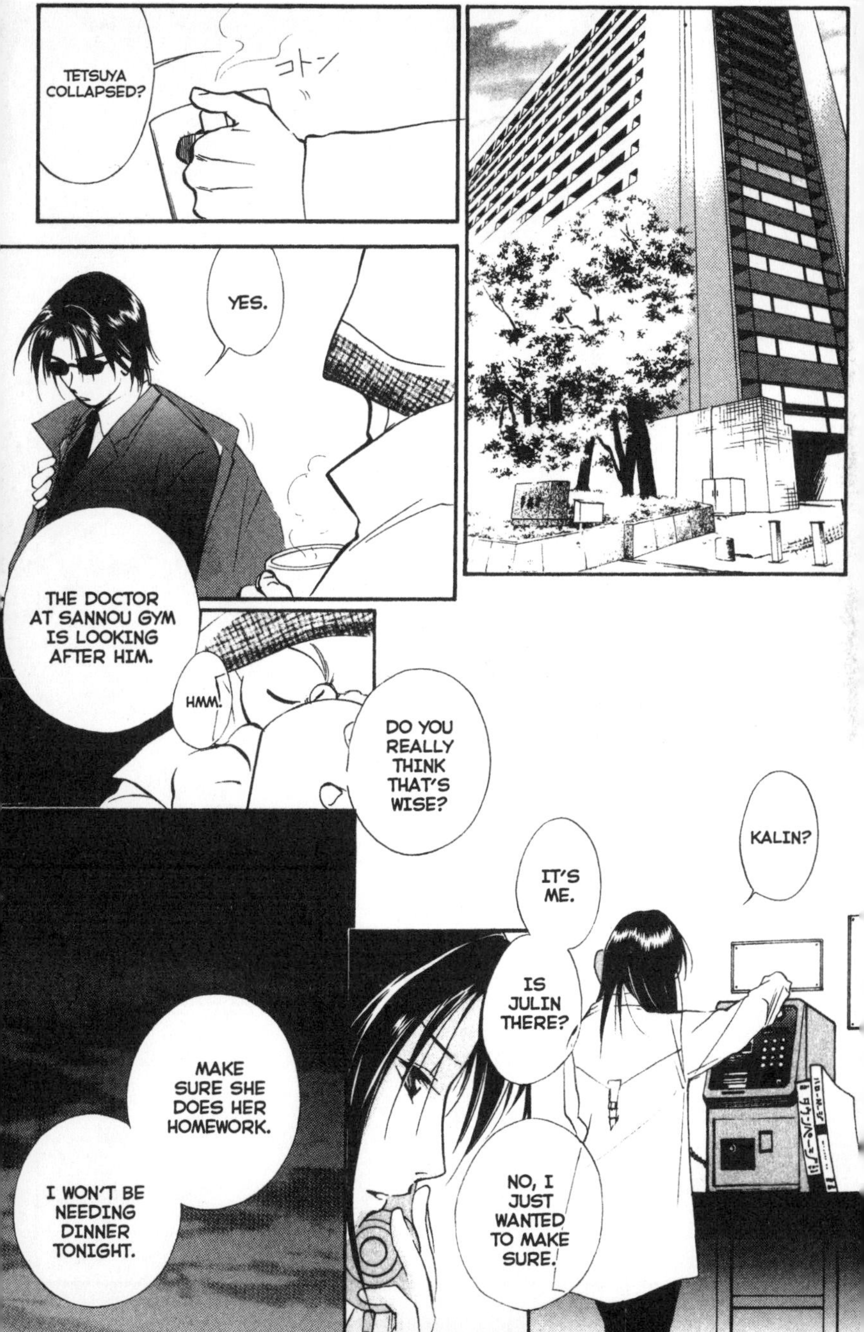
TETSUYA COLLAPSED?
コトン
YES.
THE DOCTOR AT SANNOU GYM IS LOOKING AFTER HIM.
HMM.
DO YOU REALLY THINK THAT'S WISE?
KALIN?
IT'S ME.
IS JULIN THERE?
NO, I JUST WANTED TO MAKE SURE.
MAKE SURE SHE DOES HER HOMEWORK.
I WON'T BE NEEDING DINNER TONIGHT.

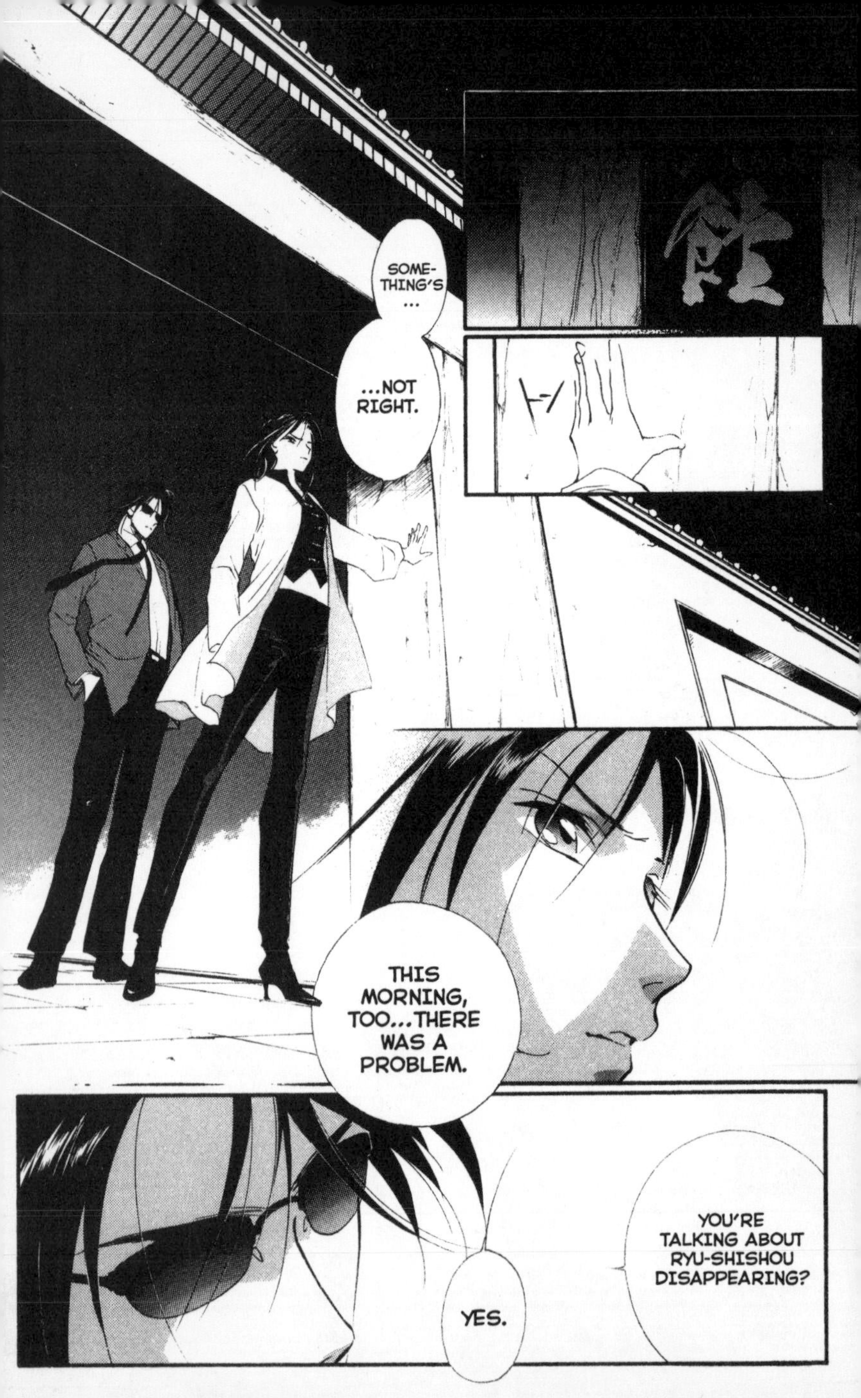
SOME-THING'S...
...NOT RIGHT.
THIS MORNING, TOO...THERE WAS A PROBLEM.
YOU'RE TALKING ABOUT RYU-SHISHOU DISAPPEARING?
YES.

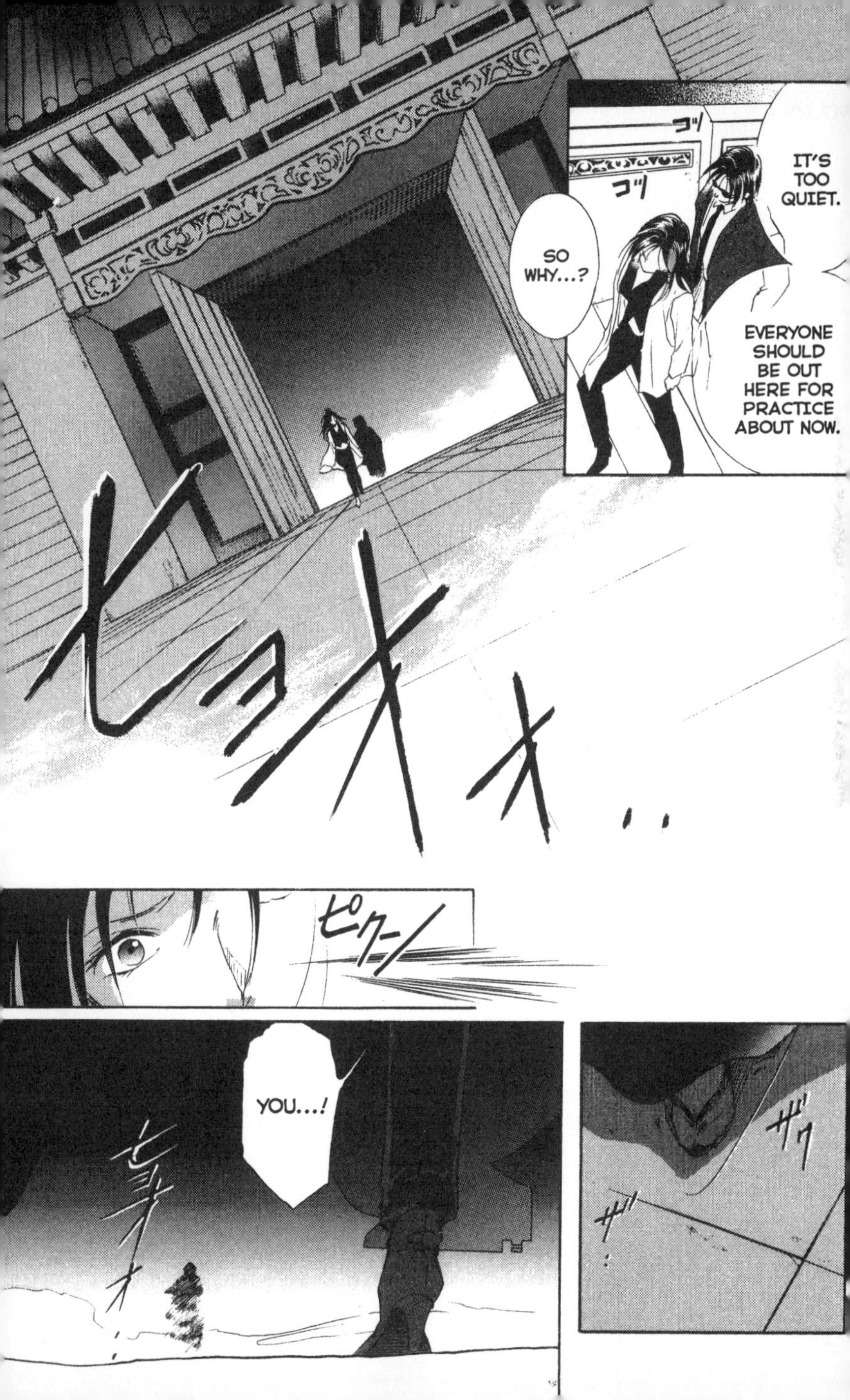
コツ
コツ
IT'S TOO QUIET.
EVERYONE SHOULD BE OUT HERE FOR PRACTICE ABOUT NOW.
SO WHY...?
YOU...!

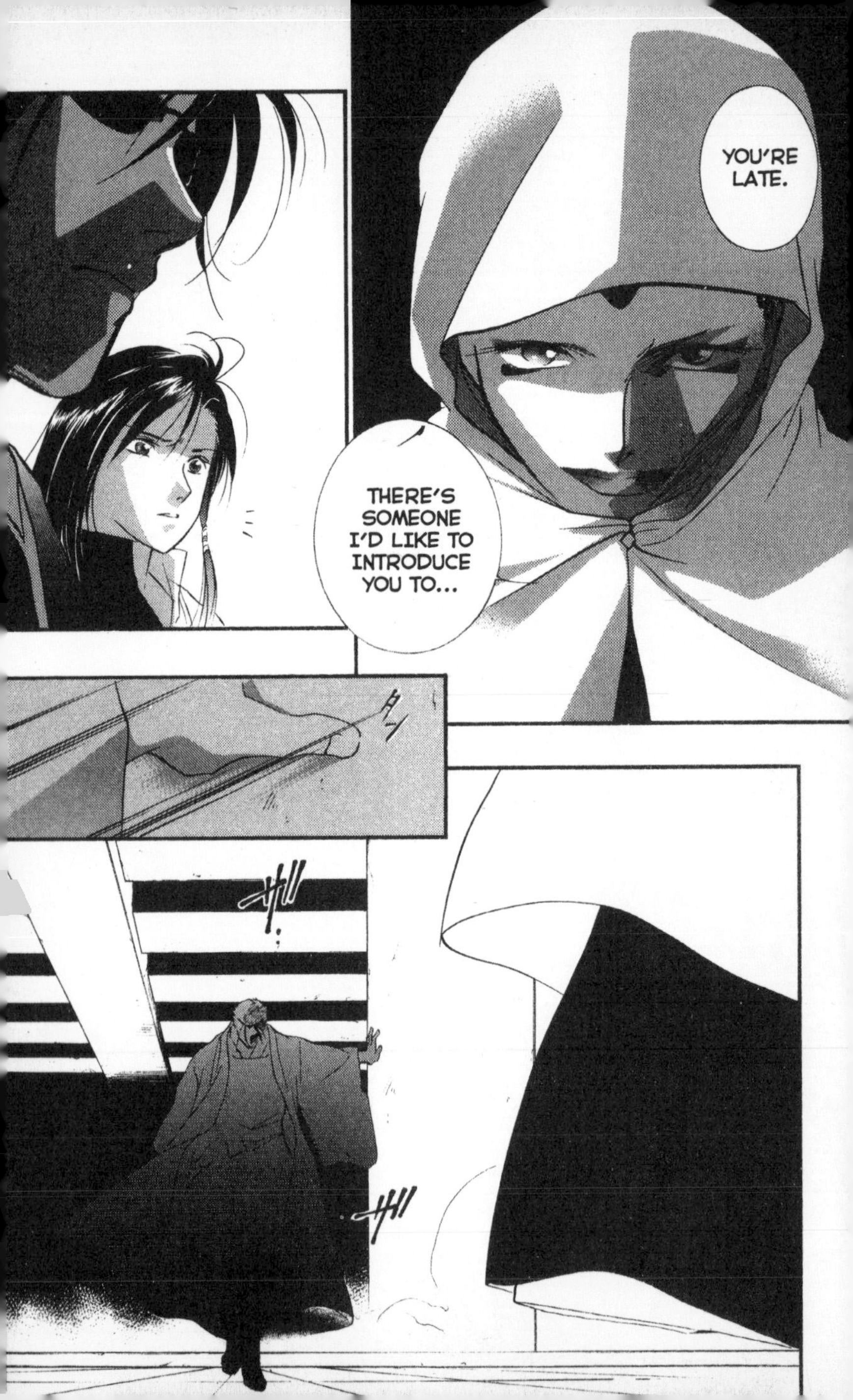
YOU'RE LATE.
THERE'S SOMEONE I'D LIKE TO INTRODUCE YOU TO...

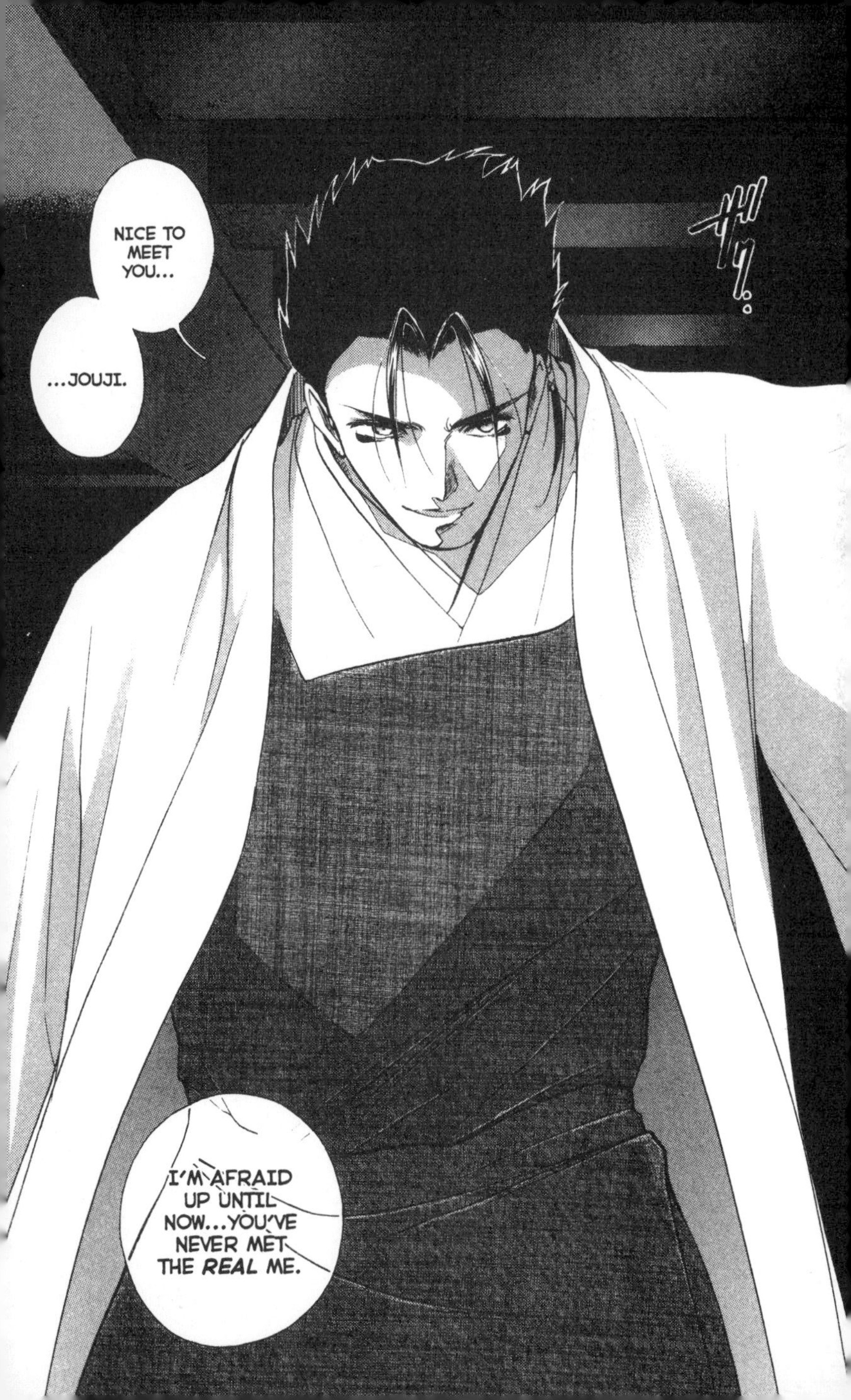
NICE TO MEET YOU...
...JOUJI.
I'M AFRAID UP UNTIL NOW...YOU'VE NEVER MET THE *REAL* ME.

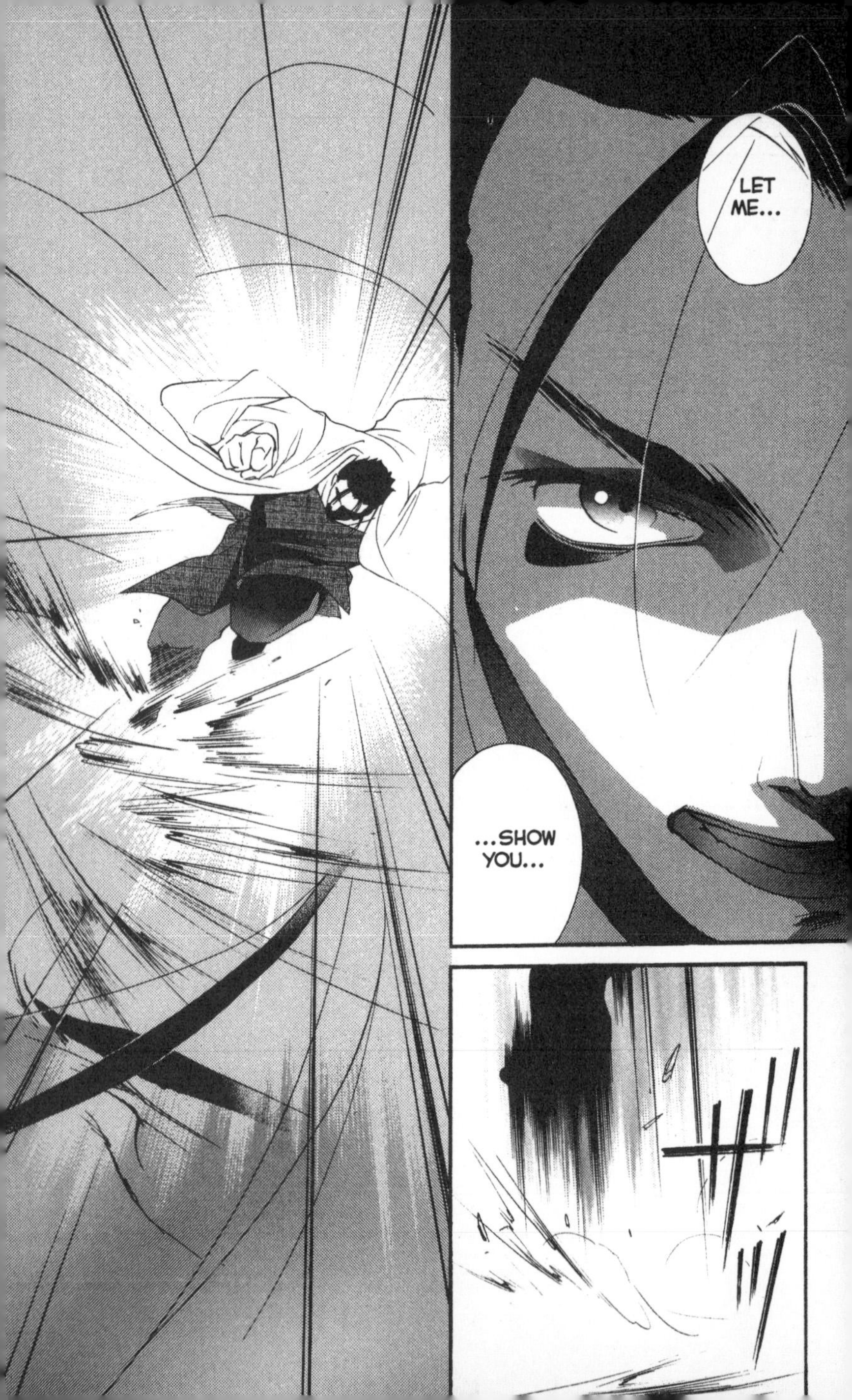
LET ME...
...SHOW YOU...

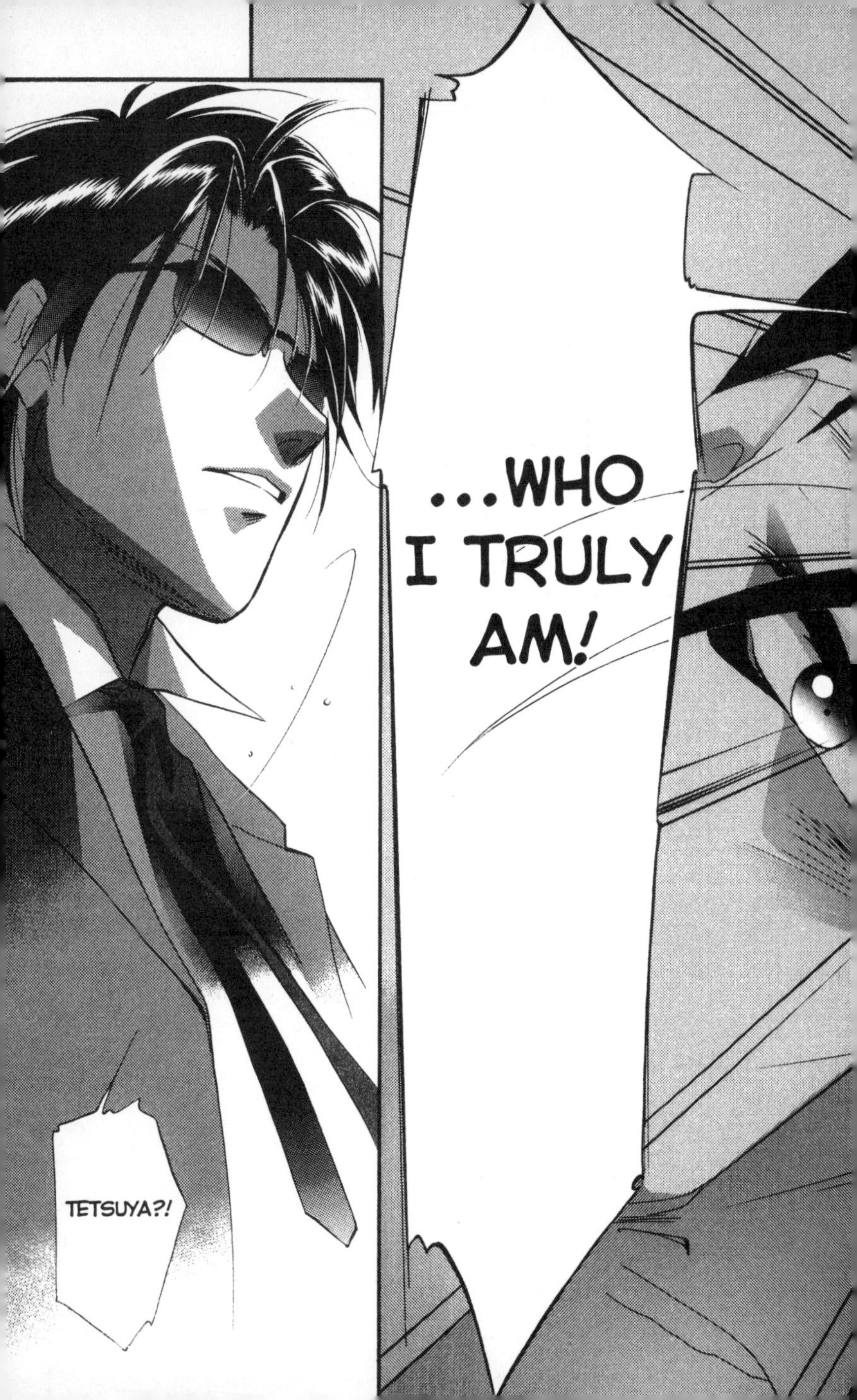
...WHO I TRULY AM!
TETSUYA?!

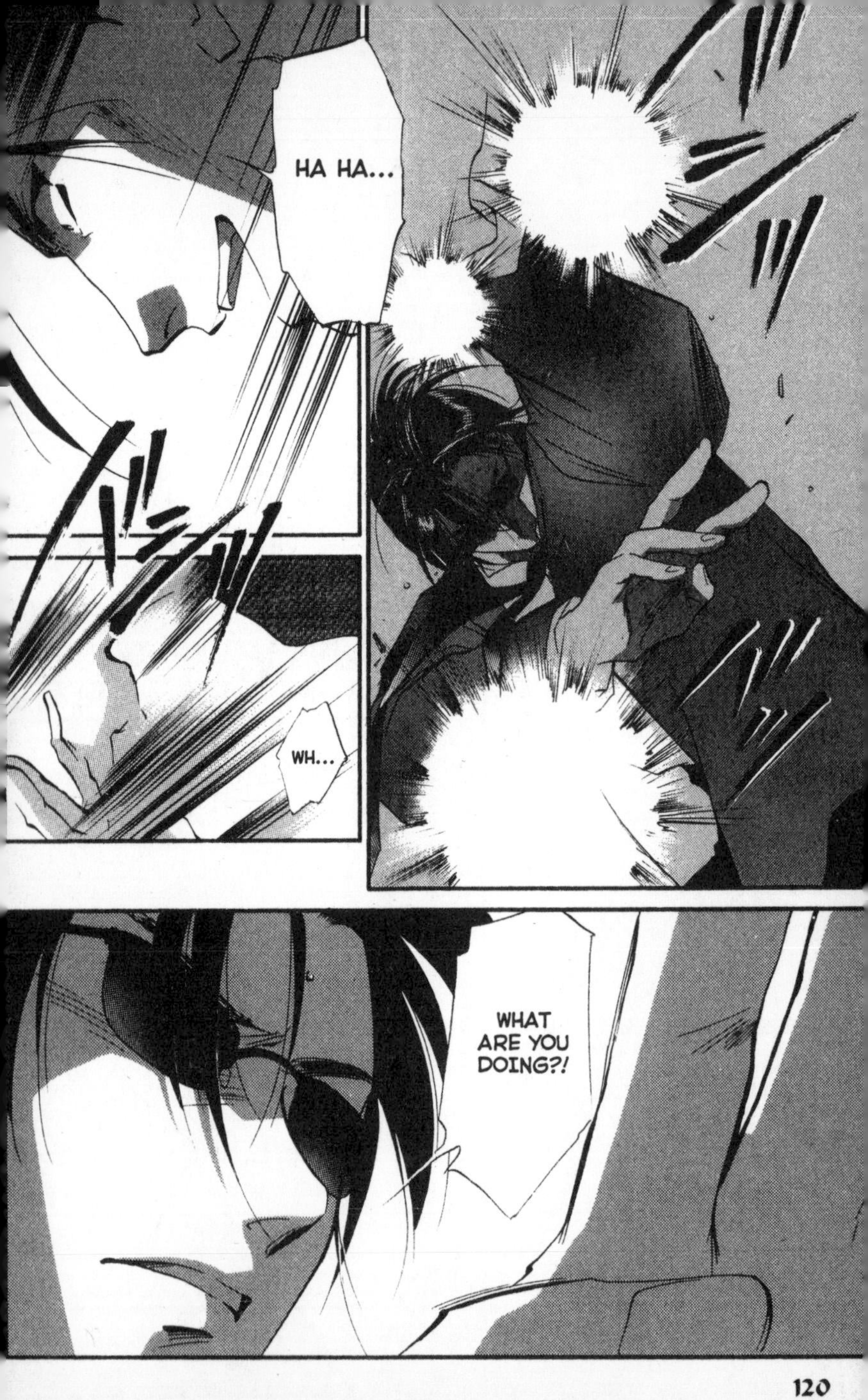
HA HA...
WH...
WHAT ARE YOU DOING?!

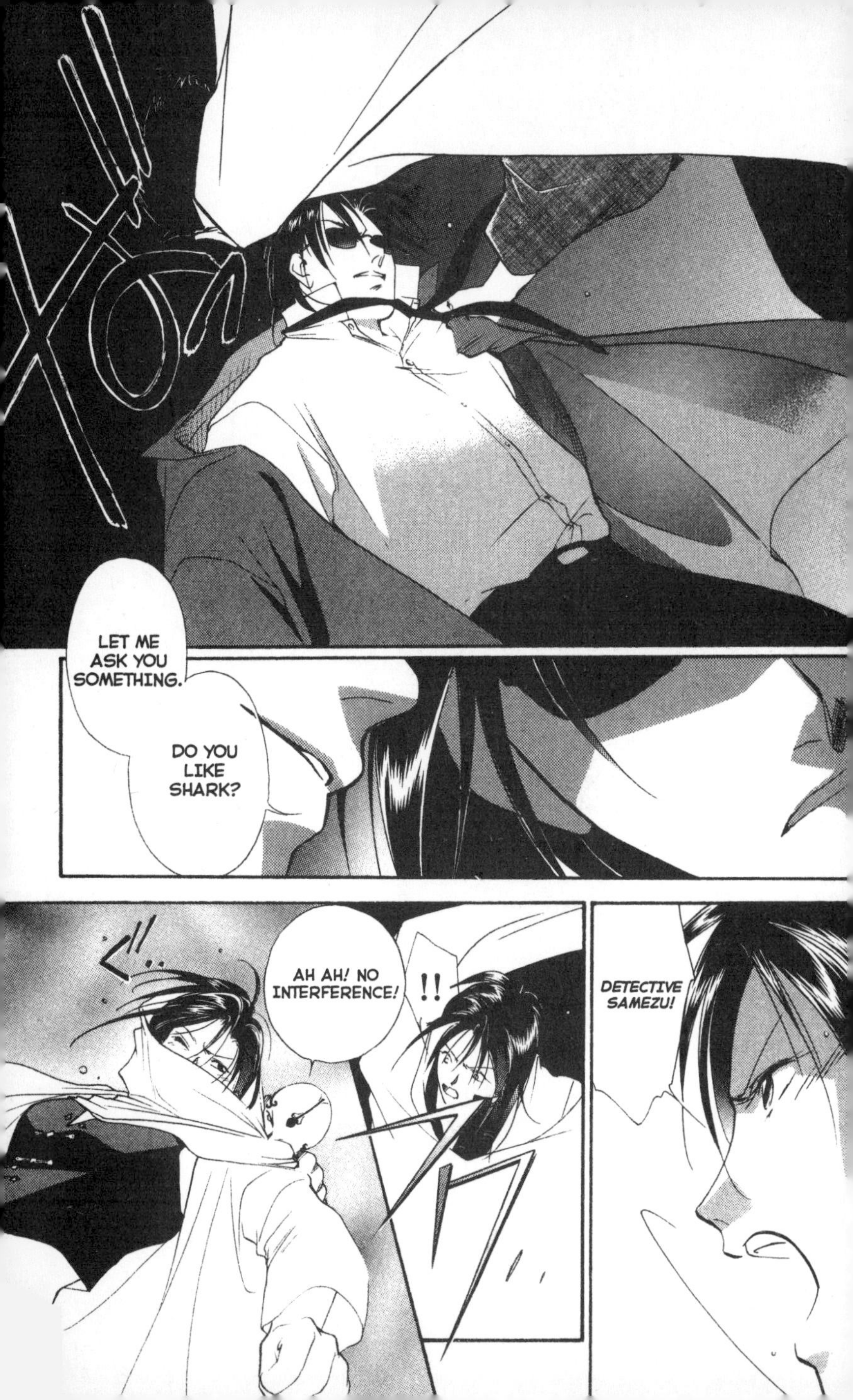
LET ME ASK YOU SOMETHING.
DO YOU LIKE SHARK?
DETECTIVE SAMEZU!
!!
AH AH! NO INTERFERENCE!

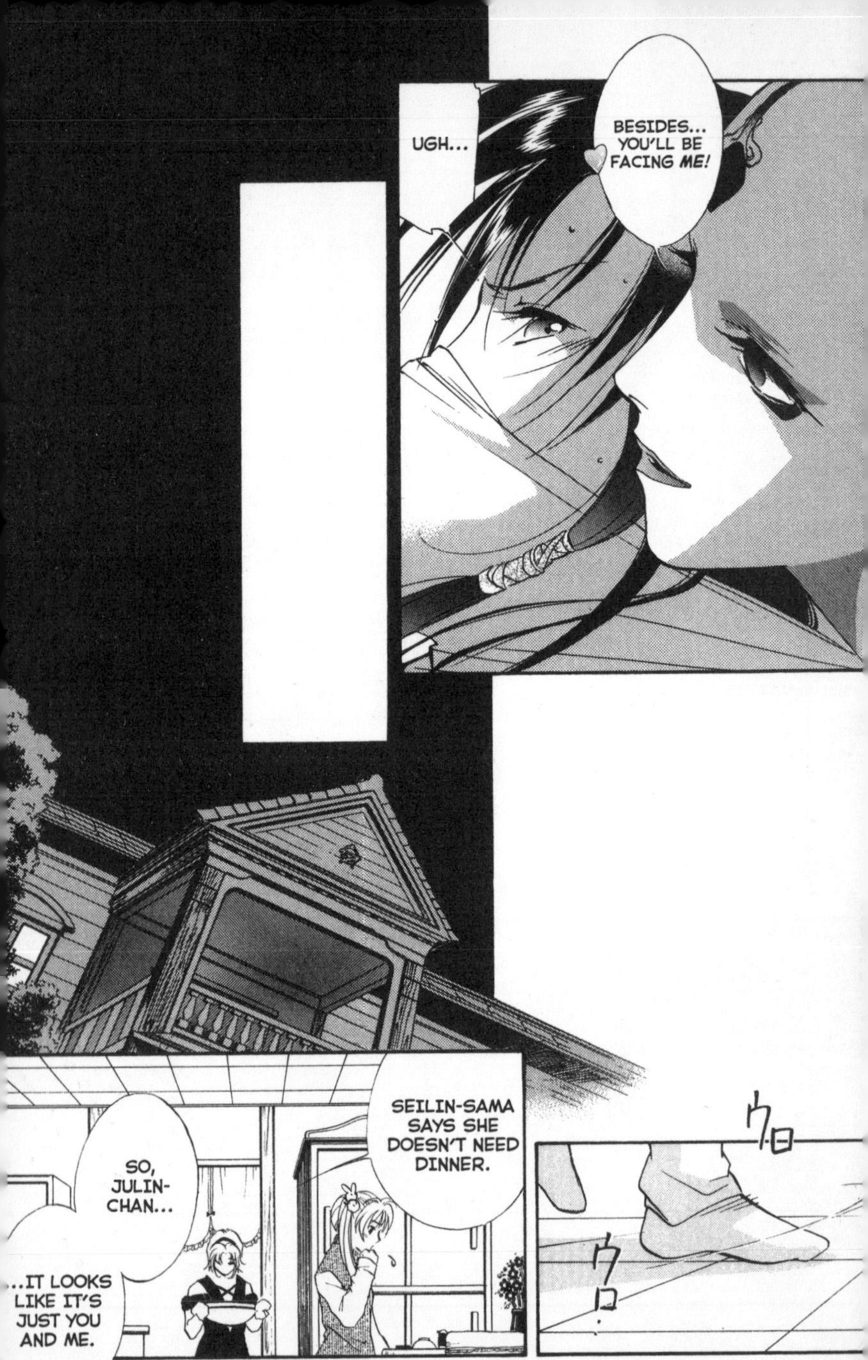
BESIDES... YOU'LL BE FACING *ME!*
UGH...
ウロ
ウロ
SEILIN-SAMA SAYS SHE DOESN'T NEED DINNER.
SO, JULIN-CHAN...
...IT LOOKS LIKE IT'S JUST YOU AND ME.

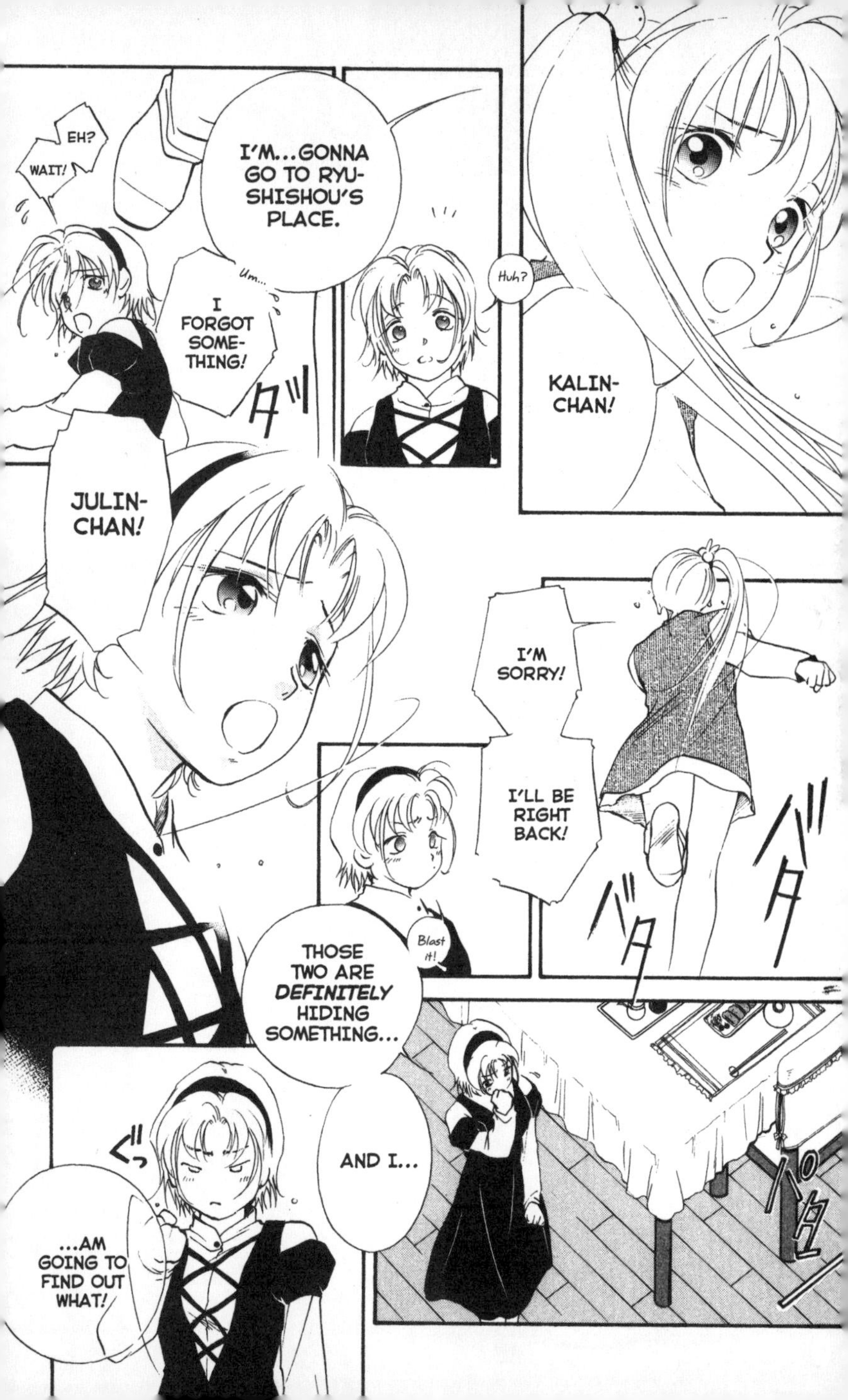

KALIN-CHAN!
Huh?
I'M...GONNA GO TO RYU-SHISHOU'S PLACE.
EH?
WAIT!
Um...
I FORGOT SOMETHING!
ダッ
I'M SORRY!
I'LL BE RIGHT BACK!
バタ
バタ
Blast it!
JULIN-CHAN!
THOSE TWO ARE *DEFINITELY* HIDING SOMETHING...
パタ
AND I...
...AM GOING TO FIND OUT WHAT!
ぐっ

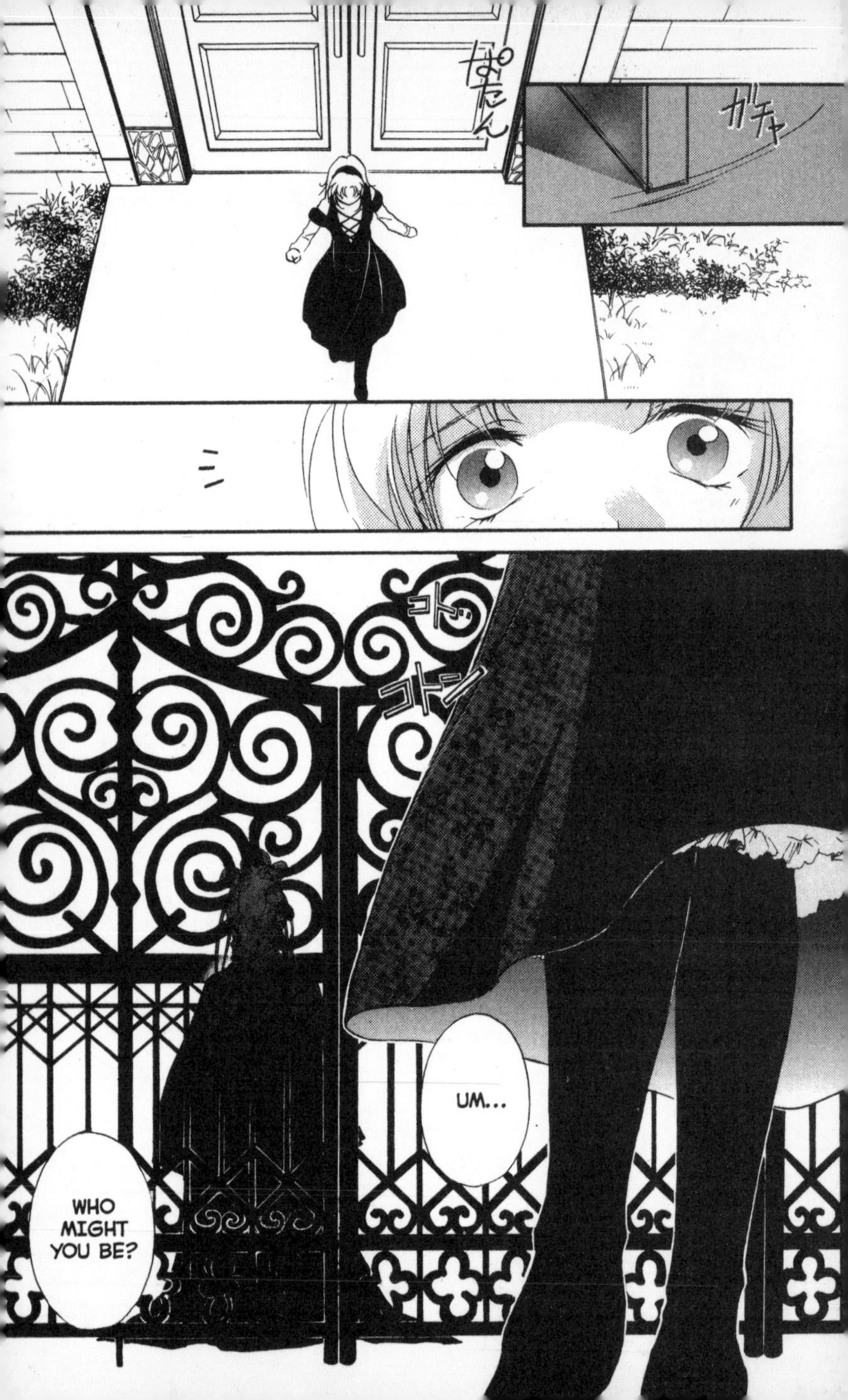
ガチャ
ぱたん
コト…
コトン
UM...
WHO MIGHT YOU BE?

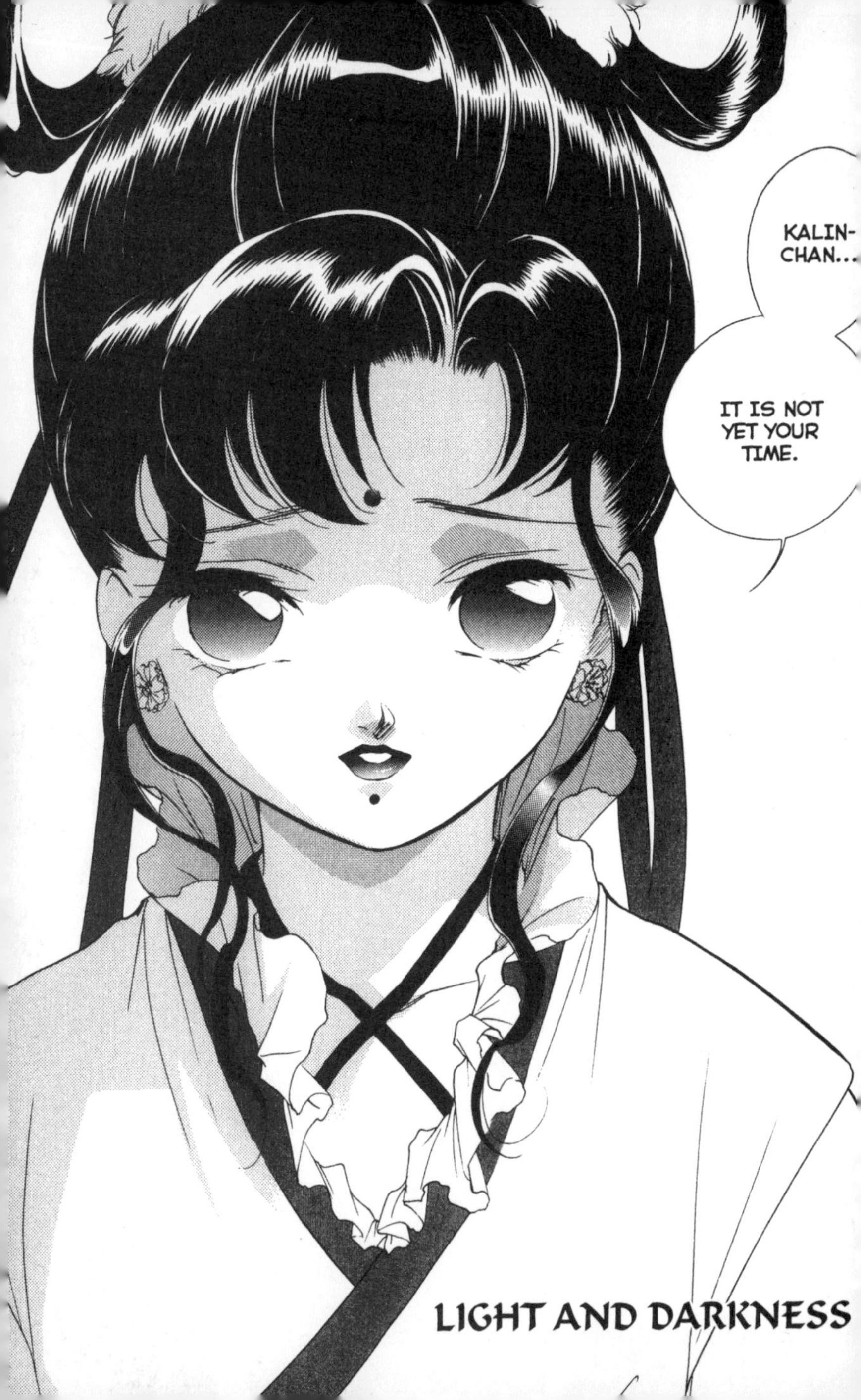
KALIN-CHAN...
IT IS NOT YET YOUR TIME.
LIGHT AND DARKNESS

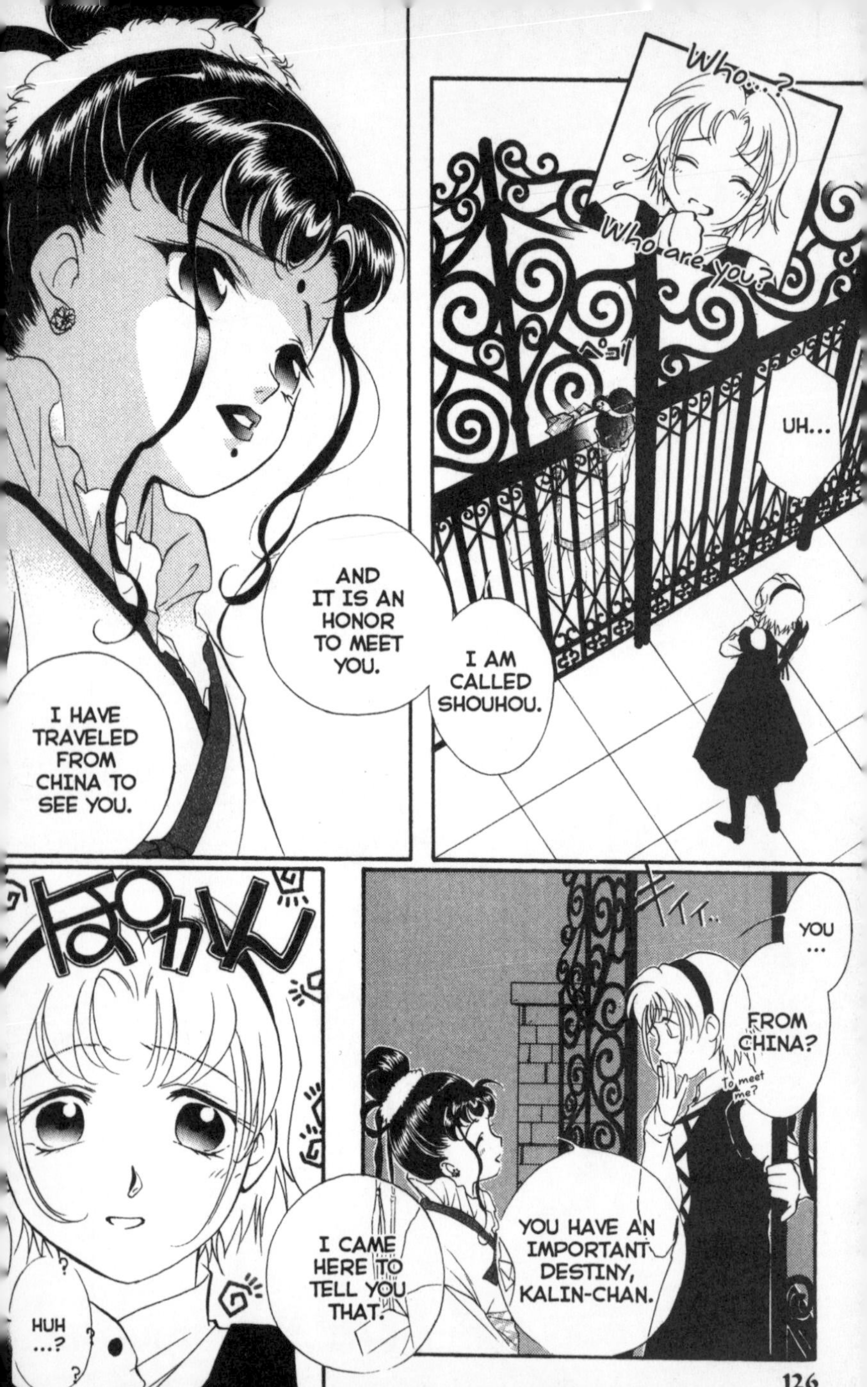
Who...?
Who are you?
ペコリ
UH...
I AM CALLED SHOUHOU.
AND IT IS AN HONOR TO MEET YOU.
I HAVE TRAVELED FROM CHINA TO SEE YOU.
キイイ..
YOU ...
FROM CHINA?
To meet me?
YOU HAVE AN IMPORTANT DESTINY, KALIN-CHAN.
I CAME HERE TO TELL YOU THAT.
HUH ...?

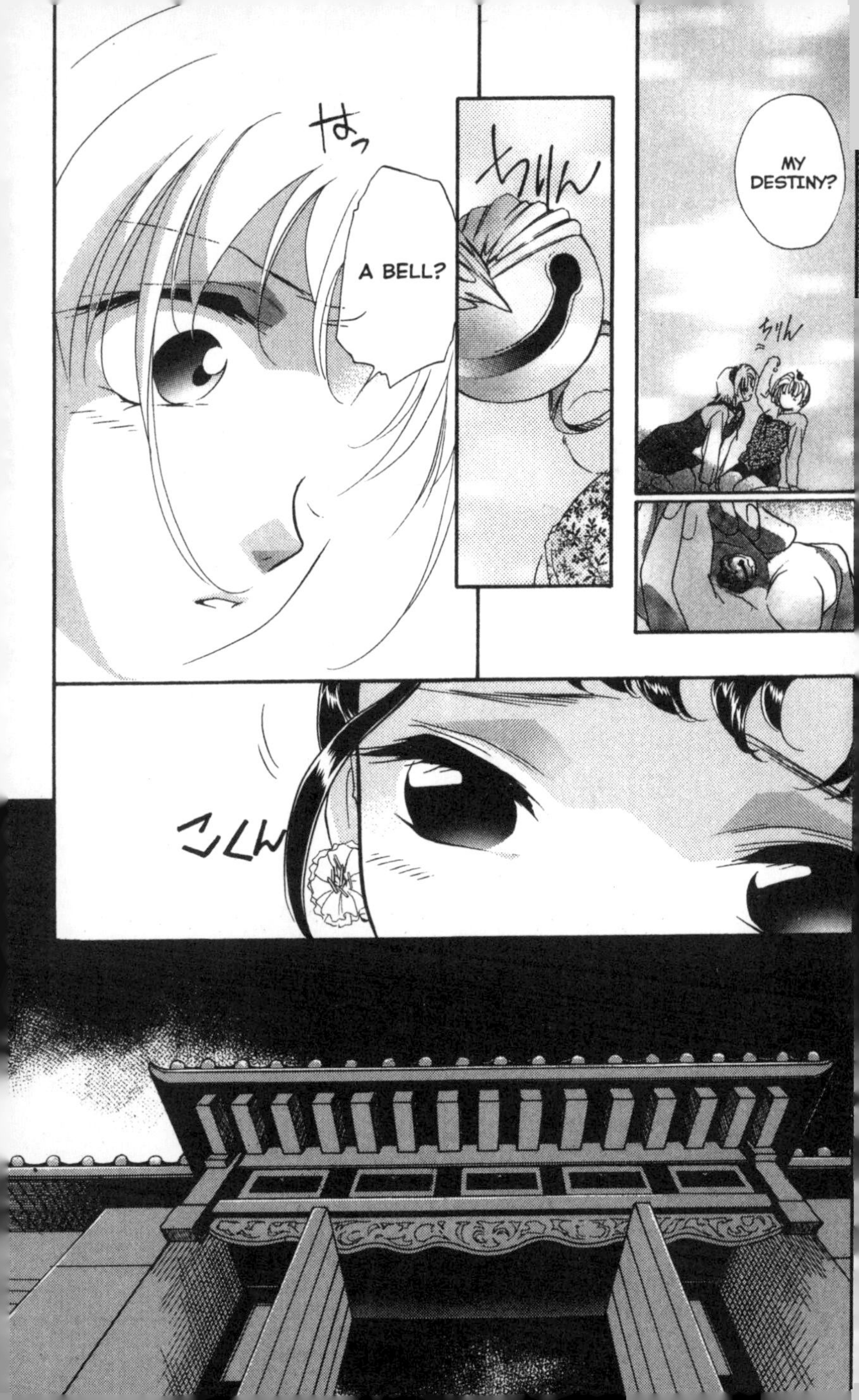
MY DESTINY?
ちりん
ちりん
はっ
A BELL?
こくん

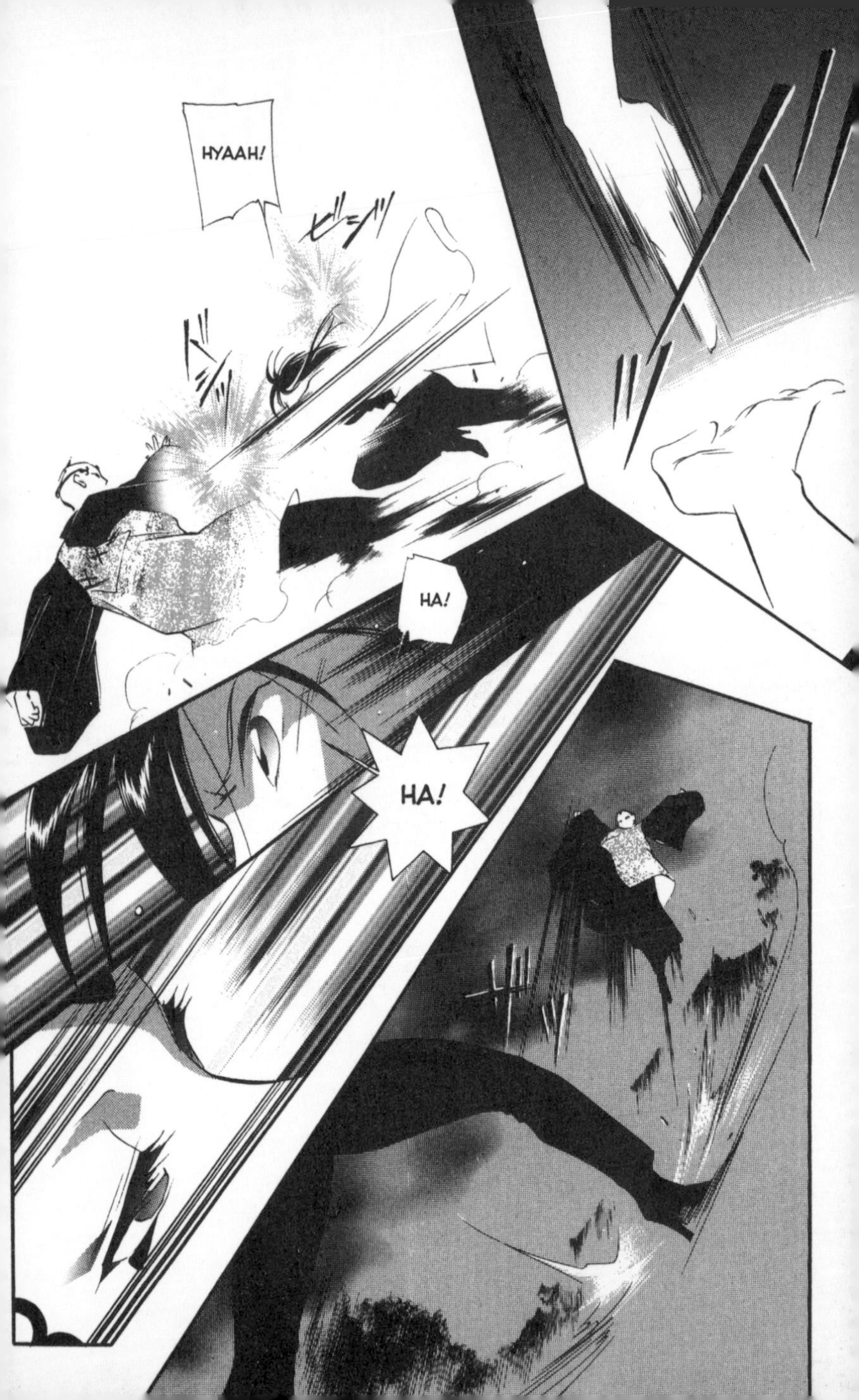
HYAAH!
HA!
HA!

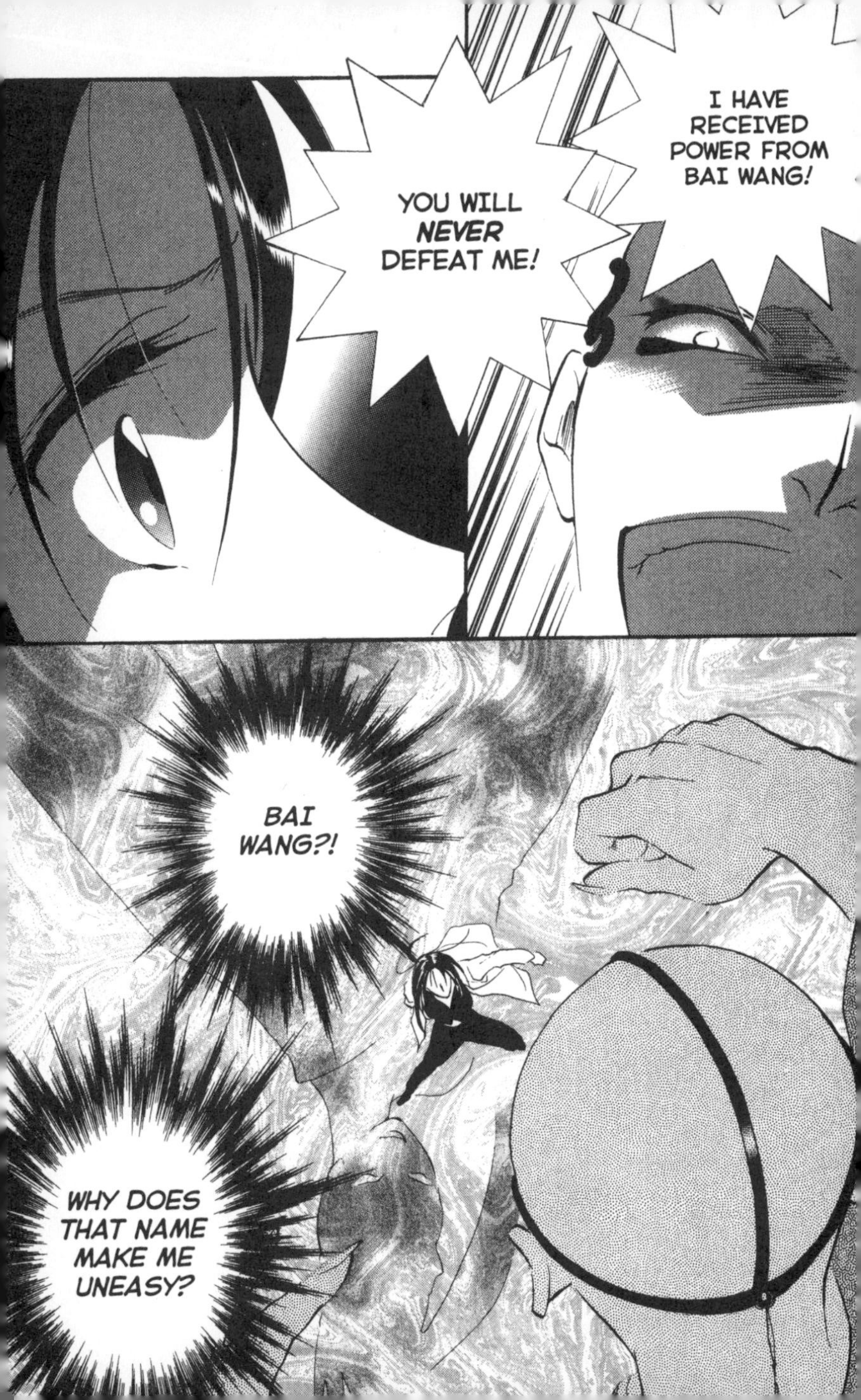
I HAVE RECEIVED POWER FROM BAI WANG!
YOU WILL NEVER DEFEAT ME!
BAI WANG?!
WHY DOES THAT NAME MAKE ME UNEASY?

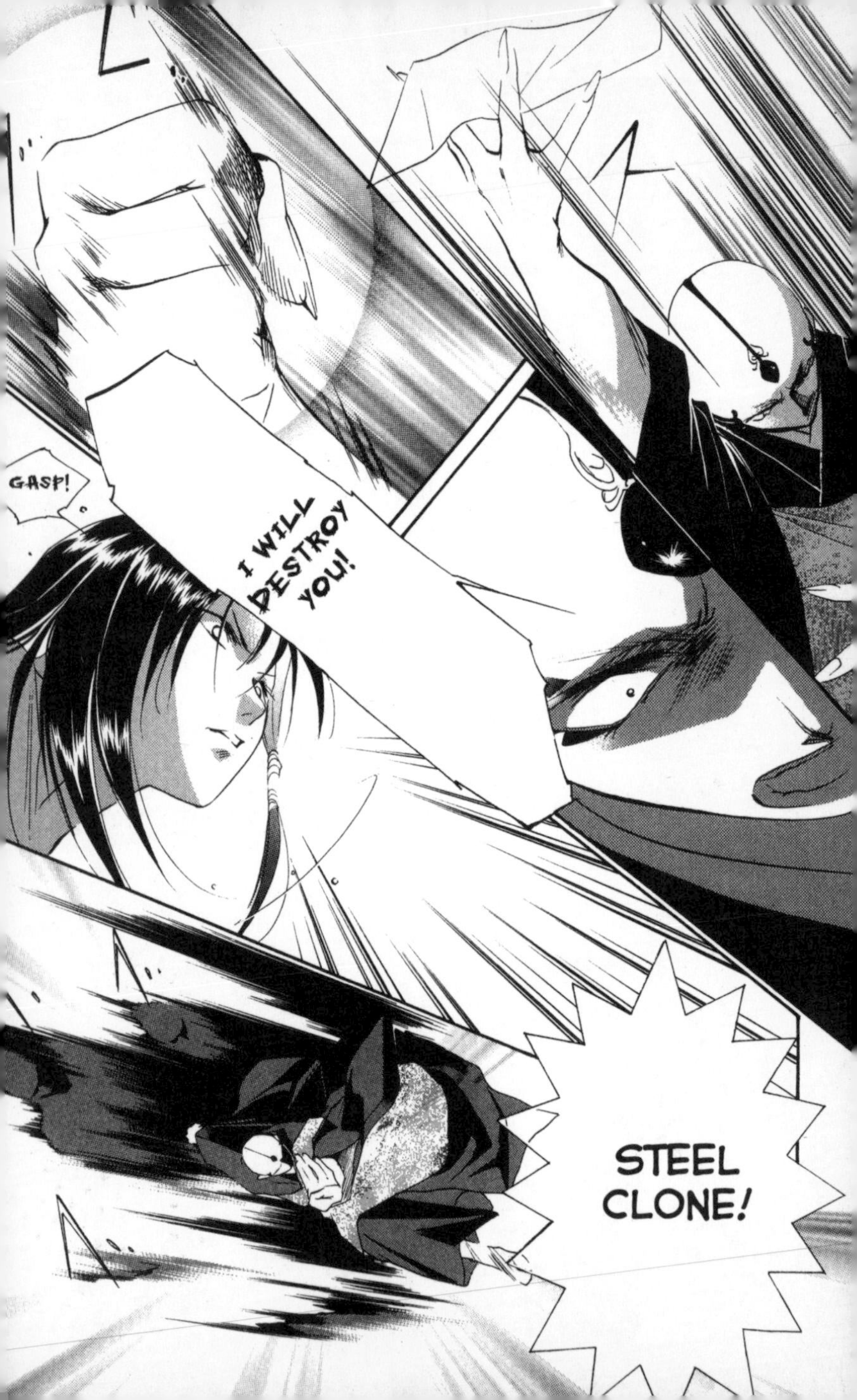
I WILL DESTROY YOU!
GASP!
STEEL CLONE!

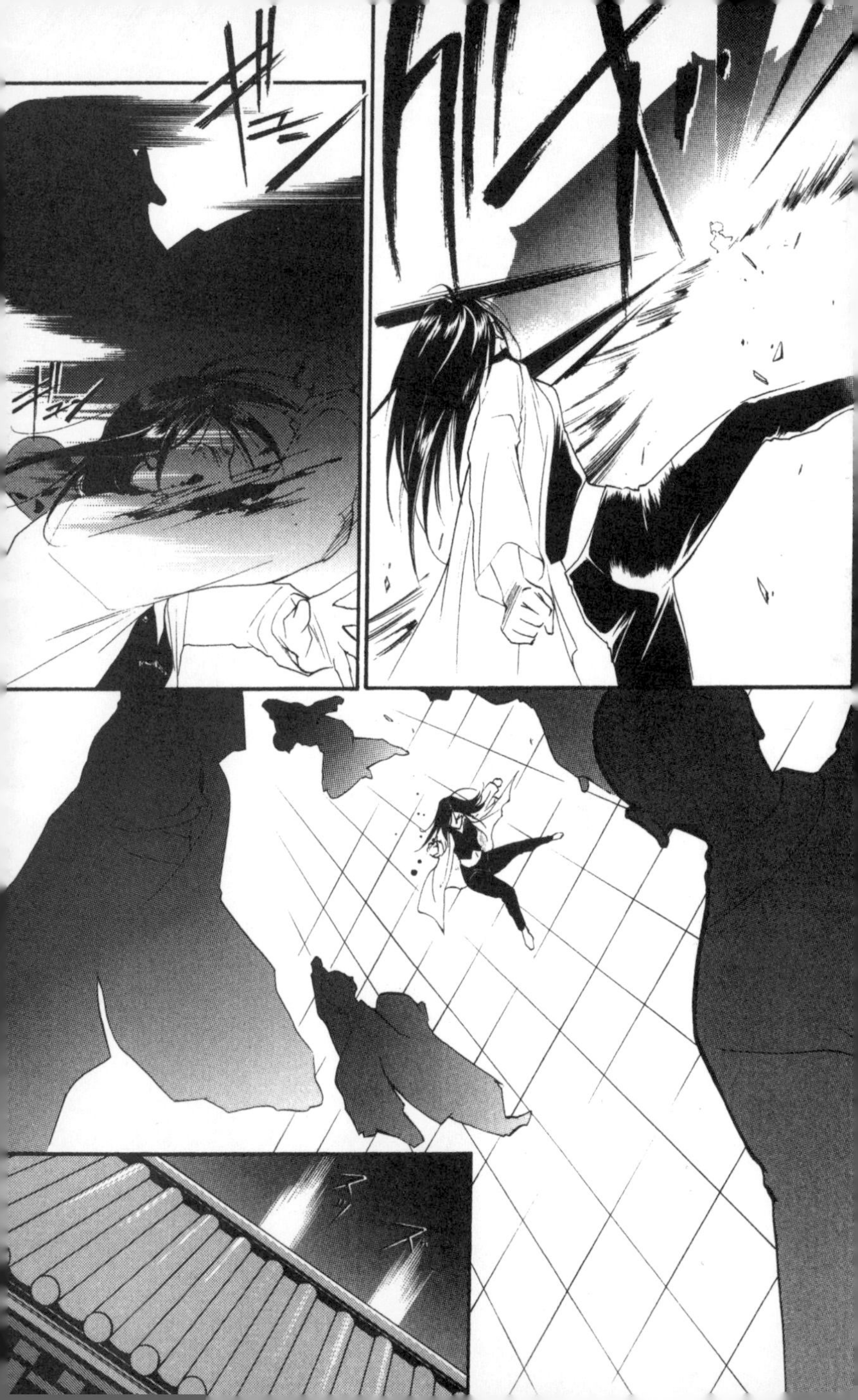
ギュ
ギュッ
ズッ
ズ

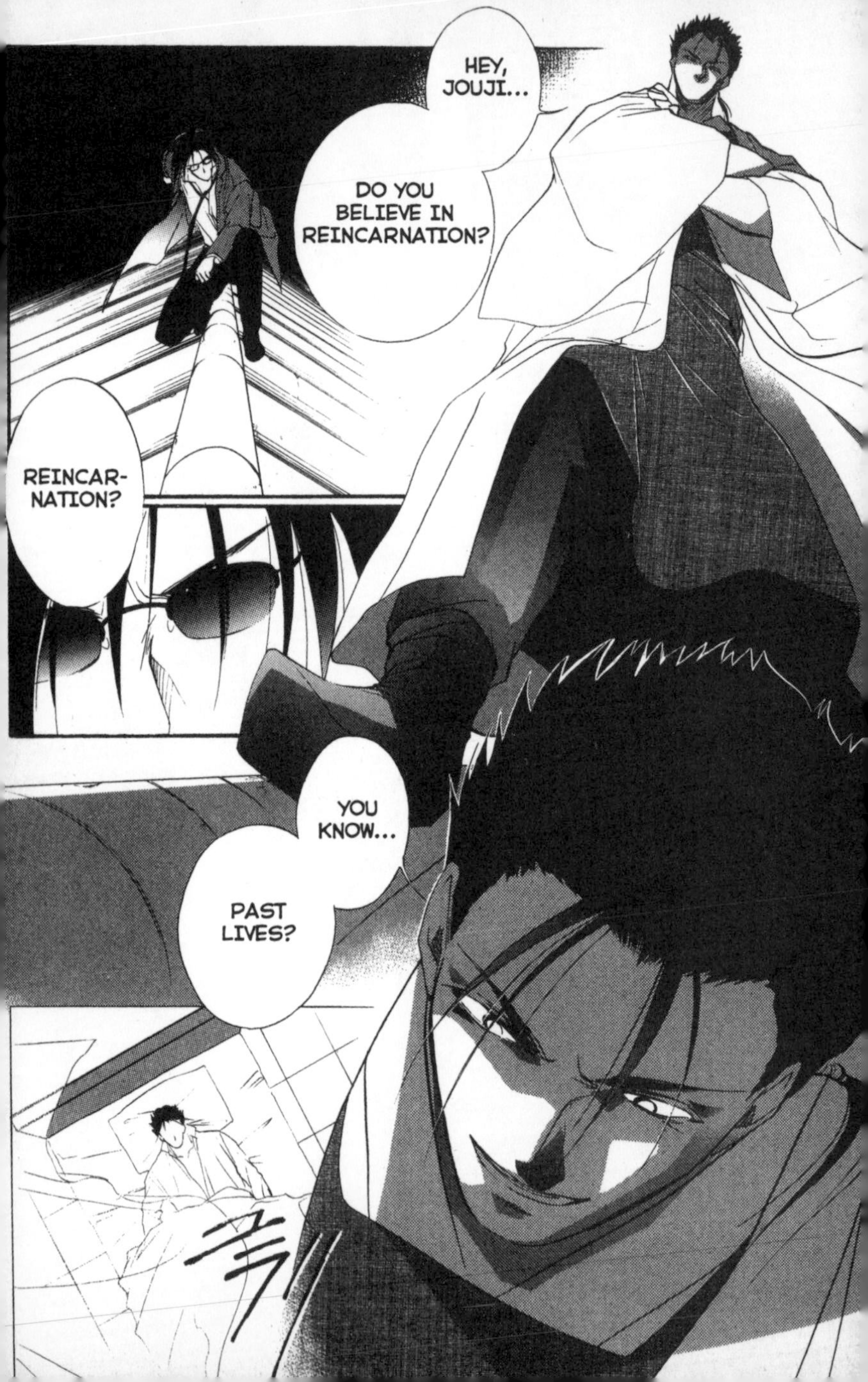
HEY, JOUJI...
DO YOU BELIEVE IN REINCARNATION?
REINCAR-NATION?
YOU KNOW...
PAST LIVES?

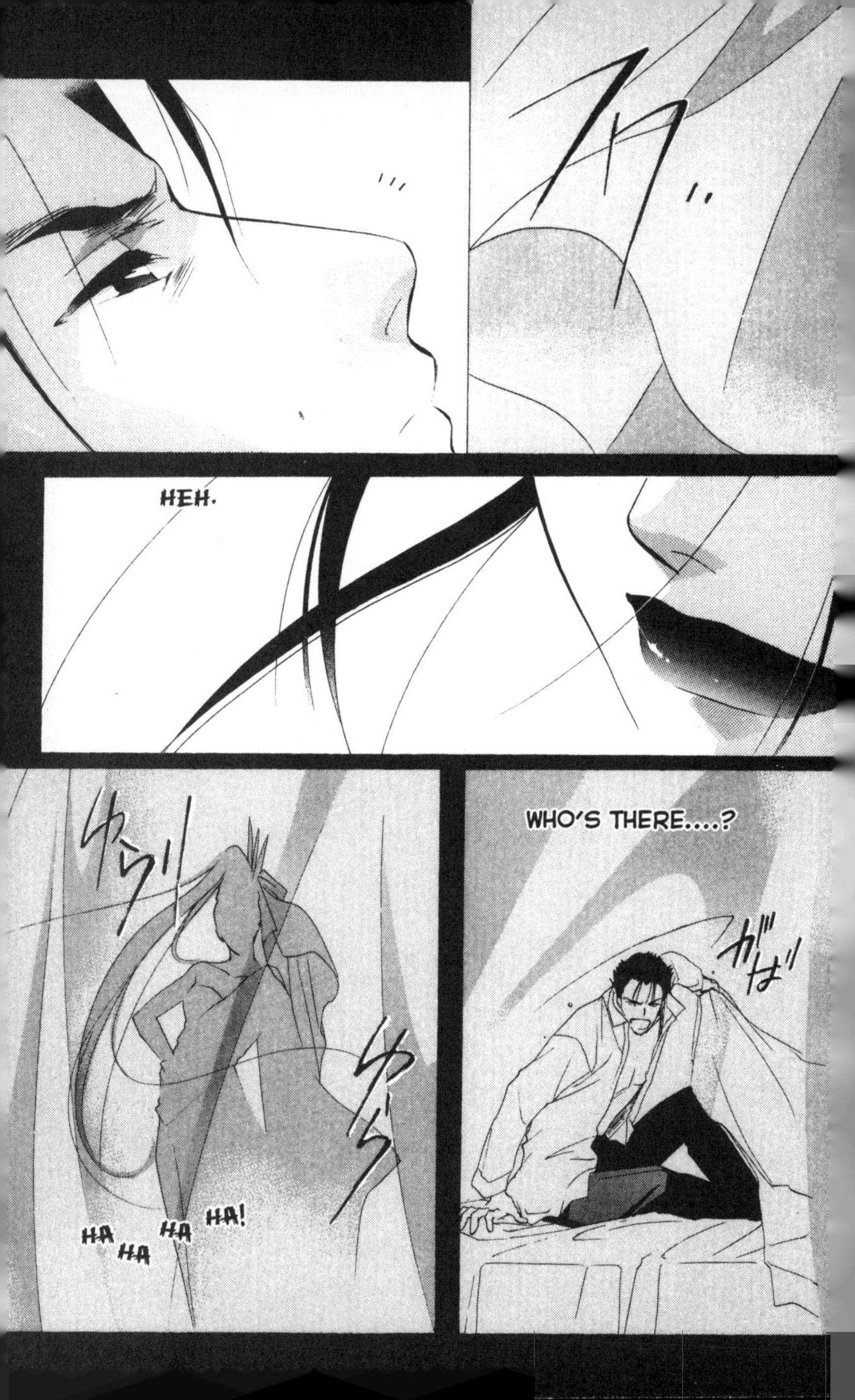
HEH.
WHO'S THERE....?
がば
ゆらり
ゆら
HA HA HA HA!

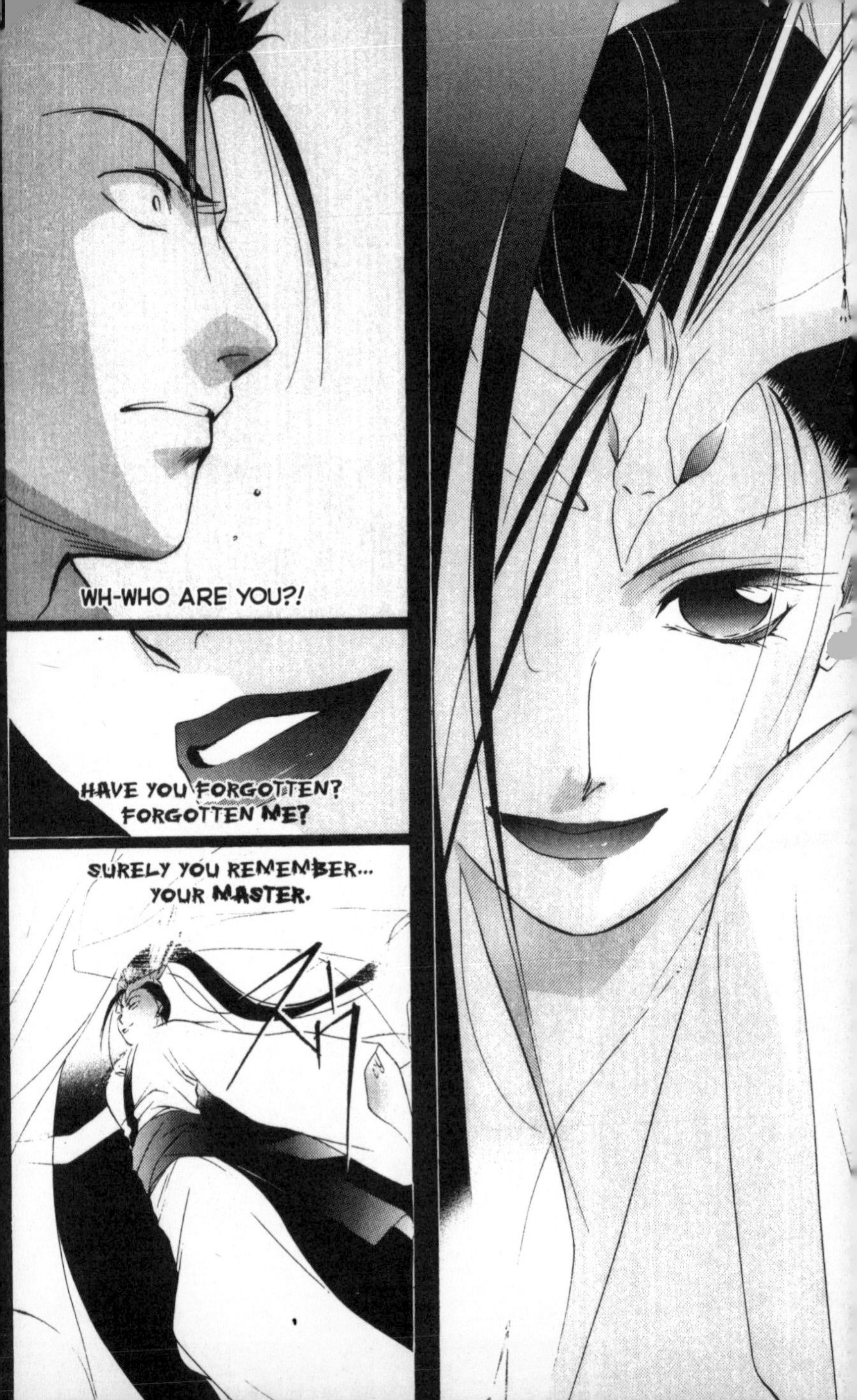
WH-WHO ARE YOU?!
HAVE YOU FORGOTTEN? FORGOTTEN ME?
SURELY YOU REMEMBER... YOUR MASTER.

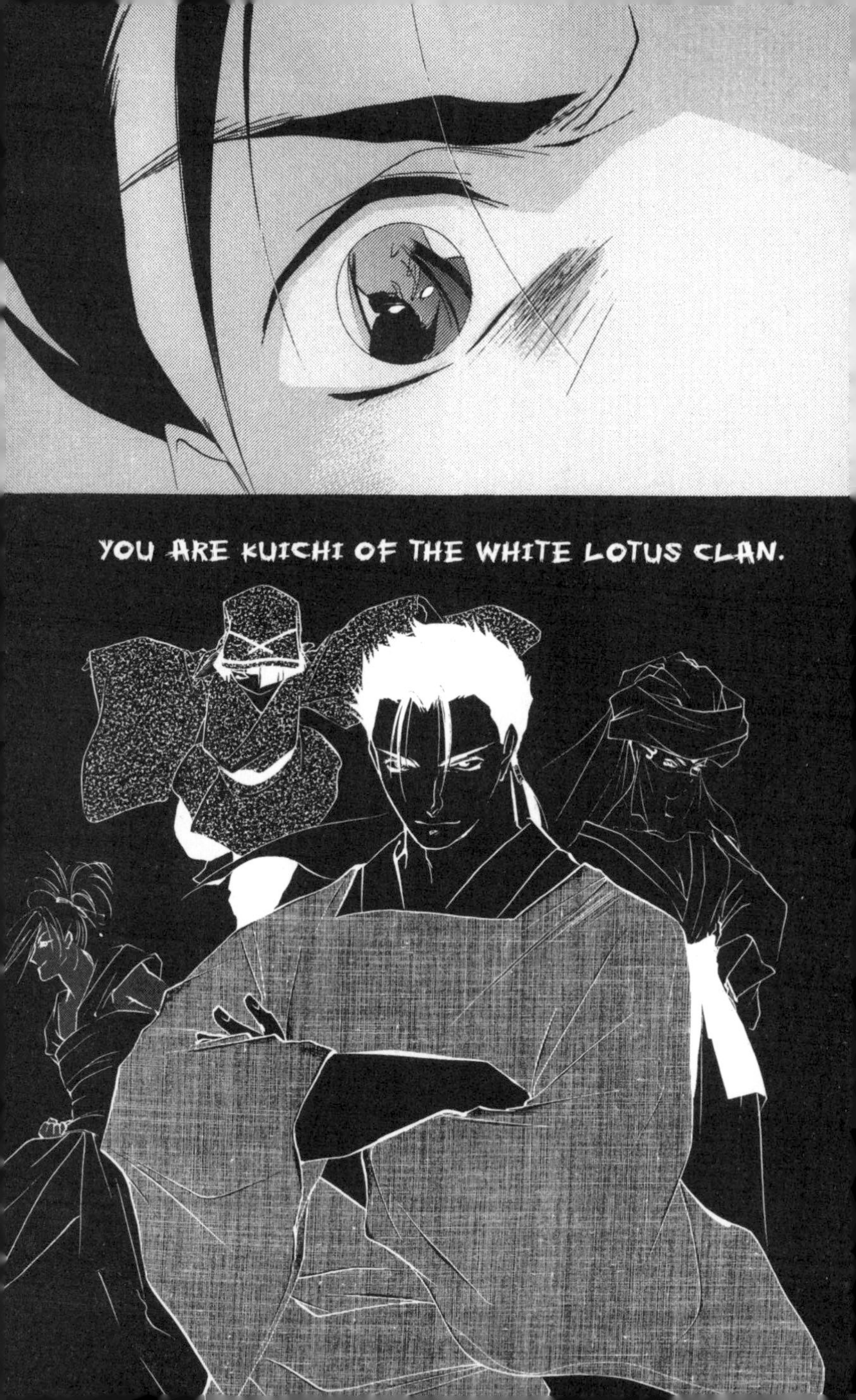
YOU ARE KUICHI OF THE WHITE LOTUS CLAN.

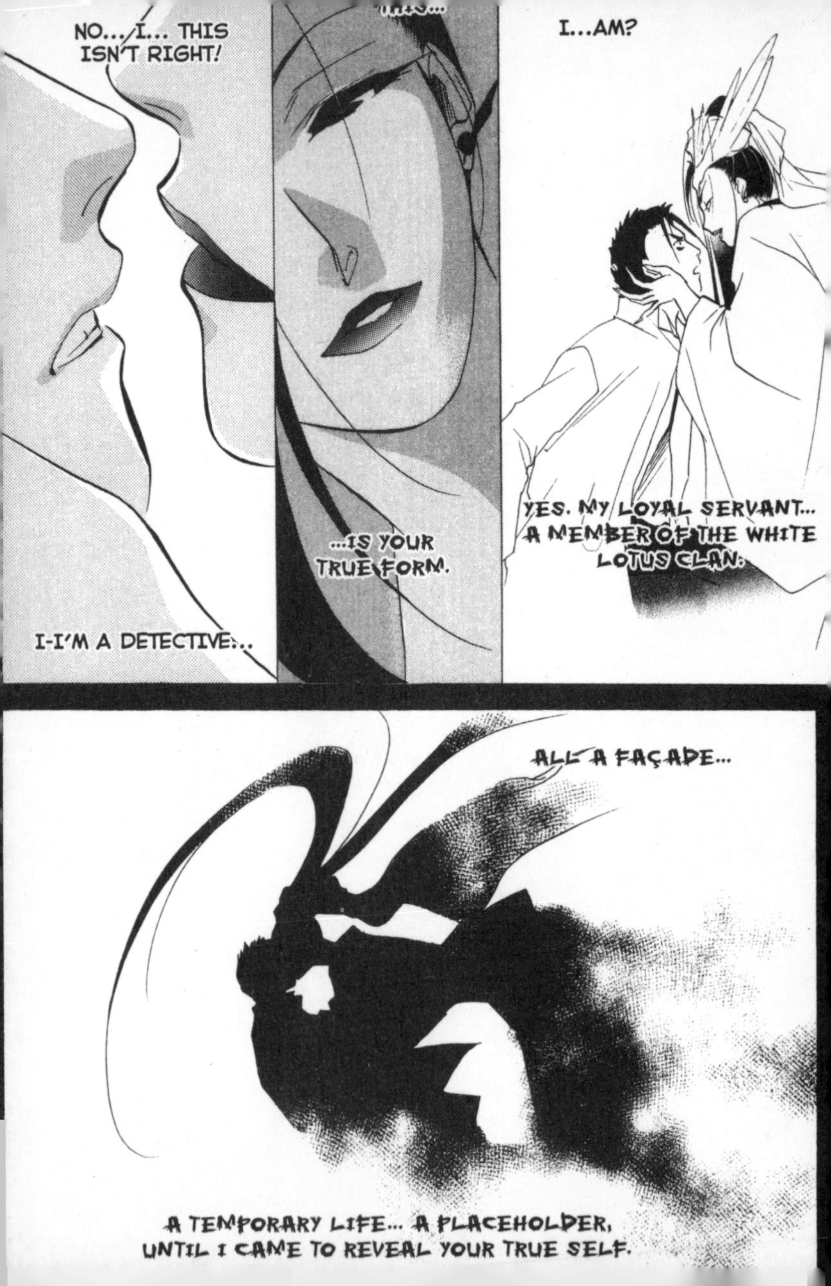
I...AM?
YES. MY LOYAL SERVANT... A MEMBER OF THE WHITE LOTUS CLAN.
...IS YOUR TRUE FORM.
NO... I... THIS ISN'T RIGHT!
I-I'M A DETECTIVE...
ALL A FAÇADE...
A TEMPORARY LIFE... A PLACEHOLDER, UNTIL I CAME TO REVEAL YOUR TRUE SELF.

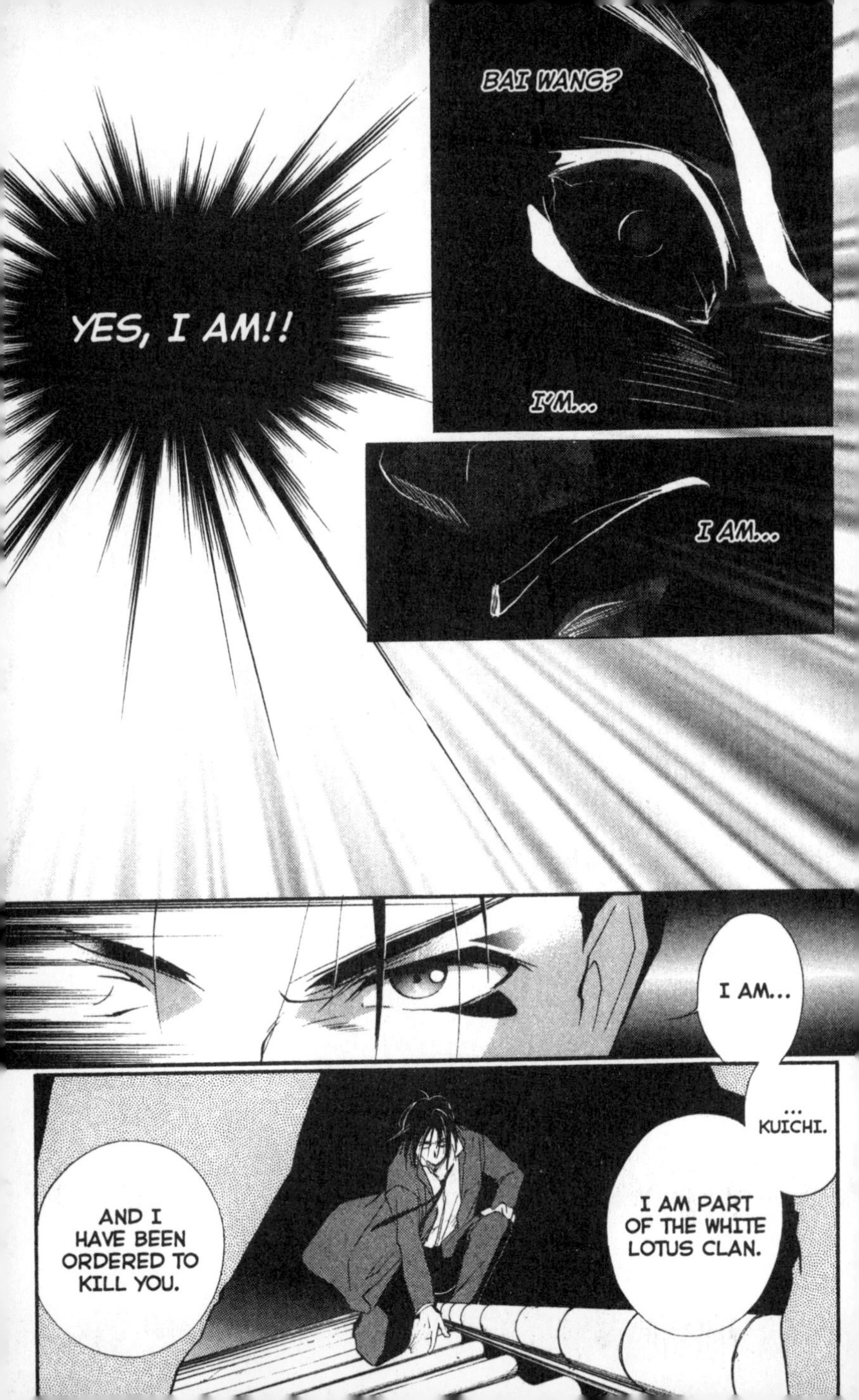
BAI WANG?
I'M...
I AM...
YES, I AM!!
I AM...
... KUICHI.
I AM PART OF THE WHITE LOTUS CLAN.
AND I HAVE BEEN ORDERED TO KILL YOU.

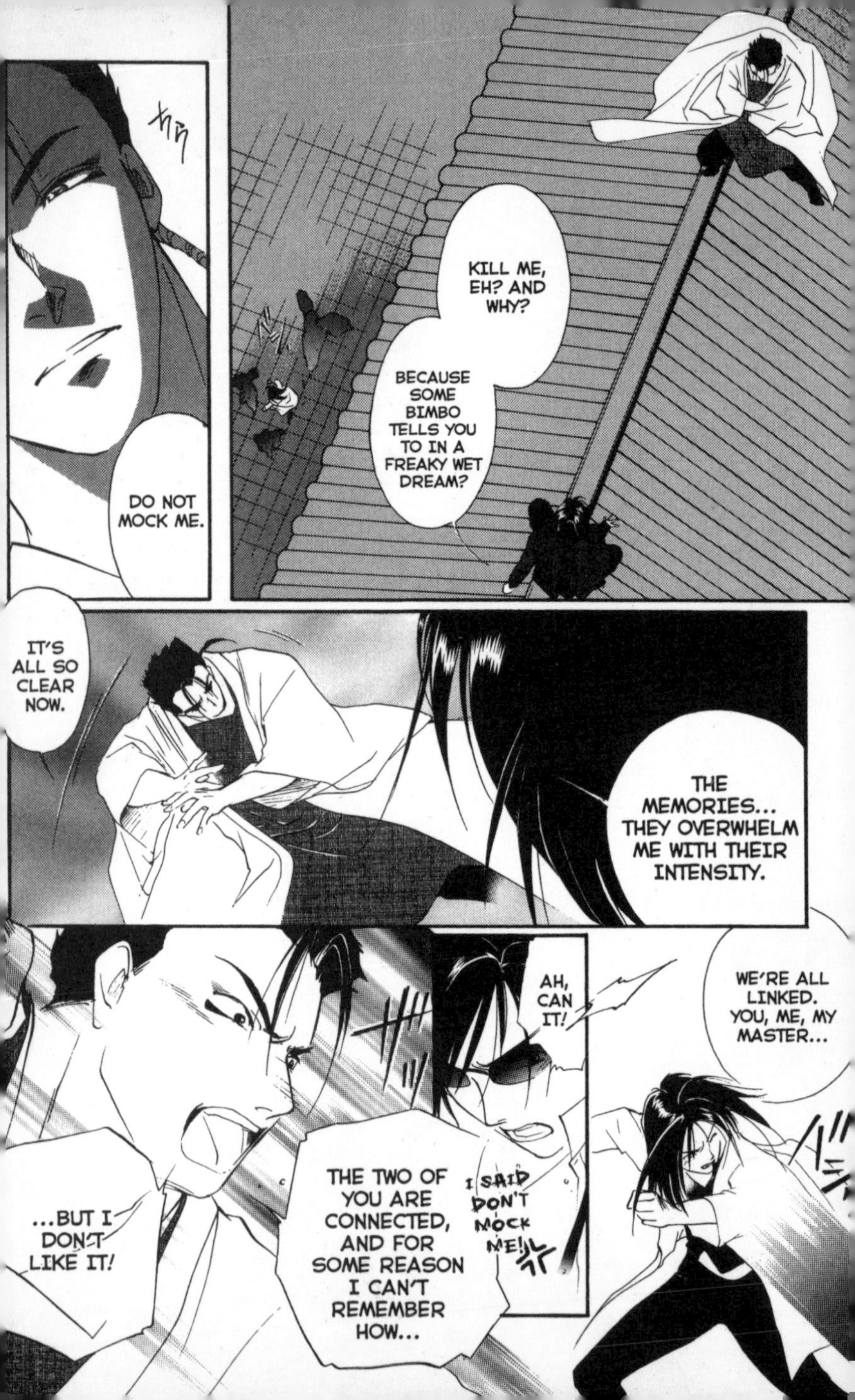
KILL ME, EH? AND WHY?
BECAUSE SOME BIMBO TELLS YOU TO IN A FREAKY WET DREAM?
DO NOT MOCK ME.
IT'S ALL SO CLEAR NOW.
THE MEMORIES... THEY OVERWHELM ME WITH THEIR INTENSITY.
WE'RE ALL LINKED. YOU, ME, MY MASTER...
AH, CAN IT!
I SAID DON'T MOCK ME!
THE TWO OF YOU ARE CONNECTED, AND FOR SOME REASON I CAN'T REMEMBER HOW...
...BUT I DON'T LIKE IT!

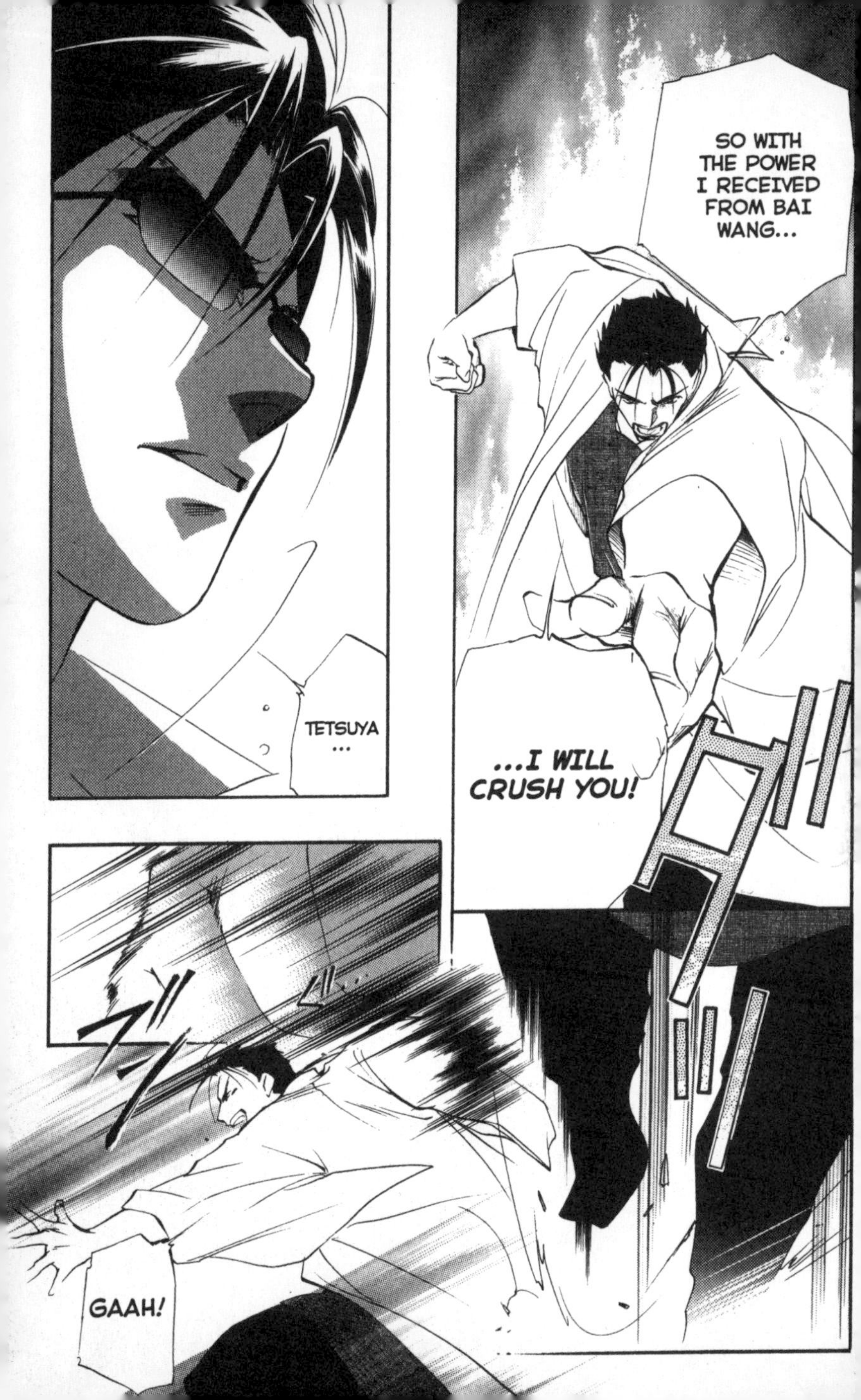
SO WITH THE POWER I RECEIVED FROM BAI WANG...
...I WILL CRUSH YOU!
TETSUYA ...
GAAH!

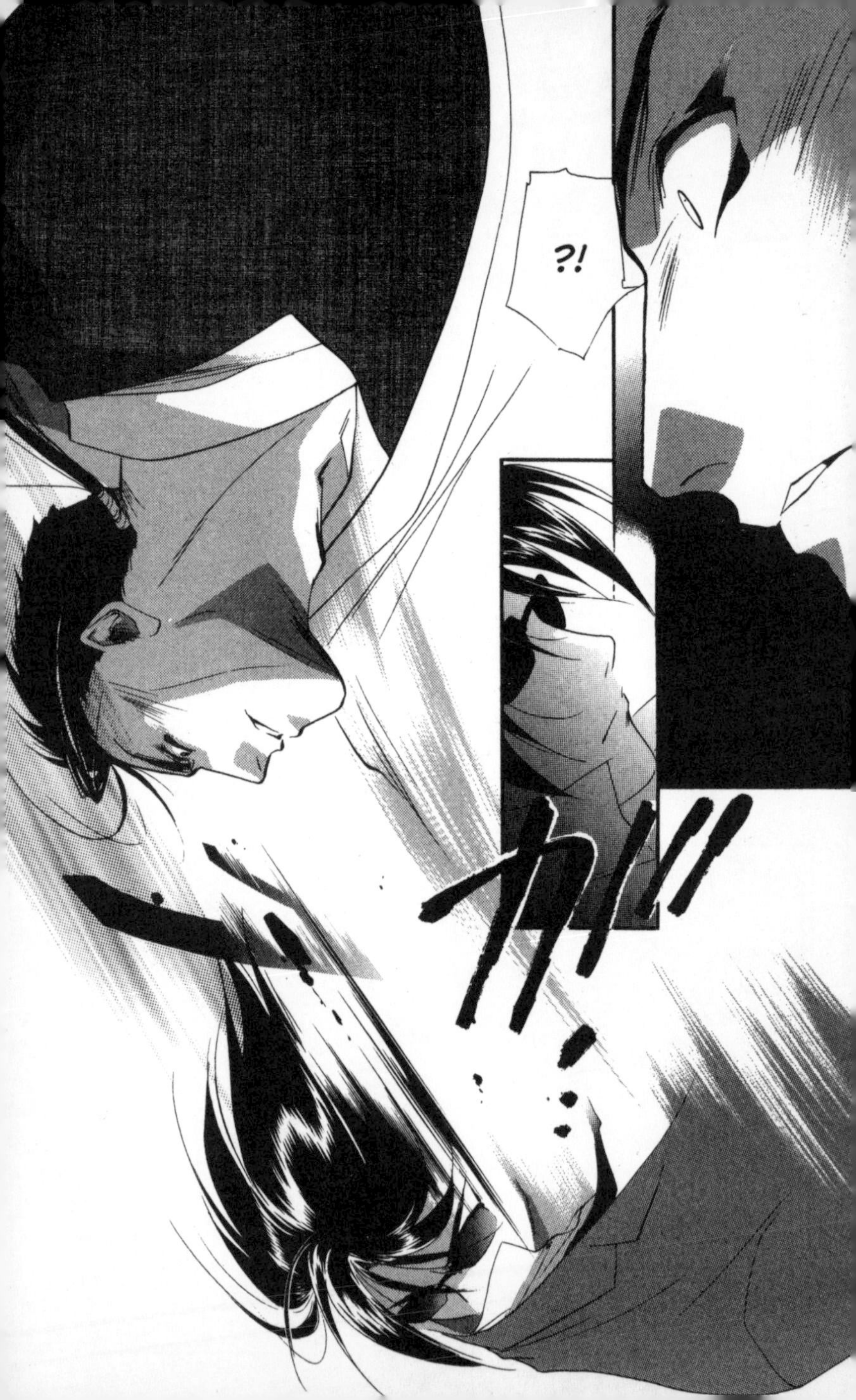
?!

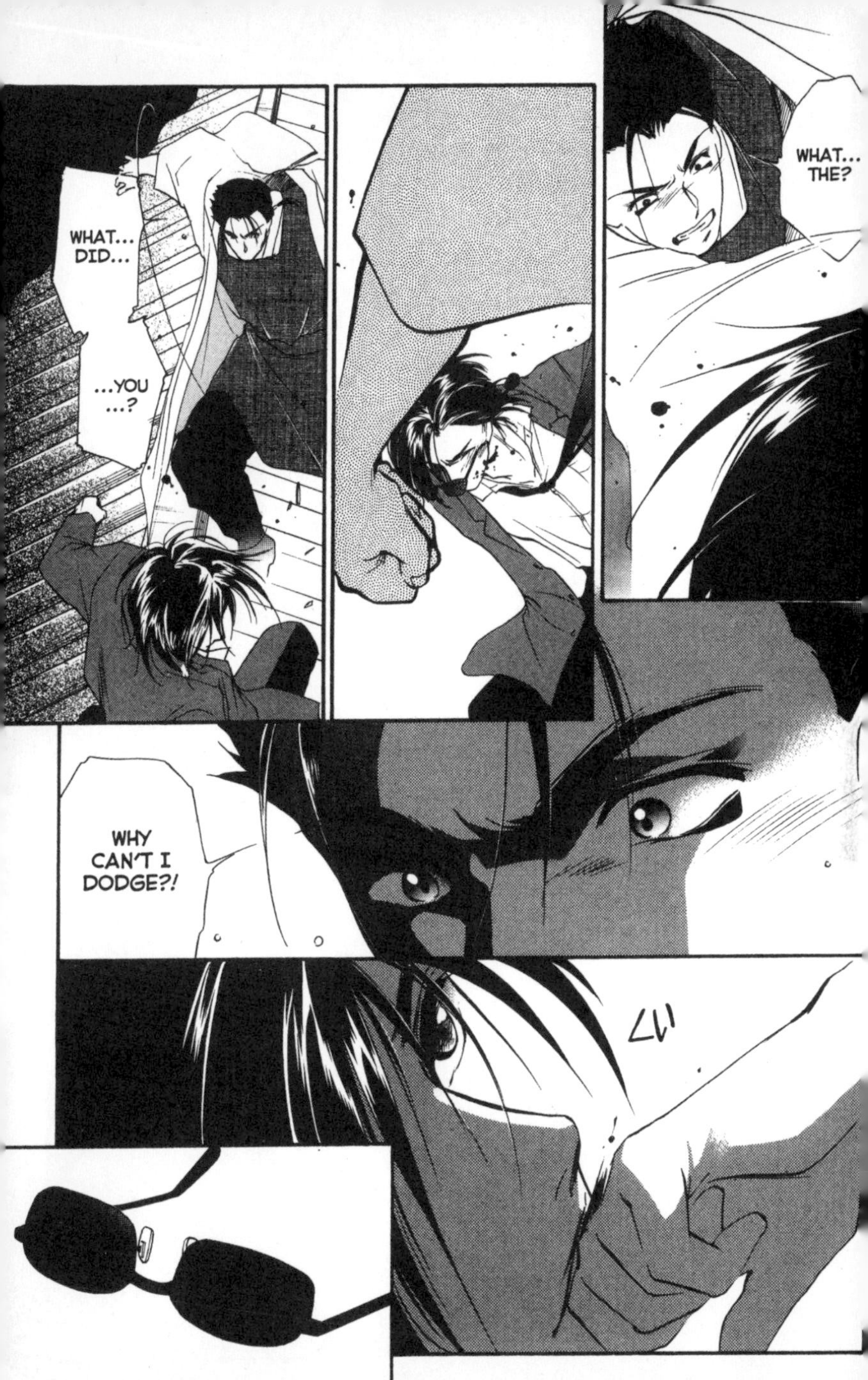
WHAT... THE?
WHAT... DID...
...YOU ...?
WHY CAN'T I DODGE?!
くい

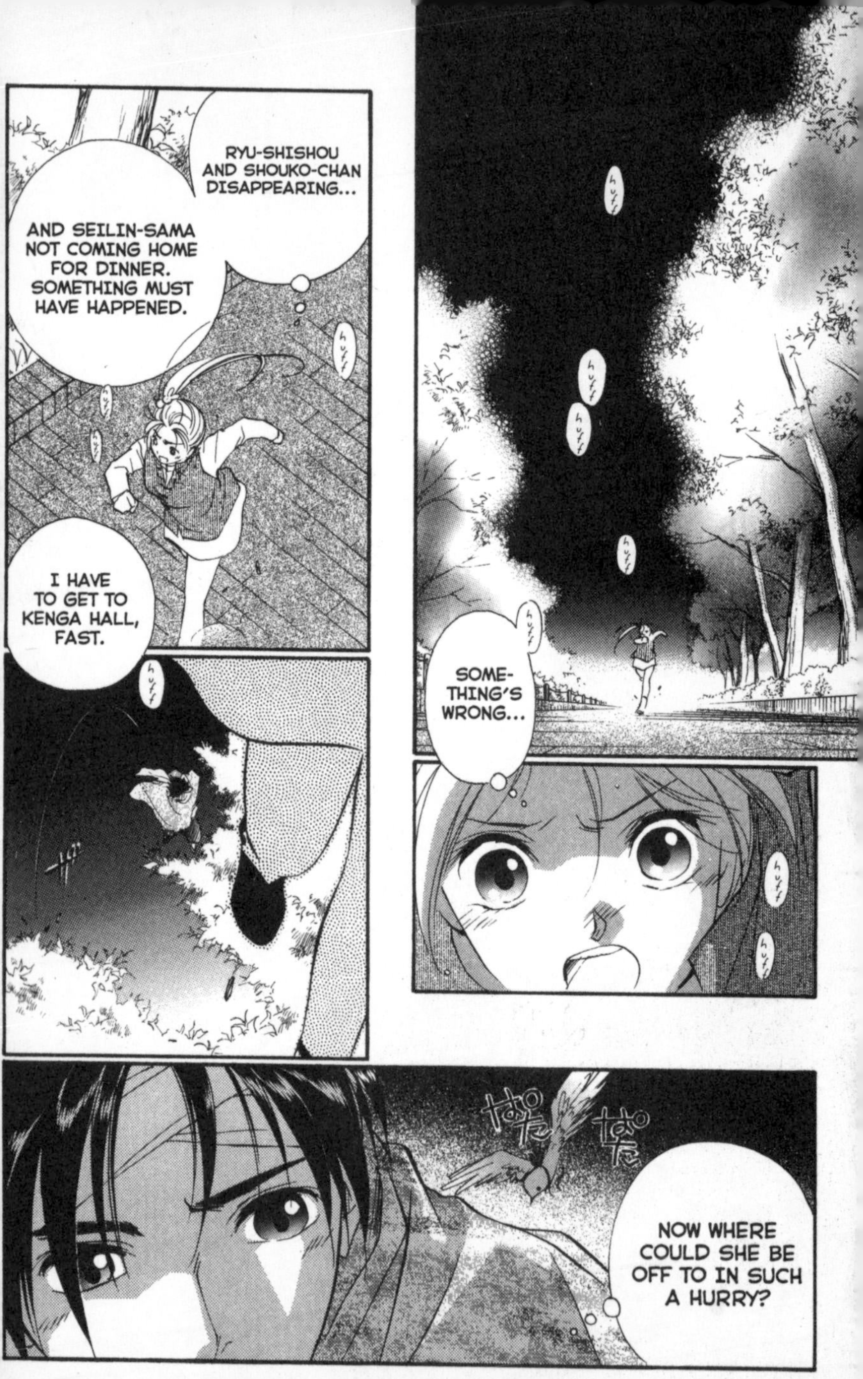
SOME-THING'S WRONG...
RYU-SHISHOU AND SHOUKO-CHAN DISAPPEARING...
AND SEILIN-SAMA NOT COMING HOME FOR DINNER. SOMETHING MUST HAVE HAPPENED.
I HAVE TO GET TO KENGA HALL, FAST.
NOW WHERE COULD SHE BE OFF TO IN SUCH A HURRY?

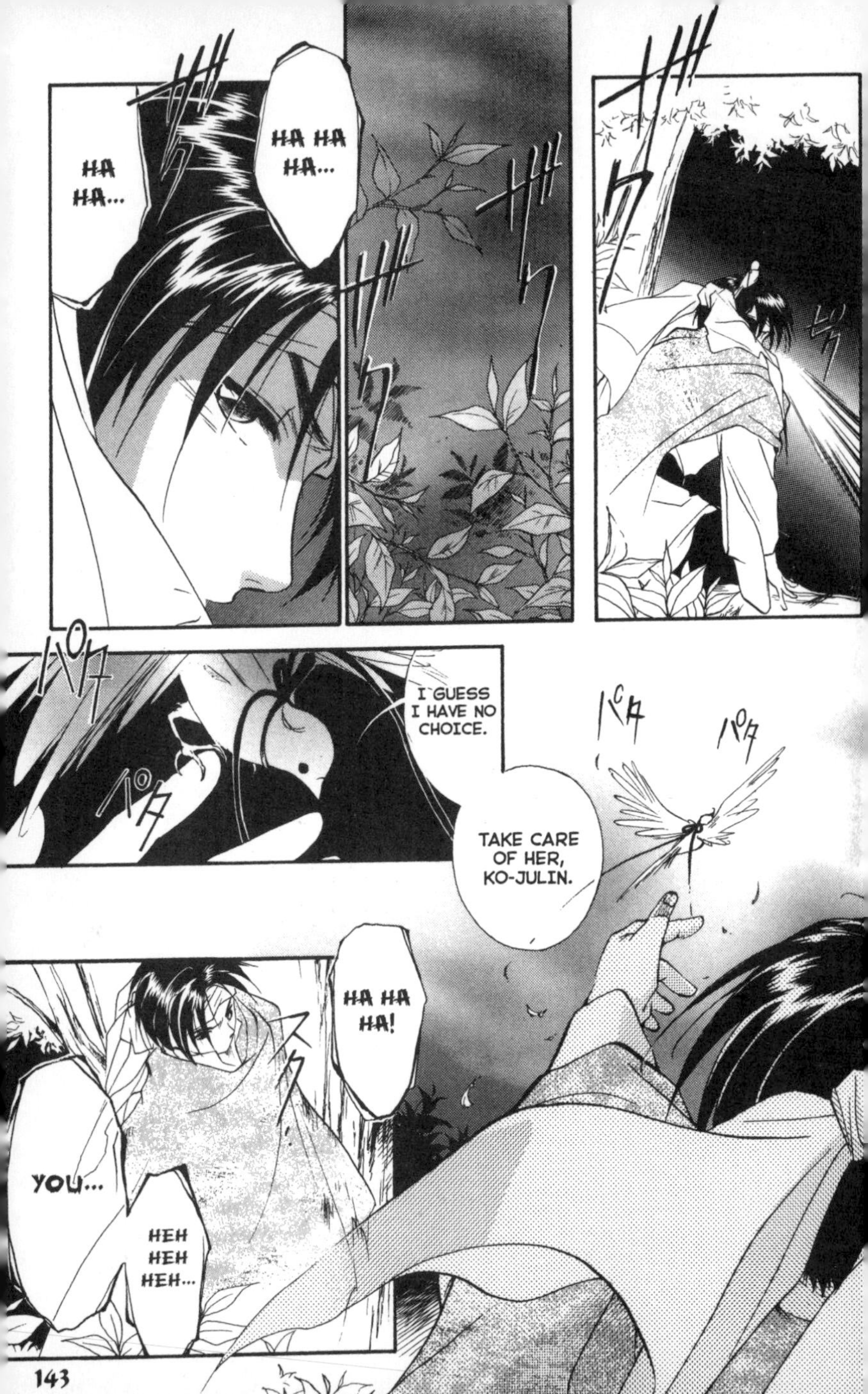
HA HA HA...
HA HA...
I GUESS I HAVE NO CHOICE.
TAKE CARE OF HER, KO-JULIN.
HA HA HA!
YOU...
HEH HEH HEH...

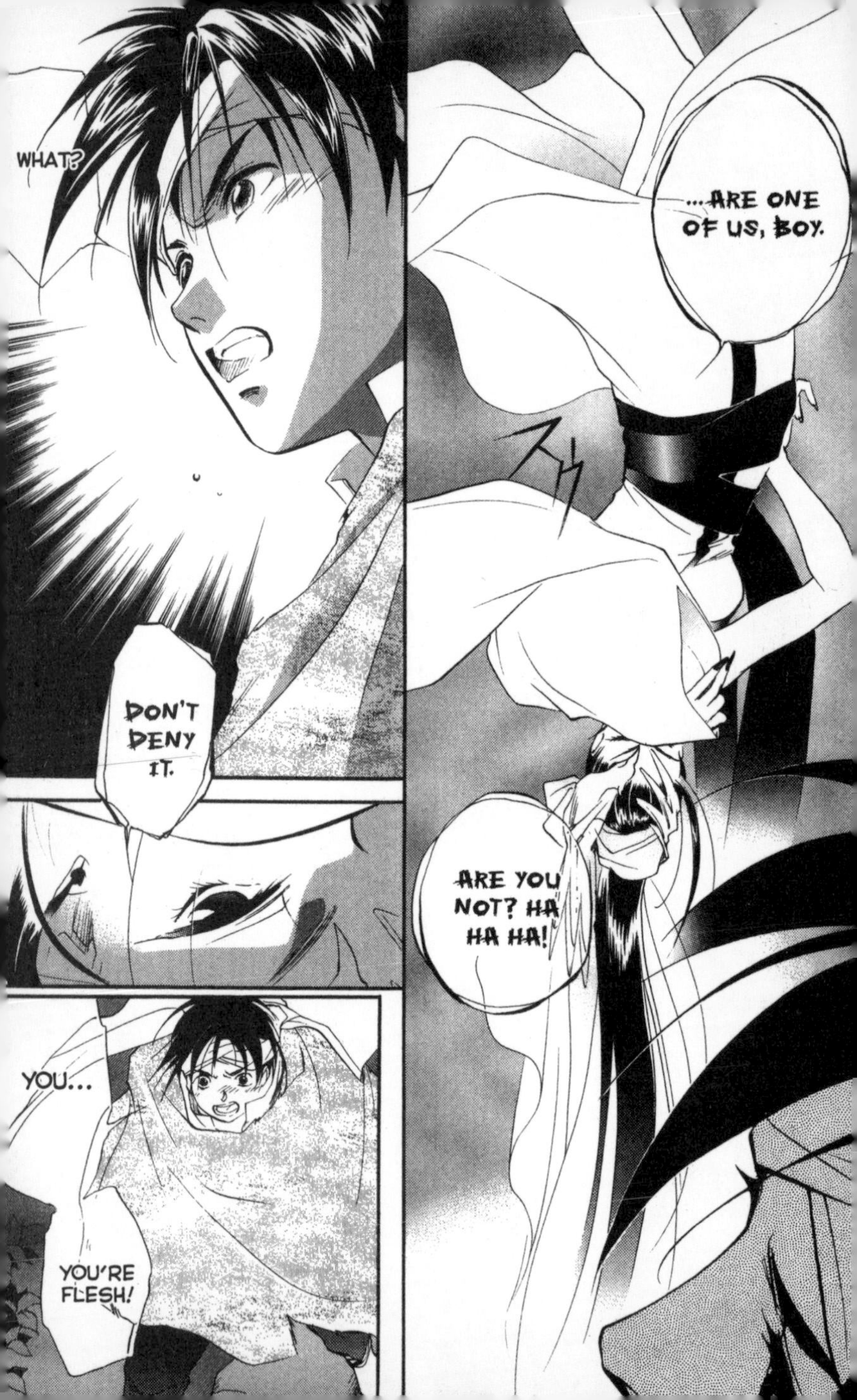
...ARE ONE OF US, BOY.
ARE YOU NOT? HA HA HA!
WHAT?
DON'T DENY IT.
YOU...
YOU'RE FLESH!

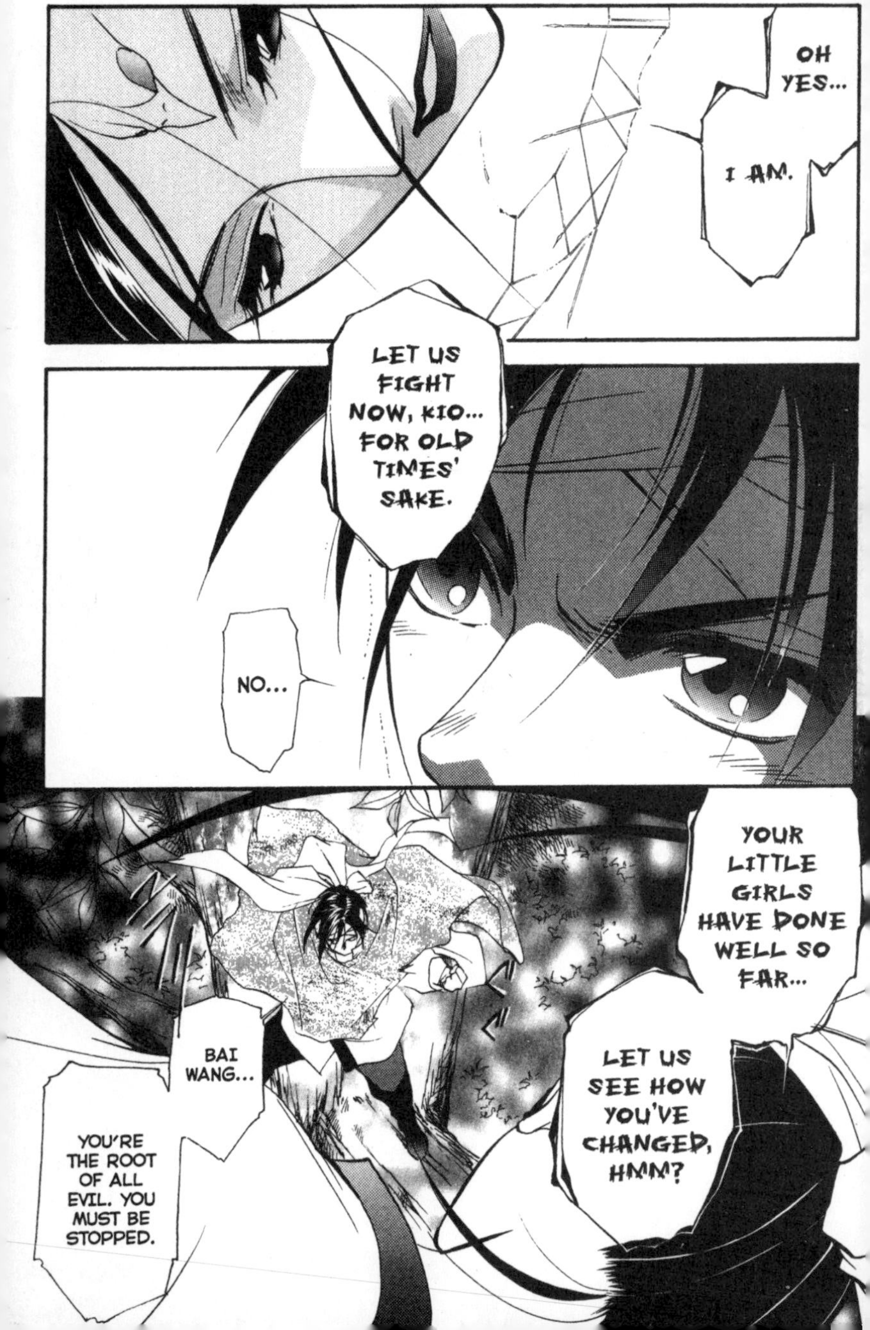
OH YES...
I AM.
LET US FIGHT NOW, KIO... FOR OLD TIMES' SAKE.
NO...
YOUR LITTLE GIRLS HAVE DONE WELL SO FAR...
LET US SEE HOW YOU'VE CHANGED, HMM?
BAI WANG...
YOU'RE THE ROOT OF ALL EVIL. YOU MUST BE STOPPED.

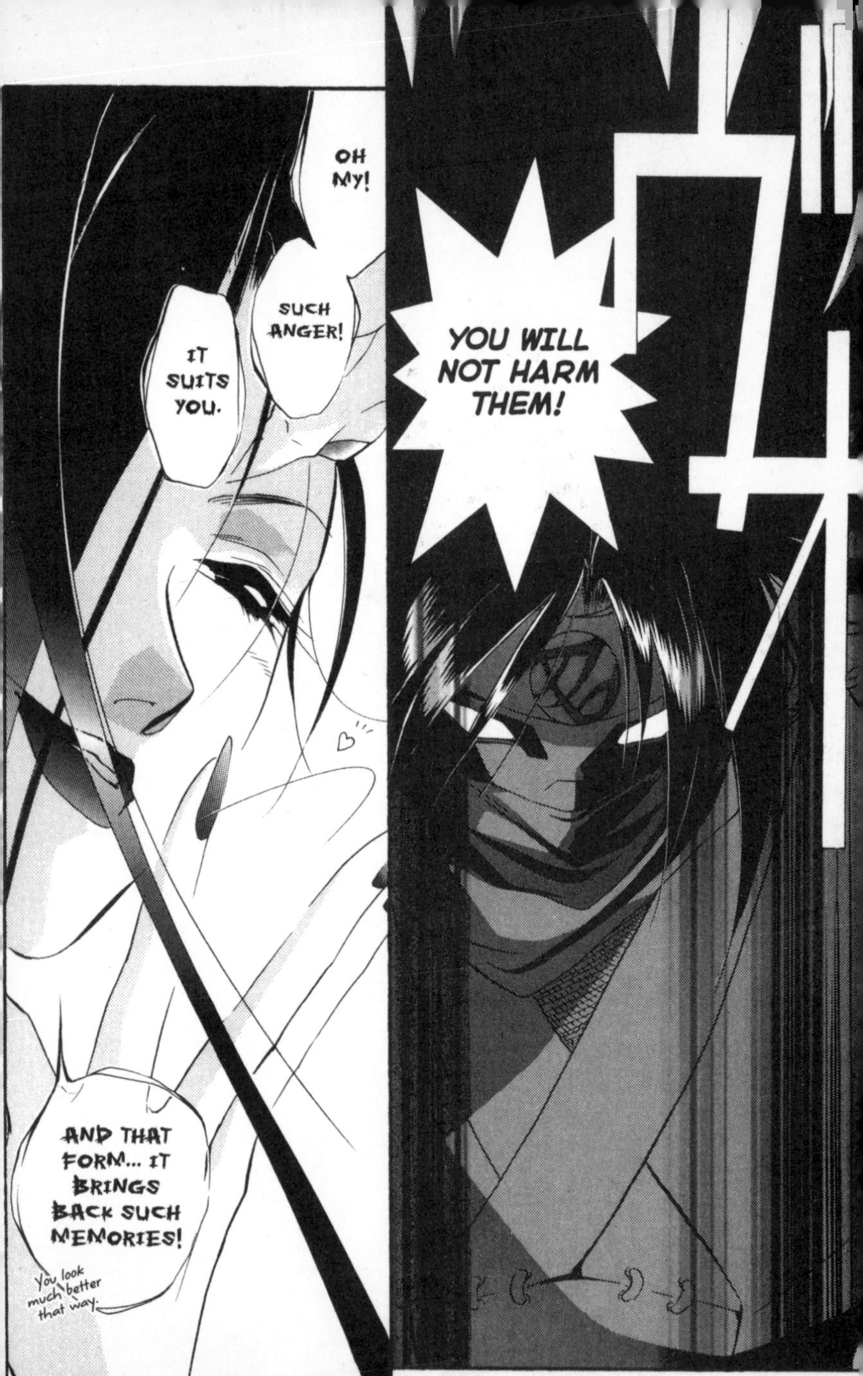
YOU WILL NOT HARM THEM!
OH MY!
SUCH ANGER!
IT SUITS YOU.
AND THAT FORM... IT BRINGS BACK SUCH MEMORIES!
You look much better that way.

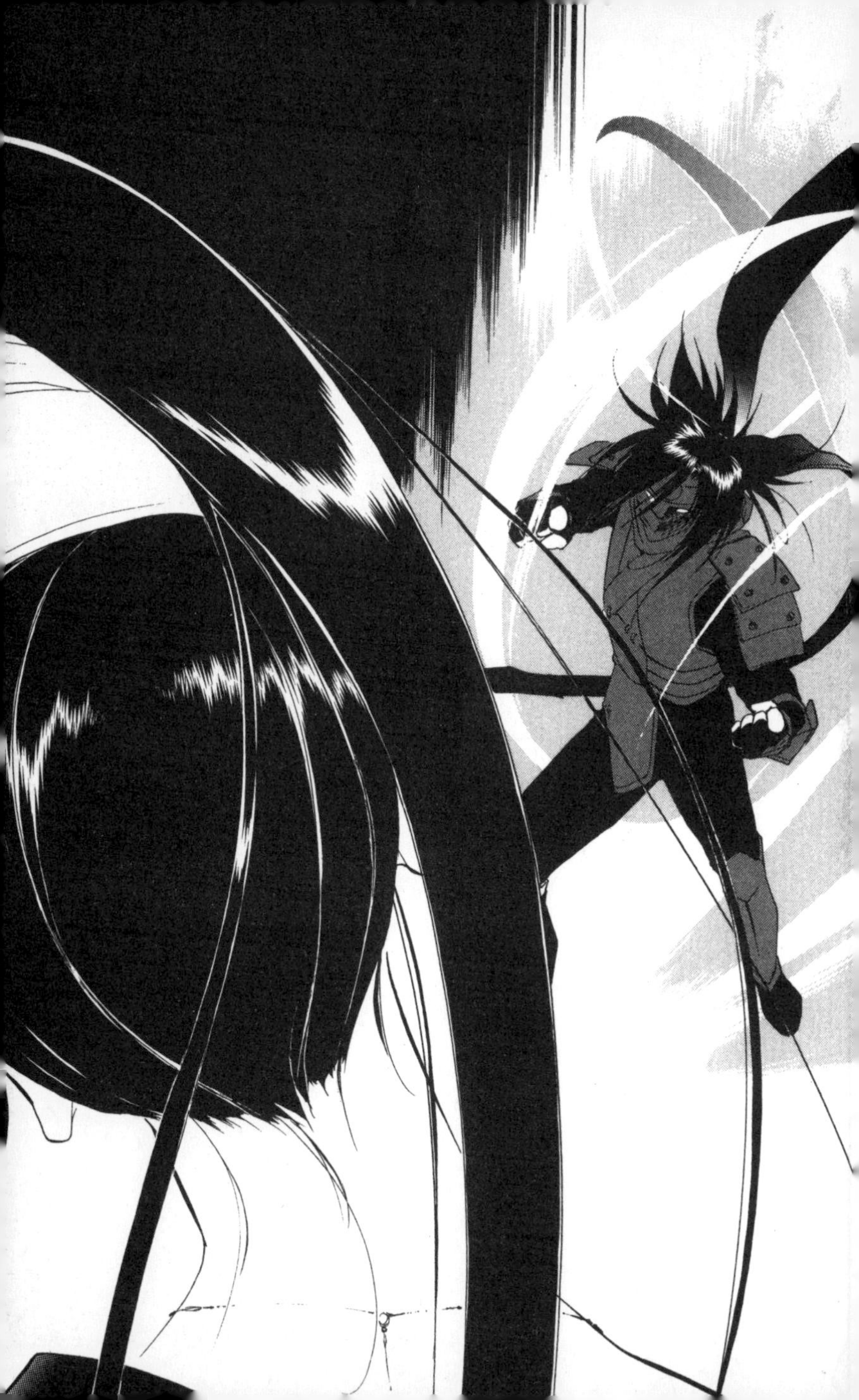

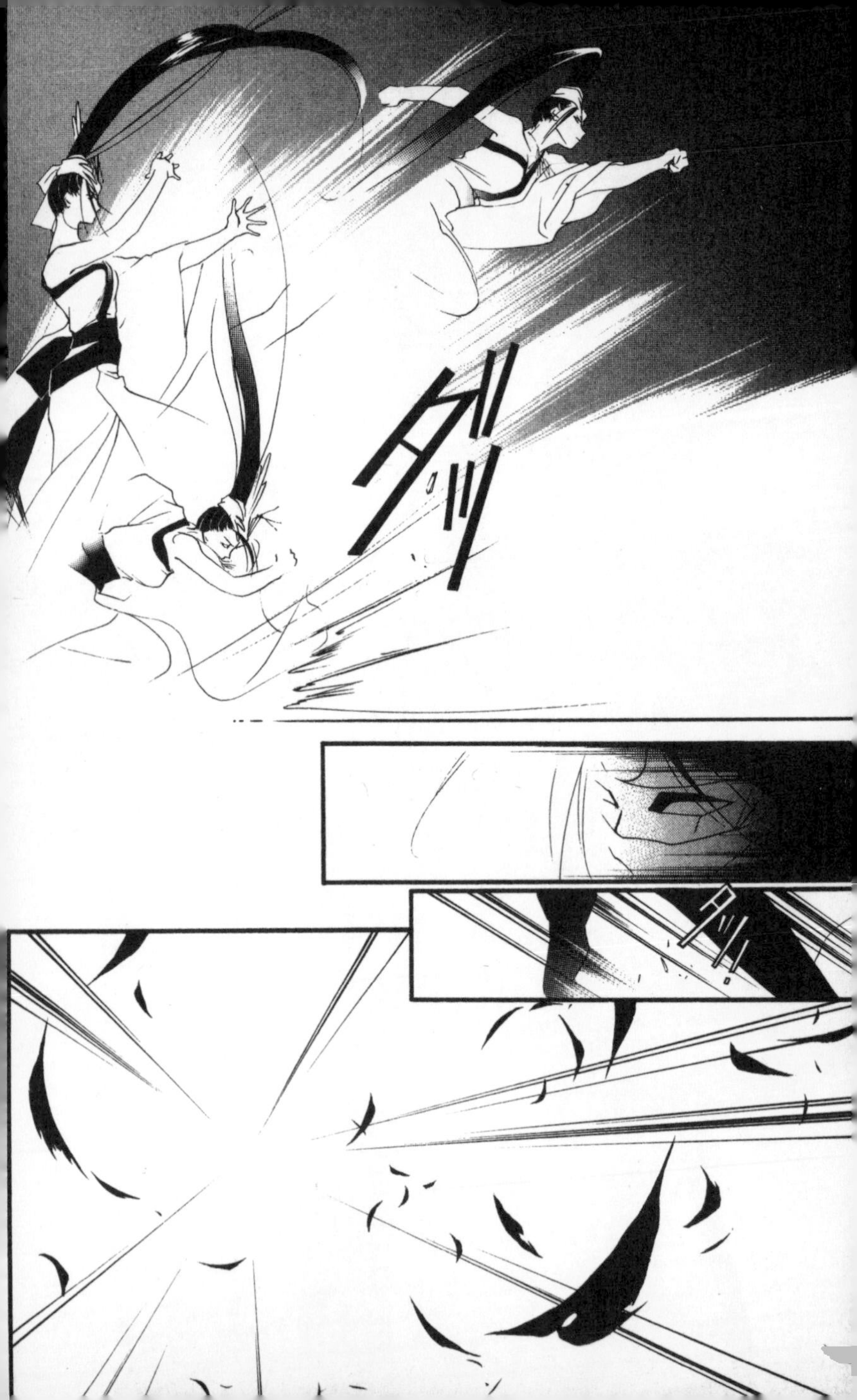
ダッ
ダッ

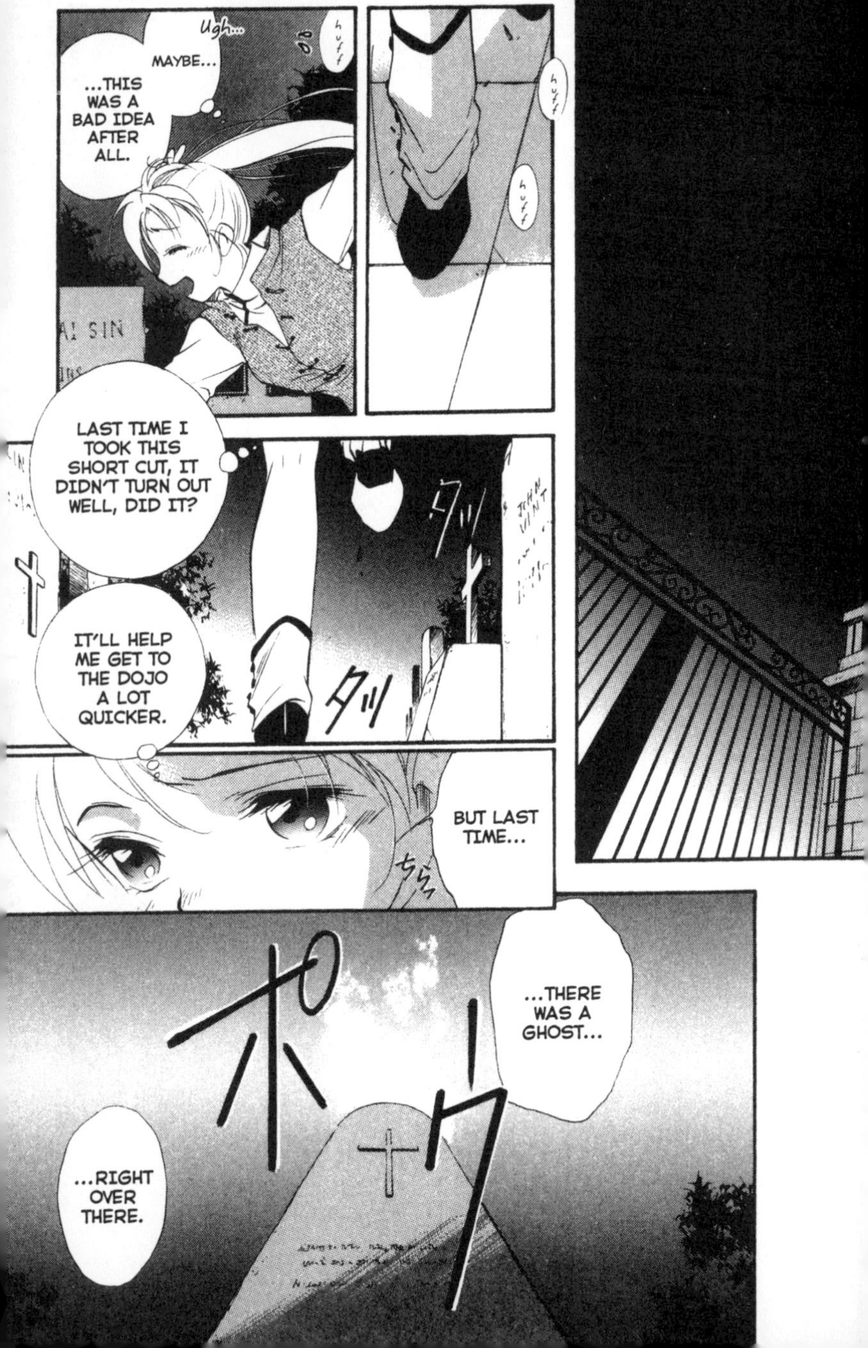
huff
huff
Ugh...
MAYBE...
...THIS WAS A BAD IDEA AFTER ALL.
LAST TIME I TOOK THIS SHORT CUT, IT DIDN'T TURN OUT WELL, DID IT?
タッ
タッ
IT'LL HELP ME GET TO THE DOJO A LOT QUICKER.
BUT LAST TIME...
...THERE WAS A GHOST...
...RIGHT OVER THERE.

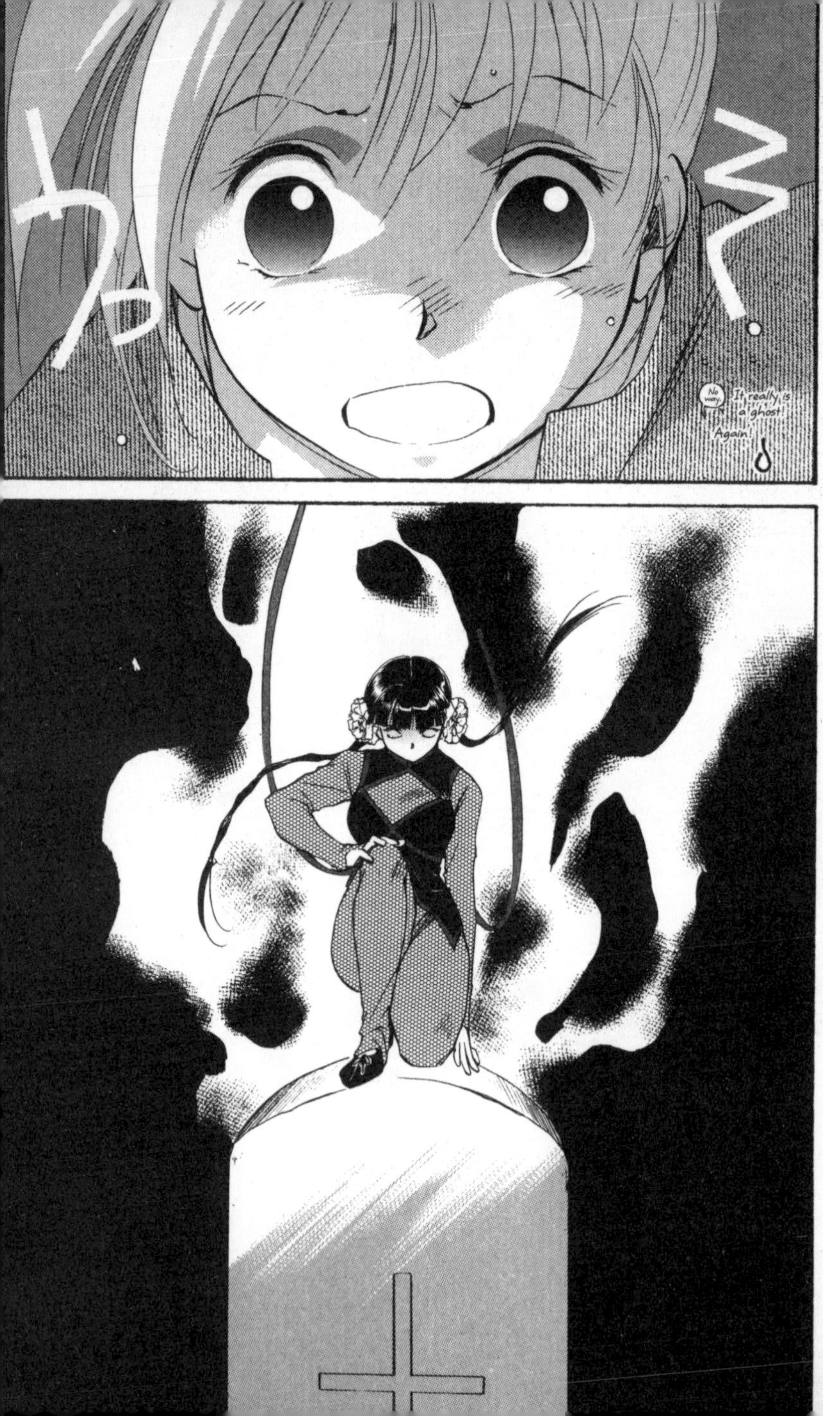
It really is a ghost!
Again!
No way.

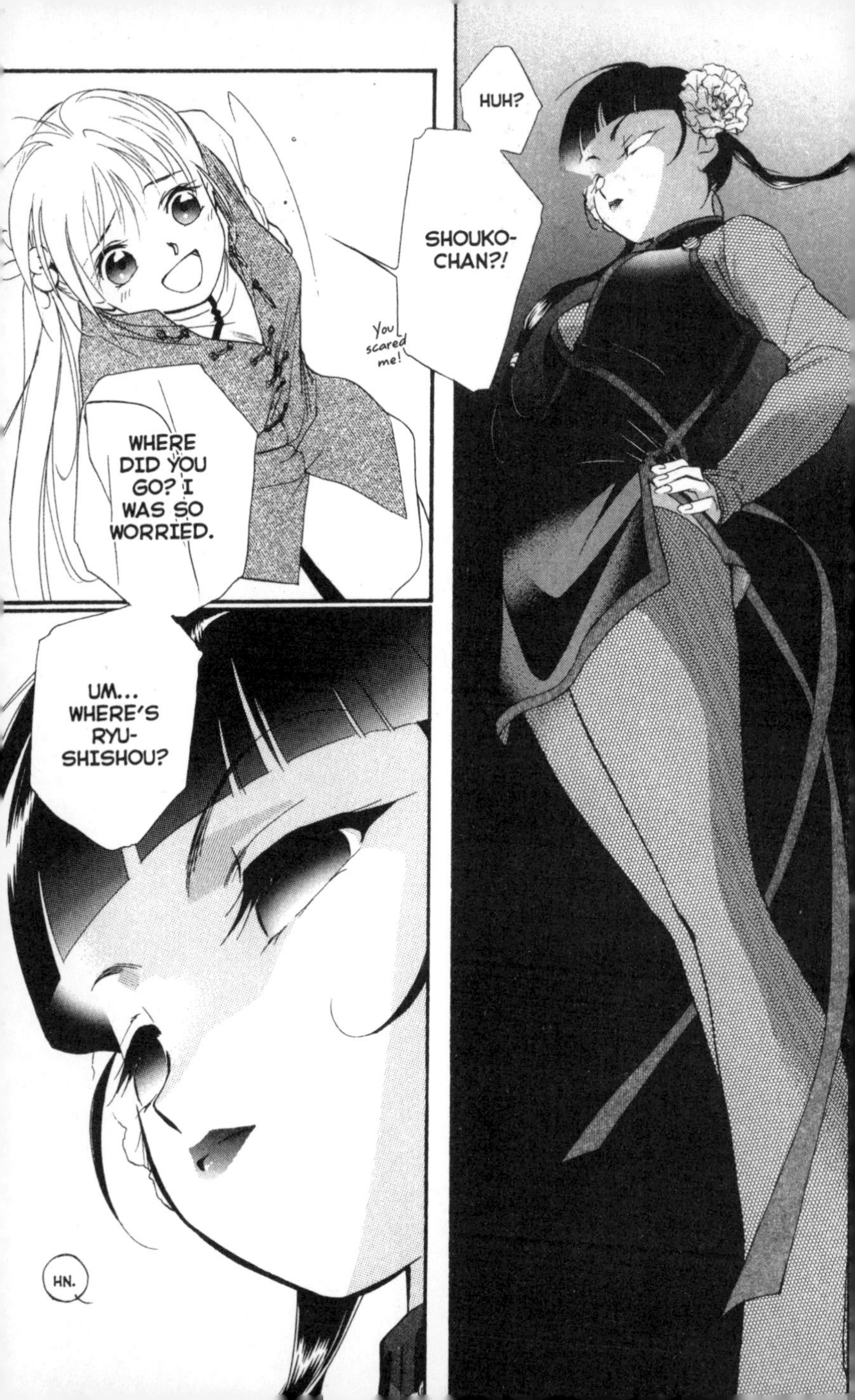
HUH?
SHOUKO-CHAN?!
You scared me!
WHERE DID YOU GO? I WAS SO WORRIED.
UM... WHERE'S RYU-SHISHOU?
HN.

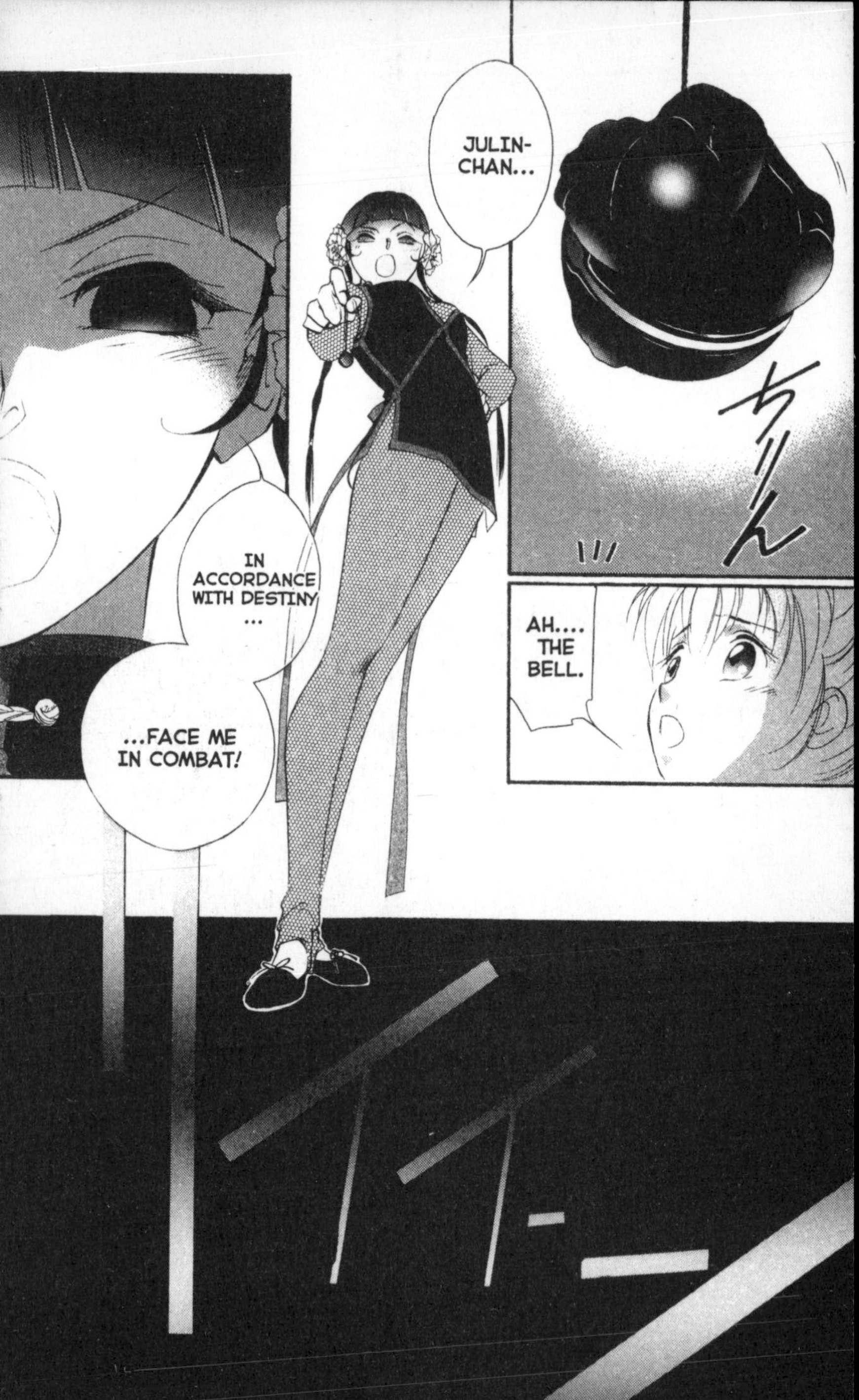
ちりん
AH.... THE BELL.
JULIN-CHAN...
IN ACCORDANCE WITH DESTINY ...
...FACE ME IN COMBAT!

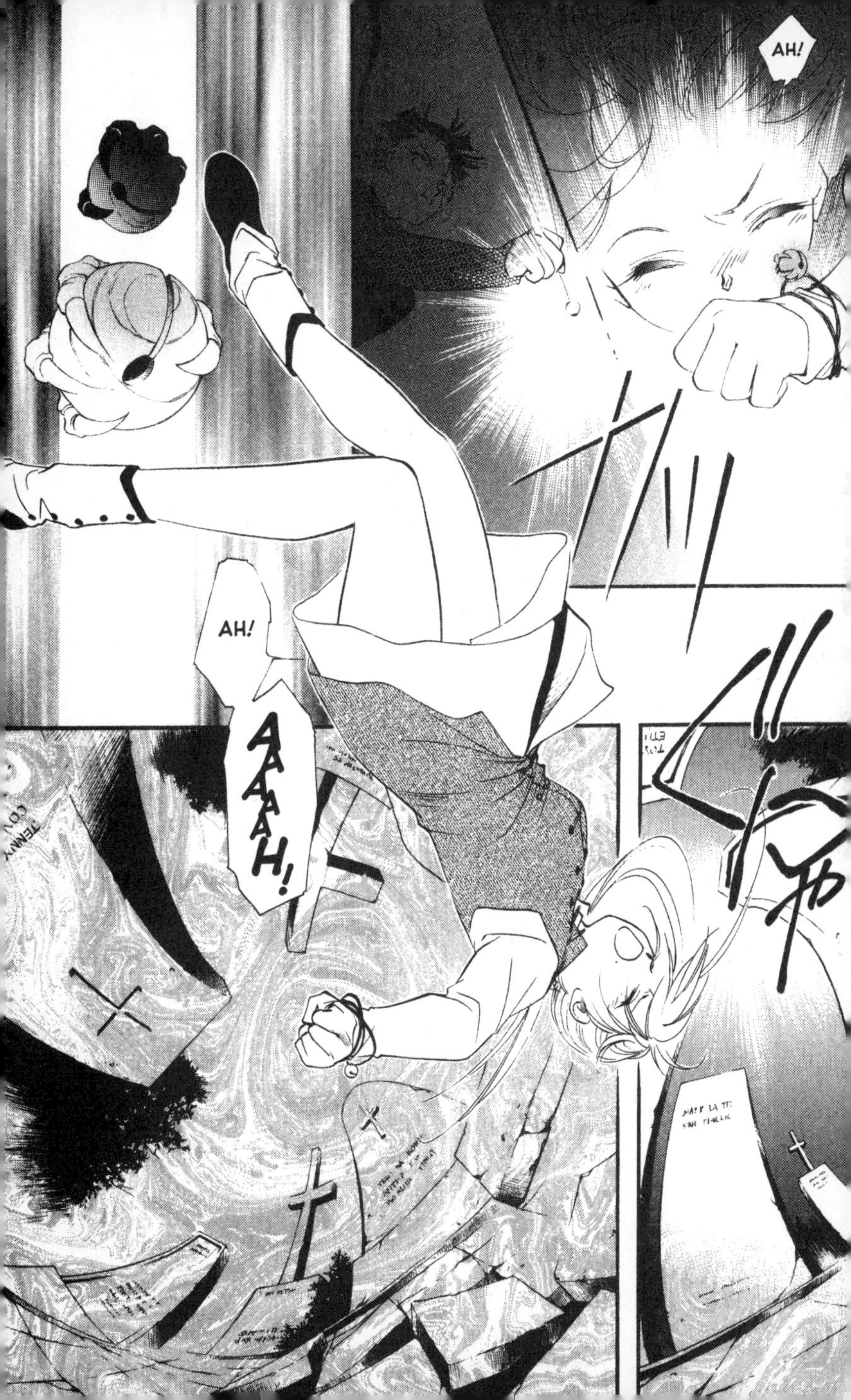
AH!
AH!
AAAAH!

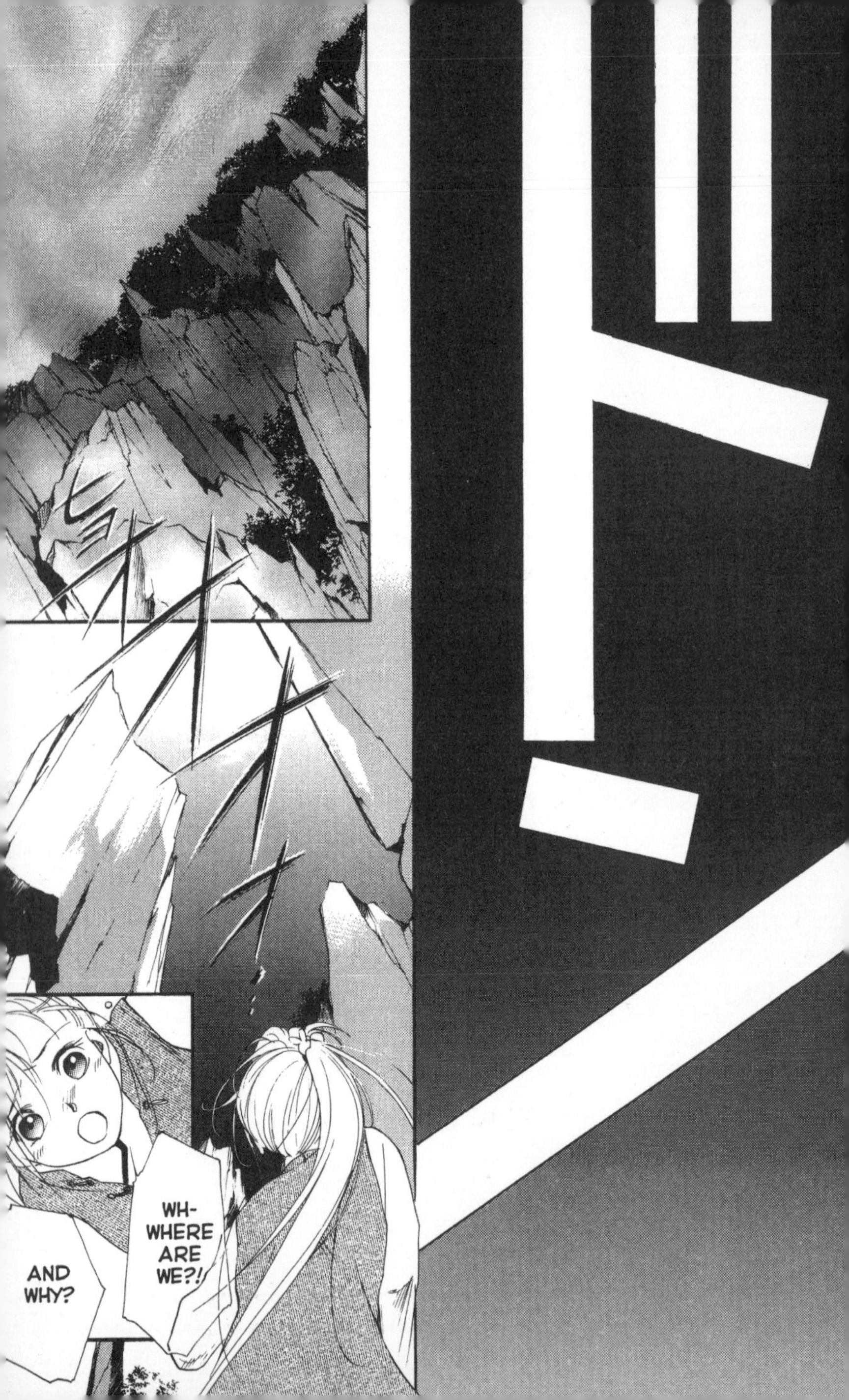
ドン
WH- WHERE ARE WE?!
AND WHY?

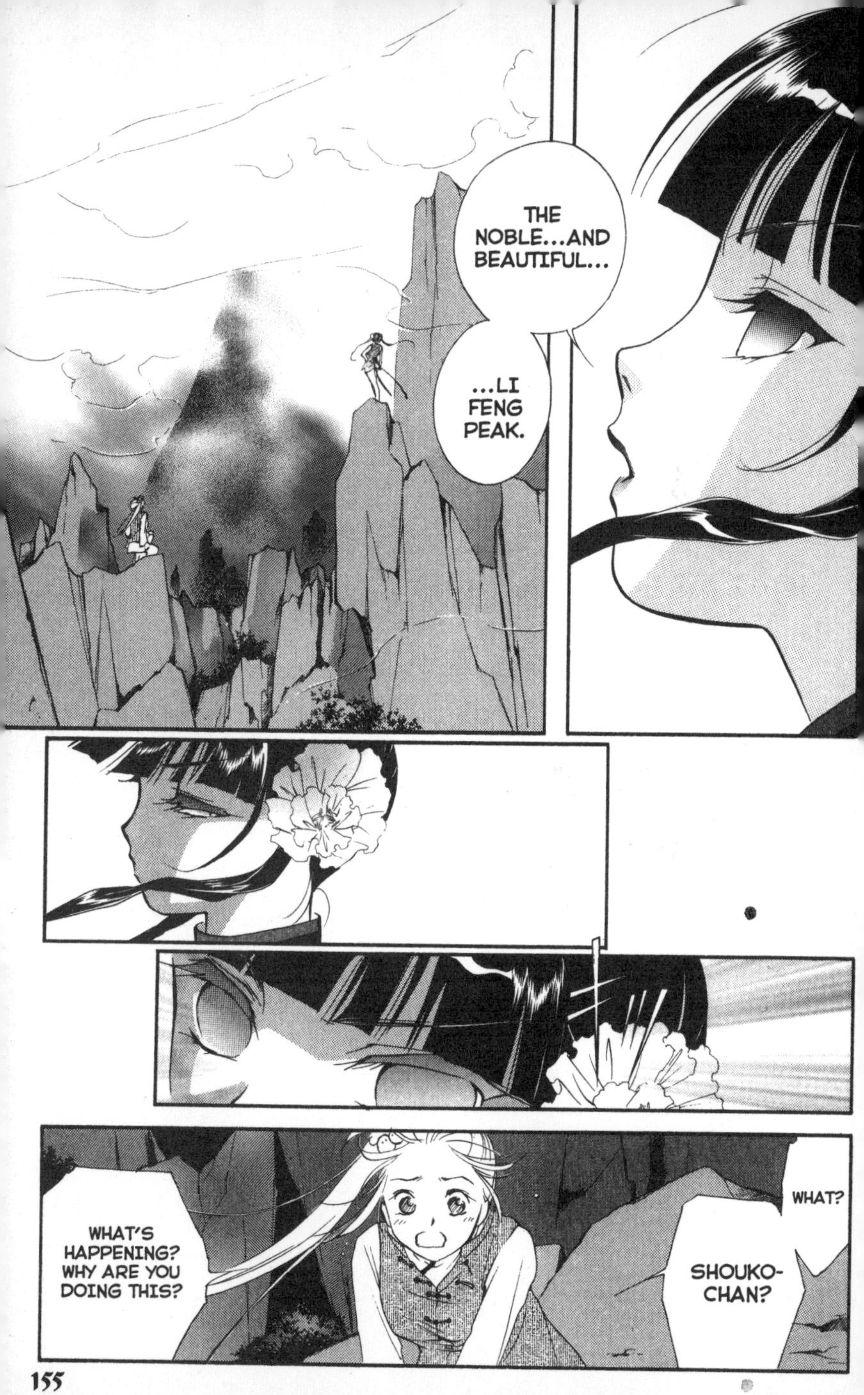
THE NOBLE...AND BEAUTIFUL...
...LI FENG PEAK.
WHAT?
SHOUKO-CHAN?
WHAT'S HAPPENING? WHY ARE YOU DOING THIS?

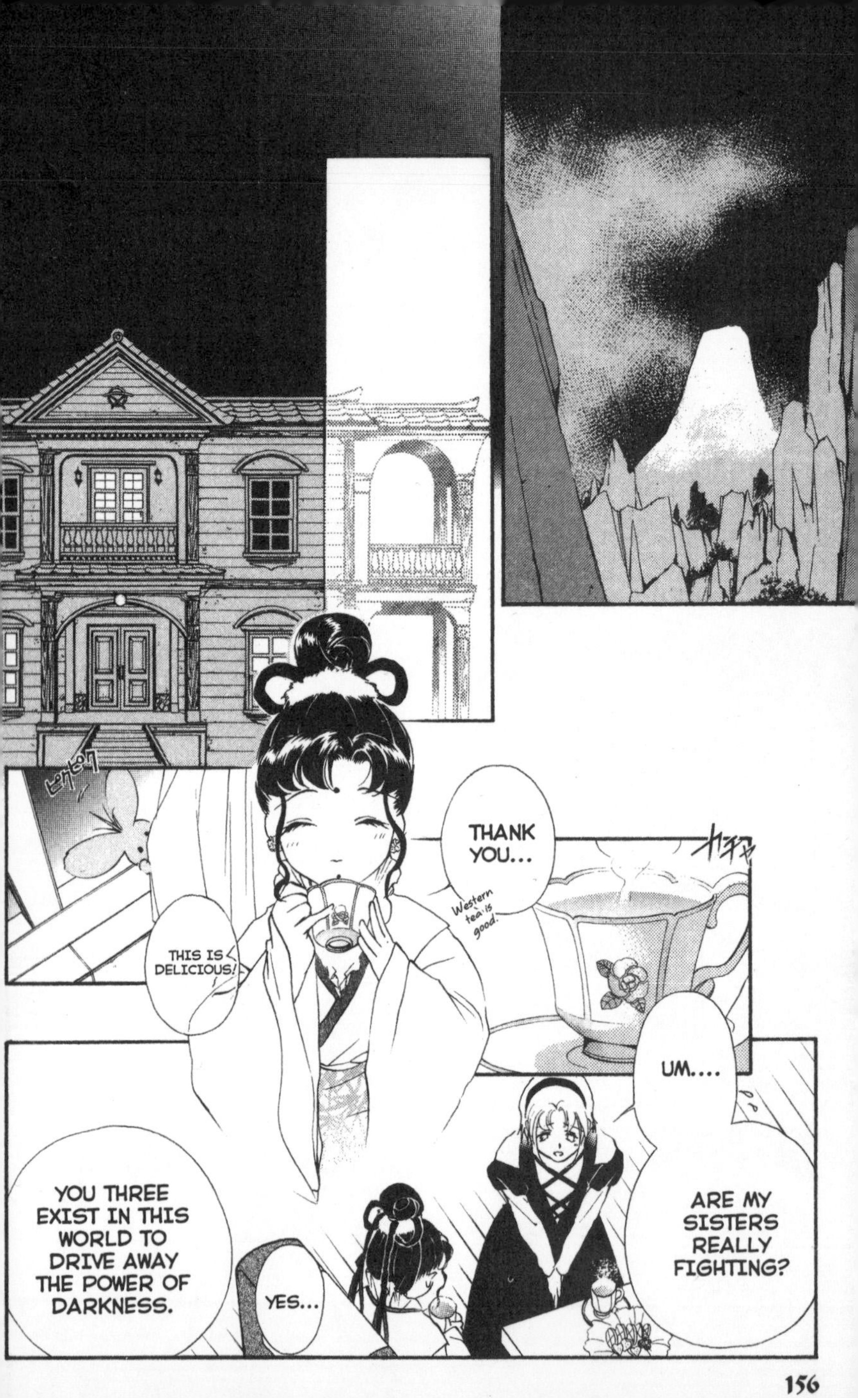
THANK YOU...
Western tea is good.
THIS IS DELICIOUS!
UM....
ARE MY SISTERS REALLY FIGHTING?
YES...
YOU THREE EXIST IN THIS WORLD TO DRIVE AWAY THE POWER OF DARKNESS.

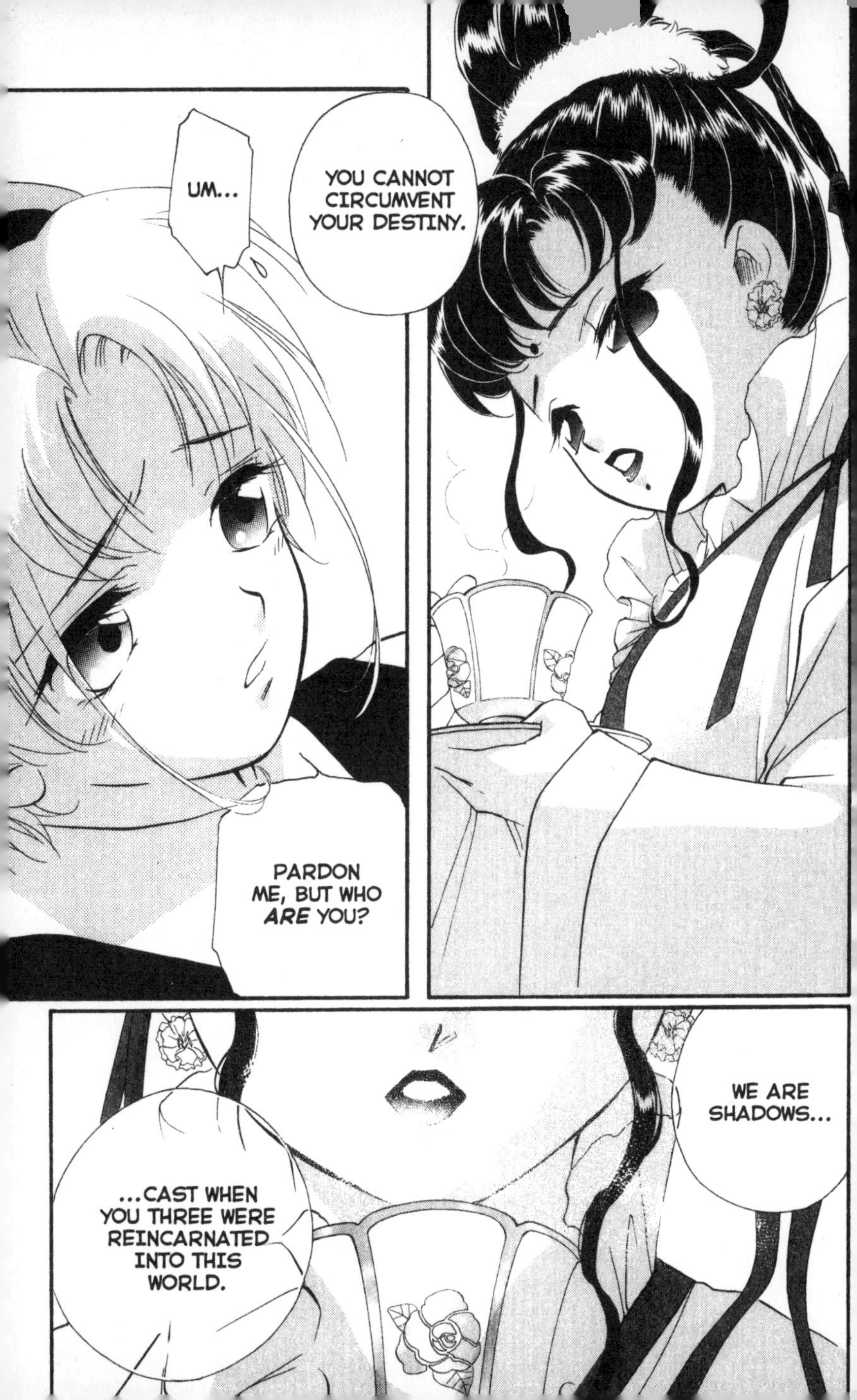
YOU CANNOT CIRCUMVENT YOUR DESTINY.
UM...
PARDON ME, BUT WHO *ARE* YOU?
WE ARE SHADOWS...
...CAST WHEN YOU THREE WERE REINCARNATED INTO THIS WORLD.

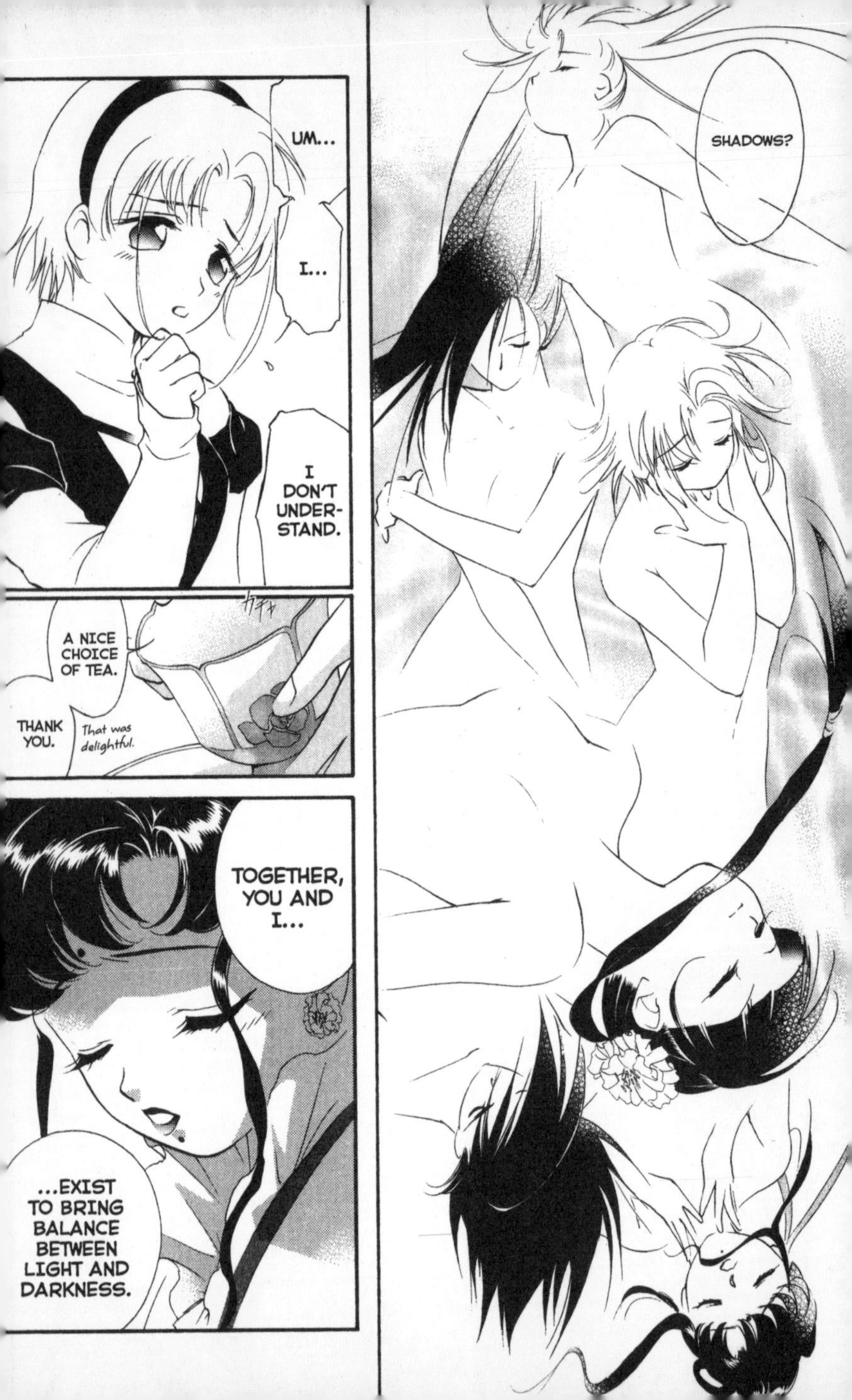
SHADOWS?
UM...
I...
I DON'T UNDERSTAND.
A NICE CHOICE OF TEA.
That was delightful.
THANK YOU.
TOGETHER, YOU AND I...
...EXIST TO BRING BALANCE BETWEEN LIGHT AND DARKNESS.

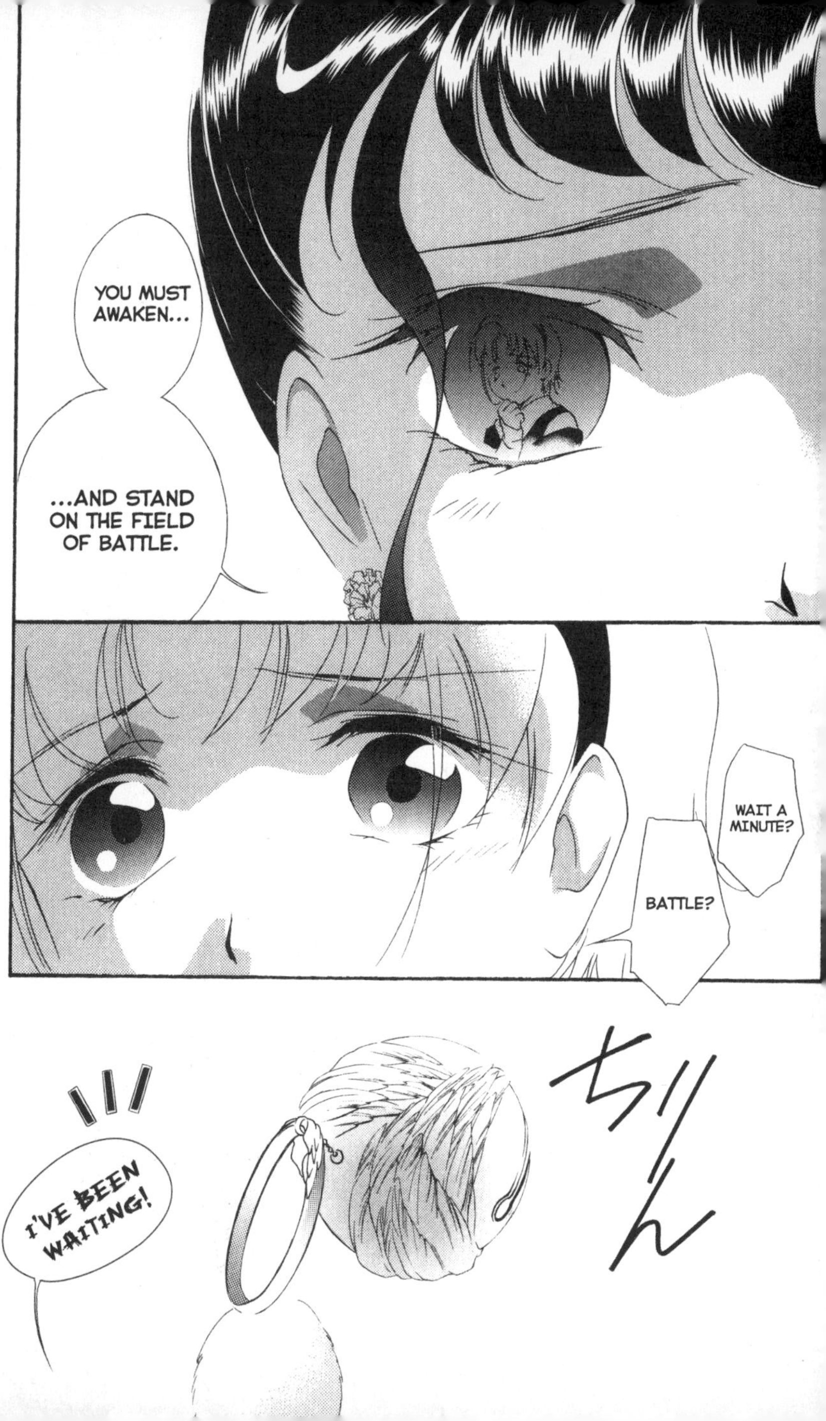
YOU MUST AWAKEN...
...AND STAND ON THE FIELD OF BATTLE.
WAIT A MINUTE?
BATTLE?
ちりん
I'VE BEEN WAITING!

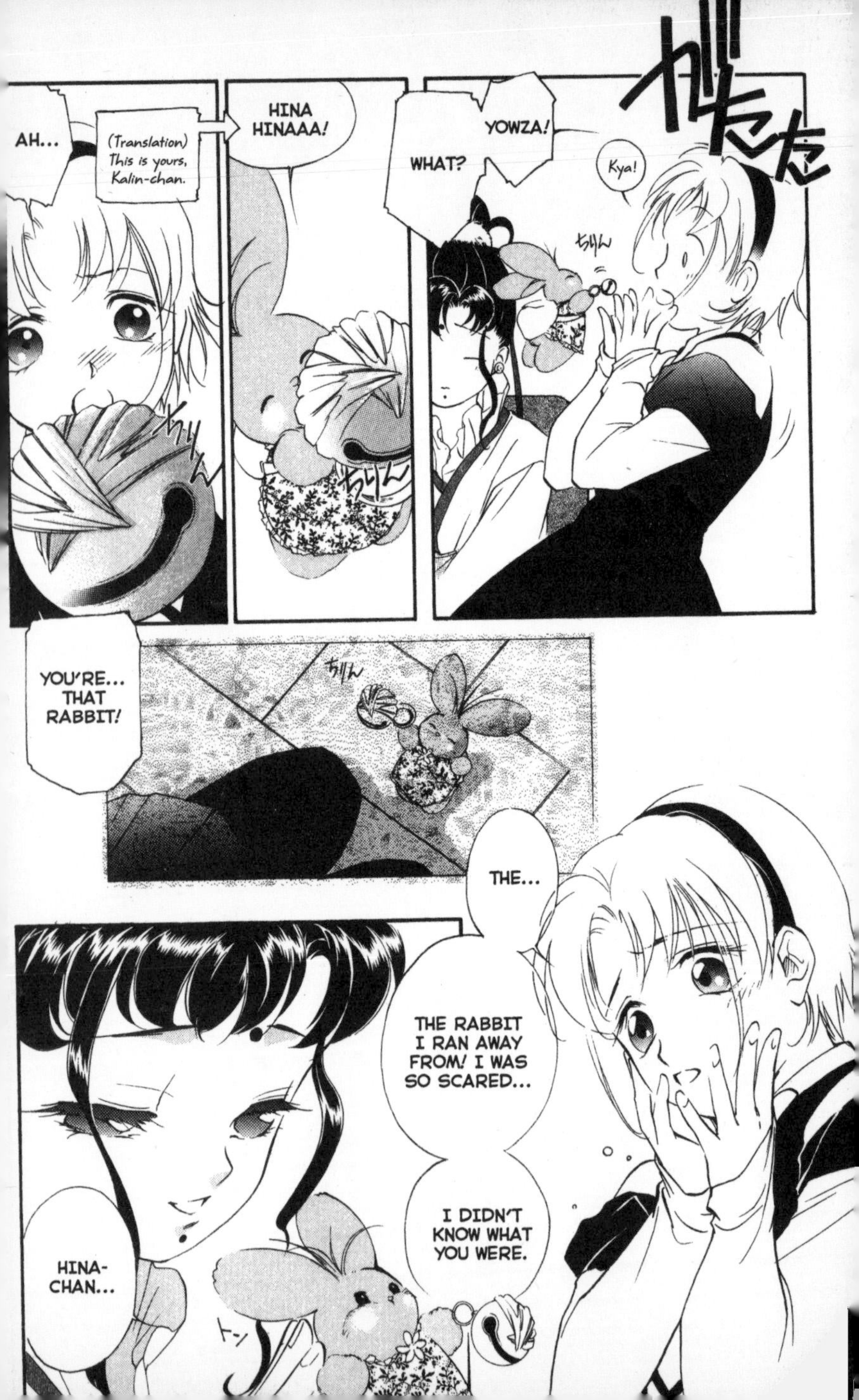
がたた
Kya!
ちりん
YOWZA!
WHAT?
HINA HINAAA!
ちりん
(Translation) This is yours, Kalin-chan.
AH...
ちりん
YOU'RE... THAT RABBIT!
ちりん
THE...
THE RABBIT I RAN AWAY FROM! I WAS SO SCARED...
I DIDN'T KNOW WHAT YOU WERE.
HINA-CHAN...
トン

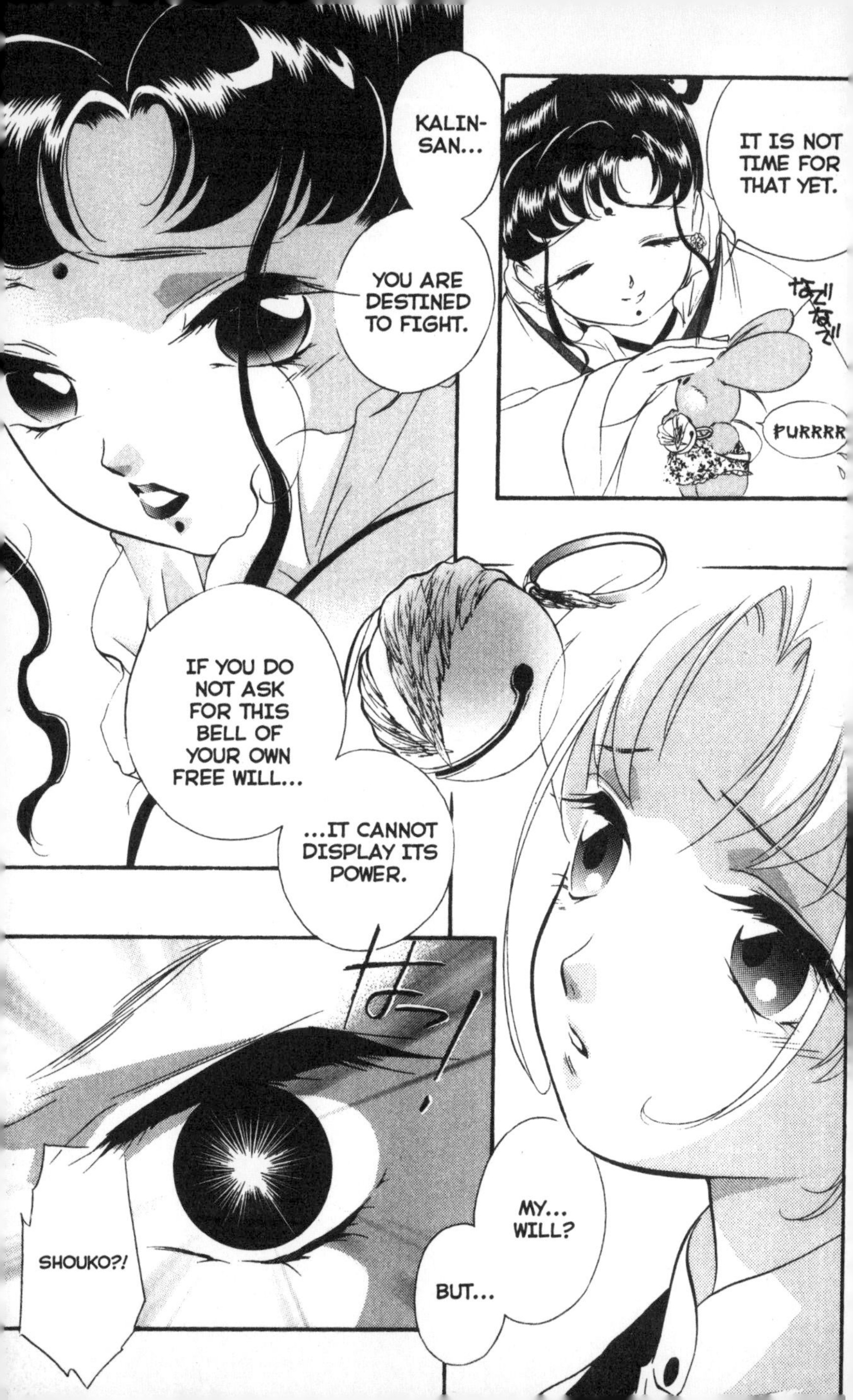

IT IS NOT TIME FOR THAT YET.
なで!! なで!!
PURRRR
KALIN-SAN...
YOU ARE DESTINED TO FIGHT.
IF YOU DO NOT ASK FOR THIS BELL OF YOUR OWN FREE WILL...
...IT CANNOT DISPLAY ITS POWER.
MY... WILL?
BUT...
はっ!
SHOUKO?!

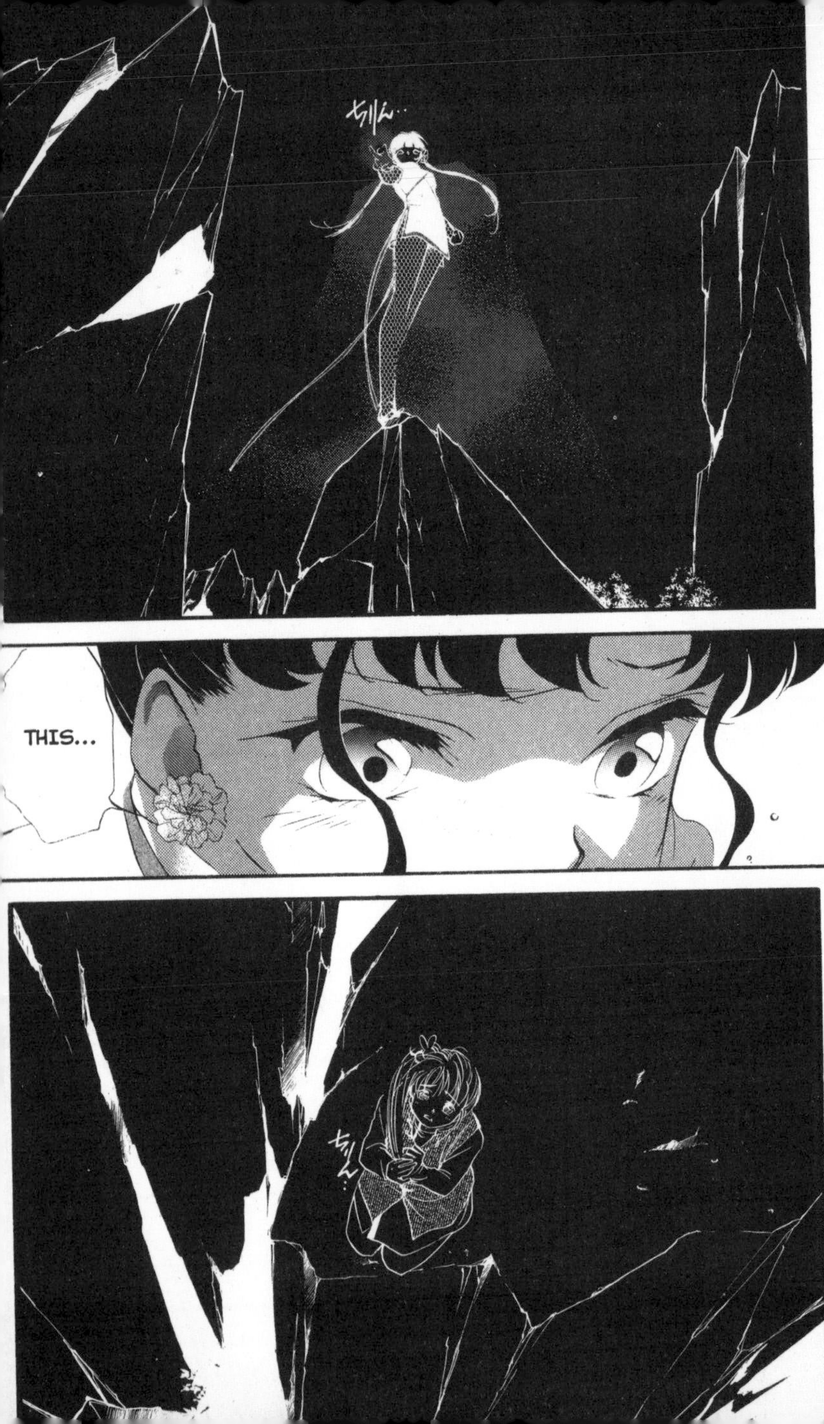
ちりん…
THIS...
ちりん…

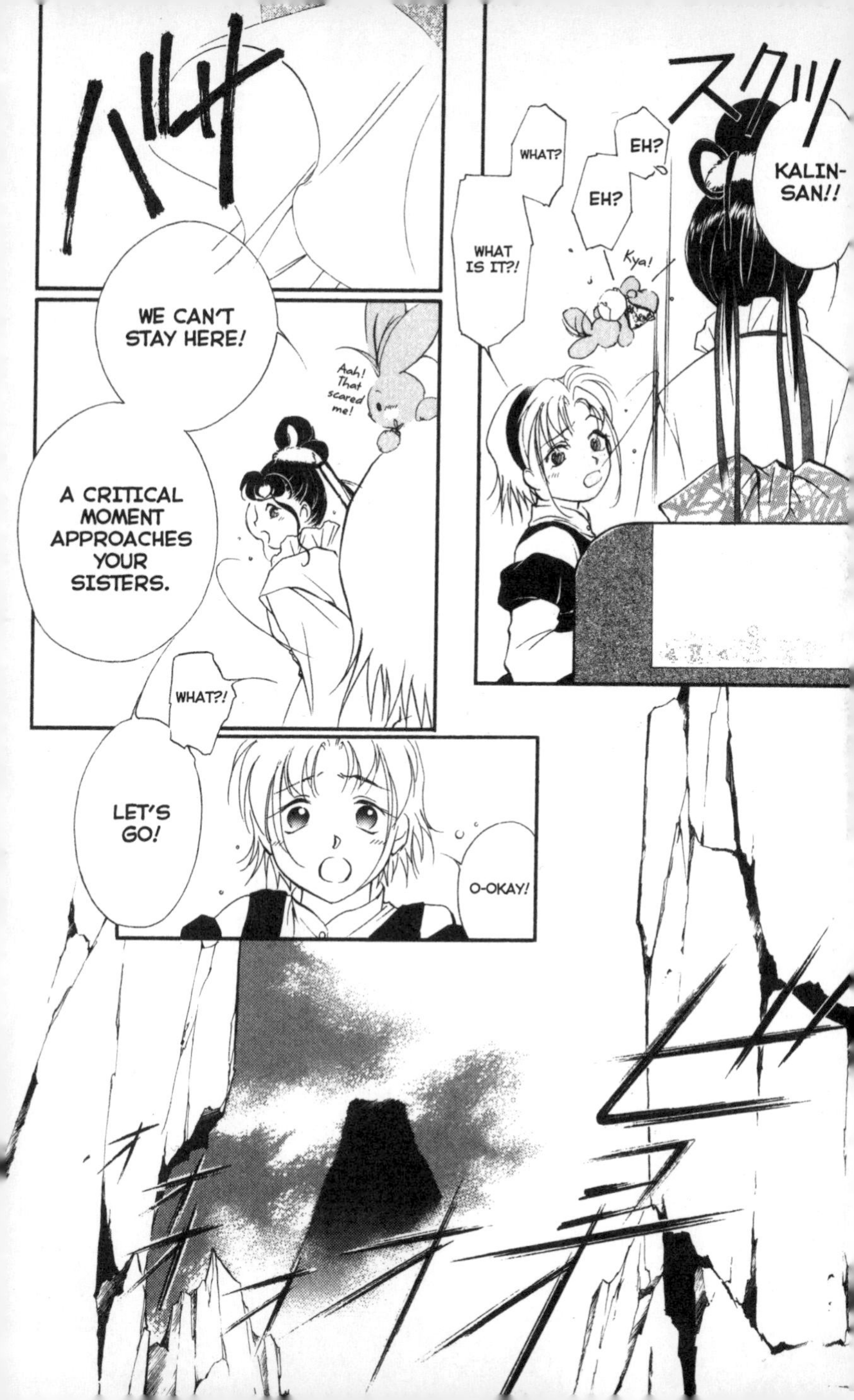
KALIN-SAN!!
EH?
EH?
Kya!
WHAT?
WHAT IS IT?!
WE CAN'T STAY HERE!
A CRITICAL MOMENT APPROACHES YOUR SISTERS.
Aah! That scared me!
WHAT?!
LET'S GO!
O-OKAY!

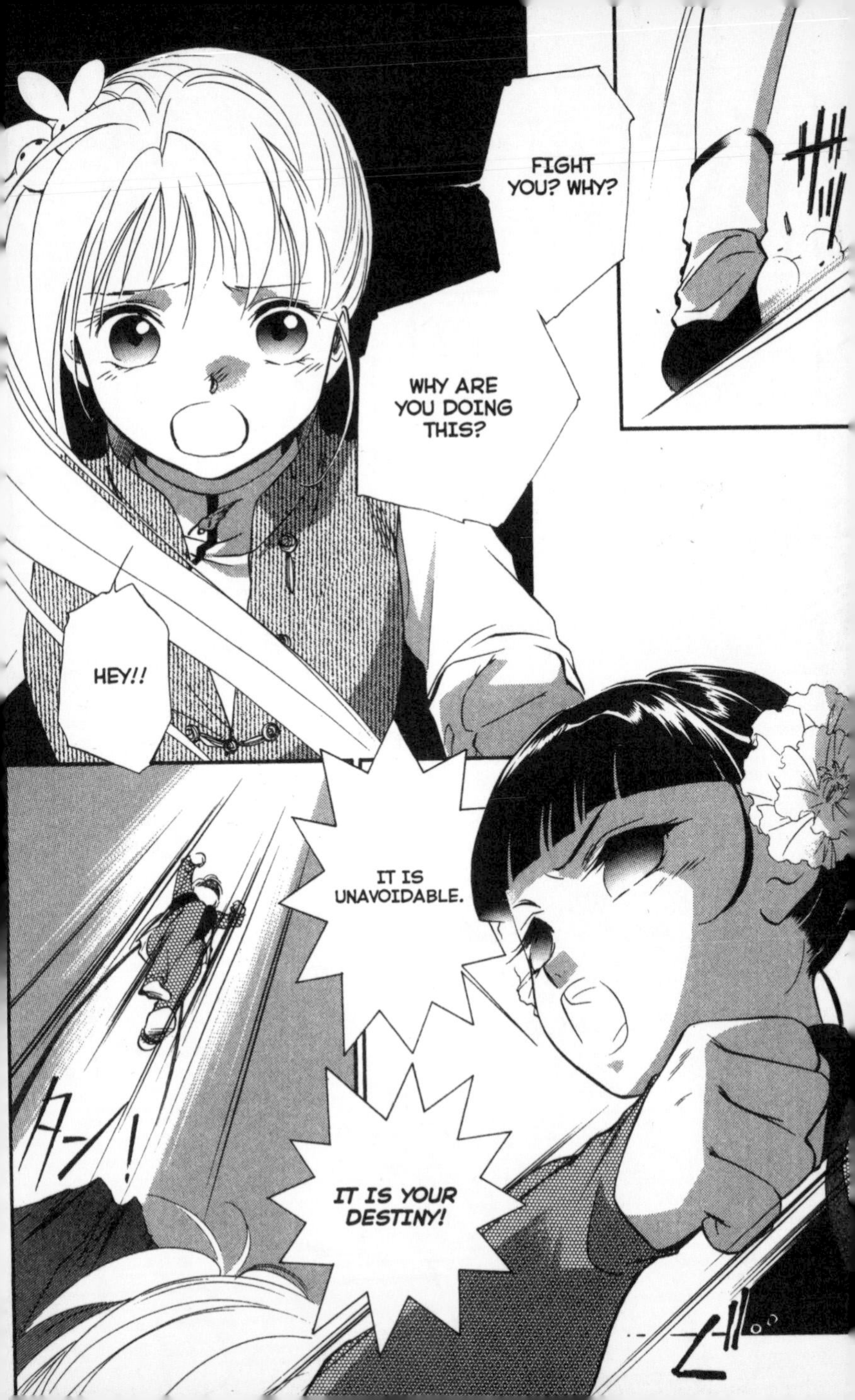
FIGHT YOU? WHY?
WHY ARE YOU DOING THIS?
HEY!!
IT IS UNAVOIDABLE.
IT IS YOUR DESTINY!

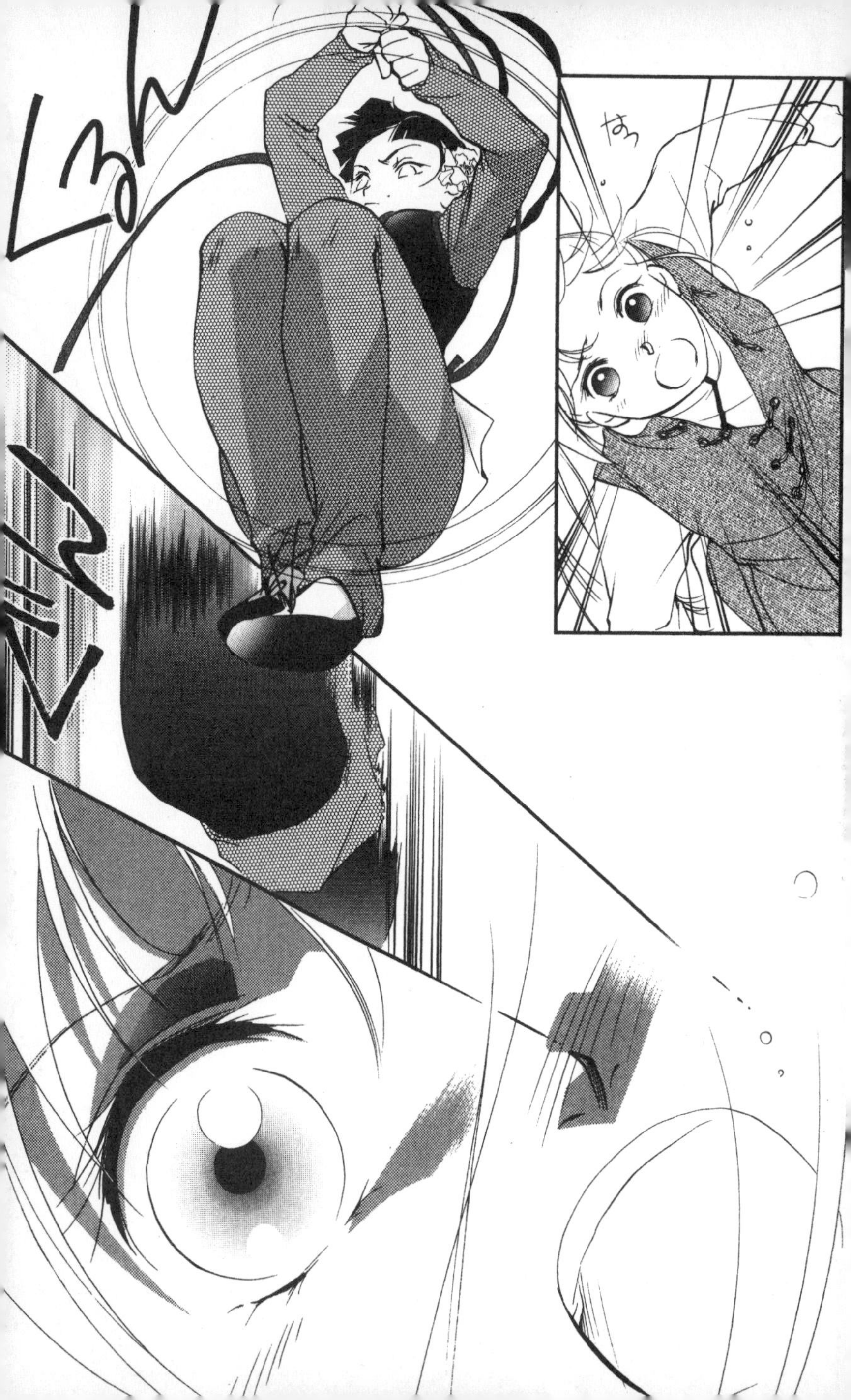
はっ
くるん

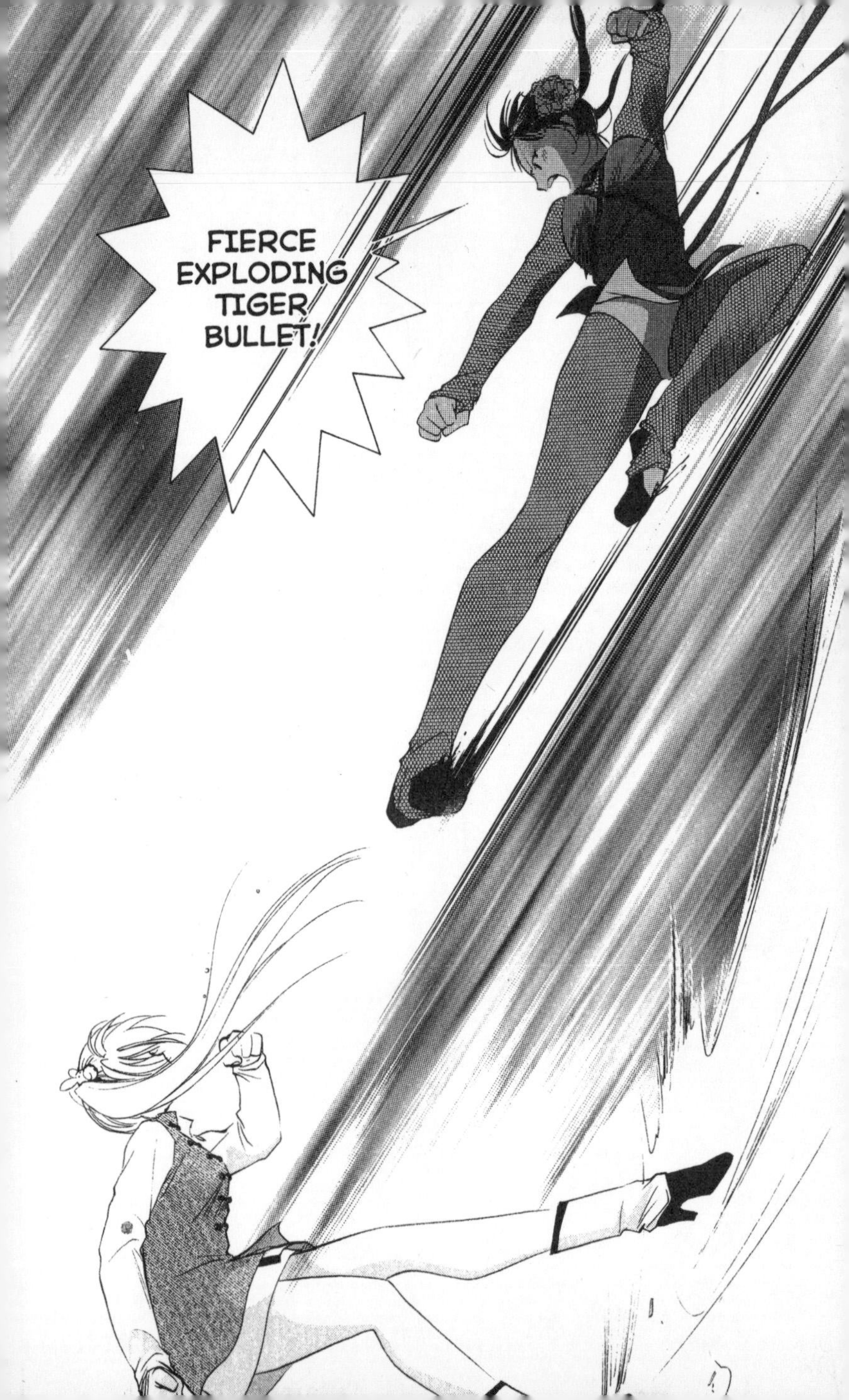
FIERCE EXPLODING TIGER BULLET!

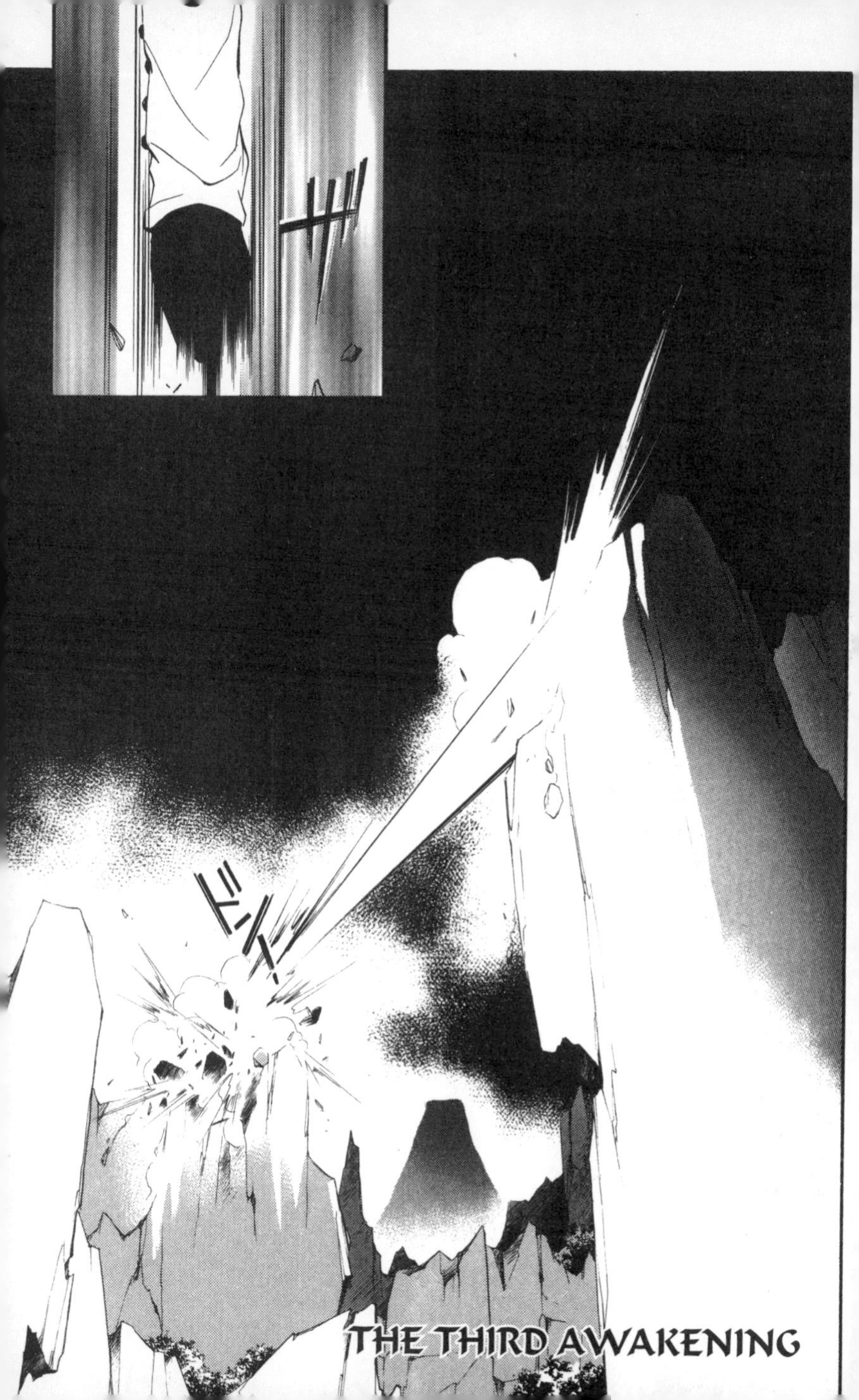

THE THIRD AWAKENING

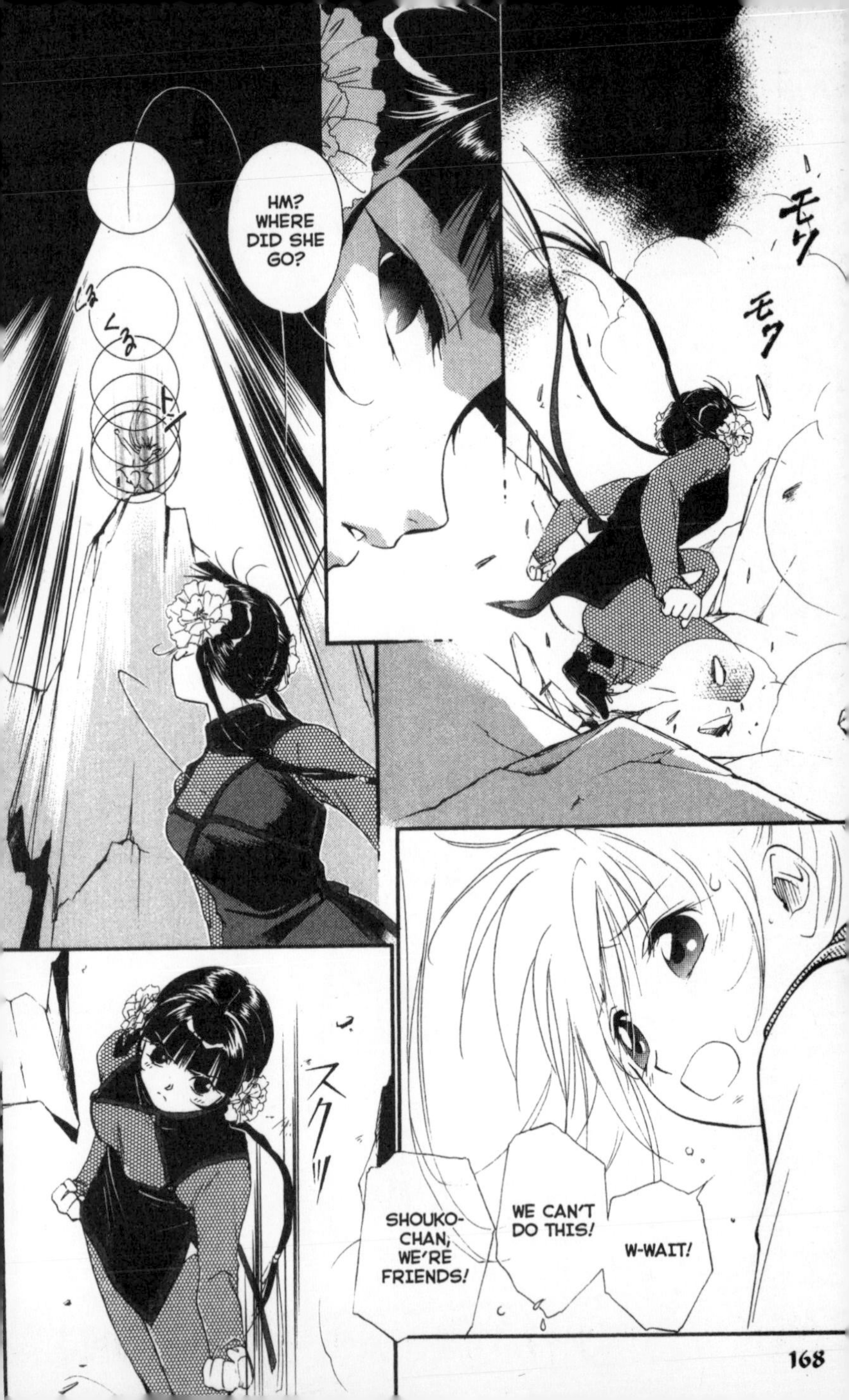
モク
モク
HM? WHERE DID SHE GO?
くるくる
W-WAIT!
WE CAN'T DO THIS!
SHOUKO-CHAN, WE'RE FRIENDS!
スク

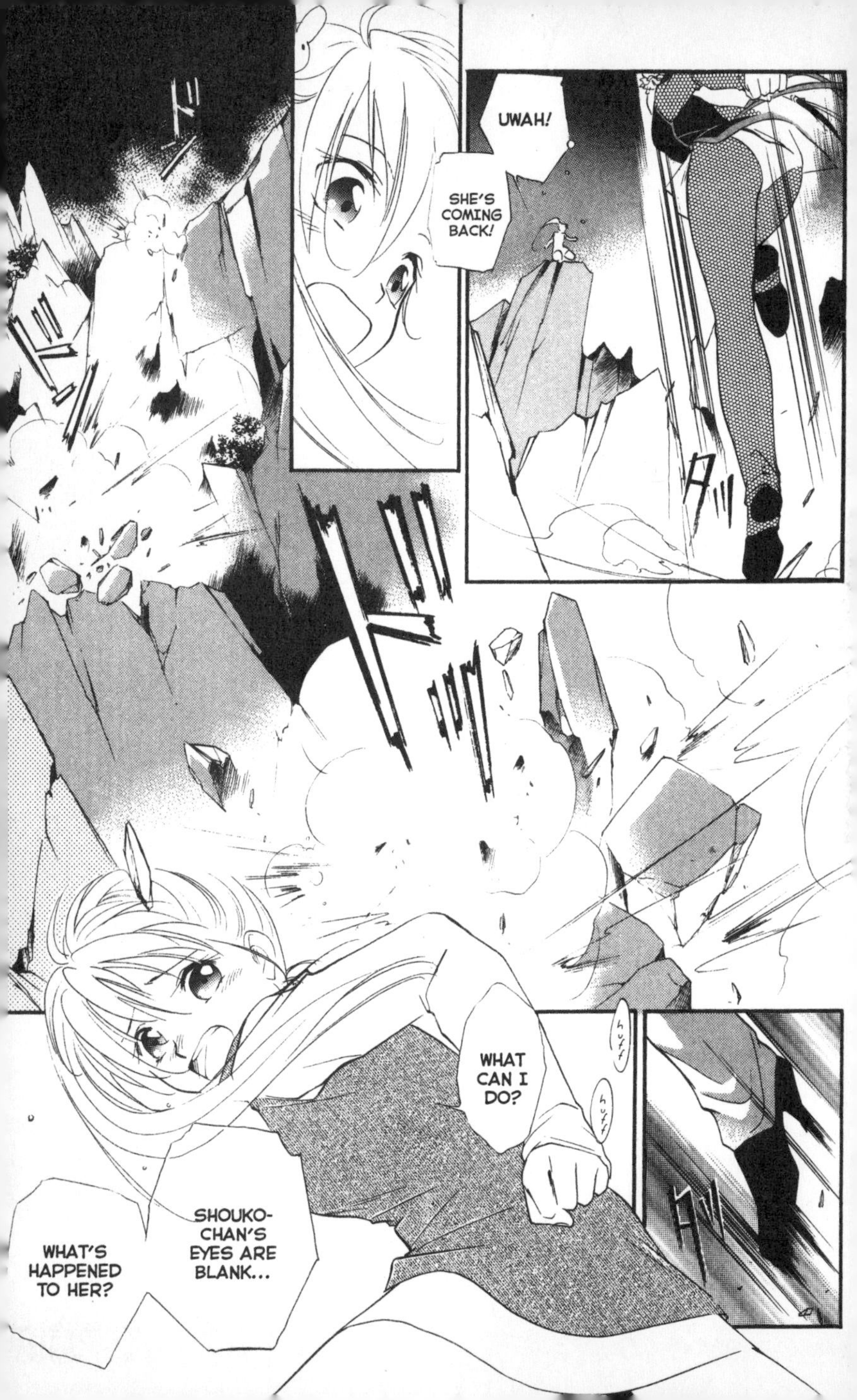
UWAH!
SHE'S COMING BACK!
huff
huff
WHAT CAN I DO?
SHOUKO-CHAN'S EYES ARE BLANK...
WHAT'S HAPPENED TO HER?

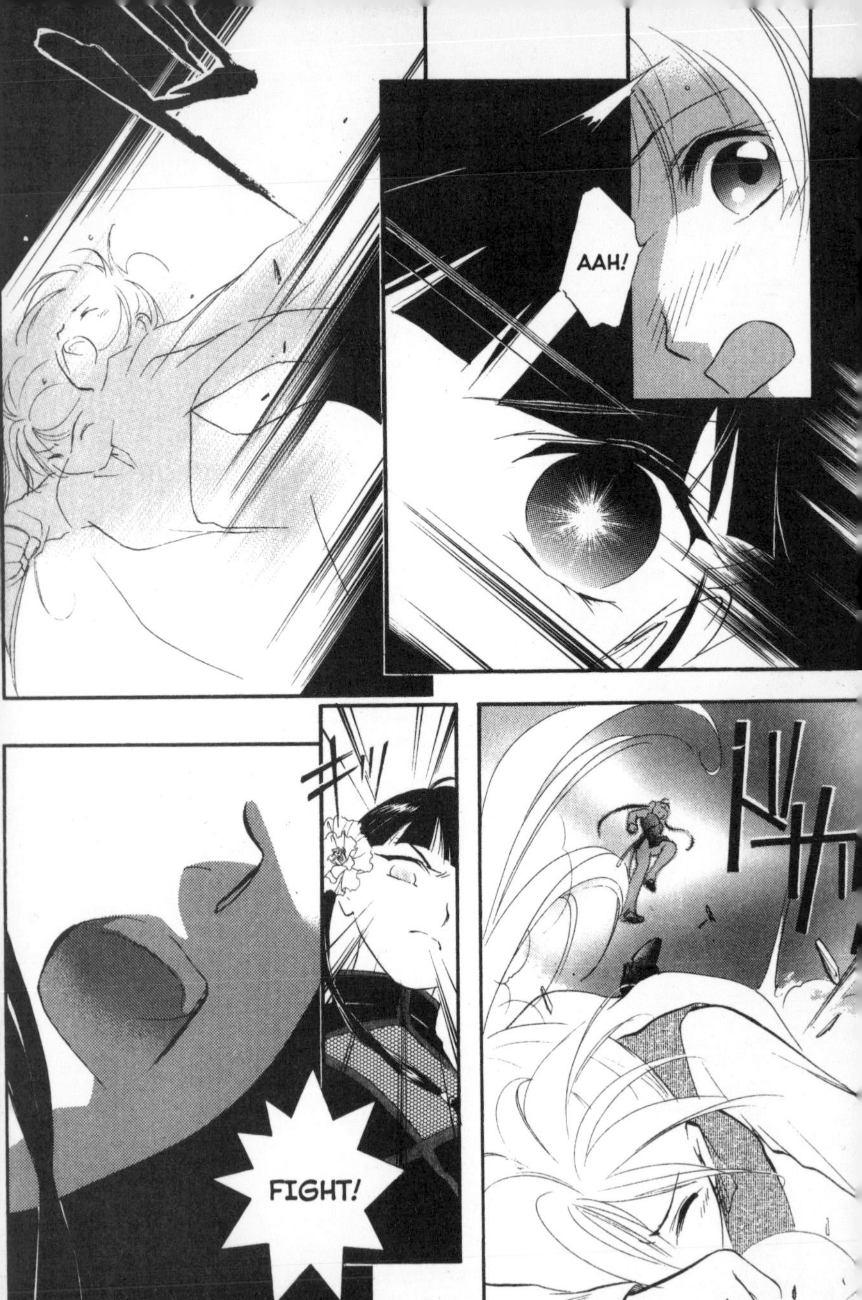
AAH!
FIGHT!

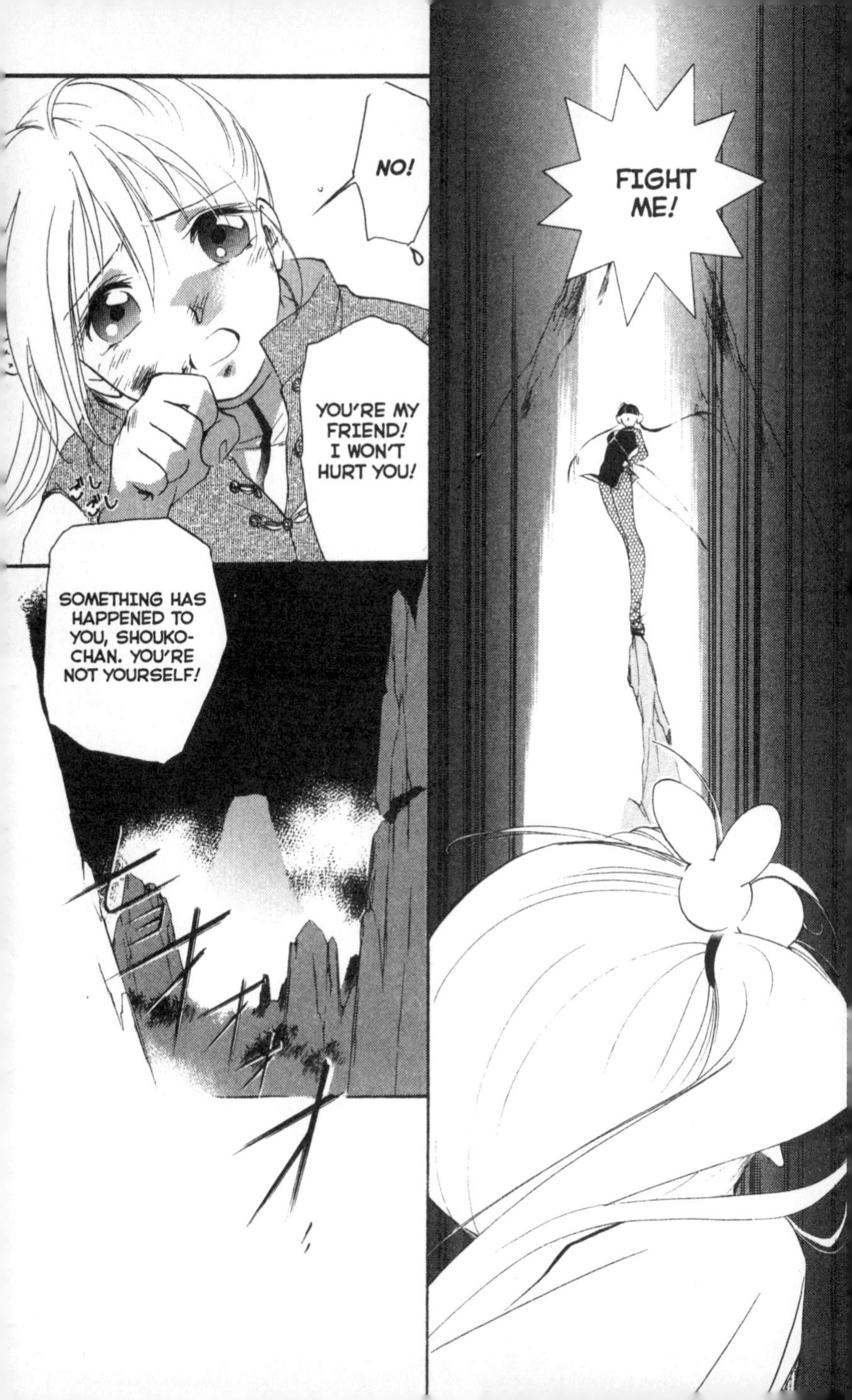
FIGHT ME!
NO!
YOU'RE MY FRIEND! I WON'T HURT YOU!
SOMETHING HAS HAPPENED TO YOU, SHOUKO-CHAN. YOU'RE NOT YOURSELF!

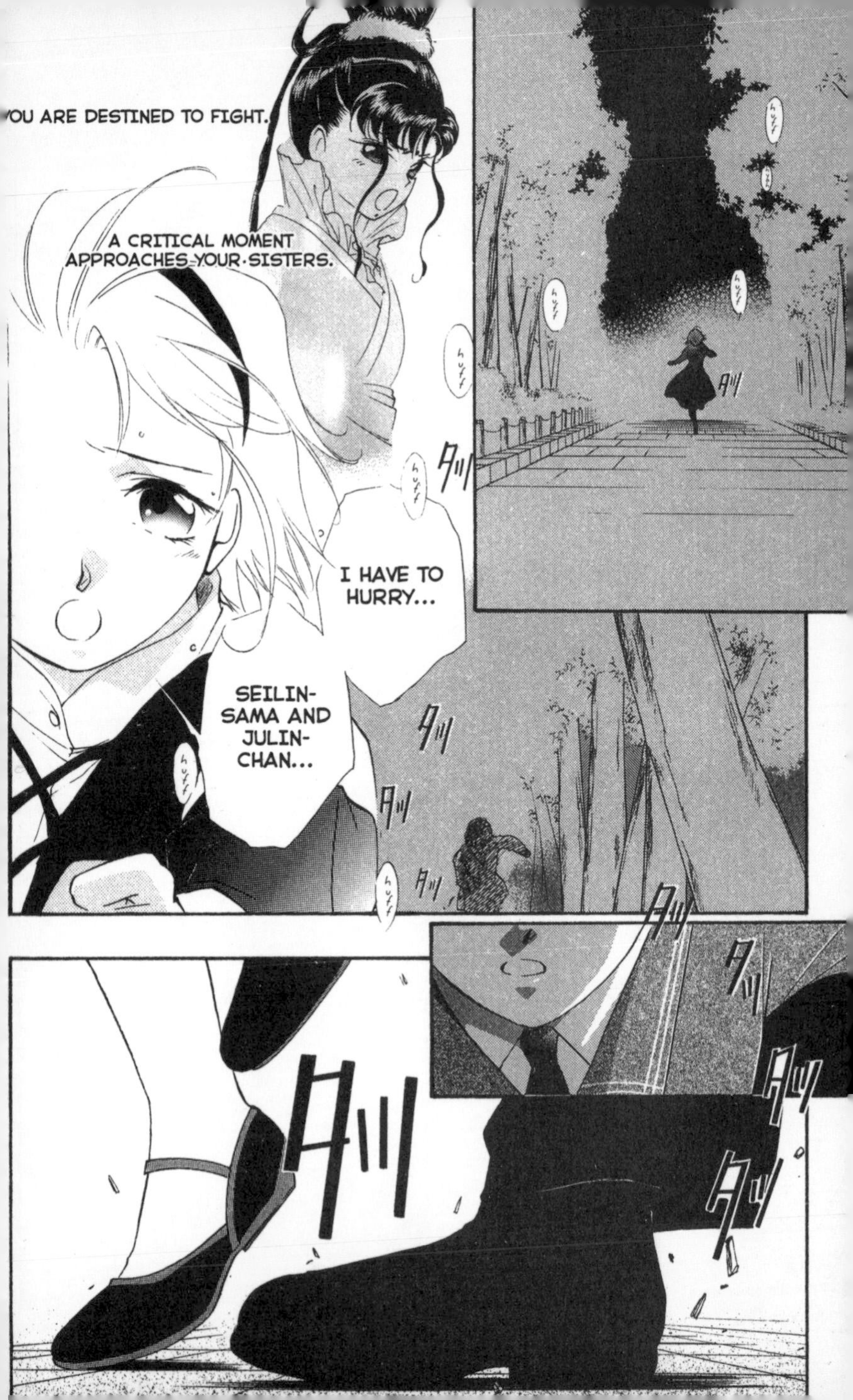
YOU ARE DESTINED TO FIGHT.
A CRITICAL MOMENT APPROACHES YOUR SISTERS.
I HAVE TO HURRY...
SEILIN-SAMA AND JULIN-CHAN...

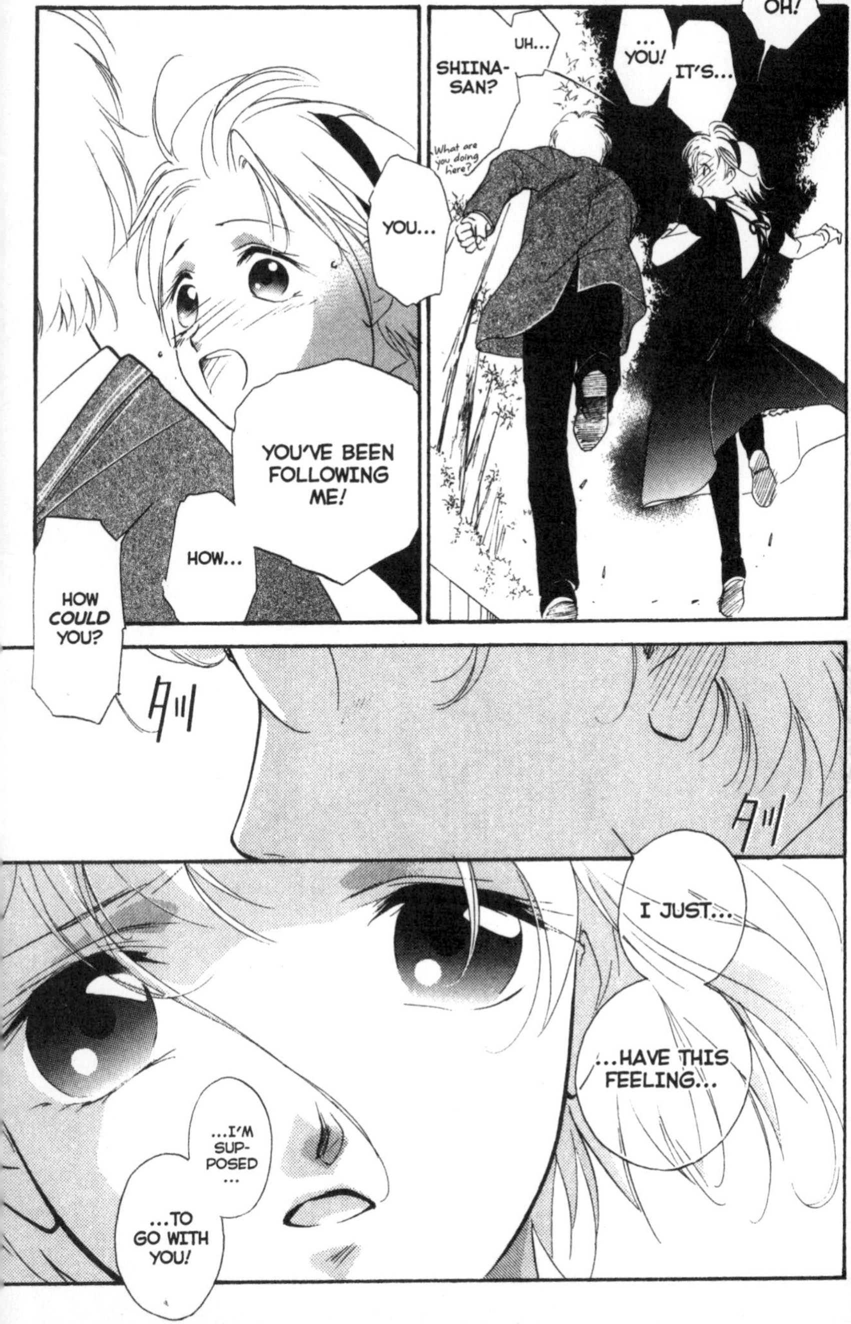
OH!
IT'S...
...YOU!
UH...
SHIINA-SAN?
What are you doing here?
YOU...
YOU'VE BEEN FOLLOWING ME!
HOW...
HOW COULD YOU?
I JUST...
...HAVE THIS FEELING...
...I'M SUPPOSED...
...TO GO WITH YOU!

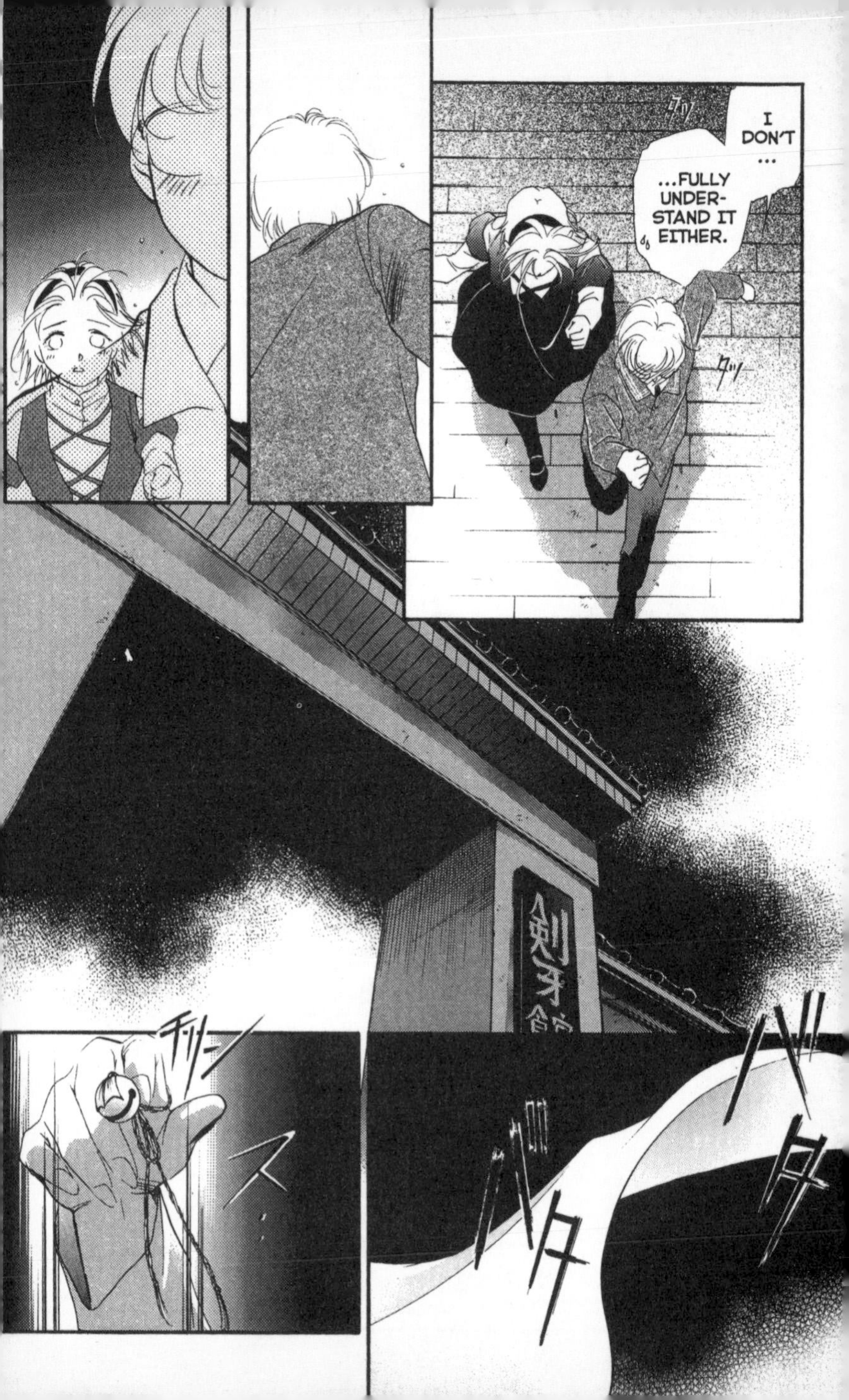
I DON'T ...
...FULLY UNDER-STAND IT EITHER.

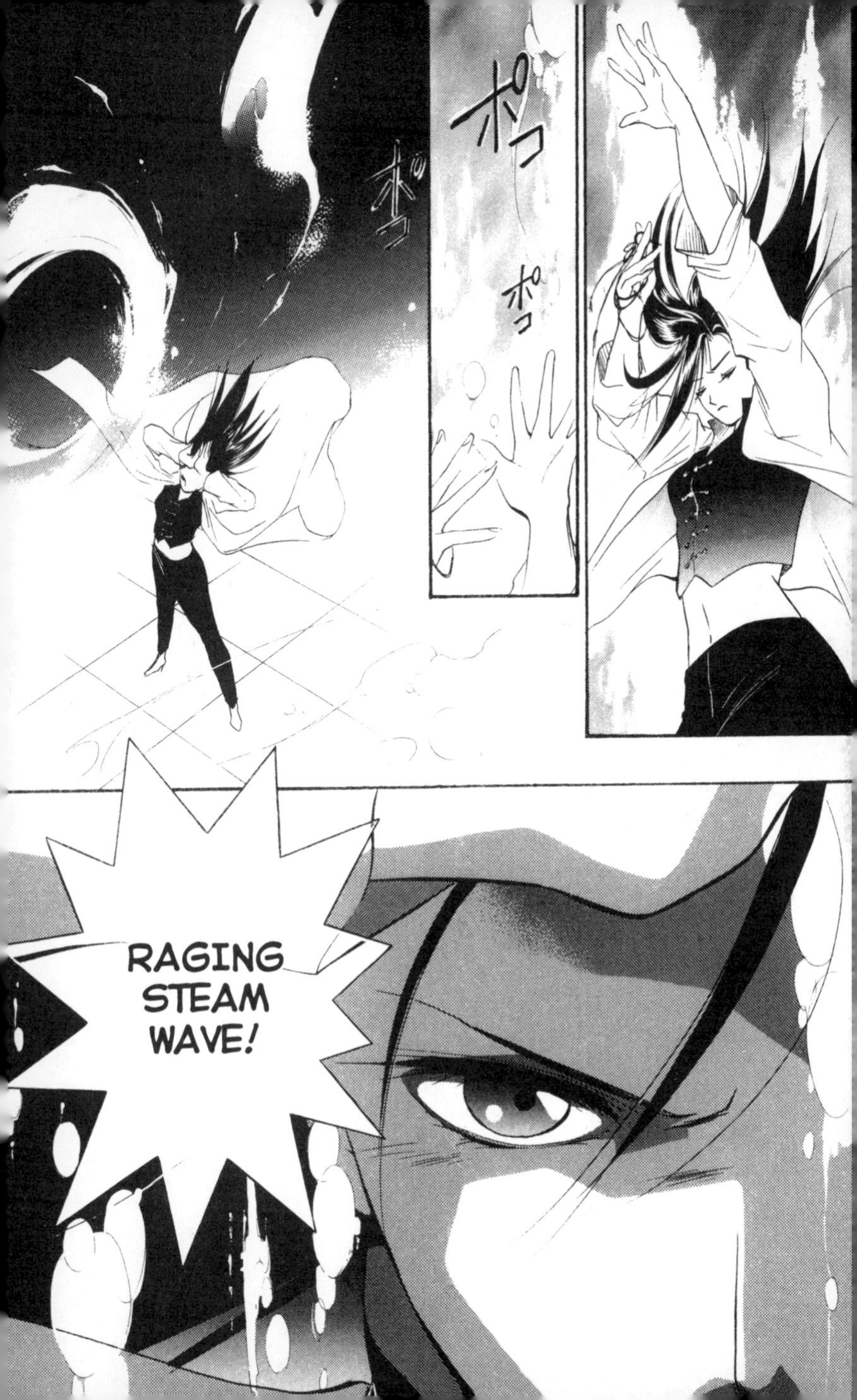
ポコ
ポコ
ポコ
RAGING STEAM WAVE!

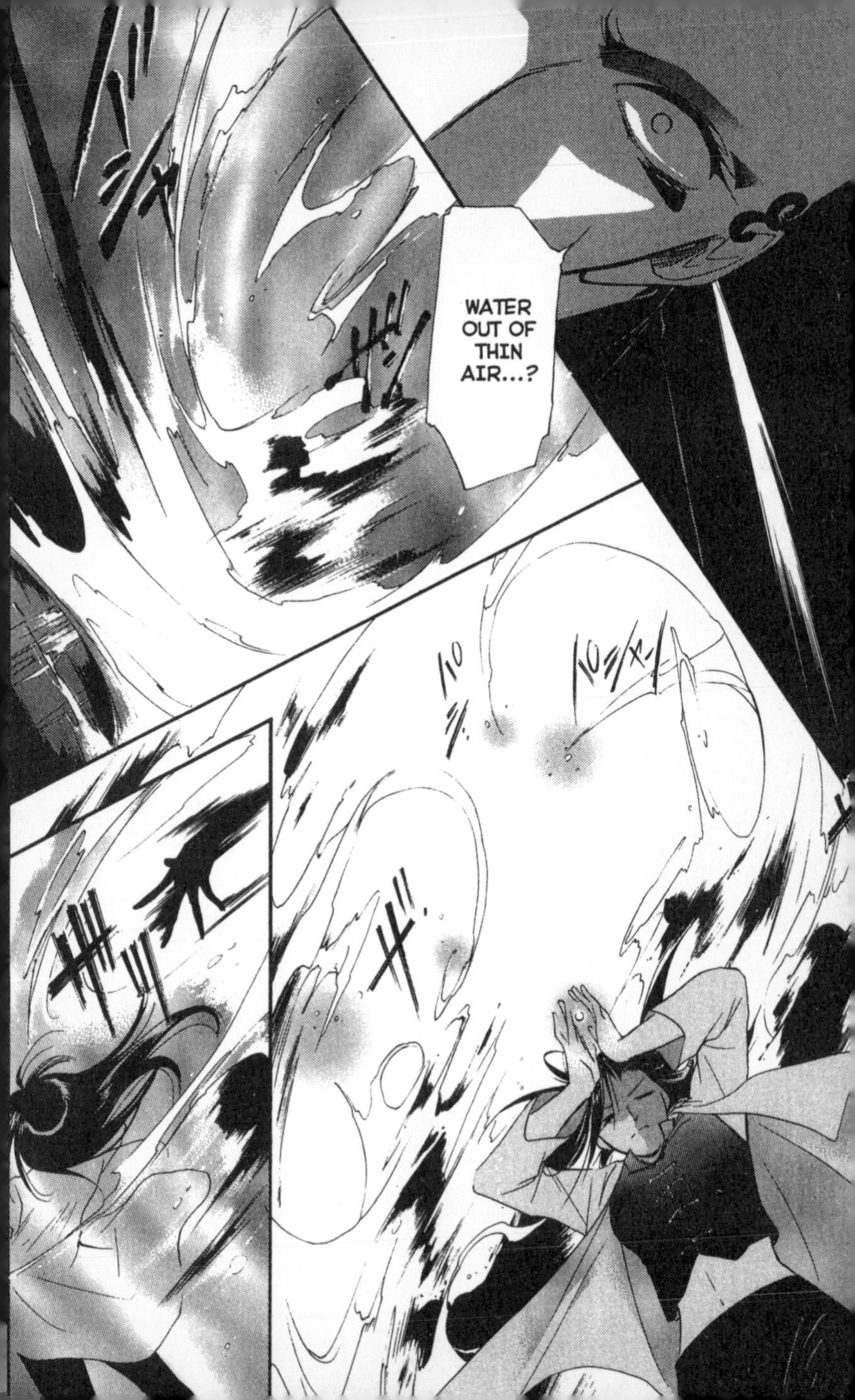
WATER OUT OF THIN AIR...?

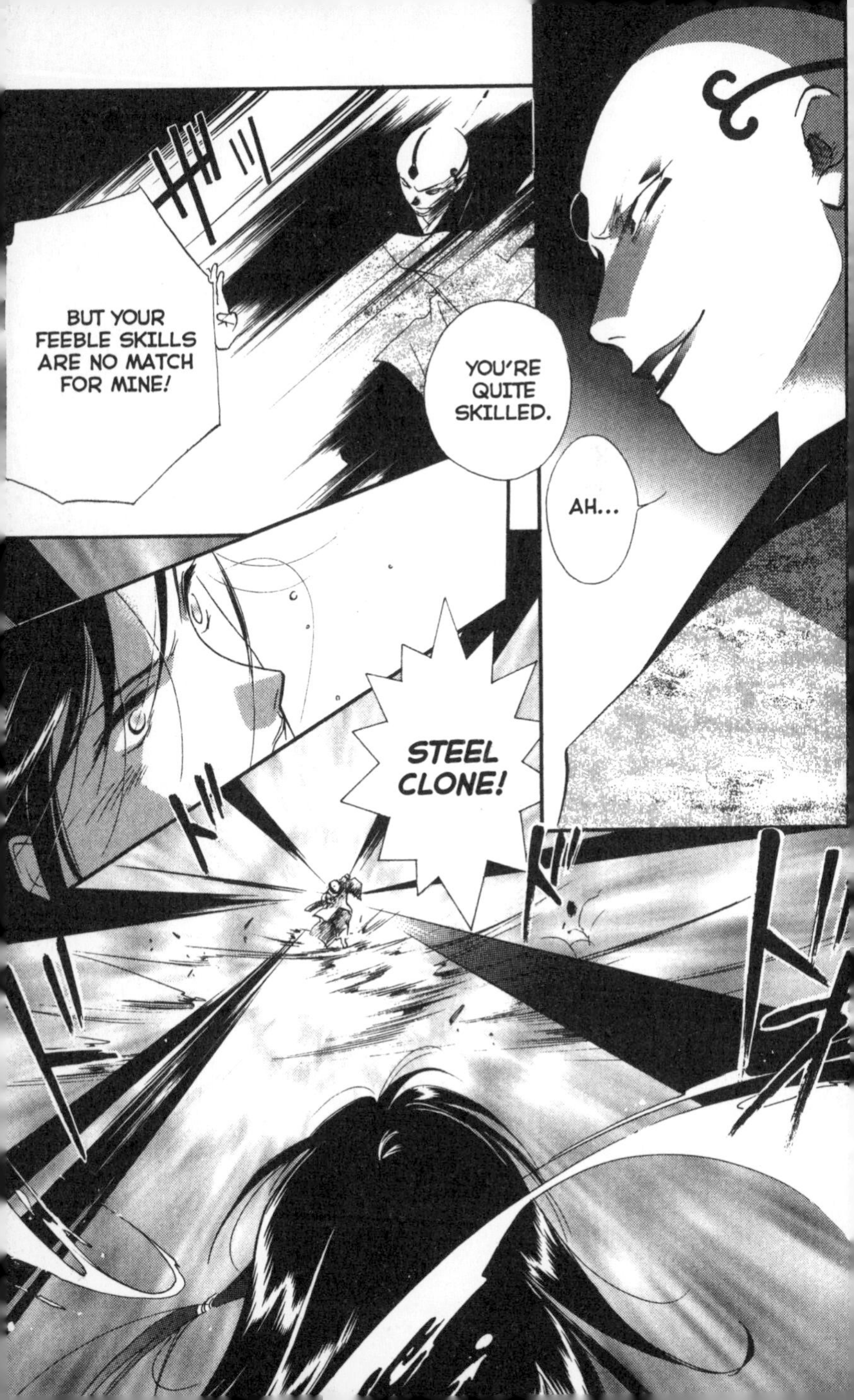
YOU'RE QUITE SKILLED.
AH...
BUT YOUR FEEBLE SKILLS ARE NO MATCH FOR MINE!
STEEL CLONE!

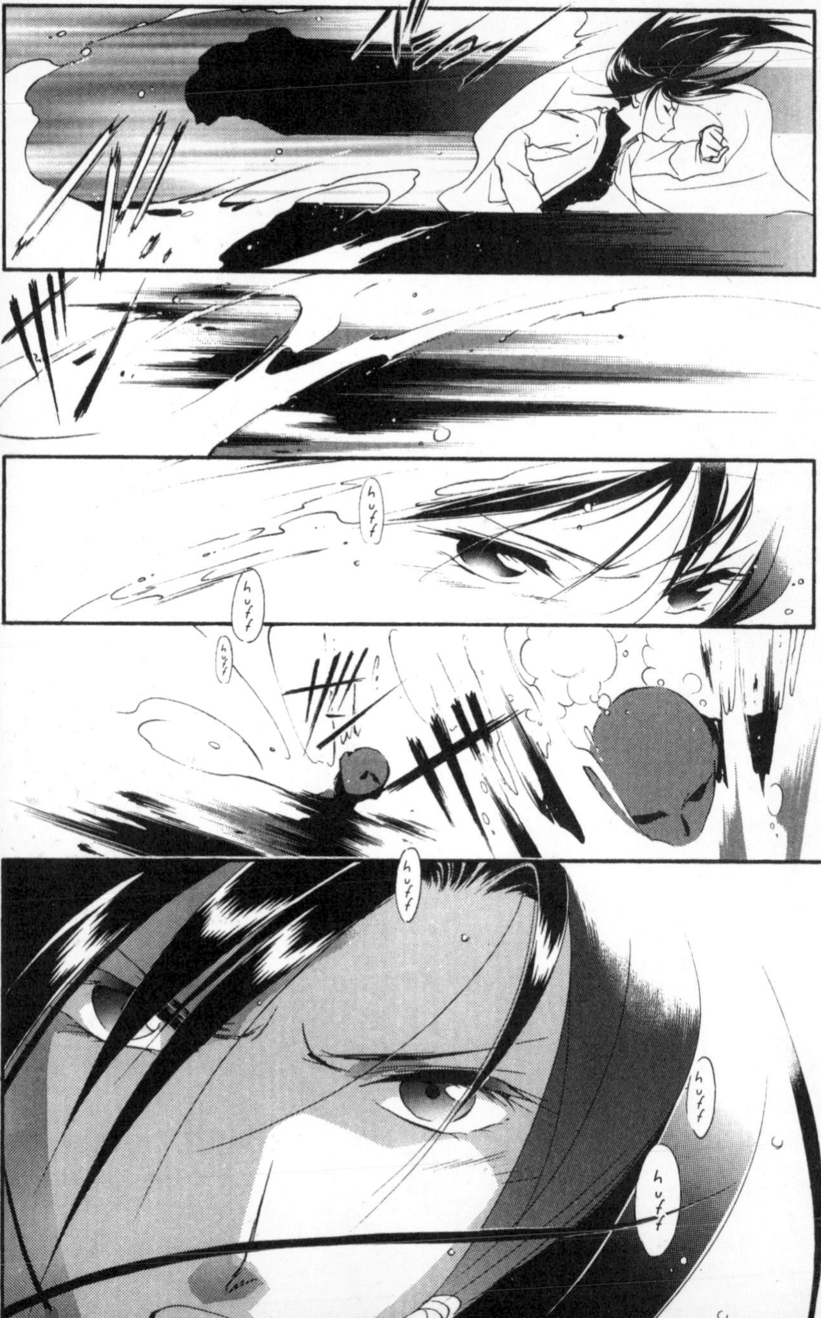
huff
huff
huff
huff
huff
huff

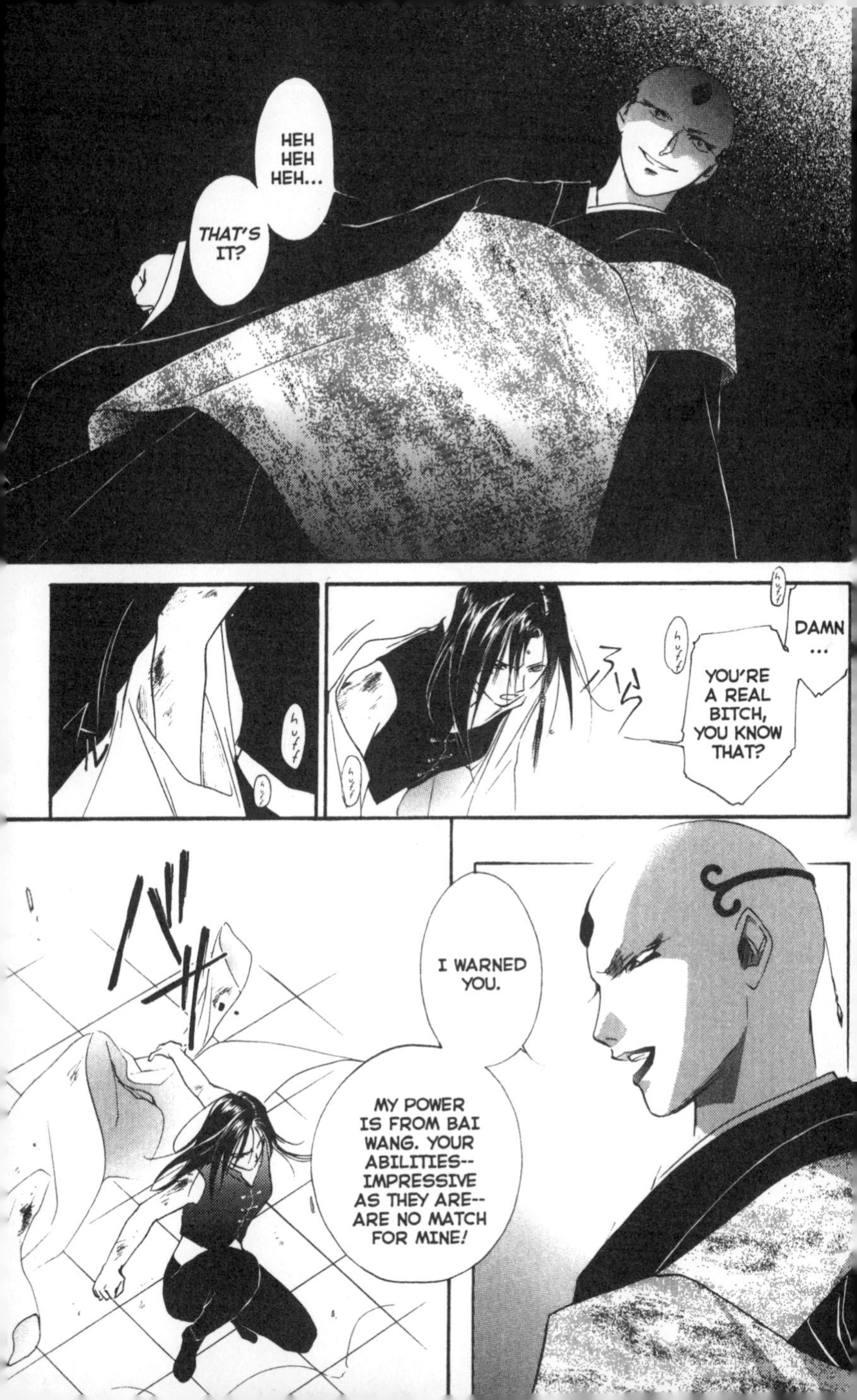
HEH HEH HEH...
THAT'S IT?
DAMN ...
YOU'RE A REAL BITCH, YOU KNOW THAT?
I WARNED YOU.
MY POWER IS FROM BAI WANG. YOUR ABILITIES-- IMPRESSIVE AS THEY ARE-- ARE NO MATCH FOR MINE!

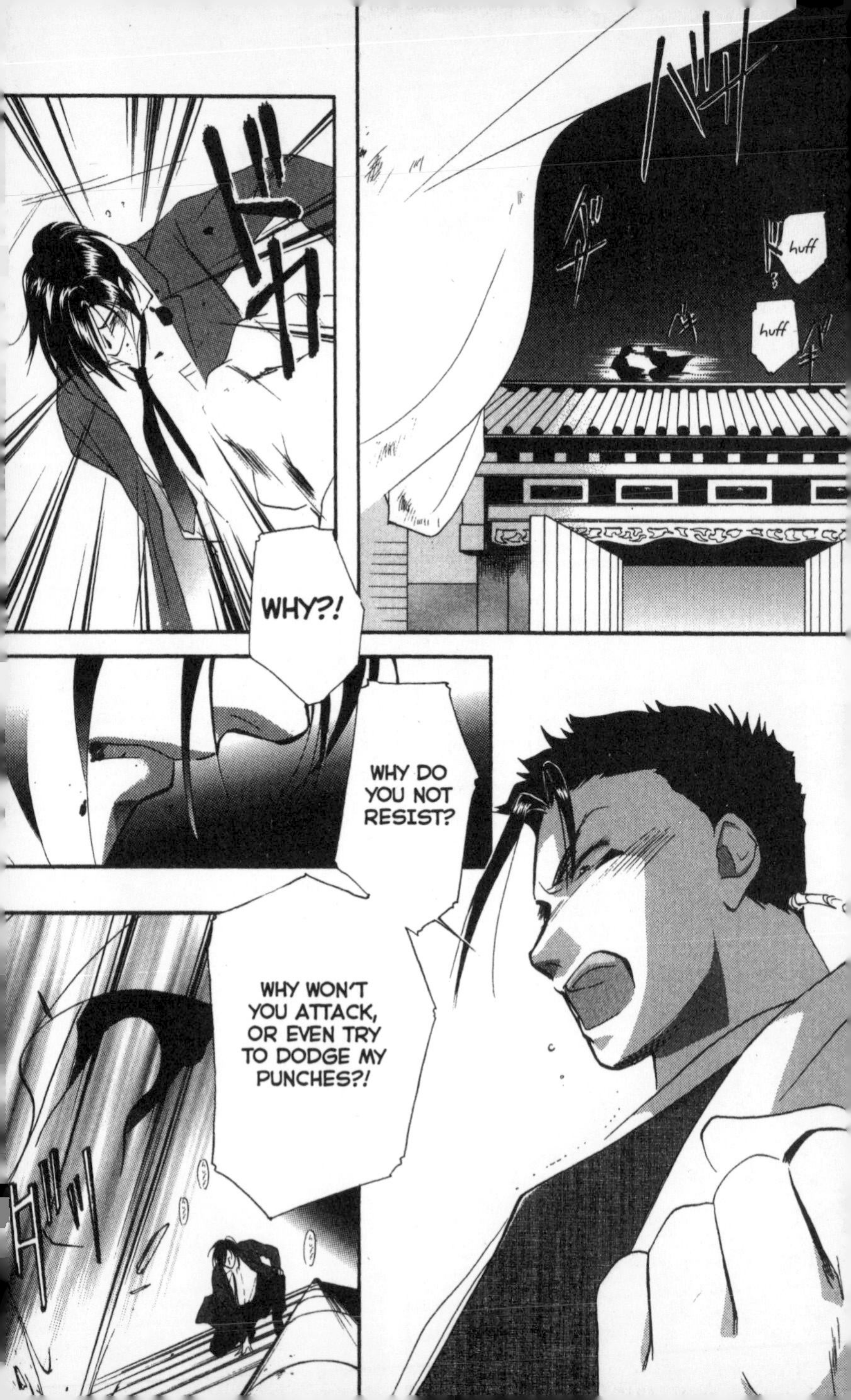
huff
huff
WHY?!
WHY DO YOU NOT RESIST?
WHY WON'T YOU ATTACK, OR EVEN TRY TO DODGE MY PUNCHES?!

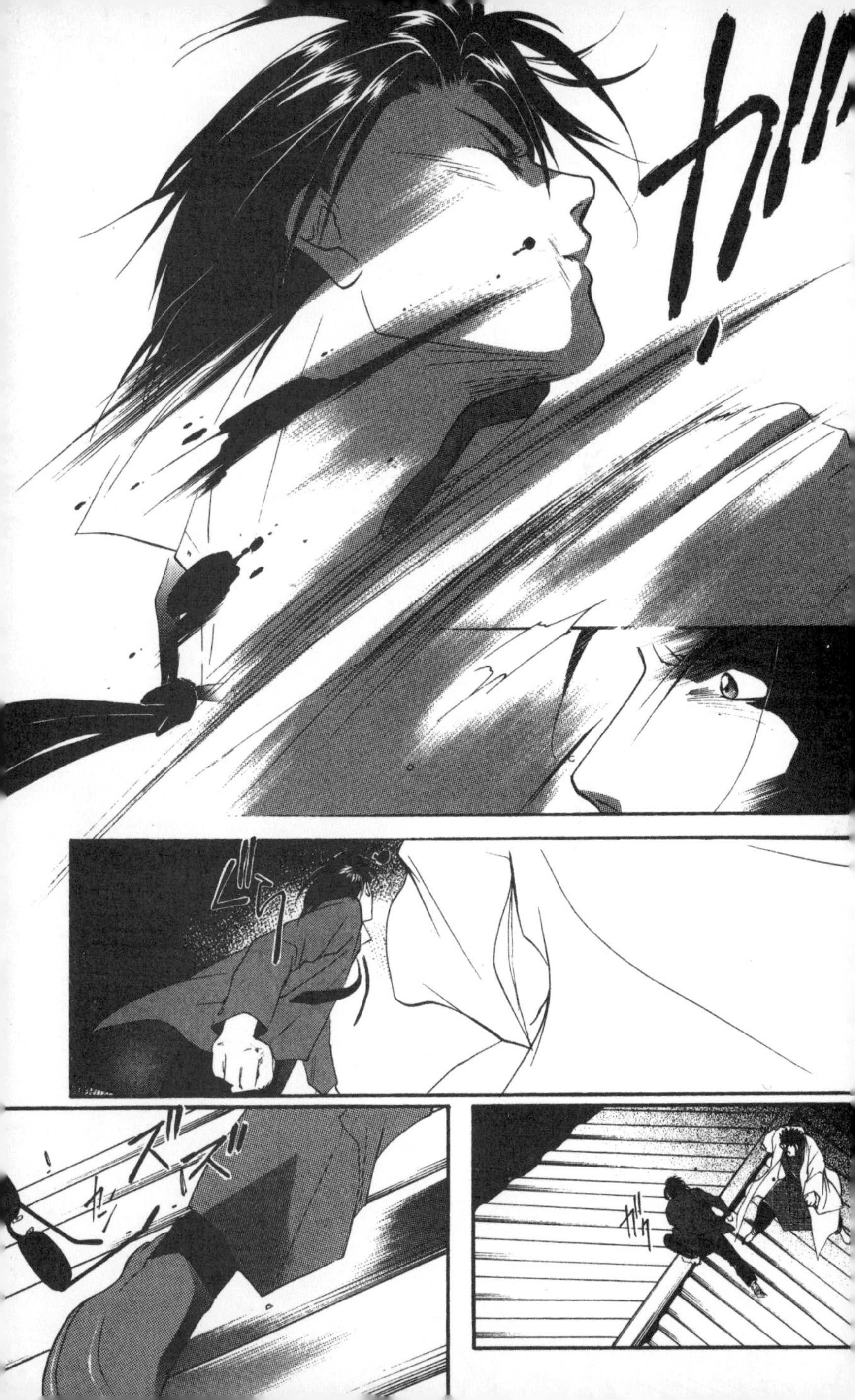
ガッ
ぐいっ
ガク
ズズ
カン
!

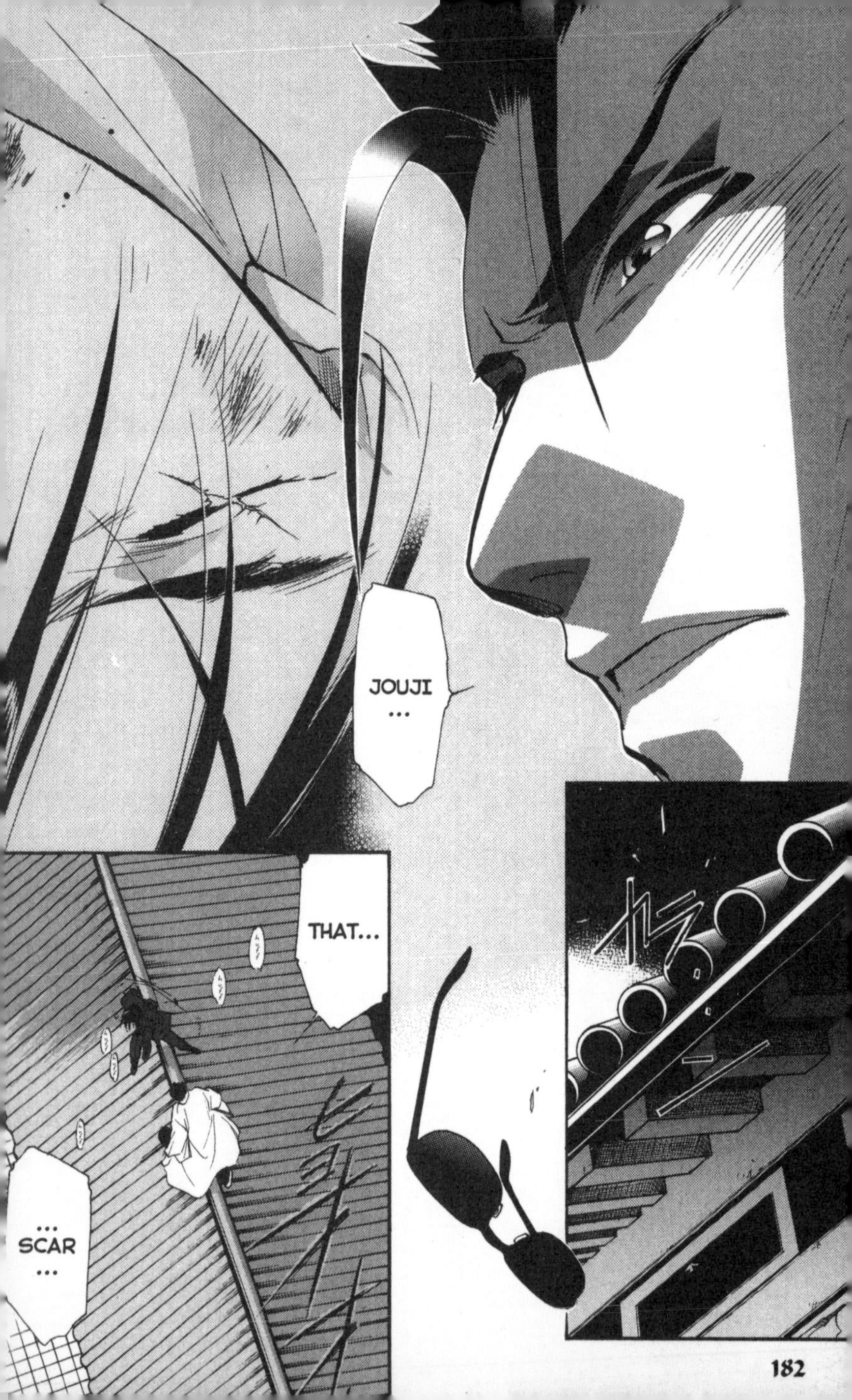
JOUJI ...
THAT...
... SCAR ...

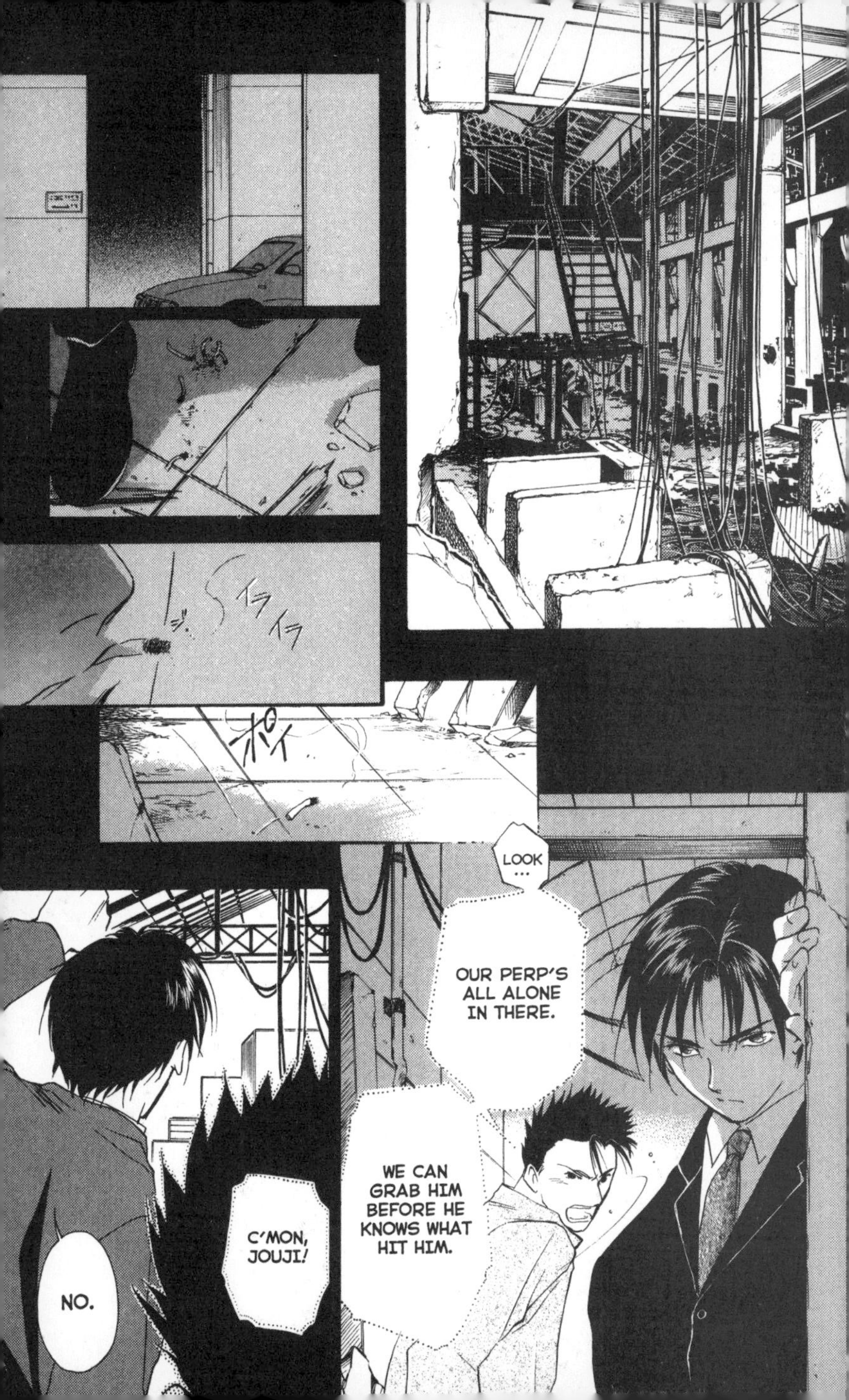
ジ…
イラ イラ
ポイ
LOOK…
OUR PERP'S ALL ALONE IN THERE.
WE CAN GRAB HIM BEFORE HE KNOWS WHAT HIT HIM.
C'MON, JOUJI!
NO.

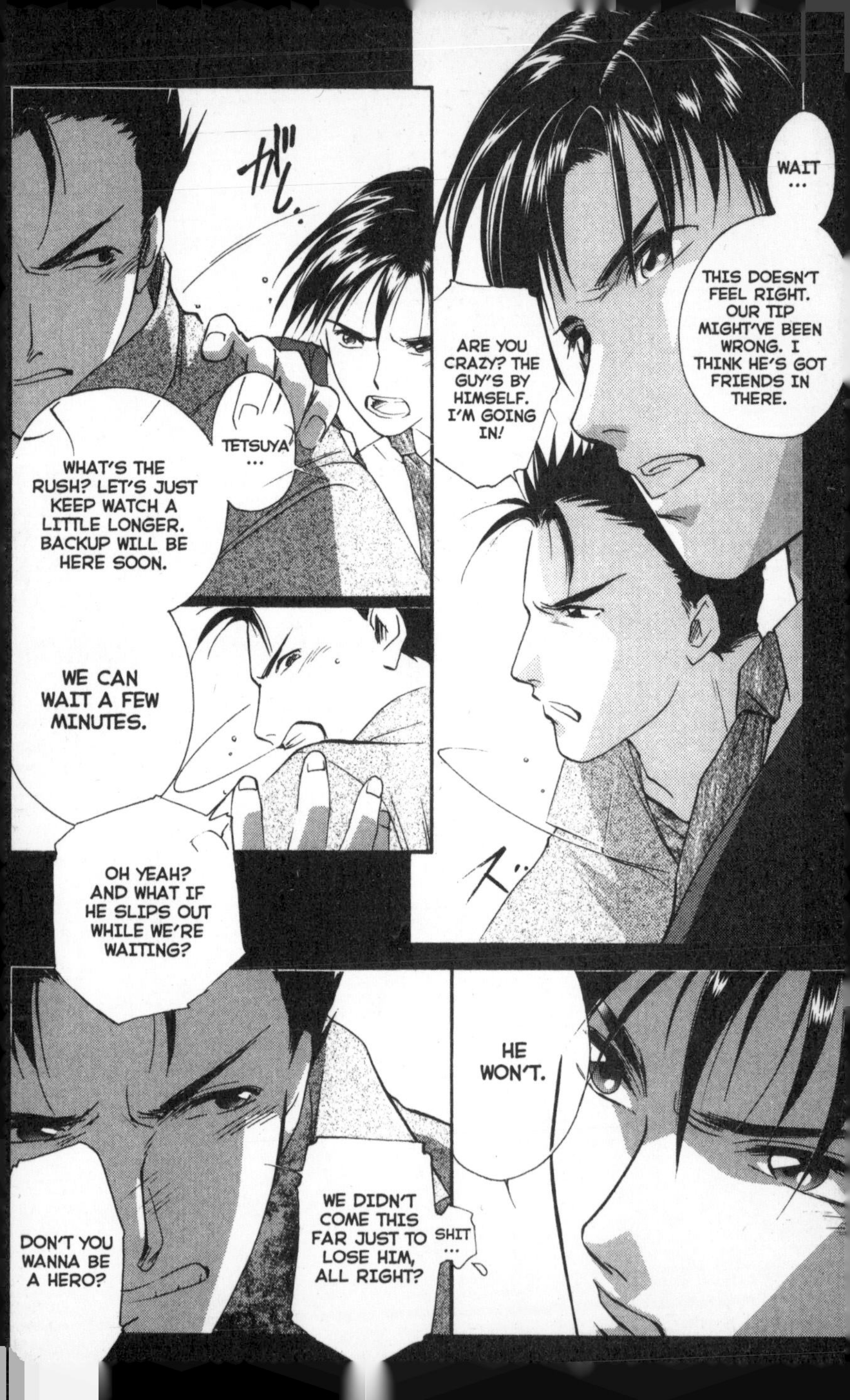
WAIT ...
THIS DOESN'T FEEL RIGHT. OUR TIP MIGHT'VE BEEN WRONG. I THINK HE'S GOT FRIENDS IN THERE.
ARE YOU CRAZY? THE GUY'S BY HIMSELF. I'M GOING IN!
ス..
がし
TETSUYA ...
WHAT'S THE RUSH? LET'S JUST KEEP WATCH A LITTLE LONGER. BACKUP WILL BE HERE SOON.
WE CAN WAIT A FEW MINUTES.
OH YEAH? AND WHAT IF HE SLIPS OUT WHILE WE'RE WAITING?
HE WON'T.
SHIT ...
WE DIDN'T COME THIS FAR JUST TO LOSE HIM, ALL RIGHT?
DON'T YOU WANNA BE A HERO?

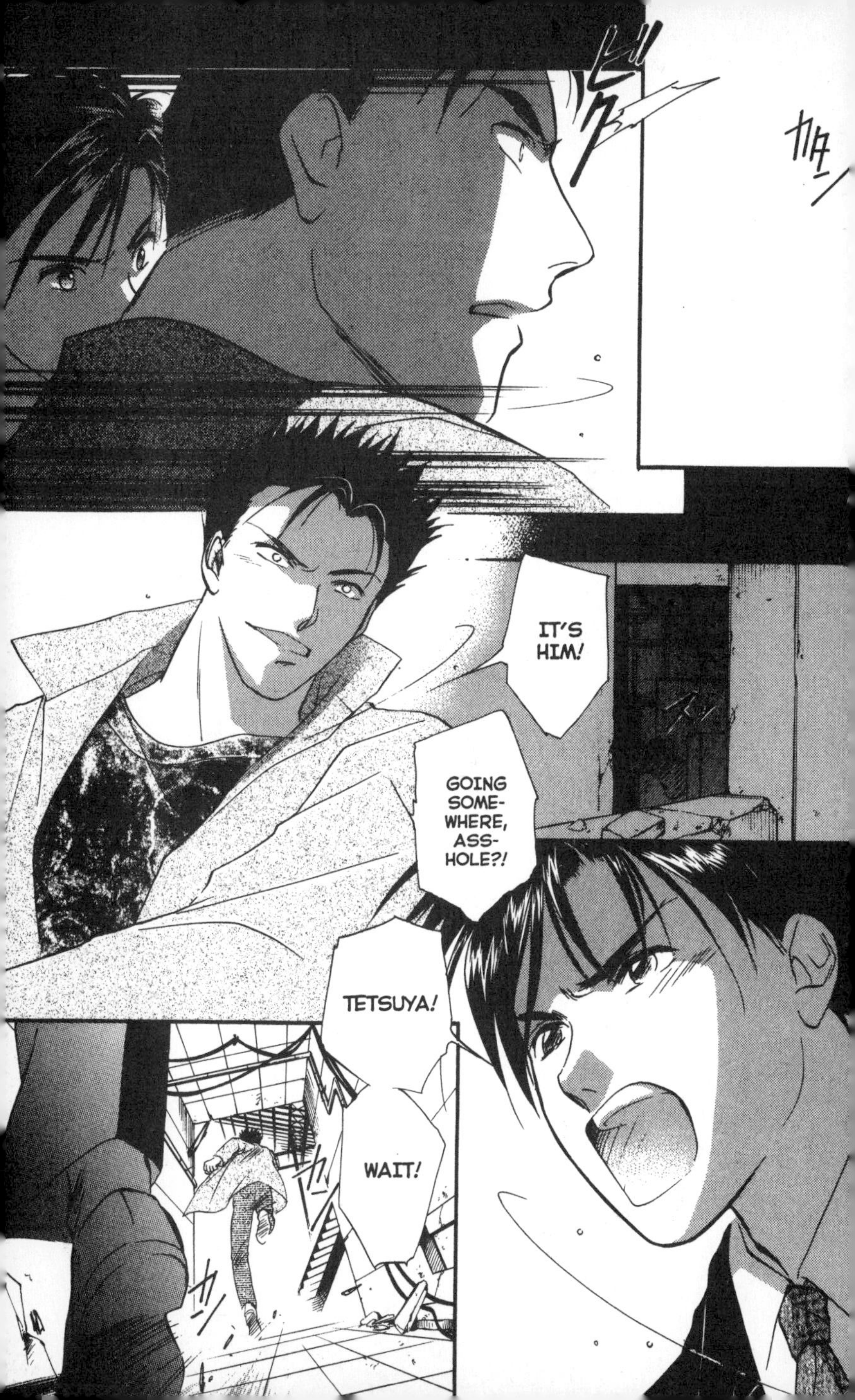
IT'S HIM!
GOING SOME-WHERE, ASS-HOLE?!
TETSUYA!
WAIT!

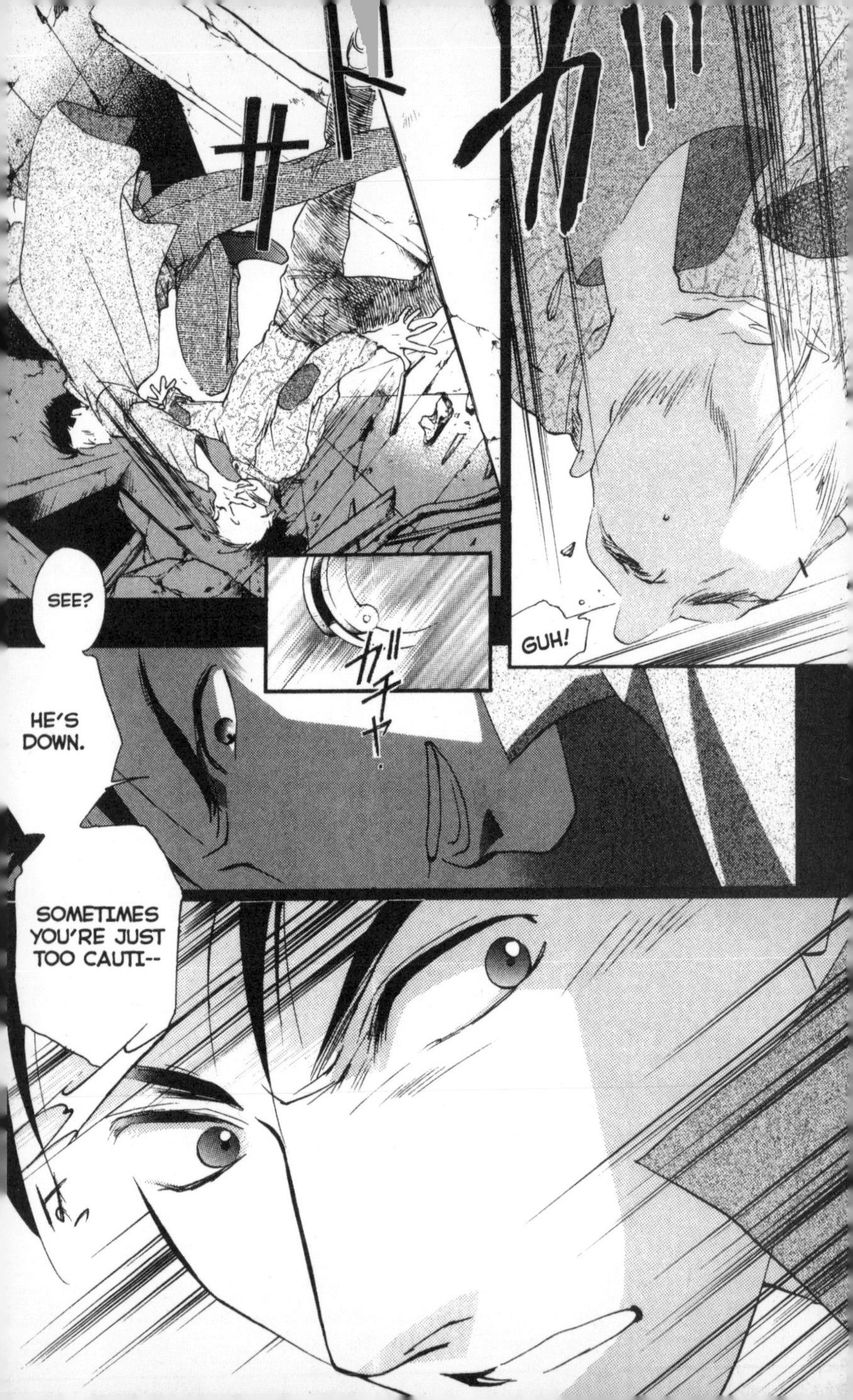
ガ
GUH!
ドサ
ガチャ
SEE?
HE'S DOWN.
SOMETIMES YOU'RE JUST TOO CAUTI--
はっ

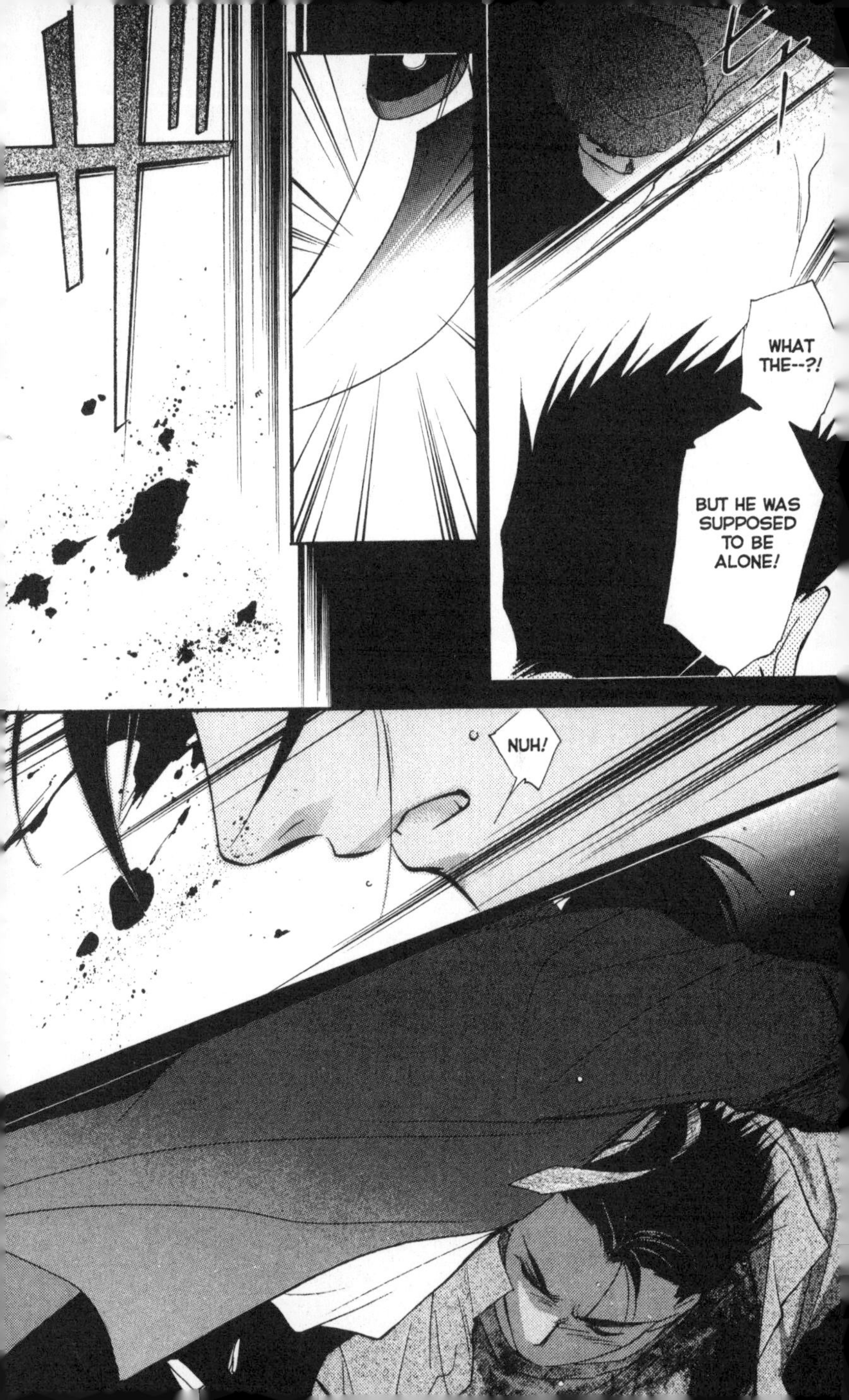
WHAT THE--?!
BUT HE WAS SUPPOSED TO BE ALONE!
NUH!

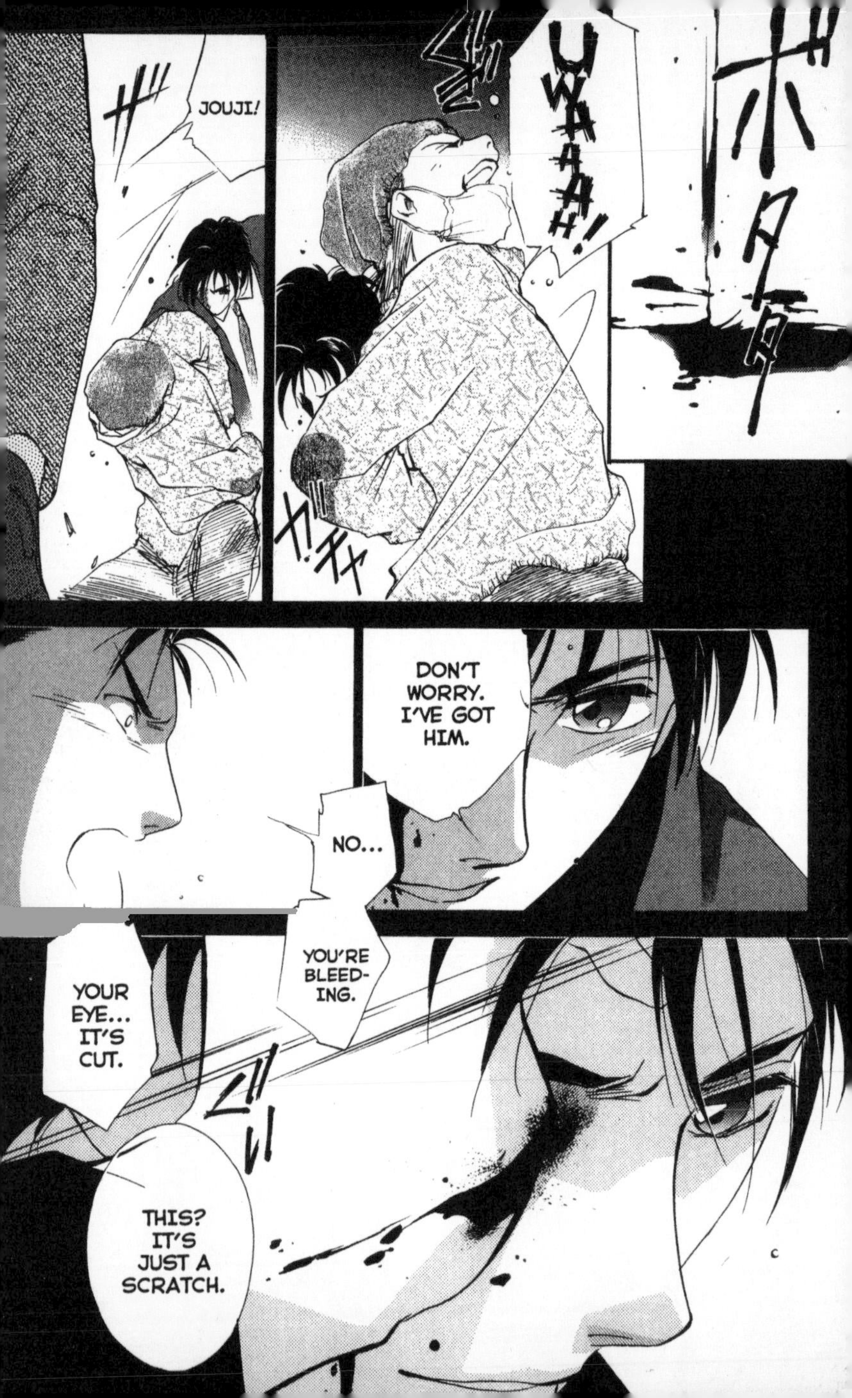
ボタタ
UWAAAH!
ガチャ
JOUJI!
DON'T WORRY. I'VE GOT HIM.
NO...
YOU'RE BLEEDING.
YOUR EYE... IT'S CUT.
THIS? IT'S JUST A SCRATCH.

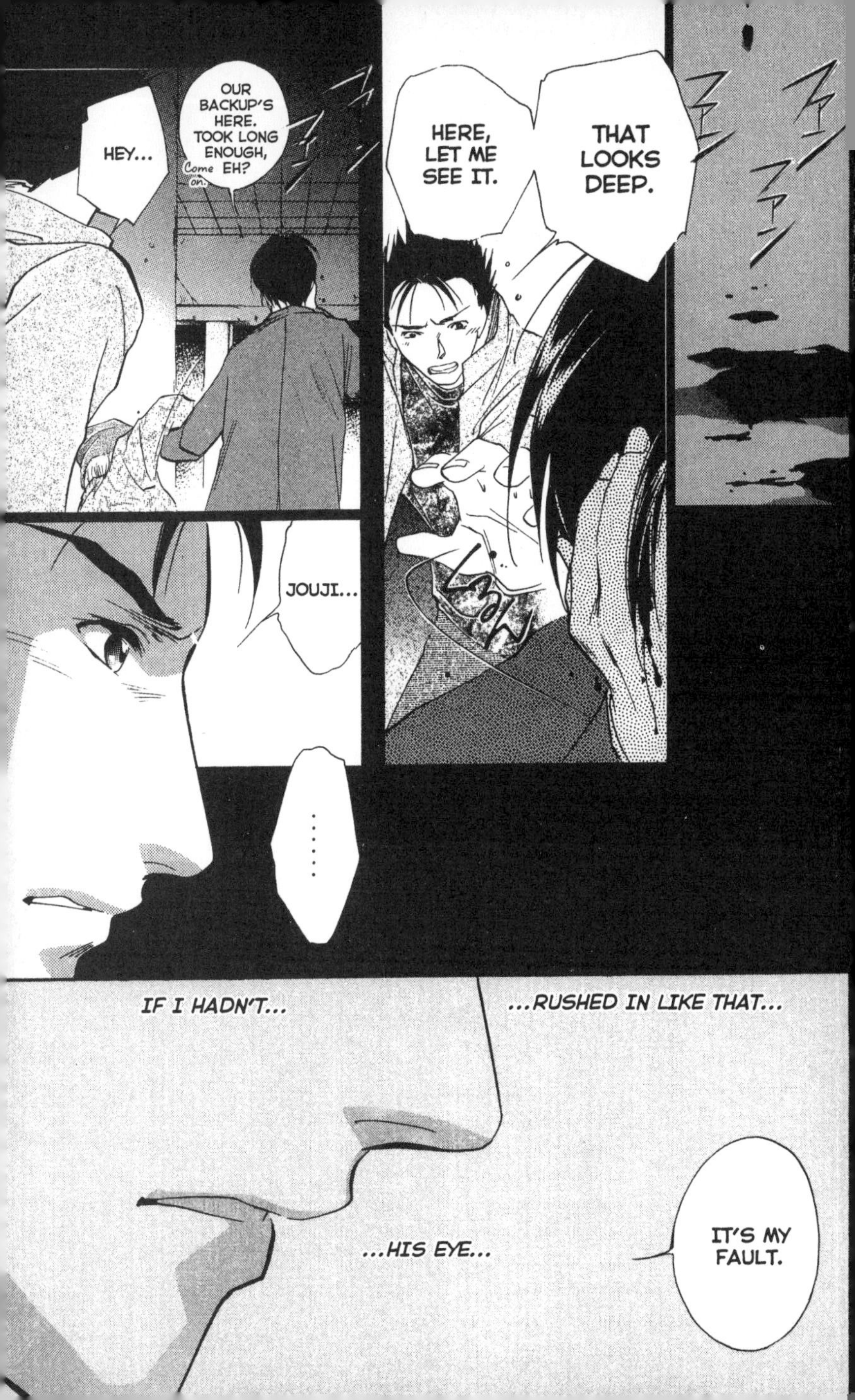
THAT LOOKS DEEP.
HERE, LET ME SEE IT.
OUR BACKUP'S HERE. TOOK LONG ENOUGH, EH?
Come on.
HEY...
JOUJI...
......
IF I HADN'T...
...RUSHED IN LIKE THAT...
...HIS EYE...
IT'S MY FAULT.

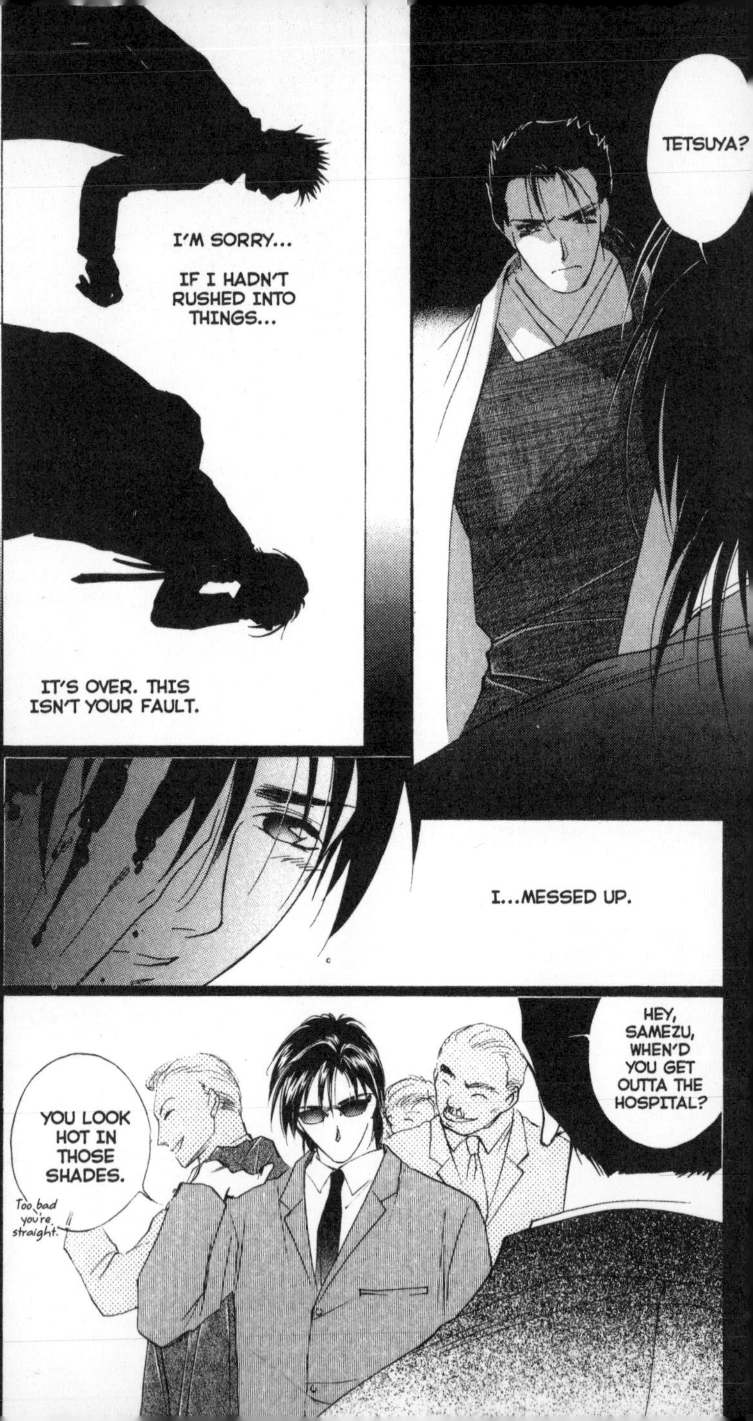
TETSUYA?
I'M SORRY...
IF I HADN'T RUSHED INTO THINGS...
IT'S OVER. THIS ISN'T YOUR FAULT.
I...MESSED UP.
HEY, SAMEZU, WHEN'D YOU GET OUTTA THE HOSPITAL?
YOU LOOK HOT IN THOSE SHADES.
Too bad you're straight.

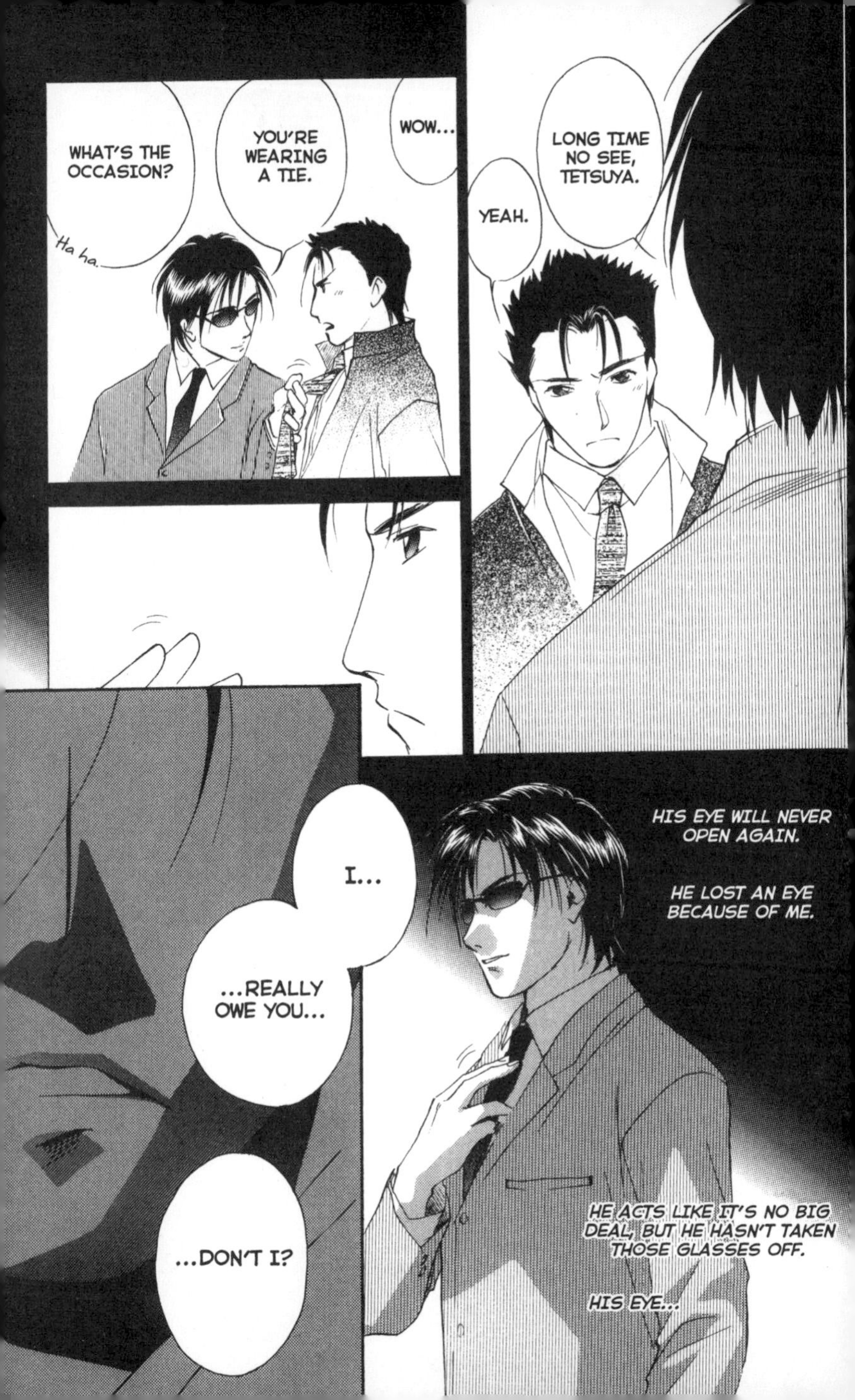
LONG TIME NO SEE, TETSUYA.
YEAH.
WOW...
YOU'RE WEARING A TIE.
WHAT'S THE OCCASION?
Ha ha.
HIS EYE WILL NEVER OPEN AGAIN.
HE LOST AN EYE BECAUSE OF ME.
HE ACTS LIKE IT'S NO BIG DEAL, BUT HE HASN'T TAKEN THOSE GLASSES OFF.
HIS EYE...
I...
...REALLY OWE YOU...
...DON'T I?

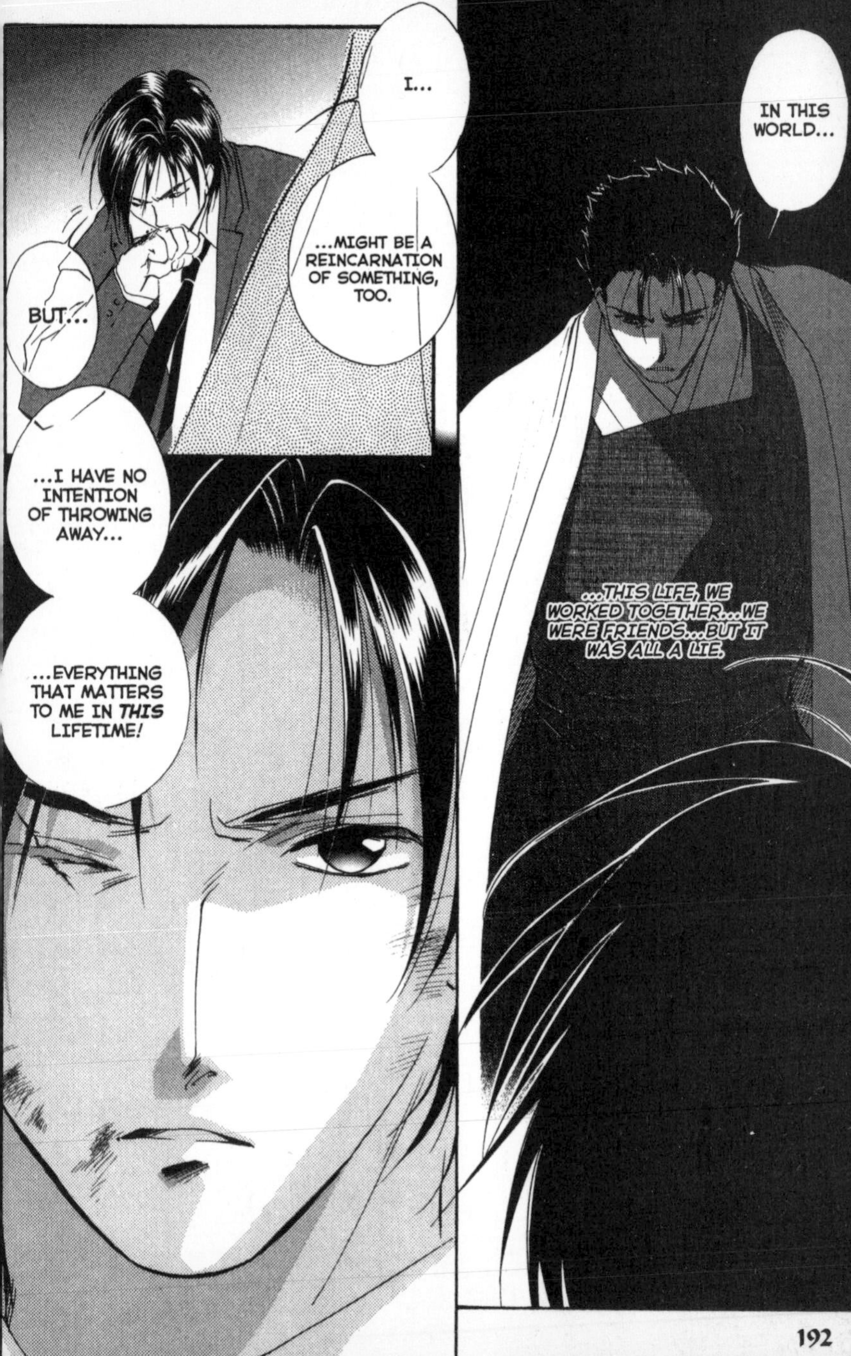
IN THIS WORLD...
...THIS LIFE, WE WORKED TOGETHER...WE WERE FRIENDS...BUT IT WAS ALL A LIE.
I...
...MIGHT BE A REINCARNATION OF SOMETHING, TOO.
BUT...
...I HAVE NO INTENTION OF THROWING AWAY...
...EVERYTHING THAT MATTERS TO ME IN *THIS* LIFETIME!

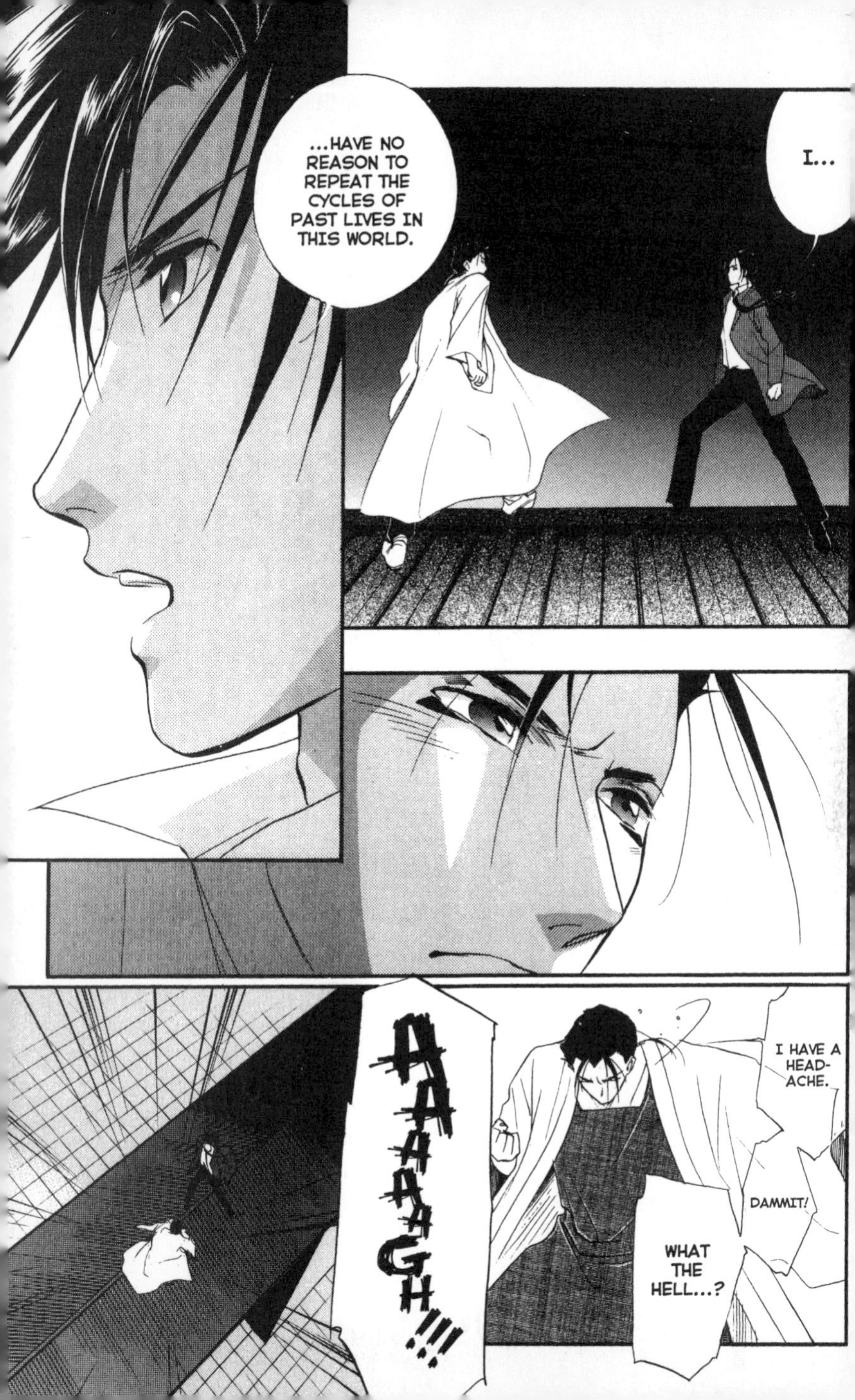
I...
...HAVE NO REASON TO REPEAT THE CYCLES OF PAST LIVES IN THIS WORLD.
I HAVE A HEAD-ACHE.
DAMMIT!
WHAT THE HELL...?
AAAAAGH!!!

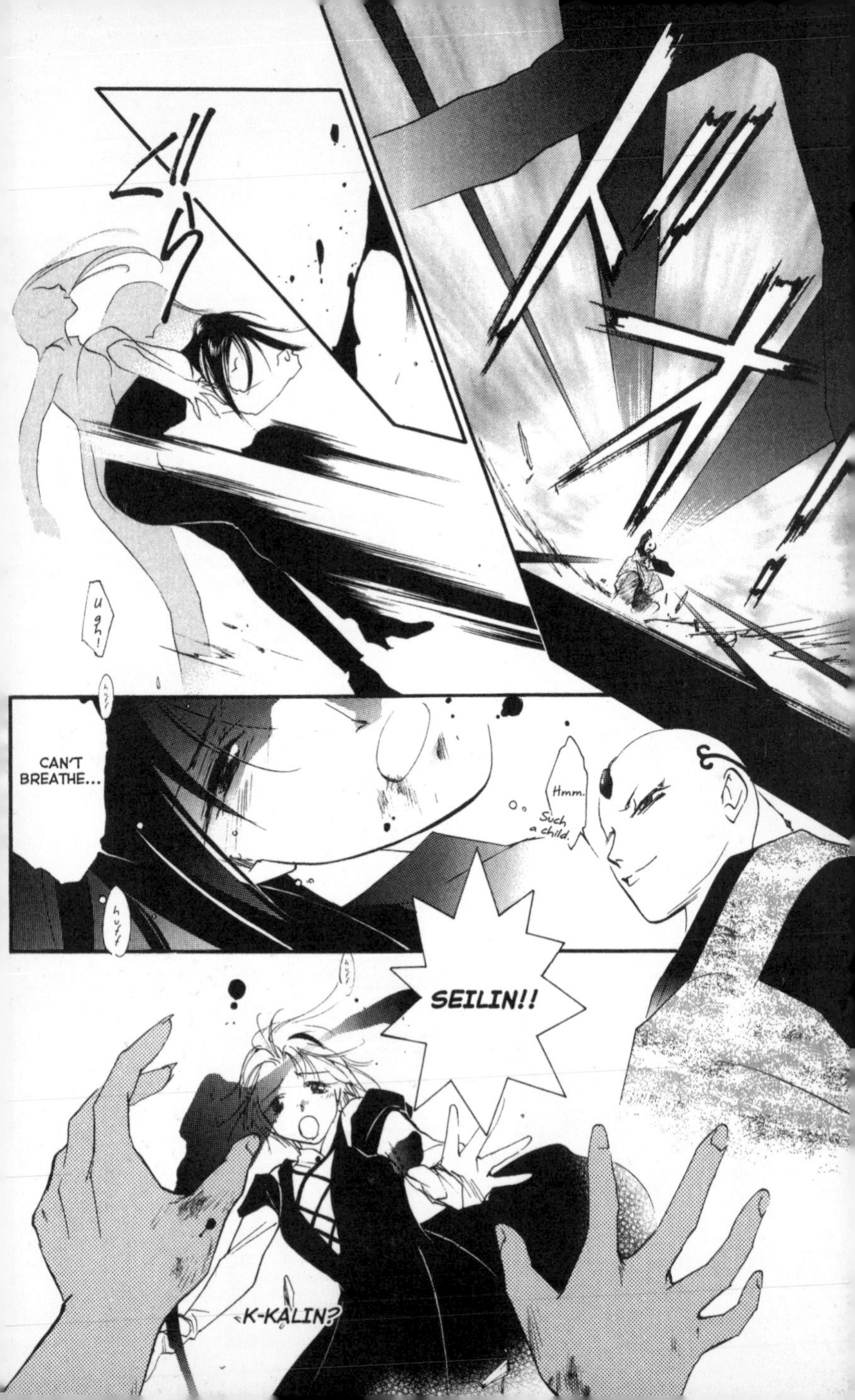
ugh!
Hmm.
Such a child.
huff
CAN'T BREATHE...
huff
huff
SEILIN!!
K-KALIN?

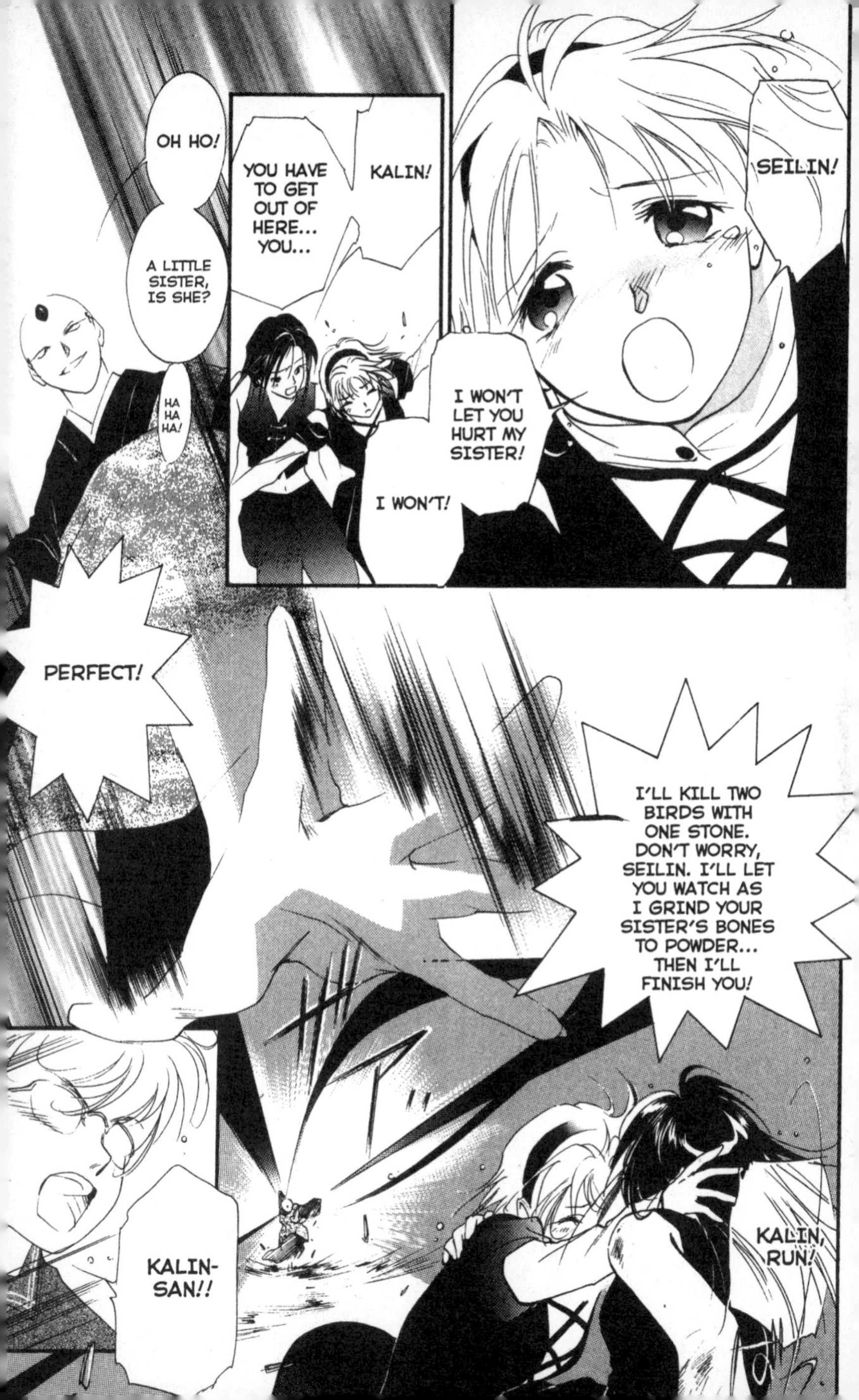
SEILIN!
KALIN!
YOU HAVE TO GET OUT OF HERE... YOU...
I WON'T LET YOU HURT MY SISTER!
I WON'T!
OH HO!
A LITTLE SISTER, IS SHE?
HA HA HA!
PERFECT!
I'LL KILL TWO BIRDS WITH ONE STONE. DON'T WORRY, SEILIN. I'LL LET YOU WATCH AS I GRIND YOUR SISTER'S BONES TO POWDER... THEN I'LL FINISH YOU!
KALIN, RUN!
KALIN-SAN!!

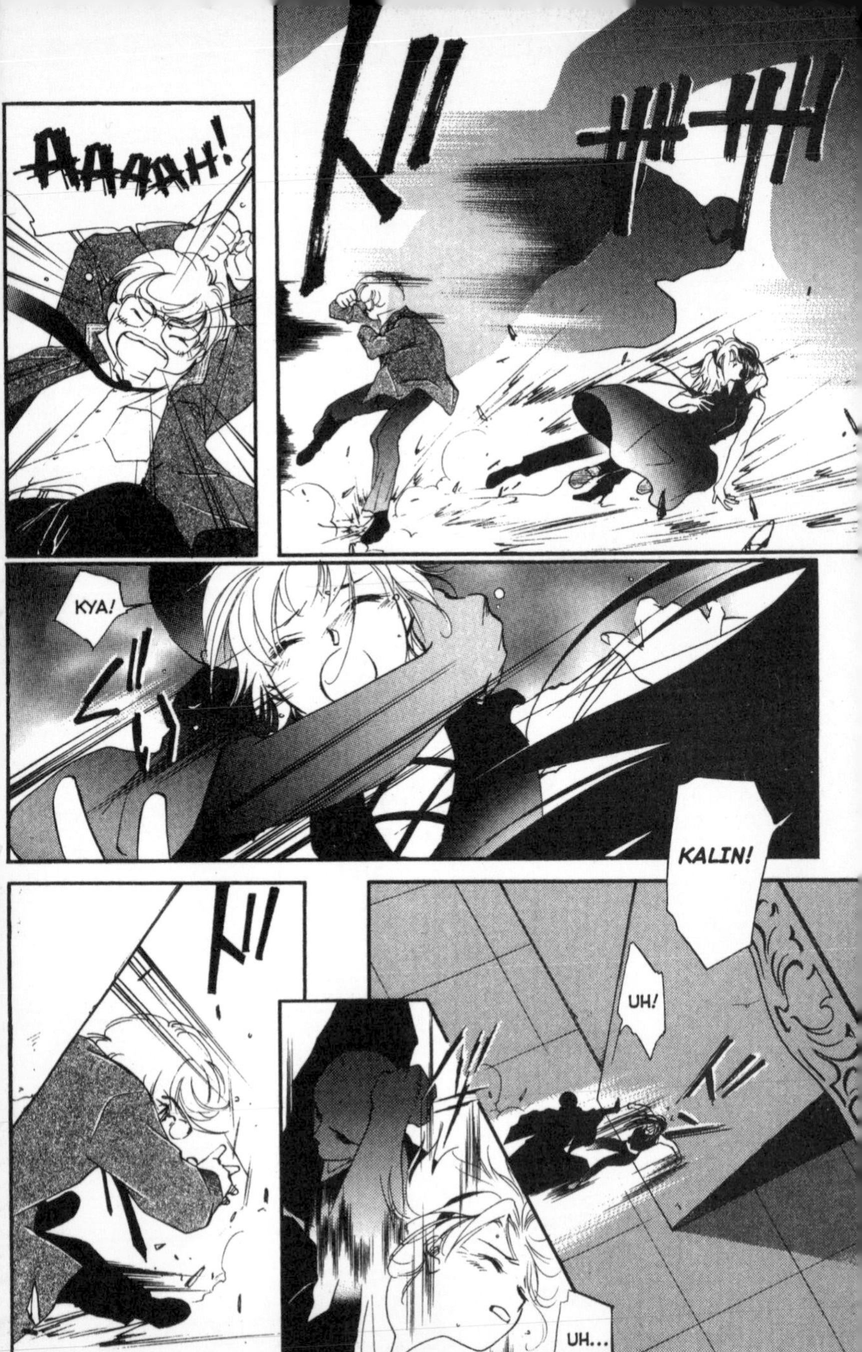
AAAAAH!
KYA!
KALIN!
UH!
UH...

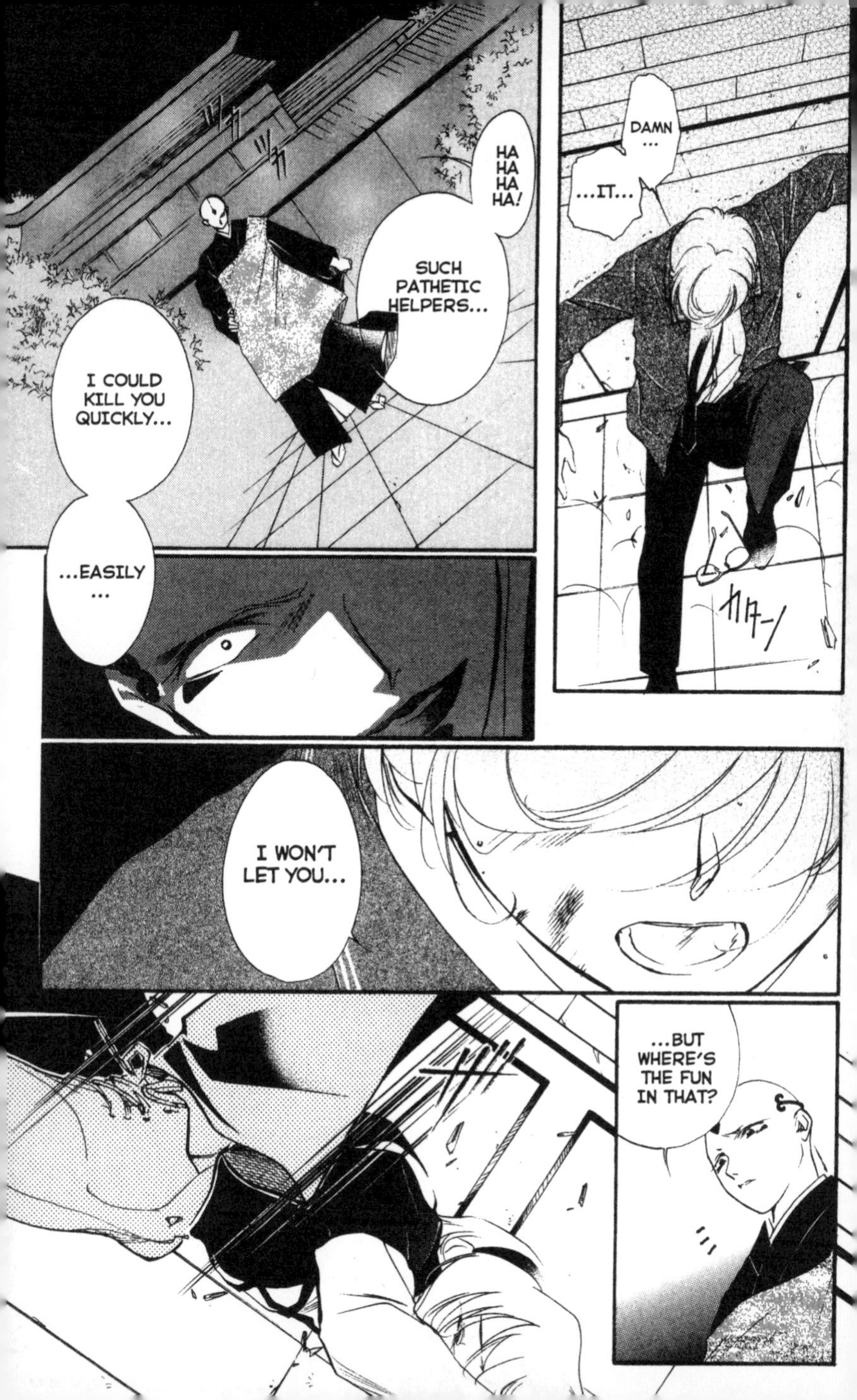
DAMN...
...IT...
HA HA HA HA!
SUCH PATHETIC HELPERS...
I COULD KILL YOU QUICKLY...
...EASILY...
I WON'T LET YOU...
...BUT WHERE'S THE FUN IN THAT?

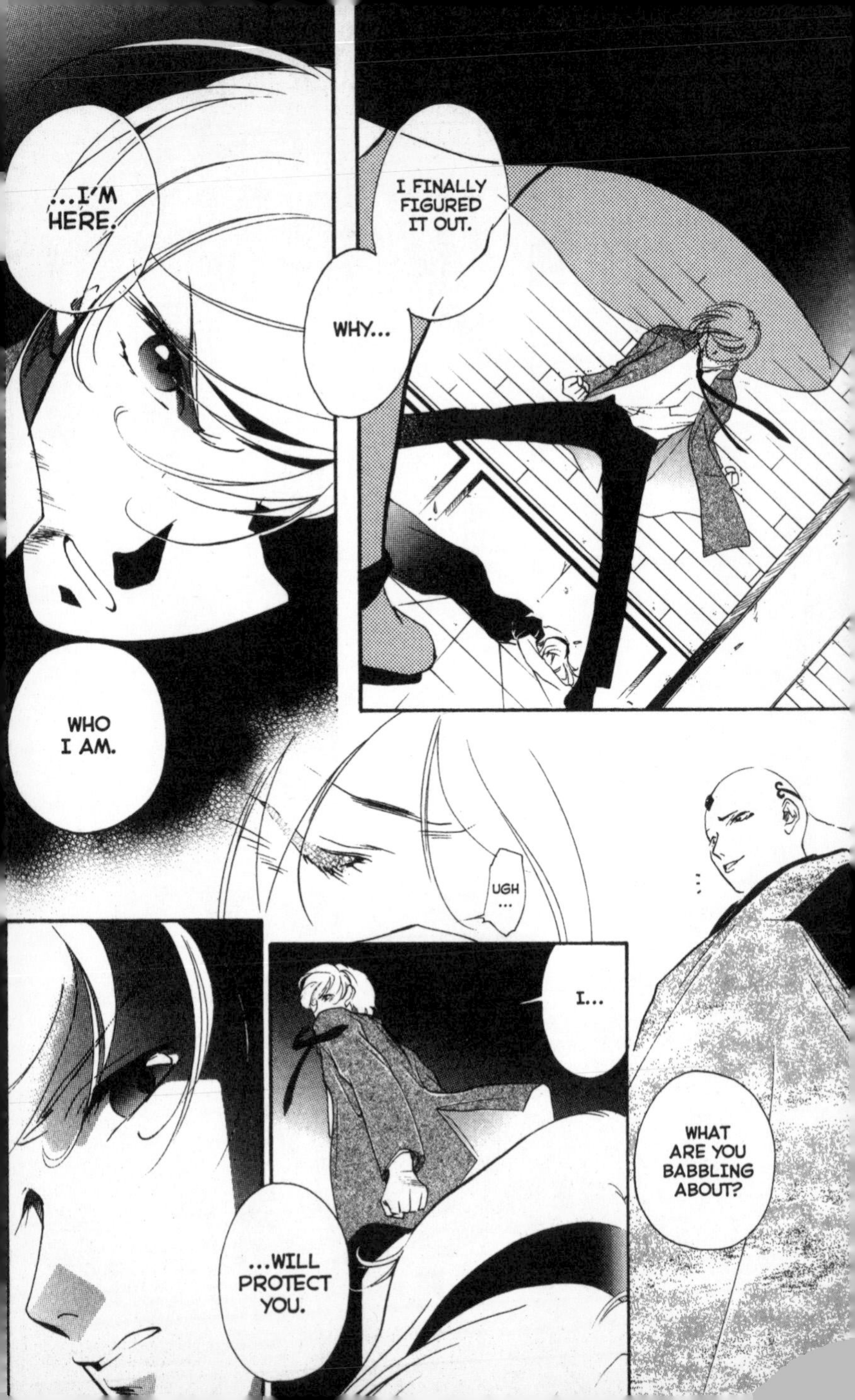
I FINALLY FIGURED IT OUT.
WHY...
...I'M HERE.
WHO I AM.
...
UGH...
WHAT ARE YOU BABBLING ABOUT?
I...
...WILL PROTECT YOU.

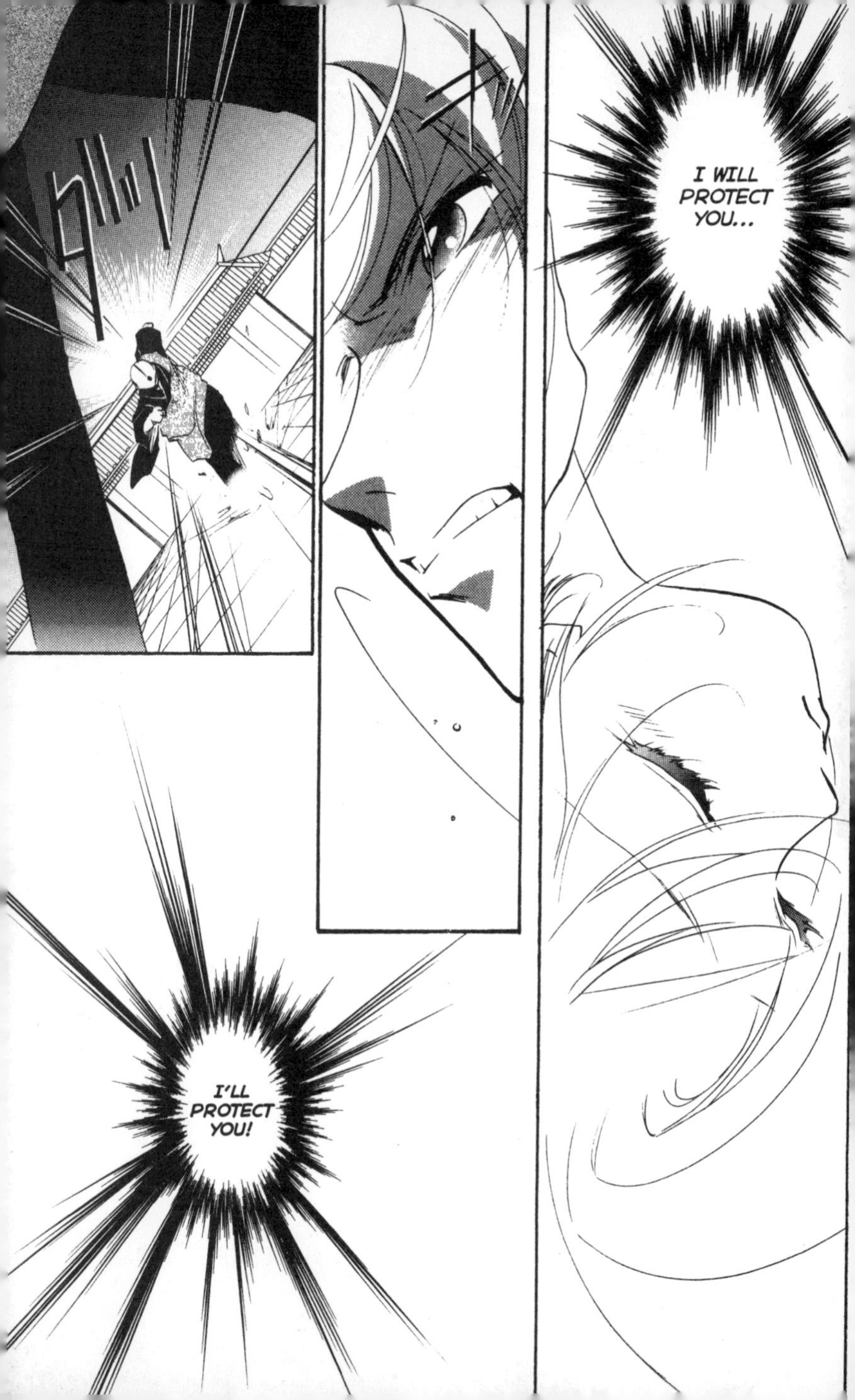
I WILL PROTECT YOU...
I'LL PROTECT YOU!

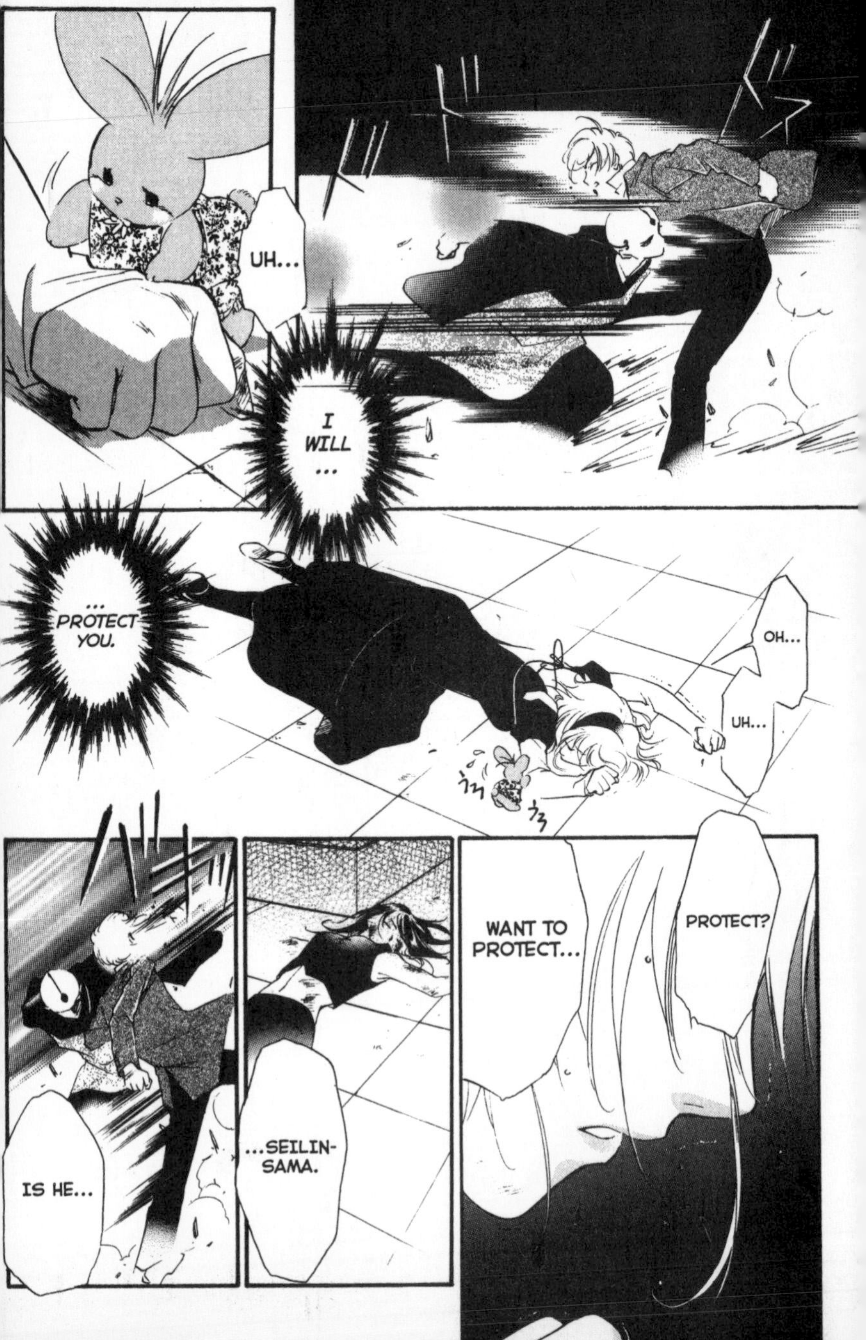
UH...
I WILL...
OH...
UH...
...PROTECT YOU.
PROTECT?
WANT TO PROTECT...
...SEILIN-SAMA.
IS HE...

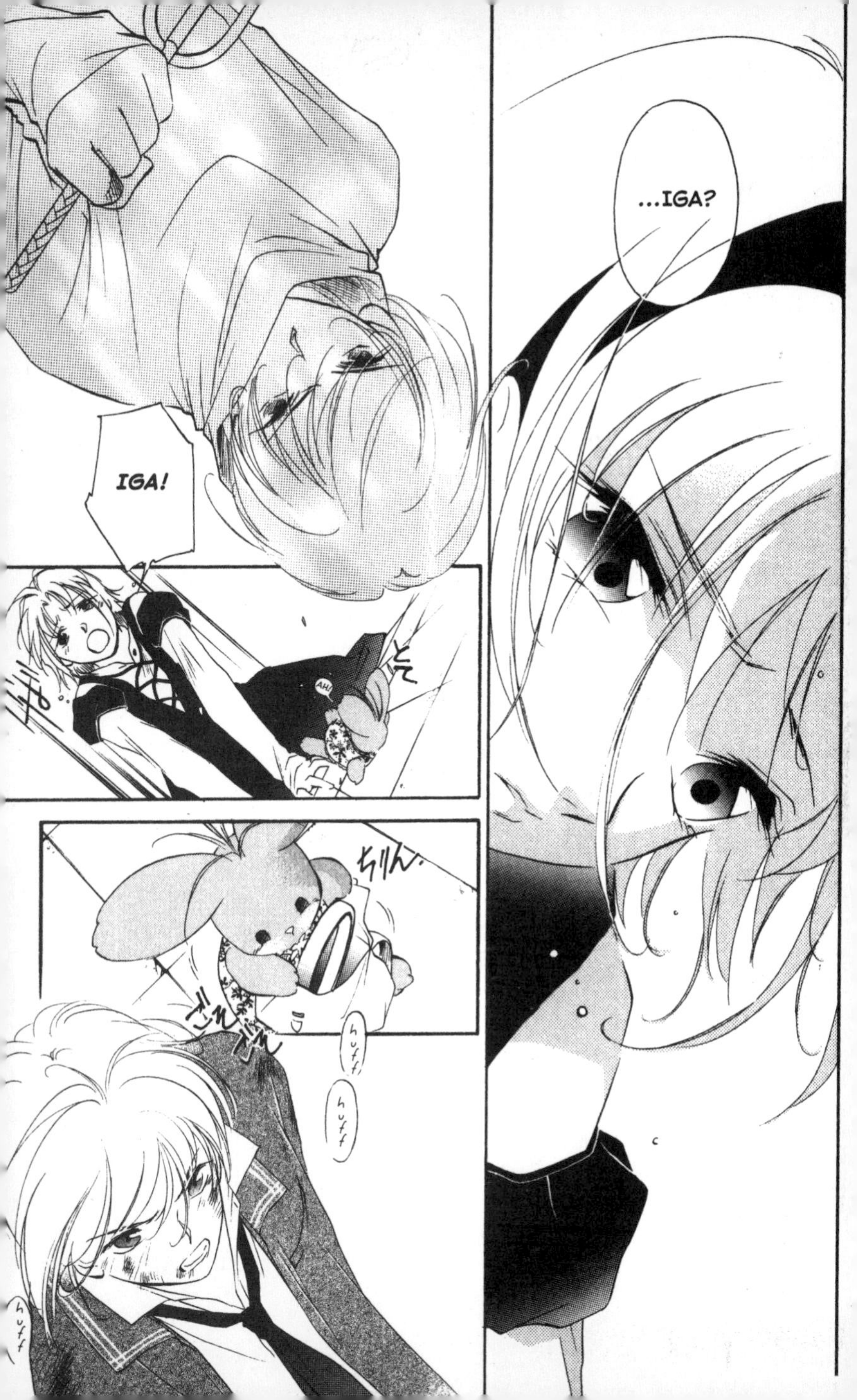
...IGA?
IGA!
AH!
huff
huff
huff

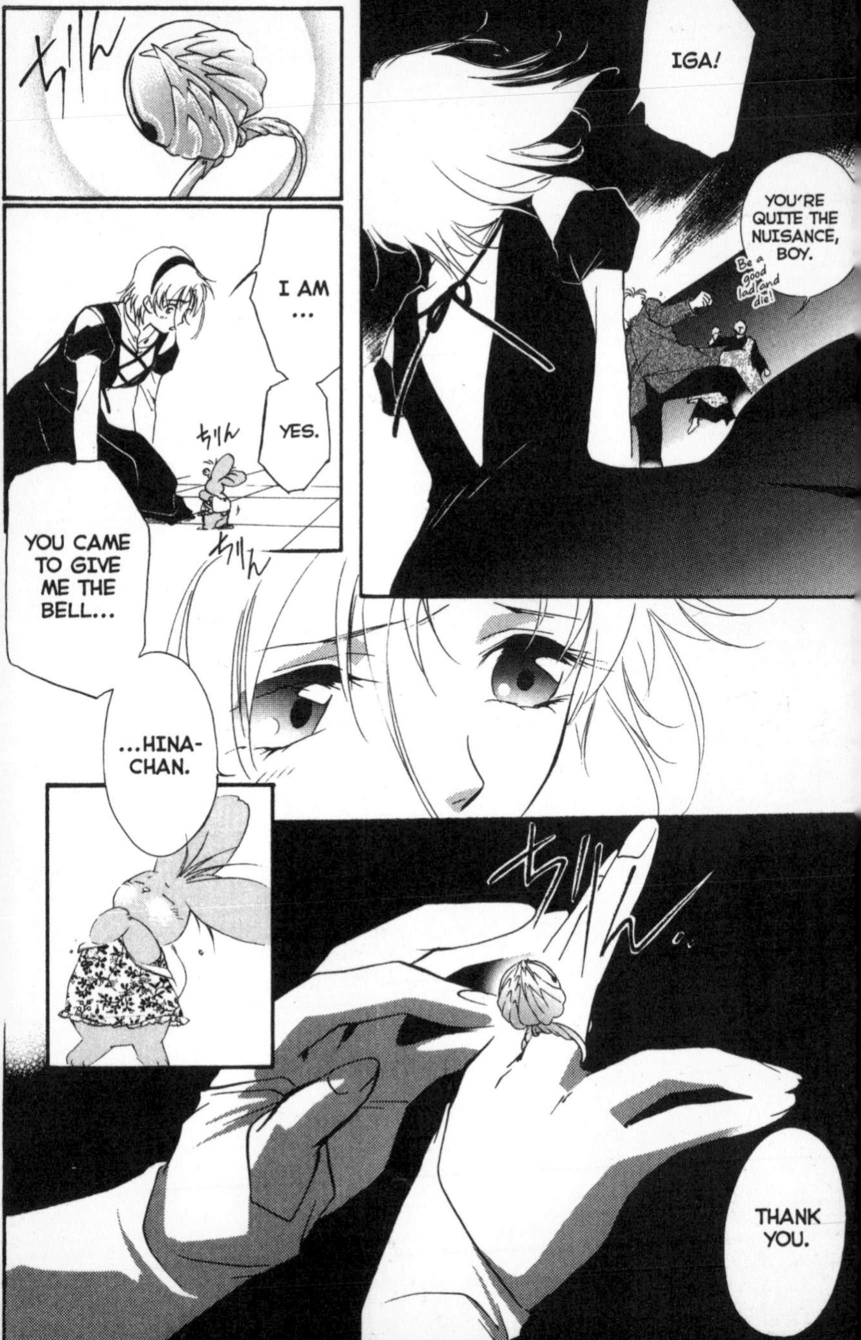
IGA!
YOU'RE QUITE THE NUISANCE, BOY.
Be a good lad and die!
ちりん
I AM ...
YES.
ちりん
ちりん
YOU CAME TO GIVE ME THE BELL...
...HINA-CHAN.
ちりん
THANK YOU.

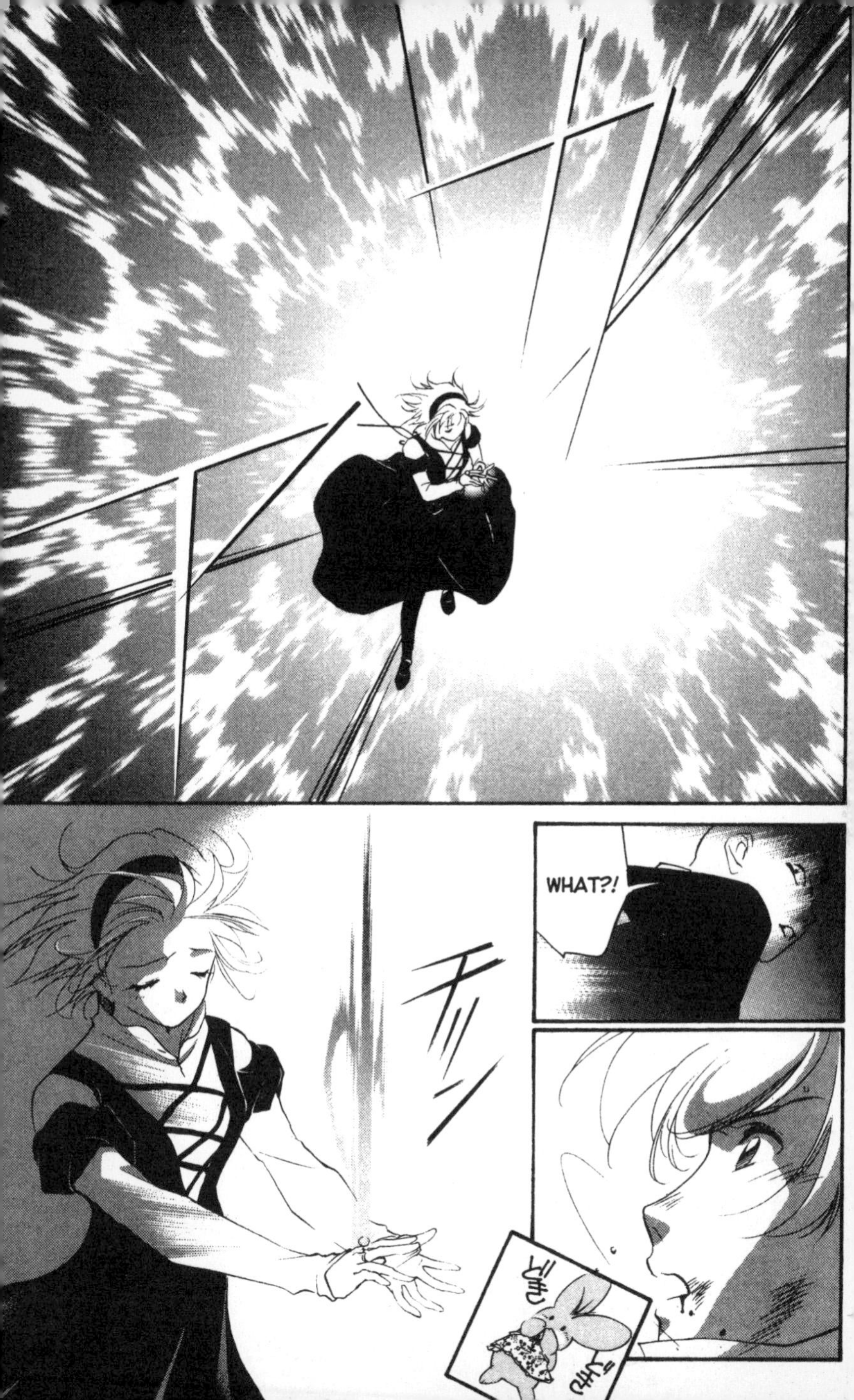
WHAT?!

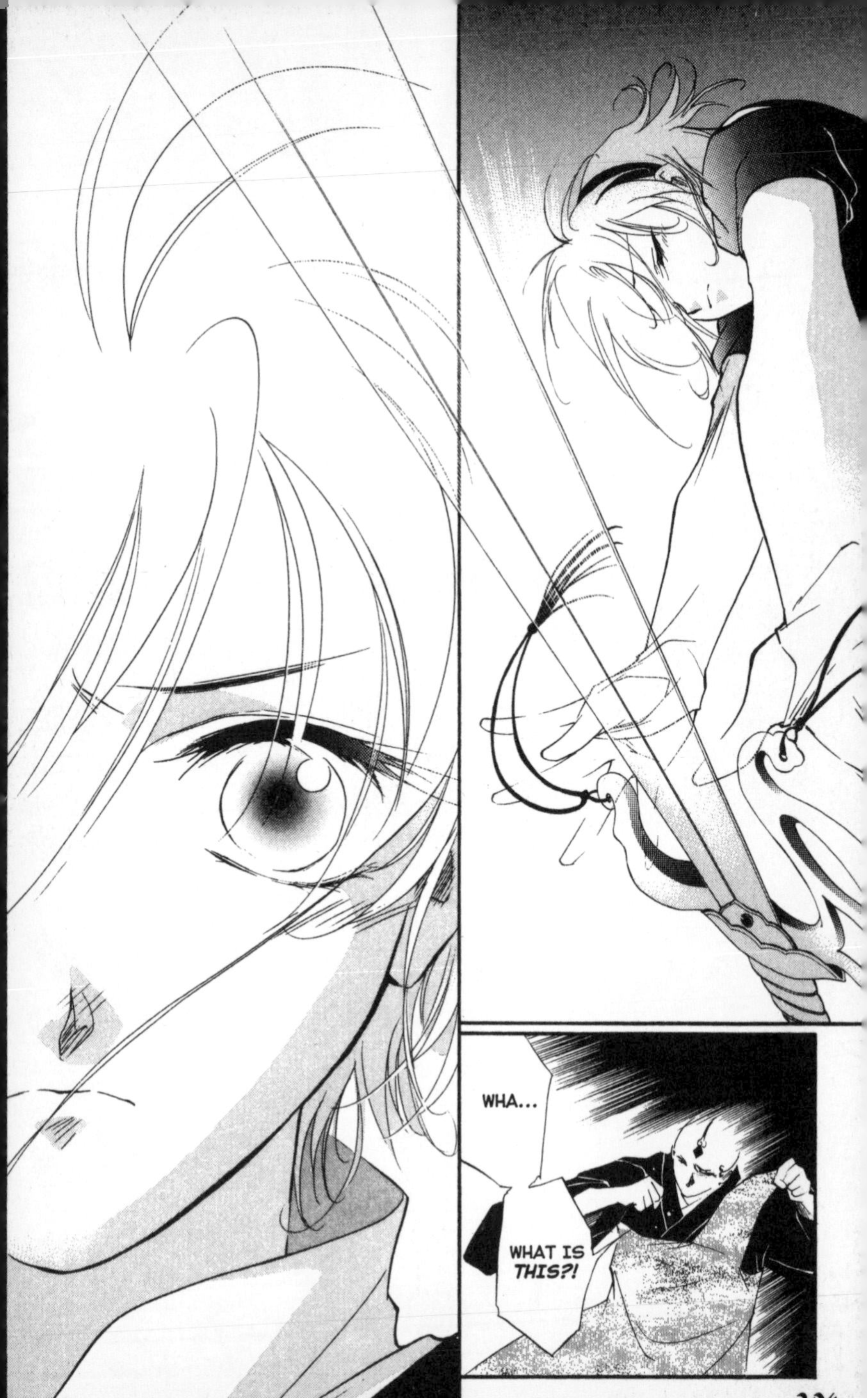
WHA...
WHAT IS *THIS?!*

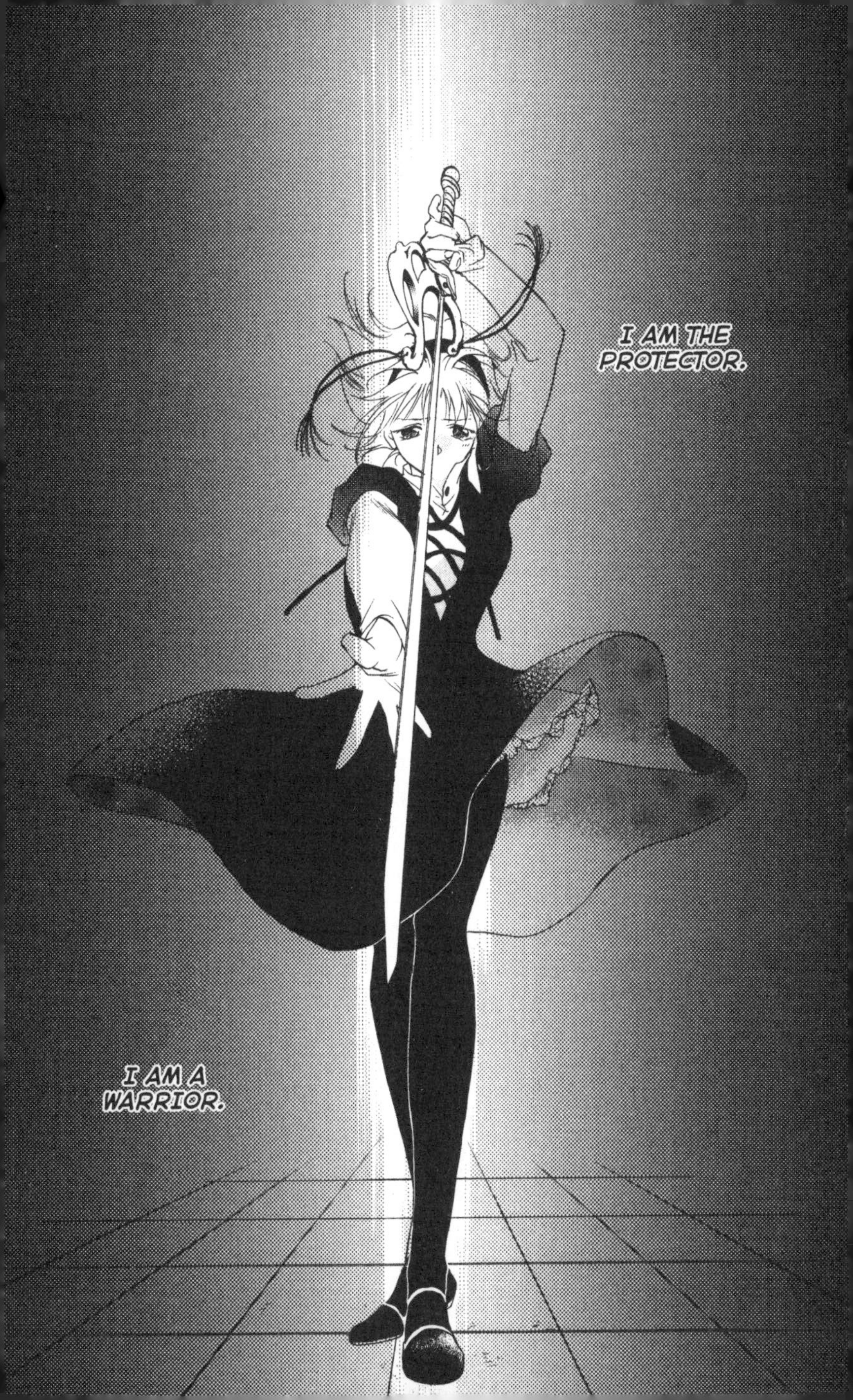
I AM THE PROTECTOR.
I AM A WARRIOR.

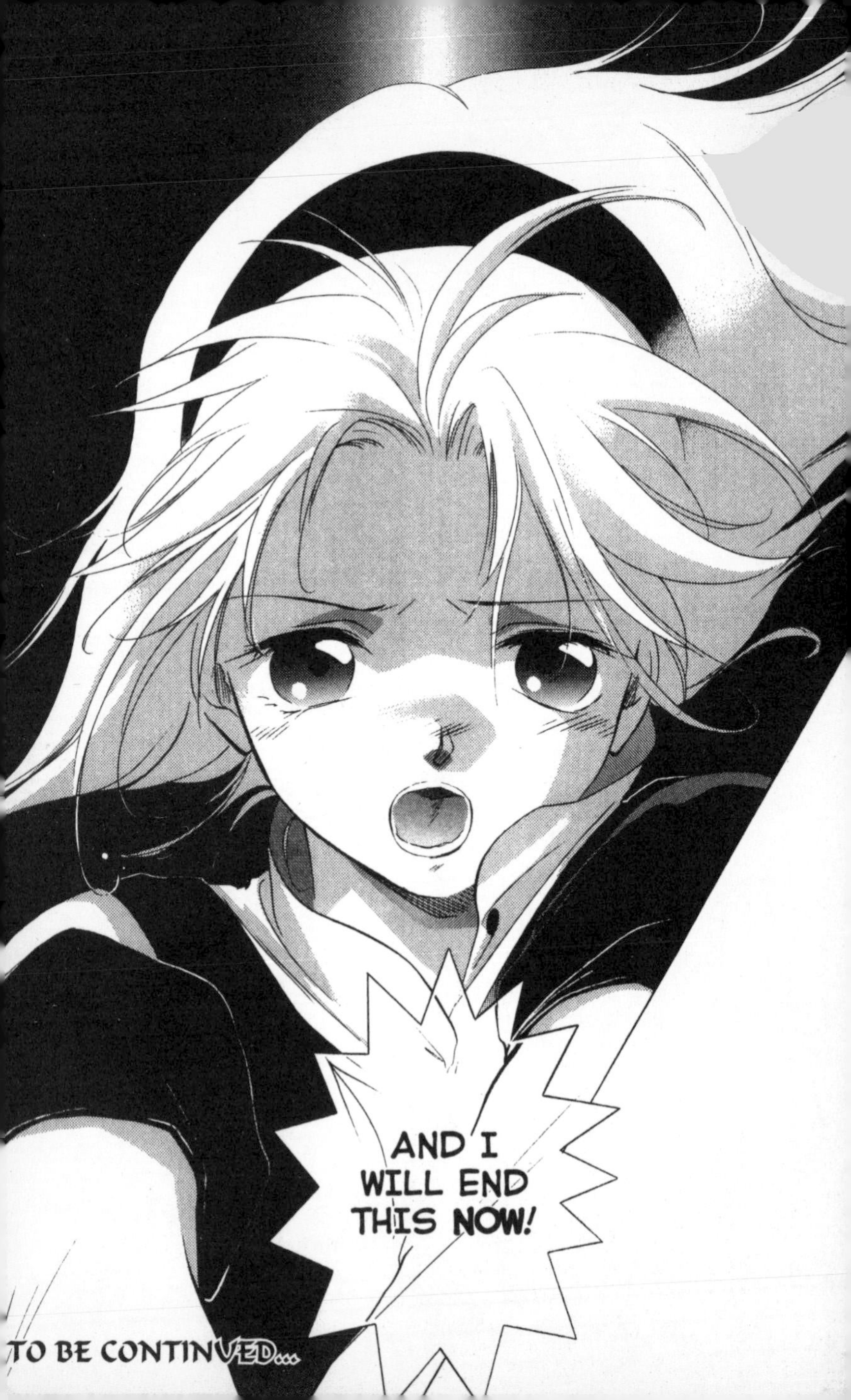
AND I WILL END THIS NOW!
TO BE CONTINUED...

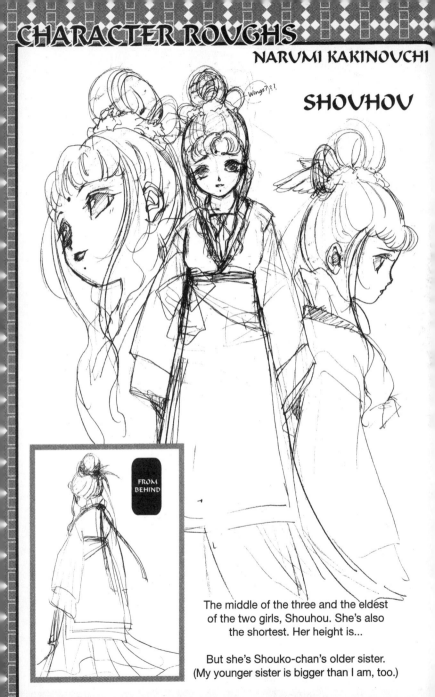

CHARACTER ROUGHS

NARUMI KAKINOUCHI

SHOUHOU

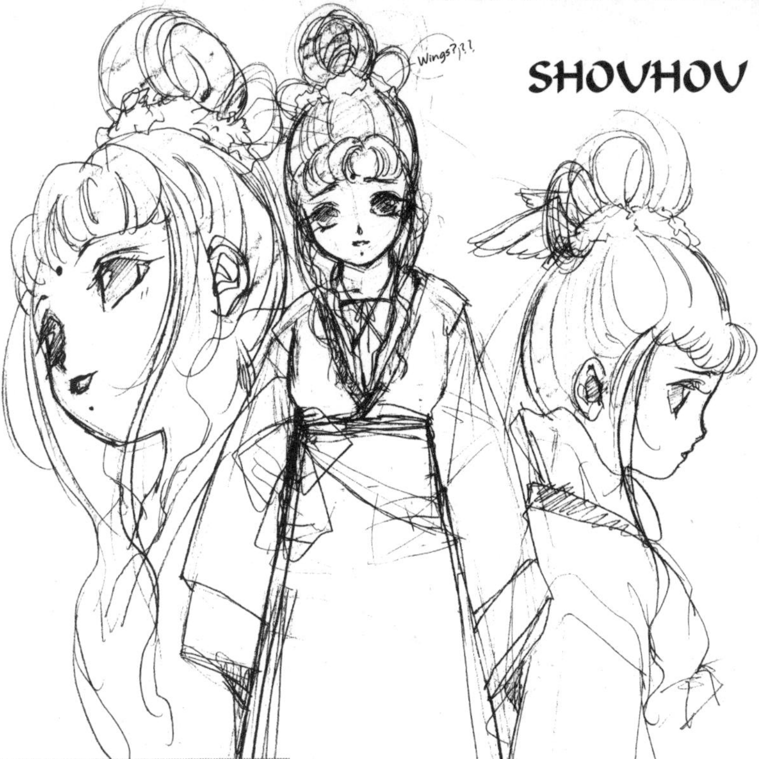

Wings?!??

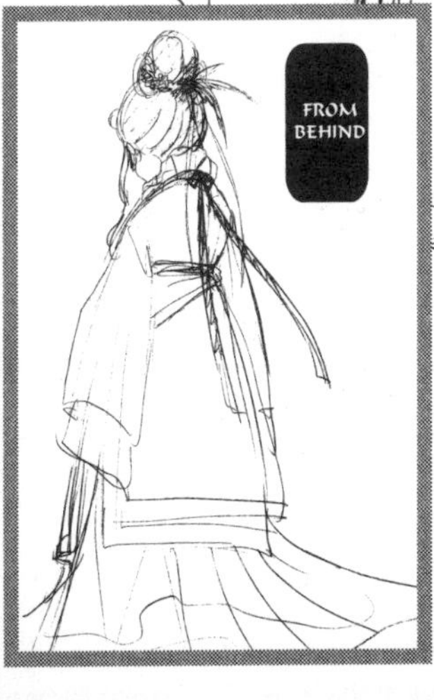

FROM BEHIND

The middle of the three and the eldest of the two girls, Shouhou. She's also the shortest. Her height is...

But she's Shouko-chan's older sister. (My younger sister is bigger than I am, too.)

IN THE NEXT VOLUME OF...

SHAOLIN SISTERS REBORN

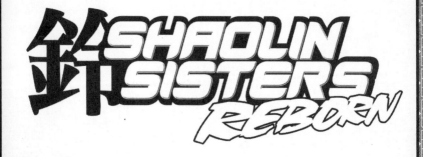

All three sisters have awakened just in time, as the evil Bai Wang grows more powerful with each passing day. And as she slowly carries out her dark plan, fate will bring the Misumi sisters to the same place they fought Bai Wang many centuries ago: Li Feng Island. On this desolate isle, three powerful forces will intertwine: the Misumis' bells of light, the Lins' bells of darkness, and the sinister powers of the White Lotus Clan. Which one will emerge triumphant? Will darkness snuff out the forces of light, or will good defy all odds and prevail? Who will survive this bloody battle? All will be revealed in the pulse-pounding conclusion of *Shaolin Sisters: Reborn*!

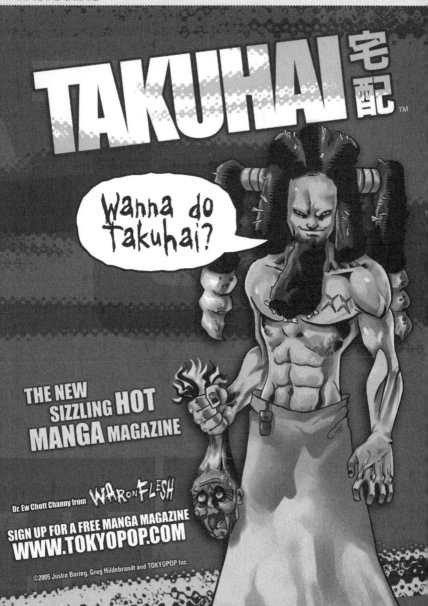

TOKYOPOP SHOP

WWW.TOKYOPOP.COM/SHOP

DRAMACON and other hot titles are available at the store that never closes!

HOT NEWS!

Check out the TOKYOPOP SHOP!
The world's best collection of manga in English is now available online in one place!

SAMURAI CHAMPLOO

KINGDOM HEARTS

DRAMACON

- **LOOK FOR SPECIAL OFFERS**
- **PRE-ORDER UPCOMING RELEASES**
- **COMPLETE YOUR COLLECTIONS**

MARK OF THE SUCCUBUS

BY ASHLY RAITI & IRENE FLORES

Maeve, a succubus-in-training, is sent to the human world to learn how to hone her skills of seduction. But things get complicated when she sets her sights on Aiden, a smart but unmotivated student at her new high school. Meanwhile, the Demon World has sent a spy to make sure Maeve doesn't step out of line. And between Aiden's witchy girlfriend, his nutty best friend, and Demon World conspiracies, Maeve is going to be lucky to make it out of our world alive!

Here is a Gothic romantic fantasy set in one of the most menacing worlds known to humans: high school.

T
TEEN
AGE 13+

FOR MORE INFORMATION VISIT: WWW.TOKYOPOP.COM

A Midnight Opera

Immortality, Redemption, and Bittersweet Love...

For nearly a millennium, undead creatures have blended into a Europe driven by religious dogma...

Ein DeLaLune is an underground Goth metal sensation on the Paris music scene, tragic and beautiful. He has the edge on other Goth music powerhouses—he's undead, a fact he's kept hidden for centuries. But his newfound fame might just bring out the very phantoms of his past from whom he has been hiding for centuries, including his powerful brother, Leroux. And if the two don't reconcile, the entire undead nation could rise up from the depths of modern society to lay waste to mankind.

A MIDNIGHT OPERA

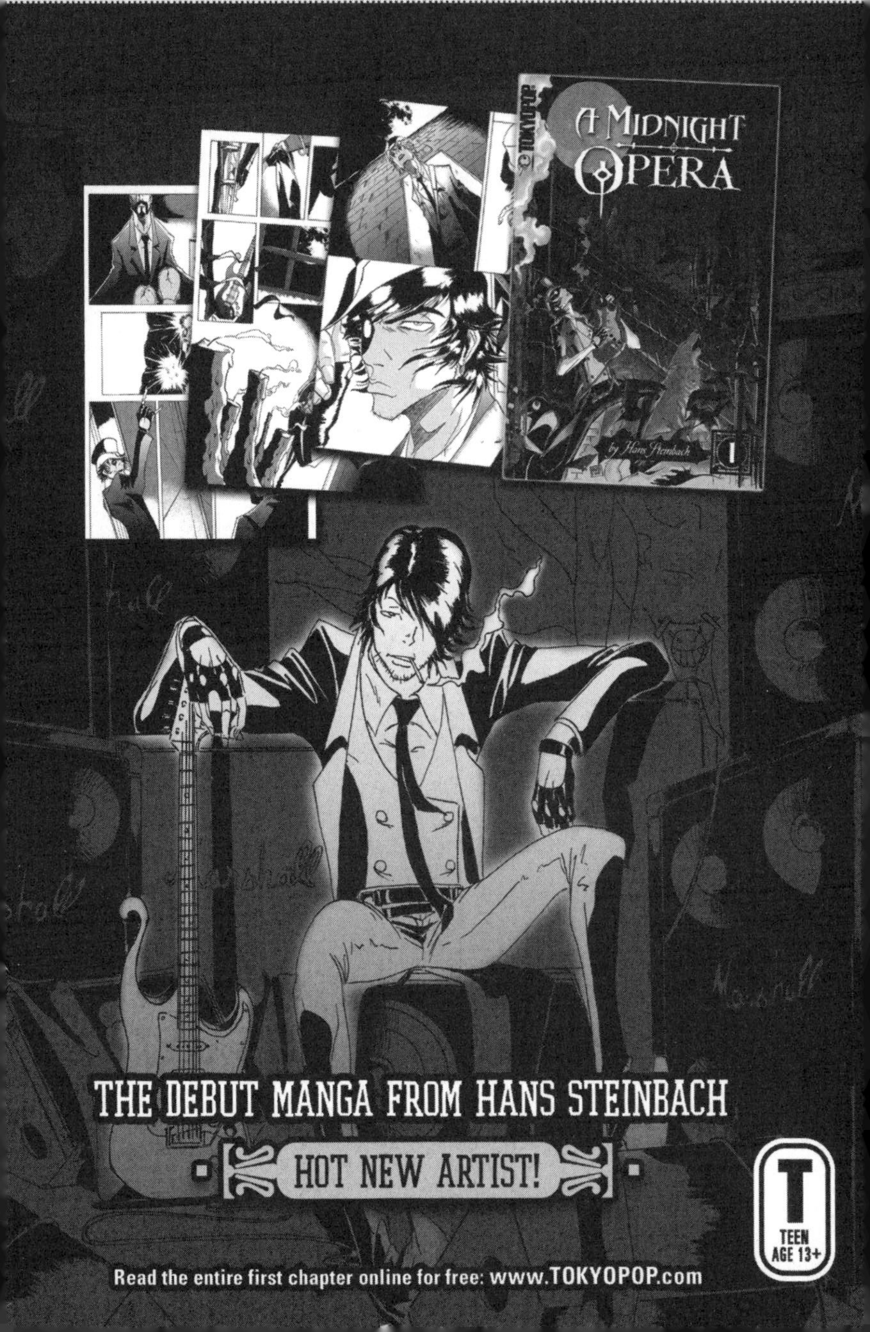
A MIDNIGHT OPERA
TOKYOPOP
by Hans Steinbach
1
THE DEBUT MANGA FROM HANS STEINBACH
HOT NEW ARTIST!
T
TEEN
AGE 13+
Read the entire first chapter online for free: www.TOKYOPOP.com

© Rivkah and TOKYOPOP Inc.

STEADY BEAT
BY RIVKAH

"Love Jessica"... That's what Leah finds on the back of a love letter to her sister. But who is Jessica? When more letters arrive, along with flowers and other gifts, Leah goes undercover to find out her sister's secret. But what she doesn't expect is to discover a love of her own—and in a very surprising place!

Winner of the Manga Academy's Create Your Own Manga competition!

T TEEN AGE 13+

© MIN-WOO HYUNG

JUSTICE N MERCY
BY MIN-WOO HYUNG

Min-Woo Hyung is one of today's most talented young Korean artists, and this stunning art book shows us why. With special printing techniques and high-quality paper, TOKYOPOP presents never-before-seen artwork based on his popular *Priest* series, as well as images from past and upcoming projects *Doomslave*, *Hitman* and *Sal*.

A spectacular art book from the creator of *Priest*!

T TEEN AGE 13+

3 Liu GOTO © SOTSU AGENCY • SUNRISE • MBS

MOBILE SUIT GUNDAM SEED NOVEL
ORIGINAL STORY BY HAJIME YATATE AND YOSHIYUKI TOMINO
WRITTEN BY LIU GOTO

A shy young student named Kira Yamato is thrown in the midst of battle when genetically enhanced Coordinators steal five new Earth Force secret weapons. Wanting only to protect his Natural friends, Kira embraces his Coordinator abilities and pilots the mobile suit Strike. The hopes and fears of a new generation clash with the greatest weapons developed by mankind: Gundam!

The novelization of the super-popular television series!

T TEEN AGE 13+

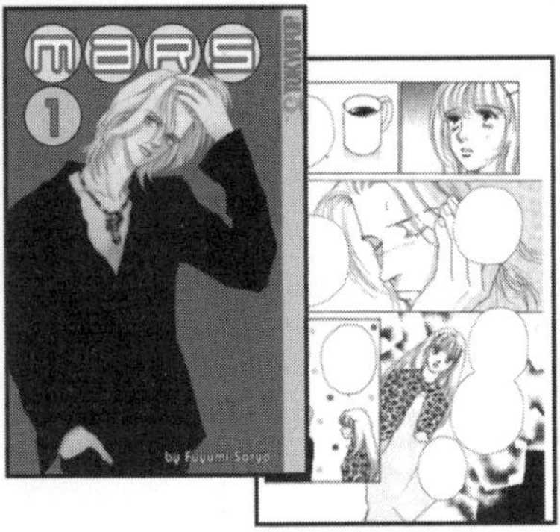
mars
1
by Fuyumi Soryo

BY FUYUMI SORYO

MARS

I used to do the English adaptation for *MARS* and loved working on it. The art is just amazing—Fuyumi Soryo draws these stunning characters and beautiful backgrounds to boot. I remember this one spread in particular where Rei takes Kira on a ride on his motorcycle past this factory, and it's all lit up like Christmas and the most gorgeous thing you've ever seen—and it's a factory! And the story is a super-juicy soap opera that kept me on the edge of my seat just dying to get the next volume every time I'd finish one.

~Elizabeth Hurchalla, Sr. Editor

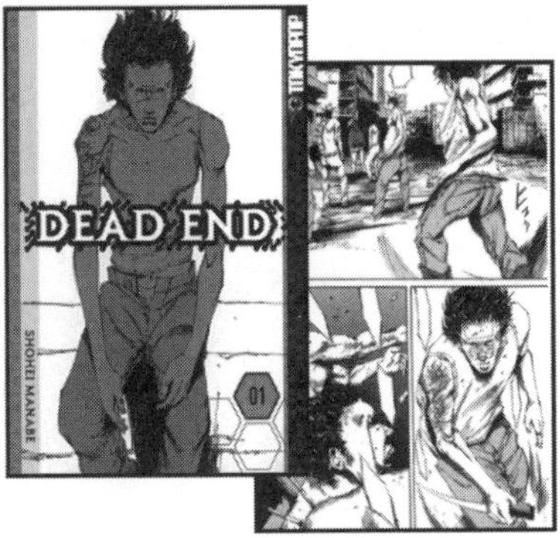
DEAD END
SHOHEI MANABE
01

BY SHOHEI MANABE

DEAD END

Everyone I've met who has read *Dead End* admits to becoming immediately immersed and obsessed with Shohei Manabe's unforgettable manga. If David Lynch, Clive Barker and David Cronenberg had a love child that was forced to create a manga in the bowels of a torture chamber, then *Dead End* would be the fruit of its labor. The unpredictable story follows a grungy young man as he pieces together shattered fragments of his past. Think you know where it's going? Well, think again!

~Troy Lewter, Editor

STOP!

This is the back of the book.
You wouldn't want to spoil a great ending!

This book is printed "manga-style," in the authentic Japanese right-to-left format. Since none of the artwork has been flipped or altered, readers get to experience the story just as the creator intended. You've been asking for it, so TOKYOPOP® delivered: authentic, hot-off-the-press, and far more fun!

DIRECTIONS

If this is your first time reading manga-style, here's a quick guide to help you understand how it works.

It's easy... just start in the top right panel and follow the numbers. Have fun, and look for more 100% authentic manga from TOKYOPOP®!